APPOINTMENT
AT THE PALACE

Mary Jane Staples

CORGI BOOKS

APPOINTMENT AT THE PALACE
A CORGI BOOK : 0 552 14908 X

First publication in Great Britain

PRINTING HISTORY
Corgi edition published 2002

1 3 5 7 9 10 8 6 4 2

Set in 11/12pt New Baskerville by
Phoenix Typesetting, Ilkley, West Yorkshire.

Corgi Books are published by Transworld Publishers,
61–63 Uxbridge Road, London W5 5SA,
a division of The Random House Group Ltd,
in Australia by Random House Australia (Pty) Ltd,
20 Alfred Street, Milsons Point, Sydney, NSW 2061, Australia,
in New Zealand by Random House New Zealand Ltd,
18 Poland Road, Glenfield, Auckland 10, New Zealand
and in South Africa by Random House (Pty) Ltd,
Endulini, 5a Jubilee Road, Parktown 2193, South Africa.

The Random House Group Limited supports The Forest Stewardship
Council (FSC®), the leading international forest certification organisation.
Our books carrying the FSC label are printed on FSC® certified paper.
FSC is the only forest certification scheme endorsed by the leading
environmental organisations, including Greenpeace. Our
paper procurement policy can be found at
www.randomhouse.co.uk/environment

MIX
Paper from
responsible sources
FSC® C018072

Printed and bound in Great Britain by Clays Ltd, St Ives PLC

The day in question was to be a memorable occasion for the Adams family. A knighthood was to be bestowed on Edwin Finch, husband of the family matriarch, mother to Boots, and known as Chinese Lady.

Chinese Lady had long been in a flustered state about it, and the closer the day came the more frequent was her need for smelling salts. It was her son-in-law Ned's opinion that Chinese Lady should have been in the honours list herself, since she was a wife, mother, grandmother and great-grandmother in no uncertain fashion. That was worth a special place, wasn't it?

'Well,' said Lizzy, 'She's going to be a Lady, Lady Finch.'

Also by Mary Jane Staples

The Adams Books

DOWN LAMBETH WAY
OUR EMILY
KING OF CAMBERWELL
ON MOTHER BROWN'S DOORSTEP
A FAMILY AFFAIR
MISSING PERSON
PRIDE OF WALWORTH
ECHOES OF YESTERDAY
THE YOUNG ONES
THE CAMBERWELL RAID
THE LAST SUMMER
THE FAMILY AT WAR
FIRE OVER LONDON
CHURCHILL'S PEOPLE
BRIGHT DAY, DARK NIGHT
TOMORROW IS ANOTHER DAY
THE WAY AHEAD
YEAR OF VICTORY
THE HOMECOMING
SONS AND DAUGHTERS

Other titles in order of publication

TWO FOR THREE FARTHINGS
THE LODGER
RISING SUMMER
THE PEARLY QUEEN
SERGEANT JOE
THE TRAP
THE GHOST OF WHITECHAPEL

and published by Corgi Books

APPOINTMENT
AT THE PALACE

THE ADAMS FAMILY

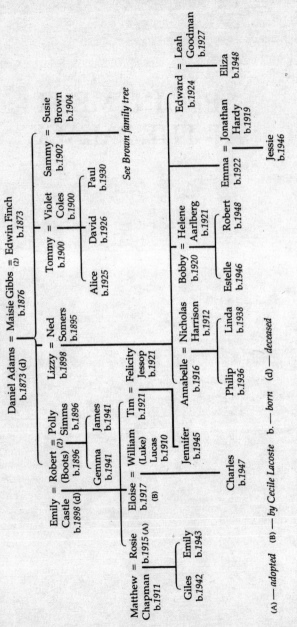

Daniel Adams (d) b.1873 = Maisie Gibbs b.1876 = (2) Edwin Finch b.1873

Emily Castle b.1898 (d) = Robert (Boots) (2) b.1896 = Polly Simms b.1896

Lizzy b.1898 = Ned Somers b.1895

Tommy b.1900 = Violet Coles b.1900

Sammy b.1902 = Susie Brown b.1904

See Brown family tree

Gemma b.1941
James b.1941

Alice b.1925
David b.1926
Paul b.1930

Edward b.1924 = Leah Goodman b.1927

Eliza b.1948

Matthew b.1911 = Rosie Chapman b.1915 (A)

Eloise b.1917 (B) = William (Luke) Lucas b.1910

Tim b.1921 = Felicity Jessop b.1921

Annabelle b.1916 = Nicholas Harrison b.1912

Emma b.1922 = Jonathan Hardy b.1919

Bobby b.1920 = Helene Aarlberg b.1921

Giles b.1942
Emily b.1943

Jennifer b.1945

Charles b.1947

Philip b.1936
Linda b.1938

Jessie b.1946

Estelle b.1946
Robert b.1948

(A) — *adopted*   (B) — *by Cecile Lacoste*   b. — *born*   (d) — *deceased*

THE BROWN FAMILY

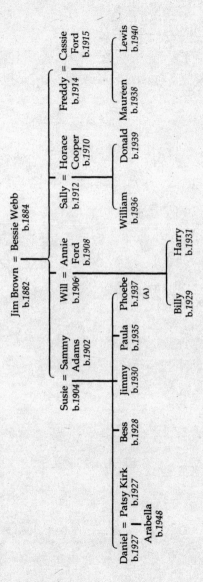

Chapter One

A winter night, a room in darkness except for the glow of a log fire and the light of a large red Christmas candle in its table holder.

Around the table sat a quartet of players, cards in their hands, faces set in expressions of concentration on this tense game of skill and chance. Not a word was spoken, and the only movements were those of hands reaching for a card from the top of either a face-down or a face-up pack, which card, after a furrowed examination, was either retained in exchange for one from the hand or discarded.

The silence was nerve-racking, the candle's flame wavering uneasily at times, as if expecting to be angrily snuffed out. Each player occasionally stole glances at the others in an attempt to read expressions and to find out if hope, triumph or despair was uppermost. Eyes reflected the candlelight, lashes quivered, and every so often one player or another took a sip of refreshment from a wine glass.

One participant expelled a sudden breath, drawing quick looks, but nothing came of it, and nothing was said. The tension mounted and the silence was such that had a pin dropped, the sound might have shattered nerves and numbed ears. Eyes flickered, cards came and went. Burning logs issued flames, and the flames cast light over the brass fender. Melting wax glistened around the top of the candle, and the closed curtains shut out the coldness of the night.

Someone coughed. Eyes darted. A cough could cover up exultation. The someone took a sip of wine. Still not a word was spoken, still the concentration was profound and secretive.

But the silence was broken at last.

A hand of cards was placed down, face upwards, and a gleeful voice heralded triumph.

'Rummy!' cried eight-year-old Gemma Adams. 'A penny from everybody and a kiss from Daddy!'

'Crikey, look at that,' said Gemma's twin brother James, 'she's got three threes, three jacks and three kings. That's the third time she's won. D'you know what, Dad, I think she keeps spare cards where she keeps her hankies.'

'Oh, that boy, he'll get himself talked about,' said Gemma, finishing her ginger beer. 'You'd best speak to him, Daddy.'

Robert Adams, known as Boots, offered her a smile instead of a promise to reform her brother. The intelligence of the twins at only eight fascinated him. They played card games with confidence and skill, and earned glowing tributes for their learning abilities from teachers at their prep school, a private establishment in Dulwich that prepared its pupils for entry into grammar school. The product of a grammar school himself, one that he considered had civilized him, Boots found it difficult to understand the Labour government's dislike of them.

He leaned and delivered a kiss on Gemma's cheek.

'There, poppet, I've paid up,' he said.

'Daddy, you haven't,' protested Gemma, 'you've got to give me a penny as well. So have Mummy and James.'

Her mother, Mrs Polly Adams, laughed. Boots's second wife, she had been married to him for nine years, and each year had flown much too fast for her. Restless, flippant and frustrated prior to her marriage, she was now the kind of woman who, as a contented wife and mother, was regarded by liberals and intellectuals as bourgeois: meaning dull, humdrum and commonplace. Polly was far from that. If, as a wife and mother, she was fulfilled – something the liberals thought self-deceptive – she was still a vivacious and entertaining woman.

She and Boots were both fifty-three, and both looked as if they had the measure of old Father Time, whose unwelcome fingers wrote their implacable lines on the faces of others. Polly's features still held a hint of the piquant flapper of the Wild Twenties, and the only real evidence of her age were the little crow's feet developing at the corners of her wide grey eyes.

She glanced at Boots, who was trying to explain to James that in all card games luck played a greater part than aces that were shiftily hidden up a sleeve or – um – elsewhere. His explanation, of course, was so droll that James was grinning all over, and Gemma giggling.

Gemma interrupted to say, 'Yes, Daddy, that's all very well, but nobody's given me any pennies yet.'

11

'Pay up, everyone,' said Boots, and Gemma received her well-won dues.

'I don't know why she keeps winning,' said James, a boyish frown appearing. 'I mean, she's only a girl.'

'I'm cleverer,' said Gemma.

'Some hopes,' said James.

Boots, who had known just how well some women had distinguished themselves as ATS officers, and listened to what they intended to make of their post-war lives, said, 'James, my lad, there's a new age dawning.'

'What d'you mean?' asked James.

'You and I, James, are going to see the rise of women into positions of power,' said Boots. 'Gemma might end up as Governor of the Bank of England.'

'What, Gemma?' said James.

'Possibly,' said Boots. 'Or even as – let's see—'

'Our Prime Minister?' suggested Polly.

'Prime Minister?' said Boots. 'That's a little over the top, perhaps. Let's say she might get to be Lord Mayor of London.'

'What, Gemma?' said James again, and looked at his sister.

Gemma yawned.

'Someone's ready for bed,' said Polly. 'Time for both of you, I think.'

'What, already?' said James, who had his father's dark brown hair and a promise of his firm features.

'We'd best go, I'm nearly worn out,' sighed Gemma, hair as darkly sienna as her mother's, her eyes as brown as her Aunt Lizzy's.

'But, Mum, it's still early,' protested James, 'you can ask Dad.'

'I don't need to ask him,' said Polly, 'I know it's

gone nine, and that means it's bed for both of you. There, look, Gemma's nearly asleep in her chair. Would you like Daddy to go up with you?'

'All right, come on, Dad,' said James, 'but I think you'll have to carry Gemma.'

Boots lifted her from her chair. She curled her arms around his neck and rested her face against his shoulder. So Boots, of course, thought one of nature's blessings to men and women were kids.

Later, when the twins were sound asleep, Polly and Boots settled down to an hour of relaxing companionship. Polly often thought a deep liking for each other's company a binding marriage factor.

'Love it,' she murmured, tucking up her legs.

'All these domestic capers?' said Boots.

'All these quiet moments,' said Polly, and smiled. 'I think I'm going to turn into your dear old dutch in a year or two. I'll get an old lady's urge for knitting. When that happens, hey-ho, old love, my vitality will have finally passed into limbo and I'll be wearing a shawl. And perhaps a pair of granny glasses.'

'I'll take a photograph of the phenomenon, frame it and hang it,' said Boots.

'And invite friends round to gawp at it, of course,' said Polly. 'Listen, old scout, it's polling day for the General Election tomorrow. Will you be voting?'

'I might make a cross in favour of Churchill's lot,' said Boots. 'The old boy deserves one more go as PM. But I sometimes think, Polly, that politicians are proliferating to our disadvantage, that the whole world will soon be full of them. They'll swamp it with their regulations. They're all civil servants at heart, with a compulsive urge to organize their citizens. Politicians with Labour, Liberal or

13

Conservative affiliations are now entering our town halls, displacing men and women of independent Ratepayers' Associations, creating strife and division instead of sensible co-operation. We need governments, central and local, of course, but unfortunately most, if not all, are made up of politicians.'

'And what do we get from them?' murmured Polly.

'Mainly, an overload of bumph,' said Boots. 'Forms in triplicate sent Sammy off his chump during the war.'

'Tommy's son Paul, isn't he an aspiring politician?' asked Polly.

'An ardent Socialist,' said Boots, 'which makes Sammy think the family's capitalist citadel is being undermined by one of its own.'

'The progress of that young man's campaign should be worth watching,' said Polly.

'It won't be dull,' said Boots. 'I understand Paul has a young lady assistant who'd like to guillotine the rich and the lordly.'

'The lordly?' Polly laughed. 'Haven't I heard from Tommy and Sammy that you've been one of the lordly from the time you were nine?'

'What you've heard,' said Boots, 'has always been in the nature of the fanciful.'

'Well, whatever,' said Polly, 'I'll fight the good fight to see you're not guillotined, old sport.'

'For that,' said Boots, 'I'll help you wind your first hank of knitting wool into a ball.'

'If I ever do get a real urge to turn into that kind of old lady,' said Polly, 'I'd prefer you to help me jump on it. By the way, I'll be needing something like an Ascot outfit in two months' time.'

'For a garden party?' said Boots.

'For Buckingham Palace on the day of your step-father's investiture in April,' said Polly. 'I promised your mother to take her with me when I go up to Bond Street. I'm to help her choose her own outfit.'

'I'm certain you'll both end up with perfect creations,' said Boots. 'Dip into our bank account for all that you need to stun the Palace sentries.'

'There's a lovely old darling you are,' said Polly.

The day in question was to represent an occasion that would make the year memorable for the Adams family. A knighthood was to be conferred on Edwin Finch, husband of the family matriarch, Boots's mother, known as Chinese Lady.

Chinese Lady had long been in a flustered state about it, and the closer the day came the more frequent was her need for smelling salts. However, there was comfort in knowing she would have the support of her nearest and dearest, for the invitation to the Palace had included Boots and his wife Polly.

It was Ned's opinion that Chinese Lady should have been included in the honours list herself, since she was a wife, mother, grandmother and great-grandmother in no uncertain fashion. Her family was legion.

Ned pointed out to Lizzy that Chinese Lady had three sons, a daughter, three daughters-in-law and one son-in-law. She had seventeen grandchildren, together with nine grandchildren-in-law and umpteen great-grandchildren.

That was worth a special place on the honours list, wasn't it?

'Well, she's already on it in a way,' said Lizzy. 'She's going to be a Lady. Lady Finch.'

15

'Ought to be a baroness as well, in her own right,' said Ned.

Lizzy said, 'But could she actually be Baroness Lady Finch?'

'Ask me another,' said Ned.

'It's all going to seem like a dream to me,' said Lizzy.

'Well, when you come to, give me a nudge,' said Ned. 'I'll be in cloud cuckoo land myself.'

Chapter Two

The following morning.

General Election day. The governing Labour Party had its sleeves rolled up. It was in a fight with the hopeful Conservative Party, led by Winston Churchill, Britain's wartime leader of renown. Neither party felt it needed to worry about the Liberals, whose fortunes had been waning since going down to a thumping defeat in the 1920s.

It was gloves off for the two main contestants, and respective Party workers were out and about, urging supporters to get to the polling booths to cast their votes. Young Socialists were reminding people of what the Labour government had done for the country and its workers. It had nationalized the Bank of England, inland transport, civil aviation, electricity and gas supplies, and iron and steel industries. And it had also created a national health service paid for by insurance contributions. Only the misguided, and the Tories, of course, said nationalization wasn't working. Businessman Sammy Adams said the trade unions were getting a bit saucy, and the farther away from his garments factory they were, the better he'd like it. You're an old-fashioned capitalist, said his

17

Socialist nephew Paul. Old-fashioned my eye, said Sammy, you've never seen me wearing a bowler hat and a cigar.

In the East Street market of Walworth, a young lady in a flapping coat and a woollen hat was working on stallholders. One had to work hard on them, or when they'd finished their day they'd give voting a miss in favour of getting home and giving their plates of meat a rest. Not many of them voted before wheeling their stalls to the market. Those who did were of the kind keen to exercise the duty and privilege of voting.

'Hey, Bert, you voted yet?' The young lady, carrying notebook and pencil, addressed a stallholder.

'Me?' said the stallholder, scarf around his neck, flat cap on his head, one hand trundling potatoes into his brass scales container. 'Talk sense, I ain't had no time to vote, and I dunno I will.'

'You'd better,' said the young lady, one Lulu Saunders, coming up to nineteen and pretty determined to make a name for herself in politics. Her straight thick black hair hung down on each side of her face, framing her horn-rimmed spectacles, from behind which her hazel eyes missed very little. 'You don't want Churchill and his capitalist mob to get in, do you?'

'What, old Winnie?' said the stallholder, emptying the weighed-up potatoes into a customer's shopping bag. 'Good bloke, old Winnie.'

'Don't make me spit,' said Lulu. 'What's he ever done for the working classes?'

'Well, I grant yer, he ain't ever done nothing for me personally,' said the stallholder, now weighing up golden-skinned onions, 'but then he ain't done nothing to upset me, either. There y'are, missus, three pounds of me best onions.' The onions followed the potatoes into the shopping bag, held by a thin but sprightly woman.

'Listen,' said Lulu, who spoke in quick, staccato fashion. 'Churchill's out. He's got to stay out. Him and his big fat cigars.'

'Here, excuse me,' said the customer, bristling, 'what's a saucy girl like you making them kind of remarks for? You ain't old enough to know nothing about Mr Churchill.'

'Help, you're not going to vote for him, are you?' said Lulu in protest.

'I don't know who I'm going to vote for till me old man gets home this evening and tells me,' said the woman, while the stallholder weighed up carrots.

'I don't believe it,' said Lulu, aghast. 'It's a maximum shocker. No woman has to vote the way her husband tells her. Missus, you've got rights. Stand up for them. Vote Labour.'

'Here, where's this saucy bit of skirt come from?' asked the woman of the stallholder.

'Oh, round the corner somewhere,' said the stallholder, tipping in carrots. 'She's all right, ain't yer, Lulu? Her dad's the MP that's called Honest John, yer know.'

'Oh, he is, is he?' said the woman. 'Well, you tell him from me it's time he put this saucy girl over his knees. A good honest spanking, that's what she wants. Did you hear her tell me how to vote?'

'Missus, stop making unfunny jokes,' said Lulu, who coveted the right to be taken seriously.

'What's going on?' Paul, younger son of Tommy

19

and Vi Adams, interceded. Like Lulu, he'd been working on stallholders and customers. They were both ardent supporters of the Labour Party, Lulu being very left-wing and desirous of doing away with capitalists, and Paul being secretary of the Young Socialists Southwark group. 'What's up, Lulu?'

'I've got problems,' said Lulu.

'There's a lot of them about today,' said Paul. 'You voted yet, Bert?' he asked the stallholder.

'Later, sonny, later,' said Bert.

'That girl's a saucebox,' said the woman, and left, her heavy shopping bag giving a slight list to her angular body.

'Listen,' said Paul, bringing Lulu away from the stall, 'it's not a good policy, upsetting our voters on polling day.'

'Leave off,' said Lulu. She and Paul were always a challenge to each other. 'That woman's not only as daft as a kite. She's a shocking example of mental paralysis. She actually votes the way her husband tells her to.'

'As long as he tells her to vote Labour, that's not our worry,' said Paul.

'Spoken like a typical male,' said Lulu.

'Lots of women need political guidance,' said Paul.

'They wouldn't if they were allowed to think for themselves,' said Lulu.

'I'm not stopping them,' said Paul.

'Yes, you are,' said Lulu, edging around shoppers. 'In a crafty way. Like most men. Some of us are going to change all that.'

'Good luck,' said Paul. 'Well, now that we've had

a hard day, let's get back to headquarters and see if optimism is prevailing.'

The Walworth Road headquarters of the Labour Party was seething with grass-roots workers and established officials, each of whom had his or her own ideas on how this election day was going. The consensus of opinion, however, was that the Conservatives were pulling in more votes than in 1945.

'I'll fall ill if they get in,' said Lulu.

'I'll ask a doctor to call,' said Paul.

'I'm thrilled you care,' said Lulu.

The following morning, Paul arrived in his office with a bottle of wine. The Labour Party had secured over three hundred seats. With some results still to come, it was estimated that three hundred and fifteen seats would be the final figure, giving it a narrow working majority. Although the total would be eighty seats fewer than in 1945, it was still a welcome victory to the supporters.

Lulu, already in the office, exclaimed, 'We won, we won!'

'So I see,' said Paul. Instead of her usual drab outfit, Lulu was actually wearing a decent dress and dark blue silk stockings. 'What're those?' he asked, pointing.

'Silk stockings,' said Lulu. 'Don't get personal. My dad treated me. He said he would if we won. Confident, he bought them in advance. Told him, of course, that I didn't go in for tarting myself up. But I had to humour him.'

'Yes, but what're those?' asked Paul, pointing again.

'What d'you mean?'

'Oh, now I see,' said Paul. 'Legs. Yes, very nice. I usually feel you haven't got any.'

'That's it, make me die laughing,' said Lulu. 'Oh well, you can't help being a head case. And who cares? Today's one in the eye for Churchill.'

'Take note, he's secured a lot more seats for his Party than last time,' said Paul, 'and he'll mount a strong opposition. The old boy's not finished yet.'

'Give over,' said Lulu, 'you're talking like a traitor to the cause of the workers.'

'I don't think so,' said Paul, 'but, anyway, we'll celebrate our victory. We'll share this bottle of wine with our lunch.'

'Oh yes?' said Lulu. 'Got ideas about me, have you?'

'Such as?'

'Getting me drunk and seducing me?'

'Not my style,' said Paul, 'but is it what you fancy?'

'That's your worst joke ever,' said Lulu. The phone rang. She picked up the receiver. 'Hello, Young Socialists' office here. What? Pardon? Oh, him. No, he's not here. Sorry. Goodbye.' She replaced the receiver.

'Who was that?' asked Paul.

'Tarty Henrietta,' said Lulu. She meant Henrietta Trevalyan, granddaughter of an ex-suffragette. Henrietta fancied making a hobby of Paul.

'Who did she want to speak to?'

'Oh, some male idiot,' said Lulu.

'That's me, I suppose,' said Paul.

'Not your fault you're retarded,' said Lulu. The phone rang again. This time Paul beat her to it.

'Hello?'

'Oh, there you are, Paul,' gushed Henrietta. 'Someone told me you weren't there. Was it that girl my granny thinks is a belly dancer?'

'That's the one,' said Paul.

'She's a bit peculiar, isn't she?'

'Some belly dancers are, I suppose,' said Paul.

Lulu, inferring how the conversation was going, breathed in deeply and fumed.

'I just wanted to say happy congratulations for the Labour Party's victory,' said Henrietta. 'And I'll come over and have lunch with you, if you'd like.'

'Lunch?' said Paul, and received a kick in his calf. Bearing the pain, he said, 'Well, I'd like that, of course, but the whole place is up in the air, and I'm already booked for an all-day celebration.'

'A jolly old knees-up?' said Henrietta.

'Something like that,' said Paul, 'but I don't know if the belly dancer will perform.'

Another kick arrived.

'I can give her a miss,' said Henrietta. 'I'll see you some other time, Paul. Don't forget I'm still madly keen about setting up a home for lonely old maiden ladies, with your help.'

'I'm still trying to work out if I've got enough spare time for that,' said Paul.

'Oh, I'm sure I can win you over, you dear thing,' gushed Henrietta.

'We'll see,' said Paul.

When he put the phone down, Lulu said at once, 'You're weak in your fat head over tarty Henrietta.'

'I've got a cure,' said Paul. 'Well, I hope I have. It's a bottle of Dr Livermore's herbal medicine for the retarded. Two spoonfuls daily.'

'Two spoonfuls?' Lulu looked scornful. 'Two

bottles, more like, in your condition. And listen. I heard your mention of belly dancer. Very funny, I don't think. Still, don't let's fall out, not on victory day.'

'Good girl,' said Paul.

During the morning, people kept coming in and going out, all expressing glad relief that the Tories had been licked. Young Socialists rang up to talk to Paul, and to thank him for organizing their supportive campaign. All in all an air of satisfaction prevailed. Everyone knew it had been a close fight, mainly because, although nationalization had strengthened the power of the trade unions, it hadn't produced the right results for the electorate. Clement Attlee's new Cabinet would effect the correct changes, for sure. Paul saw trouble ahead if it didn't. Paul could think in practical terms, while Lulu indulged in fanciful and extreme ideas.

Later, they ate their packed lunches, and Lulu consented to drink one glass of wine. Just after two o'clock, younger members from the various offices of the headquarters poured in, and it wasn't long before a good old-fashioned cockney knees-up was in full swing. Lulu, having downed three glasses of wine, after all, gave of her tipsy best, flashing her legs and stockings with her dress hitched. Paul, who often thought a female girl was struggling to emerge from Lulu's Socialist armour, felt the present struggle might be victorious.

When the end of the lively afternoon arrived and it was time to go, the flushed Lulu was straightening her dress and complaining her spectacles were steamed up.

'A small price to pay for a happy day, Lulu.'

24

'What happened?'

'Oh, a few hours of knees-up and how's-your-father,' said Paul.

'It feels like it,' said Lulu. 'What made me go in for that adolescent stuff?'

'Because you're a girl and you're pretty good at it, especially the knees-up,' said Paul.

'Piffle. It was all that red wine you poured down my throat,' said Lulu. 'Oh, all right, give us a kiss, then, for doing Churchill in the eye.'

'Well, why not?' said Paul, and gave her a lip-smacker. Her glasses fell off.

'What a swine,' she said. 'Pick 'em up.' Paul picked them up and gave them to her. She put them on, or tried to. 'What's gone wrong?'

'They're upside down,' said Paul.

She righted them and said, 'I think you'd better take me home.'

Paul did so, seeing her to her flat in Kennington, where she informed him she knew what he was after, and that if he tried to put just one foot inside her door, she'd cripple his prospects. Paul laughed and left.

Lulu's father had been re-elected by his South London constituents. He called on his daughter at her flat late that evening. Flushed with victory and a fair intake of Scotch, he was at his most convivial, although when Lulu asked him if he'd now benefit from changes in the Cabinet, he expressed frank doubts.

'You're not pushy enough,' she said. 'Make a nuisance of yourself. Fasten onto Ernie Bevin and make yourself heard in Downing Street.'

'In Downing Street,' said Honest John, 'it's dog eat dog. That's not my style. My main job is to look after the needs of my constituents. Now, how are you getting on with that young man Paul Adams?'

'He's after me,' said Lulu.

'Eh?' Honest John showed surprise. Fond though he was of his daughter, he despaired of her usual 'keep-off-the-grass' appearance. She was missing out on what made the world go round for young people. 'He's what?'

'After me,' said Lulu.

'What a day,' said Honest John.

'What d'you mean, what a day?' demanded Lulu.

'Well, victory, if a close one, for the Party, and a bloke getting after you.'

'Yes, after seducing me,' said Lulu.

'Seducing you? You sure?' said Honest John.

'Of course I'm sure,' said Lulu.

'You'll fight that, of course—'

'You bet I will,' said Lulu.

'Well, if he wins,' said Honest John, well-being knocking a hole in his head, 'I hope he'll promise to marry you.'

'You what?'

'What did I say?' asked Honest John.

'Something I can't believe,' said Lulu. 'You, my own father, as good as telling me you won't mind if Paul Adams has his indecent way with me.'

'Only after you've put up a fight, of course,' said Honest John.

'Dad, you're disgusting,' said Lulu. 'Or drunk.'

'I've had a few, I'll admit. No, I can't tell a lie, I've had more than a few, and I'm able to say I'm glad to note you're wearing a decent outfit and the silk stockings. They ought to hit Paul's eyeballs, and probably did if he had a go at you in the office. Mind, I'm against that kind of caper in the office, and you can tell him so.'

'Oh, really?' said Lulu in sarky vein. 'You don't mind outside the office? Say on the top deck of a bus?'

'Now, Lulu, no dirty talk,' said Honest John.

'Me? What d'you think's been coming out of your mouth, then? I can't believe this. My own dad.'

'Lulu, you've got to do a bit of living now and again.'

'Getting seduced? That's living?'

'Well, I suppose I don't mean exactly that,' said Honest John, who, as a widower, had a bit of a thing going with his Parliamentary lady secretary. 'More like a bit of old-fashioned lovey-dovey by your fireside.'

'Oh, I see,' said Lulu. 'I end up on the carpet, do I? Listen. I'm a modern woman. My career comes first. I don't want any bloke cluttering up my life. Or my fireside carpet.'

'Your career's going to be a struggle, Lulu,' said Honest John. 'There aren't many women MPs. In the first place, you'll find your own sex don't much fancy voting for female candidates.'

'That's because too many women vote the way their husbands tell them to,' said Lulu. 'I'll change all that. The war made a lot of women ready for changes. And if Paul Adams tries getting me on my carpet, I'll chop his legs off.'

'Pity,' said Honest John, and escaped in a rush as

Lulu gave a yell and picked up an ornament to chuck at him.

My own dad, she said to herself, my own dad, encouraging me to get myself seduced. Drunk as a kite, of course, so I'll have to forgive him.

Chapter Three

'I just don't know how I can keep up with everyone,' said Chinese Lady. She and her husband, Edwin Finch, along with Susie and Sammy, were spending an evening with Polly and Boots. The twins, energy having evaporated after a hectic day, were in bed. 'There's so many of us now.'

'In other words, old lady,' said Boots, 'we're multiplying at a confusing rate.'

'Preferable, at least, to alarming,' murmured Polly.

'It's all these marriages,' said Susie.

'The old and the new,' said Boots.

'And any that are forthcoming,' said Polly.

'I'm not worried,' said Sammy, 'I'm an admired granddad, and so's Susie.'

'Grandma,' said Susie.

'Yes, that's nice for you, Susie,' said Chinese Lady, 'but I still can't count them all, not after what's come about these last three years.'

In view of the numerousness of her great-grandchildren, it was no wonder Chinese Lady said she was losing count. And since it was known that Patsy, the American wife of Sammy's son Daniel, was pregnant with her second child, it was quite likely she would declare that her confusion could become chronic.

She frowned.

'You'll catch up, Ma,' said Sammy. He was enjoying a whisky. So were Boots and Mr Finch. Polly and Susie each had a gin and tonic, and Chinese Lady had a port. If, in these post-war austerity years, alcohol had to be rationed by retailers, Chinese Lady's sons could always rely on brother-in-law Ned to come up with a bottle or two of this, that or the other. Ned had recently been elected to the board of directors of the wine merchants in Great Tower Street. Lizzy was delighted his long and loyal service had been recognized. His standing in the City, she said, would help her – and him, of course – to feel more in keeping with her mother and stepfather when they became a lord and lady. Not quite a lord and lady, said Ned. Well, as good as, said Lizzy.

Chinese Lady came to.

'What about Tommy's daughter Alice?' she asked.

'Working at Bristol University,' said Sammy, 'and seeing a lot of our Bess.' Bess, his eldest daughter, was a student there.

'Well, I don't know that anybody's told me,' said Chinese Lady a little fretfully. 'Still, a lot of our young people have made good marriages, which is a blessing considering what the war did to a lot of families.'

Boots smiled. He rather suspected his mother was enjoying the moment. She might be seventy-three now, with an increasing amount of grey in her hair, but he would stand by his conviction that she was still sharp as a needle. He was sure she knew precisely what marriages and what births had taken place, and that her comments were to be taken as a reminder that they all belonged to a properly brought-up family with a healthy regard for procreation. On cue, she asked Sammy how old Tommy and Vi's Alice was.

'Let's see,' mused Sammy.

'She's twenty-five,' said Susie.

'Isn't it time she was engaged?' asked Chinese Lady.

'I think there's a soldier friend somewhere,' said Susie.

'He's a Scot, a regular,' said Boots, 'and overseas at the moment.'

'Well, I like to know,' said Chinese Lady.

'I'm sure Tommy and Vi will keep you informed, Mum,' smiled Susie.

'Just how many great-grandchildren are there?' murmured Polly.

'Personally,' said Boots, 'I'm foggy about the exact number.'

'Well, you didn't ought to be,' said Chinese Lady. 'Have we got them all in our birthday book, Edwin?'

'All, Maisie my dear,' said Mr Finch, 'except Daniel and Patsy's expected infant.'

'Boots,' said Chinese Lady, 'I think I'd like them all photographed in a group on the day your stepdad goes to Buckingham Palace to see our King.'

'In a group, yes, I see,' said Boots.

Polly smiled. She had long known that a request from Boots's inimitable mother was on the closest terms with an order.

'Can you arrange that, old love?' she asked.

'Probably,' said Boots, 'if you could arrange for Patsy to get a move on.'

*　　*　　*

'It's kicking,' said young Mrs Patsy Adams, seven months pregnant.

'Is it?' said husband Daniel.

'I should know,' said Patsy, putting a hand on her bulge and patting it.

'Is kicking good?' asked Daniel.

'Sure it is,' said Patsy, expecting their second child. Their first-born, Arabella, was two. 'It means we've got another healthy foetus.'

'Foetus, right,' said Daniel, 'although we don't use that word much in our family. Except for Uncle Boots and Aunt Polly, we're all a bit old-fashioned and shy.'

'Old-fashioned? Shy?' said Patsy. 'Backward, you mean.'

'Yes, that as well,' said Daniel. 'Cousin Bobby told me once that he had to explain to Helene just how shy all the blokes in our family were compared to French geezers. She fell about.'

'So will I in a minute,' said Patsy.

'Anyway,' said Daniel, 'what're we expecting this time, boy or girl?'

'Well, one or the other, I guess,' said Patsy, 'and your pa's going to give you a salary raise either way, isn't he?'

'He went cuckoo when we presented him with his first grandchild,' said Daniel. 'He'll go gaga when his second arrives, so yes, he'll raise my salary as a reward for my good work.'

'Your good work? Excuse me,' said Patsy, 'but won't I have had something to do with it?'

'Not half, and you know that,' said Daniel. 'Or you should do. I mean, you're a big girl now, Patsy.' He patted her bulge.

'Daniel, you're cute,' said Patsy, and eyed him with a smile. Twenty-two now, with dark curling hair and expressive hazel eyes, she had known him for well over five years and had married him in 1946. He was still her fun guy. If she ever missed her home town of Boston and the expansive American way of life, she had never said so, although she did say that one day she'd like to take him to the States and show him Boston. Being what he was, a smarty-pants, of course, he said he'd love to go, but did she mean she'd take him in her handbag? In answer to that, she socked him with a rolled-up magazine. It was the best answer she could think of.

'Well, whatever, Patsy,' he said now, 'I'm proud of you.' Nearly twenty-three, he was personable enough, a typical Adams with his firm features, his dark brown hair and his father's blue eyes. He worked at his dad's offices by Camberwell Green, he and his cousin Tim being joint managers of Adams Properties Ltd under the watchful eye of the chairman, Sammy himself.

At the present moment, the company was having a new factory erected in the East End. Sammy had acquired a large bomb site for the purpose. For too long, in his estimation, most of his many machinists and seamstresses had been travelling to the Belsize Park garments factory from their East End homes. The new factory in Bethnal Green would mean some of them could actually walk to their work.

The East End was presently a constructor's paradise. Slums were being swept away, high-rise blocks of council flats were going up, and a multitude of bomb sites had been cleared for commercial developers. Sammy, commercially-minded since the age of nine, jumped in with both feet, clearing the red tape of council bureaucracy with the agility of a kangaroo. In a manner of speaking. The Adams Property Company Ltd, shares held by Sammy, Boots, Lizzy, Tommy, Rosie and the family's old friend, Rachel Goodman, was prospering. It had sold, very profitably, the flats of a three-storey block built on the firm's old brewery site in Southwark. It now owned the Bethnal Green site, the Belsize Park factory, the Camberwell Green offices, the premises of a Walworth store, various private houses, a dairy farm, and three bomb sites around the Elephant and Castle, a major area of current development. Other sites there, purchased by Sammy before the war was over, had been sold at a substantial gain. Daniel and Tim were negotiating the sale of the unsold three, but holding out, under Sammy's instructions, for the best possible price.

'Negotiating, my lads,' he said, 'is a high-class word for bargaining, and bargaining an old-fashioned word for making a profit. Keep that in mind.'

'Bargaining?' said Tim.

'Profit,' said Sammy.

'We all like the sound of profit, Dad,' said Daniel.

'Very commendable,' said Sammy. 'It makes an audit look happy and keeps workers in their jobs. But watch out for the Labour Party, which considers profit evil and would like to do away with it. Can't believe it, can you? No, nor can I. But old Joe Stalin has done away with it in Russia, except, of course, for himself and his commissioners.'

'You mean commissars?' said Tim.

'Same thing,' said Sammy.

Sammy was always giving the young managers of

34

the property company sound business advice, of which Tim and Daniel took due note. Boots, general manager of the whole concern, gave them advice only when they asked for it, on the grounds that they both had enough sense gradually to evaluate for themselves what was sound and what was rocky.

Patsy, who had come to know that Daniel was much more than merely a fun guy, was very happy with his progress in the family business.

'Daniel,' she said, taking the conversation further on this particular evening, 'if you get a raise, won't Tim get one too?'

'Sure,' said Daniel.

'So you'll both benefit from my personal contribution?' said Patsy.

'Oh, Tim will get his increase as a kind of retrospective gesture for making Dad a great-uncle when Jennifer was born in '45,' said David.

'That's fair, I guess,' said Patsy.

'Dad knows an increase for both of us will stop someone from suggesting he's favouring me,' said Daniel. 'He's a wise old fruitcake.'

'Well, a raise for both of you is fair, I guess,' said Patsy, 'but should you call your pa a wise old fruitcake?'

'Why not?' said Daniel. 'He's all that and more.'

'Daniel, you're short of respect for your pa.'

'He'd say it was a compliment. By the way, don't forget we're going to Cornwall with the family for our summer holiday this year.'

'Oh, great,' said Patsy, 'but why the reminder?'

'Well, what I really meant was don't forget we'll have to think about a swimsuit for a baby girl or swimming trunks for a baby boy,' said Daniel.

'That'll be on top of a swimsuit for Arabella.'

'Daniel, you need a shrink,' said Patsy.

Saturday afternoon.

A person of the male gender watched a girl leaving the local library, a borrowed book in her hand. He'd come to know she visited the library most Saturday afternoons, as he did himself.

Advancing to the door, he opened it to watch her going on her way in the crisp sunlight of winter, her step springy. If he followed her at a distance, he might find out where she lived. Probably somewhere superior, for she looked a very well-dressed girl.

He resisted the temptation to dog her blithe footsteps, and stayed where he was. Some other time, perhaps.

'Would you mind closing that door?' called a library assistant.

He closed it and went back to studying crime novels available to borrowers.

Chapter Four

When David, elder son of Tommy and Vi Adams, was out of the RAF, and his fiancée, Kate Trimble, out of the WAAF, they made arrangements to be married. David had hopes of marital bliss and running a farm.

Kate was a cockney girl from Camberwell, and accordingly a basic townie with no great aptitude for farming. David, however, had learned to love a rural life during his years as an evacuee in Devon, where he took to the land as naturally as a copper to fingering crooks. So just before he married Kate, and after he had talked to his Uncle Sammy, he sounded her out on the prospects of running a dairy farm.

'What, me milk cows?' said Kate.

'I'll show you how,' said David.

'Oh, I bet,' said Kate, 'except I don't want anything to do with cows.'

'They're noble and gentle creatures,' said David.

'Can't we grow fruit, like oranges and bananas?' suggested Kate.

'Not in this country,' said David.

'Well, vegetables, then,' said Kate. 'Onions and carrots and things like that.'

'Not as profitable as a dairy farm,' said David, 'and

we'd get help from the new Milk Marketing Board.'

'Well, let them milk the cows,' said Kate. 'I don't suppose all civil servants sit at desks, do they?'

'Some get out and about, like school inspectors, but I don't suppose many are on close terms with cows,' said David. 'Tell you what, we'll think about hiring someone who'll do the job.'

'Now you're talking,' said Kate, 'especially as we might – well, you know.'

'Have a baby or two?' said David.

'Well, when we're married, I suppose we'll get together a bit,' said Kate.

'Yes, we probably will, a bit,' said David, thinking not for the first time that her dark auburn hair and green eyes were a perpetual reminder of his late Aunt Emily. He talked her round until Kate became quite keen for them to try their luck, especially as David's Uncle Sammy had said the family firm would buy a suitable farm for them, as long as it wasn't all the way down in Devon, which David had had in mind. Such a farm, complete with barn, dairy and farmhouse, was purchased from the elderly owner, allowing him and his wife to retire after working themselves into weathered wrinkles all through the war.

So when they were married in 1948, David and Kate took up occupation of the farmhouse. David went enthusiastically to work, and Sammy supplied more capital to enable the young newly-weds to acquire a herd of Jersey cows. Smashing milkers, said David after a month or so. Don't look at me, said Kate. David had been teaching her the basics concerning how to churn out butter and cheese, but she was still opposed to being turned into a milkmaid. So David was doing that job, while Kate, under his instruction, learned how to chat up the cows and make friends with them. She was able to clap her hands in delight when she finally succeeded in driving the herd from one field of pasture to another.

They had a stroke of luck midway through 1949. When they advertised for help, a young Italian immigrant applied. Born of Tuscan peasants, nineteen-year-old Enrico Cellino knew all about cows and dairies, and presented himself eagerly to David and Kate. He spoke good English and said he would like very much to work for them and leave his present job as a waiter in a Westerham hotel. Milk cows? Yes, he had grown up doing that, but the living was poor and, like many Italians before him, he headed for Great Britain with an immigrant's visa in 1948.

David gave him the job, and from then on Enrico kept the cows contented. At David's invitation, he left his lodgings in Westerham and installed himself in the flat above what had been a stable. There, in his spare time, he read Agatha Christie's detective novels to help his improving English, listened to the BBC music programmes on his radio, and sometimes went into Westerham.

'Doesn't he have a girlfriend?' asked Kate one day.

'What a question,' said David.

'He's got his share of good looks,' said Kate.

'And he's Italian,' said David. 'He doesn't buzz off to Westerham to look at General Wolfe's statue.'

'Isn't there supposed to be a poem about General Wolfe?' asked Kate.

'Yes, it goes like this,' said David. He quoted.

"'General Wolfe climbed up the heights
To slay the sleeping French.
But pity stayed his warrior's hand
When he saw a sleeping wench.
She came awake and gasped, 'Mon Dieu,
Tell me what you mean to do.'
'Stay like that,' said General Wolfe,
I've just got time to show you.'"'

Kate shrieked.

'My, what a lucky lot we are round here, having someone knowing larky poems,' she said. 'Anyway, if Enrico has got a girlfriend in Westerham, good luck to him, I say.'

'Even if he hasn't got any at all in Westerham,' said David, 'he's got quite a few here.'

'The cows?' said Kate.

'Well, I love 'em myself in a way,' said David.

'I must've been daft marrying a man who's potty about cows,' said Kate.

A Thursday morning.

Jimmy, younger son of Susie and Sammy Adams, was reading an airmail letter on his way to his job at his dad's Walworth store.

'Dear Jimmy,

'Well, here I am at last, writing to you as promised. Things have been hectic, but we're now settled into our new home in a suburb of New York, and Dad has settled into his new job as a Wall Street executive. It's what they call top businessmen over here. New York is thrilling, the most exciting city in the world, I should think, and so alive and heady compared to

40

poor old bashed-about London. At night Broadway is brilliant and even intoxicating. You drink in the atmosphere until you're heady, and we had a super time when Dad took all of us to see the musical hit called *Oklahoma!*. Great.

'The New York women dress very smartly, especially businesswomen. There are more of them here than there are in London. You can even see quite a few of them in Wall Street, where they have high-salaried jobs. Dad says he's never seen a single high-salaried woman in the City of London, just shorthand typists or girl clerks. He also says there'll be women executives one day on Wall Street.

'There's the other side, of course, as we all found out when we took a car ride through Harlem, a neighbourhood that's like a ghetto for poverty-stricken black people who live in its tenements. It's a kind of sullen and hostile place, which white people avoid at night.

'I've enrolled at a college of Arts and Science, and am finding it exciting and inspiring in respect of fashion design. It's giving me a greater urge to make a career as a designer. I'm very ambitious. I hope you are too.

'All for now. Lots of good wishes.

'Affectionately, Jenny.'

Jimmy grimaced. Stunning Jenny Osborne had been his girlfriend until she went to America just over a month ago. For some time her father, a City stockbroker, had been considering an invitation to join a thriving American firm on Wall Street, New York. With the blessing of his wife, he eventually accepted, and he took her, his son and two daughters with him, the whole family in a high state of excitement.

41

But it left Jimmy despondent. Nearly twenty, and as personable as most of the young Adams males, if a little more diffident, his relationship with Jenny had given him heady ideas about his future prospects with her. Accordingly, her going left him feeling that life had knocked a hole in his head. She promised to write, of course, but only a week after she'd moved out of his life, Jimmy came to the reasonable conclusion that hands across the wide Atlantic sea hardly represented much more than a relationship of penfriends.

'Buck up, Jimmy,' said Sammy, his dad, that evening.

'I wish I could,' said Jimmy, 'and I would if I could get rid of the feeling that my life's been blighted.'

'Oh, dear,' said his mother, Susie.

'Jimmy my lad,' said Sammy, 'if you'll use your mince pies you'll get to see there's no shortage of other girls. I've noticed a few meself around Camberwell Green.'

'Oh, I can see all right,' said Jimmy, 'but all I notice are the dark rolling clouds of my wintry horizon.'

'Oh, dear,' said Susie again. 'My, we have got it bad, haven't we?'

'It's bad right enough,' said Sammy. 'It must be, to make Jimmy sound like Hamlet. Have we seen that play, Susie?'

'Yes, years ago, at the Old Vic,' said Susie.

'Well, Jimmy's giving us a bit of it now,' said Sammy.

'I think I'll go and live in a dog kennel,' said Jimmy.

'Yes, all right, Jimmy love,' said Susie.

'We'll deliver a decent bone or two on your doorstep,' said Sammy.

'Sammy, that kind of joke won't help,' said Susie.

'Joke?' said Sammy. 'I feel for Jimmy living in a dog kennel, don't I?'

'Don't be upset, Mum, I'll try to live for more than a bone or two,' said Jimmy.

Jenny's letter contained the obvious implication that she was set on making a career for herself in America. Well, he had to admit that in the comparatively short time he had known her, her interest in fashion design had always seemed to mean more to her than her social interests.

Still, he thought, I don't think I'll commit suicide, or live in a dog kennel.

When he visited his Aunt Polly and Uncle Boots the following evening, Boots's reaction was similar in one respect to Sammy's. He too said there were other girls, other stunners, and that Jimmy could bowl one over by brushing up on his sex appeal.

'Pardon?' said Jimmy.

'You've got your share, young sport,' said Polly.

'But have I got enough?' asked Jimmy.

'Only the opposite sex could tell you that,' said Boots. 'Incidentally, when I was your age, sex appeal hadn't yet made its entrance.'

'Not even yours?' said Polly.

'I should explain, Jimmy, that the term itself was either unknown or forbidden,' said Boots. 'Sex was only mentioned in respect of gender, and even then not in front of one's parents. Hollywood invented sex appeal sometime in the late Thirties, applying it exclusively to its female stars. Even then, some parents were against it being mentioned in front of teenage children.'

'What am I listening to?' asked Jimmy.

'Fact,' said Boots.

'Rhubarb,' said Polly.

'Nowadays, sex appeal seems applicable to both sexes,' said Boots.

'That's true,' said Jimmy, 'but I still don't know if I've got enough of it to knock a stunner sideways.'

'Have a happy time finding out,' said Polly, 'you're an up-and-coming knockout.'

Despite all that, Jimmy replied to Jenny's letter, and in a light-hearted fashion that hid his depression.

Chapter Five

Monday morning, and Sammy was at the family's Belsize Park garments factory. He was happy. Paris, recovering from the trauma of its wartime occupation by the Germans and the shame of a large amount of collaboration, had come to life. Its fashion designers had woken up from their bad dream, and young Christian Dior had introduced what was called the New Look. This took the form of a narrow-waisted dress with a tight-fitting bodice, and a long full skirt worn over a layer of petticoats. Sammy liked that. It turned women into feminine females, which was highly welcome after the square-shouldered wartime fashions had made them look in serious need of something frilly. Under licence, the firm of Adams Fashions Ltd was manufacturing the New Look for its shops. The post-war import restrictions on fabrics prevented the firm from expanding its output, which made Sammy fret a bit.

However, much to his pleasure, his pre-war fashion designer, Lilian Chambers (née Hyams) had recently come back. She had married Bill Chambers, her local Walworth milk roundsman, some years ago. They were now living in a Hampstead flat, not far from Belsize Park. Lilian, as much of a warm-hearted Jewess as Rachel Goodman, had thought about converting to the Church of England, but Bill had said she didn't need to and so she didn't. Lizzy and Ned's son Edward, in marrying Rachel Goodman's daughter Leah at a civic ceremony, had told Leah much the same thing, and so she still followed her own religion.

Lilian was delighted to be taken on again by Sammy, whose electric outlook was always inspiring. In her old seat in the design room of the factory, she was talking about the drawbacks of the New Look. She pointed out that its tight bodice and narrow waist only suited tall, slim young women, and that it was also too lengthy for girls. Because of those faults, it was beginning to come under criticism from some women's magazines, even if its inception had been welcomed as a breath of fresh air.

'Fair enough,' said Sammy, 'so what's on your mind, pinching the design and improving it? If so, who's going to get sued, you or me?'

'We're not going to pinch any part of the New Look, I'm going to suggest a design of our own,' said Lilian, nicely buxom in her mid-fifties. 'My life, would I land us in hot soup, Sammy? Besides, we go for separates and not a dress. A skirt and a top. Think of the American-style dirndl skirt that girls are now wearing in place of the New Look. But that's also too long, in my opinion. I should have an opinion when I've been out of the game for years? Well, I have.' Lilian began to pencil outlines. 'I favour a pretty, embroidered blouse, a much shorter dirndl skirt, starched net petticoats and a saucy rustle, don't I?'

'A saucy what?' said Sam.

'Stiff petticoats rustle, Sammy, intimately.'

Sammy grinned.

'What a female woman,' he said. 'Can you come up with a sketch?'

'Watch me,' said Lilian. Deftly, artistically, she used a brush and watercolours to paint in the pencilled outline of her idea. Sammy looked on, eyes lit with blue light, as the design came into colourful being. He noted that Lilian went for a glimpse of petticoat, the merest glimpse, just below the hem of the skirt that was several inches shorter than the overlong New Look and the even longer dirndl. She chose dark blue for the skirt, and made the blouse white and embroidered in pink and blue. Just the job to make girls look highly fetching, he thought. And the blouse had to be an improvement on the New Look's restrictive bodice, for girls who didn't like to appear flat-chested.

'Lilian,' he said, 'it's my serious opinion you could earn sackfuls of French oof working for this new Paris designer, Monsewer Whatsisdear.'

'Christian Dior?' said Lilian.

'What's it matter if he's Christian or not?' said Sammy. 'He's waking up French fashions.'

'Sammy, what I earn I'd like to earn from you,' said Lilian. 'I should buzz off to Paris? Not likely. Bill hopes that we can buy a little house before we get old and rusty. His earnings as an electrician and mine with Adams Fashions should help, and could I say more?'

'Well, I like that sketch something chronic,' said Sammy, 'it's a hundred per cent female.'

'Well, Sammy love, we do need something pretty and feminine to hold off the enemy,' said Lilian.

Sammy wanted to know what enemy, and Lilian

referred him to the creeping invasion of American blue jeans. These had been worn by the farm workers and cowboys of America for many years, and had been adopted as casual wear by American teenagers during the war. Sammy tottered at the thought of them taking on in the UK. The fact was, however, he'd seen a pair or two on young blokes. He said so to Lilian. Holy Joe, he added, don't tell me you've seen them on girls. Now and again, said Lilian. I tell you, Sammy, she said, they're our creeping enemy. A girl in jeans, she said, puts a full stop on dress design.

'If they do take on here, I'll pass away,' said Sammy. 'Someone's got to inform the Yanks to keep 'em in the Wild West for their cowboys. If not, I'll buy a submarine and torpedo their imports. Anyway, you put the finishing touches to that sketch while I go and fetch Tommy and Gertie. Let's see what they think about it.'

Brother Tommy was manager of the factory, Gertie the long-serving chargehand who had worked in East End sweatshops as a girl and spent twenty-four years in the civilized conditions established by Sammy, Tommy and Boots. Gertie, nearly sixty now and close to retirement, had an affection for all three Adams brothers.

Her eyes popped when she and Tommy were shown Lilian's colourful sketch. Gertie could recognize promise or otherwise in any fashion idea, and the first thing she said came straight out of her instincts.

'Luvaduck, Mister Sammy, that's really pretty. I'll eat my Bert's old bowler if it don't prove that girls go for frills. I'd go for 'em meself if I wasn't a granny.'

48

'I like it,' said Tommy. 'But what about the materials? We're still fighting restrictions on imports.'

'There's a problem, my life, yes,' said Lilian, who had made pencilled notes of preferred fabrics. 'We'll need any amount of petticoat material. We'll be up against a shortage.'

'Blimey O'Reilly, all these never-ending shortages make me wonder who won the war, us or them,' said Tommy. Clothes rationing was still in force, and rumour had it that it would go on for at least another year. 'And as it is, the Government's never been keen on the New Look on account of its length and how much material is required. We've got serious worries about what we'll need for this new design.'

'Mister Tommy,' said Gertie, 'don't you have no faith in Mister Sammy's way of—' She paused to search for the right words.

'Finding manna in the desert?' said Lilian.

'Yes, that's it, like Moses,' said Gertie.

'Right, hop off on your camel, Sammy, and find some large bales of the kind of manna we need for launching this outfit in a big way,' said Tommy. 'We want to get Lilian's design not just into our shops but the big West End stores as well, before some French clever clogs beats us to it. That's bound to happen, y'know. I mean, look at her sketch – it's a natural.'

'I should dispute that?' said Lilian. 'I would, except it's a mistake to be too modest. Modesty in the rag trade makes buyers think you've got no self-belief.'

'Where can I get a camel?' mused Sammy. 'London Zoo, I suppose. I'll hire one and jog off to our suppliers, the ones a bloke can talk to under a palm tree.'

'Mister Sammy,' said Gertie, 'what with prospects like these and our new fact'ry going up in Bethnal Green, I ain't proposing to retire just yet. Nor Bert.'

'Couldn't manage without you and Bert,' said Tommy. Bert, Gertie's husband, was the maintenance man and assistant manager, and as loyal as she was.

'Gertie, don't retire till you're a hundred,' said Sammy. 'Well, I'm off now, I've got things to do. So long, be good.'

On his way back to Camberwell in his reconditioned Riley, purchased a few months ago because new cars were still in short supply, Sammy stopped for a quick lunchtime snack at an Italian cafe, where he thought about old Eli Greenberg, always a bloke he could talk to under a palm tree, so to speak. Yes, old Eli would know where to lay hands on large amounts of imports. He resumed his journey like a blithe spirit.

However, coming to a halt at traffic lights in Camden Town, he blinked in shock. Two young women were walking the pavement, both wearing blue jeans and windcheaters. Holy Moses, he thought, it's the enemy, two of them. The jeans, to his fashion-conscious optics, did nothing for the young women's legs except to make them look fit only for riding a horse in a faraway Indian country, somewhere in the Wild West. He turned his head, shocked eyes following the horrible sight, a sight that boded ill for the rag trade. Behind him, a car honked. The traffic started to pile up behind him and as he motored across the junction he was quivering like an Ancient Briton who'd seen his first elephant.

'Suffering cats,' he said to Camden Town, 'I'll take a week to get over this.'

When he arrived at Mr Eli Greenberg's Camberwell yard sometime later he was still a bit pale. Mr Greenberg was not suffering himself, and his white-flecked beard curled happily as he saw Sammy alight from his car. The old rag and bone merchant treasured his relationship with Sammy and the Adams family, and was a mine of information whenever Sammy wanted to know who could be useful to him in times of need.

'Sammy, vell, it's a pleasure seeing you, ain't it?' he said, lifting his black-mittened hands in greeting.

'Eli old cock,' said Sammy, 'can you put the kettle on and make me a hot cup of tea?' I'm a bit faint.'

'Sammy, are you ill?'

'I'm shocked to me core,' said Sammy, 'so I'm ill all right.'

'Vell, I'll put the kettle on and lend you an ear, von't I?' said Mr Greenberg, who, despite his many years among the cosmopolitan people of London, still spoke the kind of English he had picked up as an immigrant from Russia.

Sammy followed his old Jewish friend into his office, where Mr Greenberg put his kettle on a gas ring and listened to a highly lurid account of what could be seen walking the streets of Camden Town, which, as Sammy finally made clear, were two pairs of jeans.

'I never saw anything more painful to me eyes, Eli, not even during the war, when certain working conditions put some women into baggy trousers and boiler suits.' Sammy sighed. 'I ask you, jeans as a fashion at a time when fellers are overdue for the sight of girls in Sunday frocks every day of the week? I've got heartburn.'

'Vell, I'll be honest, Sammy,' said Mr Greenberg, pouring boiling water into a glazed brown teapot that looked as if it might have had a standing acquaintance with Queen Victoria's tea table. 'While it's true Moses vouldn't have liked it, don't I hear talk that some young wimmen find jeans comfortable?'

'Blow comfortable,' growled Sammy. 'Comfortable ought to die a death in favour of frills and nylon stockings, stockings such as we're producing on account of our helpful stocks of nylon.'

'I agree, Sammy, don't I?' said Mr Greenberg, milking two cups. 'But I hear there's imports of jeans coming in from America. Not by the thousands, not yet—'

'Not yet?' said Sammy. 'Knock it off, Eli. I had me full share of headaches last year, when the Fat Man rose up from the dead and declared war over those bales of nylon. Pour the tea and give me something to live for, even if only for five minutes.'

Mr Greenberg filled the cups with steaming tea.

'Here, Sammy,' he said.

Sammy took the proffered cup, gulped down a mouthful of the scalding liquid, then gasped something about what Old Nick's flaming brimstone was doing to his good-natured tonsils. 'Eli, my day's coming apart.'

'Sammy my friend,' said Mr Greenberg, 'don't I hear jeans are becoming a popular fashion in America?'

'It ain't a fashion, it's a disaster,' said Sammy.

'All the same,' said Mr Greenberg, shaking a sympathetic head that was crowned with his round rusty black hat, 'vhat is popular in America vun year is popular in our old country the next year, ain't it? So I think it follows, don't it, that it von't be too long before jeans vill be the fashion for young people all over.'

'What you think, Eli, is giving me a shocking pain in me elbow,' said Sammy. He drank hot tea while glooming at the prospect of the rag trade suffering competition from cowboy clobber. While the property company and other enterprises had their fond place in his working life, the rag trade had always been his first love. He would not have put the management of Adams Fashions into the hands of his son Daniel and his nephew Tim, however much faith he had in their abilities. Adams Fashions was his own cherished baby. He finished his tea. Its enlivening effect perked him up. 'Eli, I'm not going to believe female girls will buy jeans except as casual wear for Saturday daytimes, say. Girls will always go for looking like dreamboats on Saturday evenings, and for their best frocks on Sundays. The New Look helped a bit, after those gorblimey wartime fashions. What's going to help more are frills, feminine frills, and Lilian's come up with what you're going to tell me is the answer to my prayers.'

'Ah, Lilian, the happy lady, she's back with you, Sammy?' said Mr Greenberg, refilling the cups.

'She is,' said Sammy, and retailed details of the design.

'Sammy, if that don't do what it should, I will eat my hat,' chortled the delighted Mr Greenberg.

'Hope you won't have to,' said Sammy, 'hope you'll be able to leave it to the British Museum. Now listen, I need mileages of material for the blouses, skirts and petticoats. All fabrics we're getting at the moment are only sufficient for our present production of ladies' wear. Who are the chief importers of what we want now? We've got some information, but not enough.'

'You vant miles of materials, Sammy?' Mr Greenberg shook his head again. 'The Government ain't in favour of importing miles of any material. It means too much sterling leaving the country, don't it?'

'Eli, the day you and me start feeling sorry for any government is the day we get our heads examined,' said Sammy. 'So who are the biggest importers?'

Mr Greenberg sighed.

'For vunce, Sammy, I ain't able to oblige,' he said.

'Now then, Eli old cock, you've got useful acquaintances who could point me at the chief importers, haven't you?' said Sammy.

'It vouldn't do much good, Sammy,' said Mr Greenberg. 'No vun in the rag trade can get more than what is coming in on account of import restrictions, ain't it?'

'Don't I know it,' said Sammy, 'but somewhere some warehouse might be stocked up and waiting for an offer in the dark, and some importer might be looking for a cash customer.'

'Sammy,' said Mr Greenberg, 'all that's being imported this year vill already be spoken for. It's supply and demand, and supply ain't so good. And it hurts me to say I don't have time to go looking into varehouses. I'm off to Israel in three days for a visit, ain't I?'

'So you are,' said Sammy. Eli was taking his wife and his stepsons, Michal and Jacob, to the independent State of Israel. He and his wife were to stay for a month, and his stepsons intended to work for a year in a kibbutz. Sammy remembered with a great deal of pleasure how Michal and Jacob had helped lay the Fat Man low last year. 'Oh well, you enjoy yourselves, Eli, and I'll do the looking. I'll have to, bless your old sock suspenders.'

'Sammy,' protested Mr Greenberg in pain, 'I don't vear sock suspenders. They don't look so good. Not like a lady's suspenders.'

'Know what you mean,' said Sammy. 'I've seen some of those in my time. Very sexy, which sock suspenders ain't. Never worn any meself, nor have Boots and Tommy.'

He said goodbye to his old friend, told him he'd look him up as soon as he got back from Israel, then drove to his offices at Camberwell Green.

Chapter Six

'Boots, got to talk to you.'

Boots looked up as Sammy entered his office.

'Talk away, Sammy,' he said.

'I've had a day I could've partly done without,' said Sammy.

'Partly done without?' said Boots.

'I could've done with more of the other half,' said Sammy.

'The other half, yes, I see,' said Boots. 'What you mean is you enjoyed a happy morning and suffered a headache this afternoon. Or vice versa. Well, I'm listening, Sammy, so go ahead.'

'It's like this, Boots.' Sammy recited the events of the day, and how the pleasure of beholding Lilian's design had taken a nasty knock when two pairs of walking jeans had socked his eyeballs in Camden Town.

'I've spotted a few jeans myself,' said Boots.

'I feel for you,' said Sammy. 'Shocked you, didn't they?'

'I've seen worse sights,' said Boots.

'Like a pair of shorts on an elephant?' said Sammy, and spoke of how Eli Greenberg had made his headache critical by prophesying that jeans would actually become fashionable. And as for the materials needed to launch Lilian's design ambitiously, Eli had reminded him that import restrictions could turn the prospects into a dog's dinner. Eli had also said he couldn't at the moment point him at any importers or stocked-up warehouses that might be willing to deal with a cash customer.

'Did you need being reminded about import restrictions?' asked Boots.

'What I needed was being pointed at some well-stocked warehouses waiting for cash customers, like I just mentioned,' said Sammy.

'Castles in the air these days,' said Boots. 'I'm surprised you didn't know that.'

'I knew it all right,' said Sammy, 'but I had a natural attack of wishful thinking, backed up by faith in old Eli. Unfortunately, he hasn't got the time to go looking into possible sources, he's off to Israel for a visit later this week.'

'Try Hong Kong,' said Boots.

'Eh?' said Sammy.

'Hong Kong's rag trade industry is booming,' said Boots. 'Exporters are employing thousands of Chinese workers. Cheapest labour in the world. You've read about visitors who can be measured for an excellent suit one day and pick it up the next, at a cost of about twenty-one shillings, haven't you?'

'Bust my braces, so I have,' said Sammy. 'No, wait a tick, we'd have to get an import licence, whether it's for finished garments or raw material.'

'Try the relevant Ministry,' said Boots. 'Find someone in the imports and exports department. Ask for an export licence first. Exports help the tottering balance of payments. They'll be happy to issue Adams Fashions with one, and probably invite you to stay for a cup of tea and a biscuit. Accept the invitation, and over the tea make a casual request for an import licence too.'

'Sounds all right,' said Sammy, 'but try being serious.'

'Well, seriously,' said Boots, 'we're up against the economic policies of our Labour government and its poverty-stricken Treasury. We're lucky to be doing as well as we are in the rag trade.'

'But with all these restrictions on fabrics and suchlike, we're standing still,' said Sammy, 'and I ain't fond of standing still.'

Mrs Rachel Goodman, secretary and director of the firm's parent company, came in at that moment, paperwork in her hand. At forty-seven, she was still a lush-looking woman with a voice that could sound velvety.

'Oh, you're back, Sammy?' she smiled.

'With a headache,' said Sammy, and explained the reasons why his loaf of bread felt a bit chronic. Rachel listened until he reached the point concerning Boots's airy-fairy suggestion to go to work on the relevant Ministry.

Then she said, 'I don't think we'll get away with that, and I don't think Boots does.'

'I had a passing thought,' said Boots.

'But I like the sound of Lilian's design,' said Rachel. 'Just a moment while I make a phone call.'

She went back to her office, returning fifteen minutes later.

'Well?' said Sammy, now a bit fidgety.

'You mentioned warehouses to Eli, and Boots

mentioned Hong Kong to you,' said Rachel. 'Sammy, do we enter the black market?'

'Only if we don't tell Susie,' said Sammy. 'Susie's got principles. So have I, of course, only I can stretch mine a bit when I've got a hole in my head.'

'And I've got a blind eye,' smiled Boots.

'My life, Boots lovey,' said Rachel, 'don't we all know that's more than a figure of speech?' Boots's left eye had been permanently damaged during the first battle of the Somme in 1916. 'Why, and don't we all know that you and Sammy and I myself weren't brought up to embrace the improper?'

'I think you mean cuddling a spiv,' said Boots, 'but of course we don't have to go as far as kissing one.'

'Not without Susie divorcing me,' said Sammy.

'I should want to kiss Steiner and Wallis?' said Rachel.

'Who?' said Sammy.

'Owners of a new post-war warehouse,' said Rachel. 'I remembered my father speaking about their venture. Enoch Steiner is a cousin of his. The warehouse isn't in Hong Kong, it's in the London Docks. I spoke to Mr Wallis. Tomorrow, Sammy, we're to go to their warehouse at St George's Wharf, near Rotherhithe, where we'll talk to Mr Wallis.'

'We've got prospects?' said Sammy.

'At a price,' said Rachel.

'His kind of price? What a spiv,' said Sammy. 'Still, when we've got our backs to the wall, we've got to make allowances.'

'We'll need five hundred pounds cash for a deposit,' said Rachel.

'Five hundred smackers?' said Sammy.

59

'Sammy, he whistled when I told him what we were after,' said Rachel.

'OK, san fairy,' said Sammy.

'The balance to be paid on delivery to our factory,' said Rachel.

'Do I like it?' said Sammy.

'Force yourself,' said Boots, typically tolerant of what Sammy was up to, a large black market deal. In any case, he knew such deals were widespread, and that the Government hadn't been able to come up with legislation comprehensive or strong enough to deter or outwit the country's wiliest exploiters of market conditions. What legislation did exist effected no more than pinpricks.

'Yes, I like it,' said Sammy. 'I think Rachel's going to lead me to manna in a dockside oasis. Rachel, you beauty, what's in the warehouse?'

'Fabrics,' said Rachel. 'But although Mr Steiner is a distant relation, Mr Wallis isn't. That's why it will cost us a little more.'

'Two arms and a leg,' said Sammy. 'I ask myself, can I afford that much?'

'Further, everything has to be strictly confidential,' said Rachel.

'And slightly on the wrong side of the law,' said Boots.

'Still, we're grown-up now,' said Sammy. 'We can all wrestle with a bit of Old Mother Riley's principles and come out undamaged, can't we?'

'You and I, Sammy, have had a fair amount of wrestles of that kind in our time,' said Boots, 'and not even Chinese Lady has noticed any bruises.'

'I think we all agree that the business comes first,' smiled Rachel.

The following morning.

Miss Lulu Saunders arrived at the Young Socialists' office wearing a grey jersey, a dark blue jacket and light blue jeans. The jeans were such a tight fit that they shaped her hips and posterior in eye-blinking fashion.

Paul stared. He knew precisely what his Uncle Sammy thought about American jeans. That they menaced the rag trade, even if at the present moment they were few and far between.

'I don't believe what I'm seeing,' he said.

'What you're seeing cost me a packet,' said Lulu. 'They're scarce.'

'Money chucked away, since they're the wrong size,' said Paul. 'You must have used a shoe horn to get them on. Anyway, go back home and take them off.'

'Don't be funny,' said Lulu, spectacles glinting aggressively.

'Not for the first time you're wearing unsuitable office clothes,' said Paul. 'Those jeans won't do. In any case, they're not only too tight, they're too long.' The hems were turned up like cuffs around her ankles.

'It's the fashion to wear them like this,' said Lulu.

'Since when were you interested in fashion?' asked Paul.

'Since I bought 'em,' said Lulu.

'They're not suitable, I tell you,' said Paul. 'They make you look like a farmhand. So take 'em off and I'll see if I can find you a skirt.'

'Oh, feeling a bit heavy-handed today, are we?' said Lulu.

'Very,' said Paul.

'Cut the cackle and let's do some work,' said Lulu. 'What's in the post?'

'There's one letter from a member complaining that some female members turn up at meetings looking as if they represent the women road-sweepers of Moscow, not the ideals of the Labour Party.'

'Saucy bugger,' said Lulu. 'What's he consider to be the Labour Party's ideals in respect of women?'

'To make them look as if they're prospering under a Labour government, I fancy, not suffering under Stalin,' said Paul.

'Well, you've got the bit about Stalin right,' said Lulu. 'I'd be suffering like the damned under his paunch. Pity about Lenin ending up as a corpse in a glass case. I'd have suffered gladly under him. Brilliant bloke.'

'Ice-cold,' said Paul, who, like any good Labour Party man, distanced himself from the Communist ideology that turned workers into robots.

'You've got to be pitiless when you're master-minding a revolution and getting rid of capitalists, aristocrats and tsars,' said Lulu, cleaning her type-writer with its little brush. 'It beats me why people here are so finicky about getting rid of our own capitalists. We ought to have taken over Buckingham Palace for the workers long ago.'

'Join the Communist Party and write blood-curdling stuff for the *Daily Worker*,' said Paul.

Lulu sniffed.

'Show me that letter,' she said.

Paul walked over and placed it on her desk. She read it.

'Dear Mr Adams,

'My membership number is 573 and I'm writing to say I think you do a good job as our secretary and organize lively meetings that keep us on our toes, which is what you should do. I can't say I know everything about politics as I'm only nineteen and live with my grandma, my parents having gone off to Australia and forgetting to take me with them, though that's not the exact story but like it. But I do think some of our young women ought to turn up for meetings in decent clothes that don't make them look like those women road-sweepers in Moscow, it's a sort of insult to our Labour Party when they don't look as if our Government is doing a lot more good for them than the Conservatives did, though I don't hold nothing against Winston Churchill especially as my grandma's got a framed photo of him which she bought down Petticoat Lane once. Well I hope this leaves you in good health and working hard for the Party and I hope you can get your assistant to look as properly dressed as you always do yourself, yours faithfully William Albright.'

'Albright?' said Lulu. 'All batty, more like. What an oaf. You're not going to bother to answer it, are you?'

'Of course,' said Paul. 'You know our policy. Keep the enthusiasm of every member flying high.'

'His is like a balloon that needs puncturing,' said Lulu. 'Anything serious in the rest of the post?'

'It's all serious,' said Paul. 'Every letter we get comes from a member or would-be member dedicated to the advance of Socialism. If some letters read a bit funny, well, they're all written from the heart, not as a joke.'

'I like that,' said Lulu. 'Good stuff. It's got a message. True Socialism's straight from the heart. It's another name for compassion. Which we could spread around a lot more if we eliminated the capitalists. Yes, and all the stuck-up lords and ladies as well. The kind who still treat their butlers and gardeners as serfs.'

'How compassionate would that be?' asked Paul, thinking of his grandma, the future Lady Finch. She was hardly stuck-up. More of a forthcoming problem in view of the possibility that when she and Grandpa Finch received their titles, some of his Socialist friends might find out he was related to them. And what if Lulu did? She'd include him among the nobs who ought to be eliminated. 'Yes, come on, how compassionate?'

'Socialism has got to be practical,' said Lulu. 'Can't let compassion get in the way of lopping off a few heads.'

'You're not talking about Socialism,' said Paul, 'you're talking about the French Revolution, as copied by Lenin and Stalin. If you keep on like that, I'll get you drummed out of the Young Socialists, with all your buttons stripped off. Hope it'll make your jeans fall down. Now, let's do some work. I'll give you the usual kind of letters that only require the usual kind of appreciative answers. You know the form. While you're typing them, I'll scribble down answers to the more interesting letters.'

'Pass the usual ones over,' said Lulu. 'By the way, my jeans are built not to fall down.'

'No, your bum's in the way,' said Paul.

'Here, d'you mind?' said Lulu.

'Slip of the tongue,' said Paul.

Lulu growled. But as it came from a young lady, the growl sounded halfway to falsetto.

Rachel and Sammy were at the warehouse owned by Steiner and Wallis Ltd. They were closeted with the bloke who had let them know he was Mr Wallis, partner of Mr Steiner. He'd escorted them to a sparsely furnished office with the quick, tactful discretion of a man conscious that his visitors hoped to do the kind of business that could be called un-official. About fifty, he was well-furnished himself, being large and burly. However, he had a genial approach, and even if he sometimes spoke out of the corner of his mouth, his eyes had a frank and honest look. Rachel's lush brunette aura and her handsome figure added an appreciative note to his geniality. The morning being cold, she was dressed to kill in a black fur hat and a beige leather coat with a dark brown fur collar. She exuded richness, both of purse and appearance.

'Well, y'know,' said Mr Wallis, eyeing her with friendly admiration, 'it looks like this deal is going to be a pleasure.'

'For all concerned?' said Sammy, sporting a good-looking trilby.

'Mine especially,' said Mr Wallis, smiling at Rachel.

'Well, let's get down to discussing what you can do for us,' said Sammy.

'Right,' said Mr Wallis. There was no-one else about, and he was able therefore to open the dialogue without being overheard. 'Sorry Mr Steiner don't happen to be here. Got some business appointment in Clapham. But I'll do me personal best for you, and I can't say fairer, can I? What's your exact requirements, might I ask?'

'Here's a list,' said Rachel, and gave him a slip of paper containing details of fabrics and materials, and the amounts required of each. Mr Wallis perused it and blew out his cheeks.

'Well, you did give me some idea on the phone,' he said, 'and I can see this ain't peanuts. Mind, Steiner and Wallis don't deal in peanuts. Nor farthings.'

'Point is, can you supply?' asked Sammy.

'Well, seeing Mrs Goodman here is kind of related to me partner, Enoch Steiner, we'll oblige you,' said Mr Wallis. The next words came out of the corner of his mouth, despite the absence of any third parties. 'Not for farthings, mind. Understood?'

'Understood,' said Sammy. 'Say five per cent on top of the going market rate?'

'Plus the cash deposit, as agreed with Mrs Goodman,' said Mr Wallis, 'and we'll accept a cheque for the prime amount on delivery.'

'A cheque?' said Rachel. 'Will you?'

'I'll have to make the books look right,' said Mr Wallis reasonably. 'It's the deposit that'll fix the deal. Understood?'

'Two hundred quid?' said Sammy.

Mr Wallis looked pained.

'That ain't what I agreed with Mrs Goodman,' he said. 'Not for what you want. Five's the figure.'

'Well, it hurts a bit,' said Sammy. Five hundred quid was two years wages for one of his shorthand typists. 'But no real problem. What day for delivery?'

Mr Wallis gave that thought, then said, 'Seven days. Yes, I'll guarantee that.'

'A week?' said Rachel.

'An order like you want has got to come from Liverpool,' said Mr Wallis. 'We've got a place up there for certain bulk imports, y'know. But we'll look after the cartage. Be a pleasure. Now,' said the corner of his mouth, 'if you could let me have the deposit, we could say the deal's done.'

'Much obliged,' said Sammy, and handed over five hundred pounds in banknotes. 'D'you know where our factory is?'

'Only if we've done business with you before,' he said. 'I don't recollect Mrs Goodman saying you had.'

'We haven't,' said Sammy, 'but we're willing to start now.'

'Well, you won't be on our files,' said Mr Wallis, 'so write your address down, Mr Adams.'

'Here's our factory address,' said Sammy, and wrote it down on the back of one of his business cards.

'That's the place for delivery?' said Mr Wallis.

'That's it,' said Rachel.

'No problem,' said Mr Wallis decisively.

'Can we take a look at what stocks you've got here?' asked Sammy.

'What we've got is all in bales,' said Mr Wallis, 'but there's samples you can see. Same kind of stuff we've got in Liverpool. Follow me.'

He led them into the heart of the cavernous warehouse, where bales were stacked. The main doors of the place were open, and a forklift truck was being used by a gang of four men to load bales into a large van.

'You're doing business today?' said Rachel.

'Every day,' said Mr Wallis. 'There's the samples.'
A table against one wall was laden with fabric pieces.
'You take a look, while I just have a word with me customer.'

He made his way far down to the open doors to speak to one of the men, while Sammy and Rachel inspected the samples.

'Sammy, just what we need,' said Rachel.

'Quality stuff,' said Sammy.

'I'm happy,' said Rachel.

'Handing over all those smackers don't hurt so much now,' said Sammy.

'Sammy, payment by cheque for the order means we can show the purchase in our books,' said Rachel.

'That'll stop our accountants asking questions about how we managed to cope with orders for our own New Look,' said Sammy.

'What d'you think of Wallis?'

'Ready to do the deal,' said Rachel.

'So would I be with all those readies in my pocket,' said Sammy.

Mr Wallis returned, his large figure conveying an impressive amount of genial satisfaction.

'Everything to your liking, Mr Adams?' he said.

'It will be if Monday's consignment coincides with the invoice,' said Sammy.

'You'll have no worries about that,' said Mr Wallis.

'Then we'll settle the invoice on delivery,' said Sammy.

'You'll have to, as agreed. But I said you can pay by cheque, didn't I?'

'Fair enough,' said Sammy.

Mr Wallis saw them out through the office, shook hands with them, treated himself to a final admiring look at Rachel and her figure, and said goodbye.

Sammy drove Rachel back to their Camberwell offices and reported to Boots. Boots said the most satisfactory aspect of the deal was payment by cheque in return for an invoice on delivery.

'Where does the cash deposit come from?' asked Rachel.

'Private funds,' said Sammy, 'half out of my pocket and half out of yours, Boots.'

'Thought it would,' said Boots. 'You're still sharp, Junior.'

'Don't mention it, old soldier,' said Sammy.

Rachel smiled.

Chapter Seven

Over breakfast the next day, Paula said, 'Daddy, don't forget that on Saturday you're taking me to stay with David and Kate at their farm for the weekend.'

'We'll take your fur coat as well,' said Sammy, 'it'll be cold out there in the wilds of Kent.'

'I don't have a fur coat,' said Paula, now fifteen and looking all of sixteen, with her long legs and burgeoning figure. She was as lively as a skittish filly, and as talkative as a cricket. 'Crikey, d'you mean you're going to buy me one before Saturday?'

'Well,' said Sammy, 'I'm not exactly sure I—'

'I am,' said Susie. 'You're not going to buy her anything of the kind, not at her age.'

'Well, I'm blessed,' said Paula to Jimmy, 'anyone would think I'm only ten.'

'Crying shame,' grinned Jimmy.

'Yes, isn't it?' said Phoebe, who, at thirteen, was piquantly pretty, and had enjoyed nine happy years with her adoptive and caring family. 'Mummy, I could be going with Paula to David and Kate's farm if I hadn't been invited to Lily Johnson's birthday party.'

'Never mind, lovey,' said Susie, 'Daddy will treat

you to some extra pocket money so that you can take Lily a nice present.'

'Oh, thanks, Daddy,' said Phoebe, 'you're ever such a sport.'

'My pleasure,' smiled Sammy.

Jimmy said, 'You're playing happy this morning, Dad.'

'Yes, as if you've just found pirates' treasure in Ruskin Park,' said Phoebe.

'Dad hasn't been digging up the park,' said Jimmy, 'he's simply got himself on the right side of a business deal.'

'He's good at doing business deals,' said Paula.

'Don't we know it,' said Susie, who had her suspicions about this latest one.

'Got to keep Adams Fashions on the move,' said Sammy.

'Yes, so you can also keep me and Phoebe and Mum in style,' said Paula, 'and buy me a fur coat when I'm a young woman. Grandma Finch told me once it's what a husband and father is for, to provide for his wife and daughters, and see that they don't have to go to jumble sales for their clothes.'

'Or their fur coats,' said Jimmy.

'Daddy's ever such a generous provider,' said Phoebe.

'One day my pocket will get used to the strain,' said Sammy. 'One day.'

Rachel entered his office midway through the morning. She looked worried.

'Sammy?'

'What's up?' asked Sammy.

'My life, you should ask?' she said. 'I've been

costing out the exact figures for the delivery from Steiner and Wallis. It's really serious money. So I decided to phone them and to get them to agree the total. Sammy, there was no answer. The line was dead. So I rang the operator and was told the number had been disconnected yesterday afternoon.'

'Eh?' said Sammy.

'That worries you?' said Rachel. 'It worried me. I managed to get through to the area telephone manager and was told, after a lot of waffle about rules and regulations, that Steiner and Wallis had gone into liquidation and that the phone company is on the list of creditors.'

'I didn't hear that,' said Sammy, sitting up in shock. 'Or if I did, I don't believe it.'

'I knew my father's cousin, Enoch Steiner, lived in Golders Green,' said Rachel, 'so I consulted the London phone directory and found his number. I've just finished speaking to him. Sammy, we've been done to a turn, we've been had, and I'm weak at the knees, my life I am.'

'Rachel, sit down,' said Sammy. Rachel groped for the chair on the other side of his desk and seated her upset self. 'Someone hit me with a hammer and knock me conscious,' said Sammy. 'Listen, what did Steiner say about Wallis?'

'After I described that character to him, he said it wasn't Mr Wallis, that it sounded like the man in charge of the bailiffs, and that they were clearing out the warehouse on orders from the liquidators. The business had gone to the wall, Sammy. We're going to get nothing out of it. There's no warehouse at Liverpool, at least none that belong to Steiner and

Wallis. Sammy, we've been turned over by a conman, you and me both.'

'Blown up, I'd say,' growled Sammy, 'and I'm feeling seriously injured, like I'm a collection of bits and pieces. Can you see any blood?'

'I can see the ghost of five hundred pounds cash,' said Rachel.

'Painful, ruddy painful,' said Sammy.

'How did we let it happen?' asked Rachel.

'We were too ready to believe what we wanted to,' said Sammy, 'that we'd found a gold mine.' He reflected on the absence of any staff at the warehouse. Not one single office girl had been present, nor any storeman. That ought to have made him think. 'There were clues I didn't bother about. Blind O'Reilly, I fell for old-fashioned codswallop. Me, Sammy Adams. That's the first time in all me years of business I've let wishful thinking turn my brainbox into a blancmange. Still, we might not be done for yet. The geezer's not to know you've just found him out. Is your dad's cousin taking any action?'

'He would if he'd parted with all that cash himself,' said Rachel, 'but as he didn't he recommended that we contact the police.'

'Some of my best friends have been local bobbies,' said Sammy, 'but Boots and me like to solve our own business problems. Well, you know Boots and how he prefers to keep things in the family. Anyway, Rachel me old friend, as soon as your legs are working again, put your hat and coat on and we'll motor off to the docks to see if Codswallop Charley-Boy is still around.'

'Shall you tell Boots?' asked Rachel.

'Well, he's got half-shares in this particular piece of how's-your-father,' said Sammy, 'so I'd better give him the horrible details. I know what I'll get in return. He'll do his Lord-I-Am stuff and order me to corner the geezer, turn him upside down and shake him until five hundred smackers fall out of his wallet. And to do it all nice and quiet.'

'My life, Sammy,' said Rachel, 'aren't we fortunate to have a Lord-I-Am like Boots?'

'Don't make jokes like that, Rachel, I ain't in the mood,' said Sammy.

When told, Boots laughed his head off.

'Sammy old lad, you let a bailiff's man turn you over?' he said.

'You think it's funny?' said Sammy.

'In its way,' said Boots.

'Ha-bloody-ha-ha,' said Sammy bitterly.

'Well, do what you've suggested, get after him,' said Boots, 'and stand not on the order of your going.'

'You and your education,' said Sammy, 'and it still ain't funny.'

'Nor is all that cash,' said Boots. 'By the way, don't cause a riot.'

'Knew you'd say that,' said Sammy.

'Keep it in the family,' said Boots.

'Knew you'd say that too,' said Sammy, growling a bit.

'D'you want me to come with you?' asked Boots.

'Ta for the offer,' said Sammy, 'but if I find Cleverclogs, the rest is going to be me own personal pleasure, and I don't want to share it.'

'Right, off you go, then, Sammy,' said Boots, 'but mind your eye.'

*   *   *

From Camberwell Green, Sammy and Rachel, in a hurry, motored north-east towards Rotherhithe. The traffic was no help, and Sammy complained that it was highly inconvenient for other vehicles to be on the road the same time as he was. Rachel said don't boil over, Sammy, stay cool.

To which he said, 'Me, Sammy Adams, turned into a mug by a gorblimey monkey – I still don't believe it.'

'There's still hope we can pull his tail off,' said Rachel. As they passed through Peckham, she noted the blocks of flats rising to the sky and swarms of builders' men moving like busy ants on vast cradles of scaffolding. The erection of such blocks for housing people dispossessed by the wartime air raids was the Government's number one priority. Many such blocks had been finished and occupied, but Rachel wondered if they really suited families used to the privacy and neighbourliness of their old Victorian terraced houses.

Here and there some ground laid waste by bombs had been cleared and used for the erection of prefabricated dwellings. Known as prefabs, they could accommodate bombed-out couples or small families. A prefab site at least offered neighbourliness, so important to Londoners, and each dwelling had modern amenities. Several prominent figures who had gone public with their criticism had echoed Rachel's doubts in suggesting the blocks of high-rise flats, rising from concrete surrounds, were lacking that which people considered homely and comfortable about their old Victorian dwellings. Further, the flats lacked a scullery for doing the Monday washing, a back yard for hanging it out, and a front door that opened onto a street that kids could turn into a playground. A concrete surface wasn't the same as a street. A street had a soul. Concrete didn't.

'Penny for 'em,' said Sammy, stopping to let passengers alight from a tram.

'All these blocks of flats, Sammy,' said Rachel. 'I should want to live in such a flat myself? I hope I never have to.'

'Well, like my respected stepdad mentioned to me only a week ago,' remarked Sammy, driving on again, 'you can always bet that when a government puts bureaucranks in charge of any kind of enterprise—'

'Bureaucrats, I think, Sammy.'

'Same thing,' said Sammy. 'They all wear stiff collars and starched cuffs. You can bet, as my stepdad said, that they'll be short on imagination in any kind of enterprise. I personally concur with his opinion – ruddy waddling walruses, look at that in front, a horse and cart.'

'There are still some to be seen,' said Rachel.

'What I'm complaining about is that this one's holding us up,' said Sammy. Fortunately, when he reached the turn into Rotherhithe New Road, the ambling horse and cart went straight on. Sammy entered the road, on each side of which the view of the southern area of bombed Bermondsey could have looked depressing. However, clearance and development were actively under way, imparting a picture of the locality being reborn. As elsewhere in London, new buildings were going up, the work sponsored and subsidized by funds from central and local government.

It was twelve noon when they arrived at St George's Wharf, which wasn't to Sammy's liking. Given what he knew now, he'd have preferred to arrive at the crack of dawn and lain in wait for Cleverclogs. He noted the warehouse had been completely cleared of equipment and stores, and that the bailiff's men were now loading office furniture and files onto their van.

Sammy said good morning to the gang and asked a question of one.

'Is your foreman around?'

'Eh?'

'The bloke in charge. We met him yesterday, and we need to meet him again.'

'Who, old Claude?'

'What's the rest of his monicker? Not Wallis, is it?'

'Wallis? No, he's Claude Robinson, but he ain't here, mister.'

'Where is he, then?'

'Dunno. He just ain't turned up.'

'D'you know why?'

'Not me. I'm as ignorant as me mates. He could've been took sick, I s'pose.'

'Have you told the bailiff's office?'

'Can't, can we? The blower's been cut off since yesterday afternoon.'

'Well, where does this bloke, Claude Robinson, live?'

'Dunno. Half a mo, Montague might. Here, Monty, d'you know where Claude lives?'

'Not me,' said Monty. 'Ask Gerald.'

'Here, Gerald, d'you know where Claude lives?'

'Yus,' said Gerald. 'Peckham.'

'Where in Peckham?' asked Rachel.

The men looked at each other. Sammy produced a ten-bob note, and one man said to another, 'Now he's talking.'

And Gerald said, 'He's got a room over a pub.'

'What pub?'

'Black Horse.'

'Where's that exactly?'

'Dunno.'

Sammy parted with the ten-bob note, which the men accepted as if it was now their due.

'Well, then, gentlemen, so where exactly is the Black Horse pub?' asked Rachel, one with Sammy in what on the surface was a good-natured inquisition.

'Peckham High Street,' said the bloke name of Gerald.

'Ta,' said Sammy. 'Might I ask if he's got a wife and kids?'

'What, old Claude? Not him. Lady friends, that's his style, mister. And the gee-gees.'

Well, thought Sammy, so Cleverclogs isn't tied to a family, he's free to scarper. If he's got ideas about laying those five hundred smackers on a cert, then scarpering off to Australia with the winnings, I ain't standing by.

'Much obliged,' he said. 'So long. Come on, Rachel.'

The bailiff's men watched them go, eyes following Rachel more than Sammy.

'That lady's what I call decorative.'

'Like to keep her on your parlour mantelpiece, would you, Monty?'

'Be an improvement on our old tick-tock.'

Chapter Eight

With Rachel beside him, Sammy began the drive back, a stop in Peckham in mind.

'Well, Sammy?' said Rachel, after they had left the river and its bomb-scarred docklands behind.

'Point is, are we going to corner Cleverclogs, or has he done a bunk already?' said Sammy. 'Let's see what we get out of the Black Horse publican.'

'Ask nicely,' said Rachel.

'I'm not in the mood to be fussy,' said Sammy. 'Still, I'll proceed very polite, bearing in mind I'll soon be related to Lord and Lady Finch.'

'Sir Edwin and Lady Finch,' said Rachel.

'If I get copped for aggravated assault and it gets into the newspapers,' said Sammy, 'Buckingham Palace might keep my dear old ma and my respected stepdad locked out on their great day.'

'My life, should I believe the honour is still keeping the family in a giddy state?' asked Rachel.

'My dear old ma still needs her smelling salts twice a week,' said Sammy.

Rachel said Vi had told her that she'd be giddy enough to do a knees-up if the band played. Sammy said Vi was the last person to do a knees-up at Buckingham Palace, she was too placid for that.

Rachel said Vi's placid condition might fly out of a Buckingham Palace window on such an occasion.

'I should dance if I were Vi, Sammy? I would.'

'Well, if we corner old Cleverclogs, let's see what kind of a dance he'll do,' said Sammy.

They found the Black Horse pub in Peckham High Street. Sammy parked the car and they made their way into the public bar. The time was well after one, and a number of customers were imbibing their liquid lunch. Sammy and Rachel approached the bar, the while casting their eyes around for a possible sight of Mr Claude Robinson.

'What's your fancy?' asked the genial publican. He had the florid complexion of a bloke who enjoyed his own wares.

'First,' said Sammy, 'I'd like—' He stopped as his eyes caught sight of customers in the adjacent bar, the private bar. He picked out one particular customer, a burly man standing at a licensed slot machine. Well, if it wasn't artful old Claude himself. There was a large suitcase on the floor beside his right leg. It was waiting while he engaged with the one-armed bandit. Coming to, Sammy responded to the publican. 'Yes, I'd like a half of old ale,' he said. 'What's your liking, Rachel?'

'A cider,' said Rachel, and the publican began to oblige them. Sammy glanced at Rachel, winked, then directed his gaze elsewhere. She followed it, and she too saw the bloke they were after, playing the fruit machine in the private bar. She whispered, 'Is he using your dibs, Sammy, to go for the jackpot?'

'He's ready for the off,' whispered Sammy. 'Clap your peepers on that suitcase.' Up came the publican with the ale and the cider. Sammy passed the cider to Rachel.

'Elevenpence,' said the publican.

Handing him a silver bob, Sammy swallowed some ale and said, casually, 'Is old Claude around? Claude Robinson?'

The publican gave him a funny look along with a penny change.

'You a friend?' he asked.

Not being short of savvy, Sammy wisely said, 'Let's say I know him.'

'So do I, and so does my old lady,' said the publican. He became sympathetically chatty, as if he knew Sammy had something grievous on his mind apropos the character in question. 'Getting a few bob rent out of that crafty carrot for his room was like trying to raise the *Titanic* with a fishing line, I tell yer. Round here he's called Touchyer, meaning if you don't watch out he'll touch yer for a bob. He's touched more than a few in his time. And he's touched me for more tick than I care to remember. Still, he settled up this morning when he gave up his room. Told me and me old dutch that he'd had a winner and was moving to the Old Kent Road. He's likely on his way to his new lodgings now, unless he's still drinking in the private bar. First time he hasn't had a pint on the slate.' He took a look. 'There y'ar, there he is.'

Sammy took his own look.

'Yes, that's him,' he said, thinking Cleverclogs would have been well away if he'd known the curtain had gone up on his act.

'Touched yer for a packet, did he?'

'I'm still mortified,' said Sammy, swallowing more

81

ale in place of lunch. 'Well, I'll have a word with him as soon as he leaves.'

'That's it, when he leaves,' said the publican. 'I ain't permitting a punch-up on the premises.'

Rachel nudged Sammy. A man, a pint glass of beer in his hand, had come to stand beside Claude, to watch him operating the fruit machine. Claude at once moved his suitcase with his right foot until it stood between his legs. His legs purposefully cuddled it, while he continued pulling the arm of the bandit.

'Rachel,' whispered Sammy, with the publican attending to a new customer, 'he's got valuables in that case.'

'Not just an old suit, his toothbrush and a pair of pyjamas?' whispered Rachel.

'Not this side of Christmas,' murmured Sammy, and they stood close together, enjoying their liquid refreshment and watching Cleverclogs. A large woman with a small drink, a brandy, moved to stand on the other side of Claude, who gave her a quick glance. He was somewhat hemmed in now by the man and woman, and Rachel was sure his legs clasped his suitcase tighter.

Let's see, thought Sammy, would he have stuffed five hundred smackers in his luggage instead of his wallet? In a pub, where he could be crowded, yes, he might. Five hundred were a lot more valuable than a few, and would put a bulge in his wallet. Peckham had its share of eagle-eyed pickpockets.

Rachel nudged Sammy again, this time drawing his attention to the fact that the suitcase was moving once more, rising from the floor as Claude took a firm grip of the handle and hefted it. He said something to the man and woman, and they made way for him.

Sammy finished his drink and put the glass down. Rachel relinquished what was left of her cider.

'So long and ta,' said Sammy to the publican, and he and Rachel left the public bar in quick, synchronized togetherness. Their exit coincided with that of the quarry through the open door of the private bar. Sammy executed a movement that blocked Claude's further progress.

'Hello, hello,' said Claude amiably, 'I think you're standing in my way. Would you mind shifting?'

'Yes, I would mind,' said Sammy, an inch taller than his man, if not barrel-chested, 'so don't ask again.'

'Half a mo,' said Claude, 'do I know you?'

'You know both of us,' said Rachel, and Claude gave her an admiring once-over.

'Strike me stupid, how could I forget?' he said. 'Where was it we met? I know, Ascot sometime. No, wait a tick, I tell a lie. At the Epsom Derby last year, of course, wasn't it?'

'Leave off,' said Sammy, 'or I'll call a copper.' A bus rumbled by, and Claude eyed it like a man wishing he was among the passengers. 'Just hand me back the loot,' said Sammy, 'and we'll part with not a lot of hard feelings.'

'Eh?' said Claude, keeping a tight hold on the handle of his suitcase.

'You heard,' said Sammy.

'I heard all right,' said Claude, 'but I didn't hear correct, did I?'

'Yesterday,' said Sammy, choosing to be crisp and deliberate, 'you were at St George's Wharf in charge of the bailiff's men clearing out Steiner and Wallis's warehouse.'

'Was I?' Claude gave it thought, then came up with a genial smile. 'Well, so I was, yes, working out me last day on the job. No prospects, y'know, for a bloke like me.'

'Some regular pickings, though, of bankrupt stocks, I daresay,' suggested Sammy.

'Here, live and let live,' said Claude. 'Well, wherever we all met, been a pleasure to see you and your missus again, but I've got a train to catch.'

'This lady's not my missus,' said Sammy.

'Well, hard luck, mate,' said Claude.

'She's a witness to your thieving performance of yesterday,' said Sammy, solidly perched on the pavement and giving not an inch. 'So hand the dibs back while you're still in one piece.'

'Come again?' said Claude.

'Don't do it here, Sammy,' said Rachel, 'too many people about for you to spread blood over the pavement.'

'Look, I don't have time to listen to jokes,' said Claude, 'I've still got a train to catch. But tell yer what, if you think I'm carrying oof that don't belong to me, you're welcome to search me, wallet as well. Go on, try me.' He put his suitcase down and opened up his jacket.

Sammy and Rachel both knew for sure then that the smackers weren't on his person.

'You try,' said Rachel. 'Start by opening up your case.'

'I ain't having you or him lifting me silver-backed hairbrushes,' said Claude, and picked his case up with haste and purpose. 'Got to get that train. See

84

you next Derby Day.' He did a quick sidestep and took off. That is, he made the attempt, but Sammy, on the alert, thrust out a firm foot and tangled up his legs. Tripped, Claude fell heavily, letting go of his suitcase. Sammy pounced. Pedestrians stopped to look down at the grounded man.

'What's 'e doing down there?' asked an elderly bloke.

'Drunk, I suppose,' said a woman. 'Took a drop too many in this pub.'

'Bleedin' disgraceful,' said the elderly bloke. He bent to address Claude, now trying to sit up. 'Ought to be ashamed of yerself.'

'Sod off,' said Claude, and climbed to his feet. The elderly bloke and the woman retreated from his burly frame and what they considered was his drunken condition. Drunks as big as him could be dangerous when they were upright. He turned. 'I'm suing you for assault, you— Here, where's the bugger gone with his tart?'

'Heading for that copper,' said the woman, and disappeared with the elderly bloke before the drunk turned evil.

'Sod my eyeballs,' breathed Claude, hoarse with disbelief, 'they've nicked my bloody case.' He saw them, talking to a copper on the beat. The sight of the bluebottle galvanized him into performing a disappearing act of his own.

Sammy was asking where the Peckham railway station was.

'It's Queen's Road station,' said the bobby, 'and Queen's Road is straight ahead, sir. You'll find the station entrance on the left.'

'Thank you, officer,' said Rachel with a lush smile.

'Pleasure, madam,' said the smitten bobby, and off went Sammy and Rachel, Sammy in secure possession of the suitcase. They took a roundabout route to get back to the parked car, where Sammy placed the case in the boot. He let Rachel have the privilege of opening it. She sprang the locks and lifted the lid, then searched among clothes and other items. It did not take long for her to come up with something favourable, a man's vest wrapped around a fat object, which turned out to be a well-stuffed brown envelope. They took the envelope into the car, and from it Rachel extracted a wad of banknotes. She counted them. The original number had been a hundred, all fivers. Two were now missing.

'He probably settled his owings with that,' said Rachel.

'Cheap at the price,' said Sammy. 'When a business bloke loses his marbles, like I did yesterday, and it costs him only a tenner, I reckon that's a reward for being honest, upright and deserving, except for occasionally forgetting I attended Sunday School. Only occasionally. Rachel me old friend, I could kiss you.'

My life, thought Rachel, wouldn't I like him to?

But she said, 'No, I don't think so, Sammy.'

'Well, would you like some lunch?' asked Sammy.

'Thanks, but I'm not hungry,' said Rachel, 'I'm full up with adrenalin. Sammy, how cool you were. Boots would have been proud of you.'

'If he gives me a pat on the head, it won't surprise me,' said Sammy, 'but it'll give me a feeling I'm still in short trousers. Right, let's get back to the office. On the way we'll stop at a baker's shop and treat ourselves to a decent fruit cake we can have with a pot of tea.'

'Who's going to say no?' said Rachel. 'Sammy, what do we do with Claude's case?'

'We'll pull up outside the Black Horse on our way back, and I'll dump it at the door of the private bar,' said Sammy.

Which he did, without knowing that Claude was talking to the publican and trying to rent his room again.

Back at the office, where Rachel unwrapped a fruit cake and one of the girls put the kettle on, Sammy reported the success of the outing to Boots. Boots complimented him on a job well done, and gave him a figurative pat on the head.

'Sometimes,' said Sammy, 'I think I'd like to see you in charge of the lions at the zoo.'

'Why?' asked Boots.

'Lions bite when you pat 'em on the head,' said Sammy.

Boots laughed.

'All the same, sterling work, Sammy old lad.'

'What's the use?' muttered Sammy, but he was grinning when he reached his office. It was a work of art to get under Boots's skin. Talk about the original cool cucumber with knobs on. But there was one thing that had shaken him to the core. The Belsen concentration camp. The sights and sounds had knocked him sideways, and stayed on his mind for a hell of a time. The hanging of top Nazis responsible for what went on in such places satisfied him to some extent. It was no secret that he was now following reported progress on the hunt for Dr Mengele, the sadist who'd performed hideous experiments not only on Jewish inmates at Auschwitz, but on their children too. Mengele had disappeared, and Sammy knew Boots wanted him found and slowly hanged.

Good luck, old soldier, thought Sammy.

He'd been there, at Belsen, when British troops uncovered the unbelievable.

Just before he left at the end of the day, Boots had a word with Sammy.

'Sammy, you realize there's still a problem?'

'Tell me,' said Sammy.

'You still need a regular large supply of fabrics if you're to launch Lilian's design successfully,' said Boots.

'Might I point out it's not my exclusive problem?' said Sammy. 'It's yours as well.'

'Pass me half your headache,' said Boots. 'But not now. Sometime tomorrow.'

'Pardon me for not laughing,' said Sammy.

'Love to Susie,' said Boots.

'Had a good day, old love?' asked Polly when he arrived home.

'Busy but peaceful,' he said, 'so let me tell you about the kind of day Sammy had.' He did so. Polly, as vivacious as ever, shrieked with laughter.

'Everything happens to Sammy,' she said.

'Sammy's way of life has always invited the eventful, sometimes favourable, sometimes troublesome and sometimes slightly bruising,' said Boots. 'It's all made a great survivor of him in the world of tough business.'

'You're both survivors in your different spheres

and your different ways,' said Polly. 'Old sport, you're both the kind of men who won the Empire, Sammy as a contractor and you writing the scripts.'

'Not quite,' said Boots. 'I spent my formative years as a junior clerk and Sammy spent his running a market stall. As for the Empire, it's falling apart.'

'Had to happen, old darling,' said Polly. 'When the war ended, and the men came home, that was it. They retired from their labours on behalf of this old island and its Empire to take care of their families, and their gardens or their back yards. Heigh-ho, good luck to all of them, and very special good luck to you and Sammy. By the way, your mother now has her Buckingham Palace outfit sorted out for next month, and I have mine, even though I'll only be standing outside waiting for you. We had a fitting in Bond Street today, and she carried off the occasion like a duchess, even if she said afterwards that she'd never met such superior shop assistants in all her life. Your stepfather will be proud of her, and I hope you'll be proud of me. I'll be collecting both outfits next week.'

'What's the damage?' smiled Boots.

'Aren't you lucky, old top, it's only thirty guineas.'

'How much?' said Boots.

'It's not a lot, considering Bond Street is dressing me,' said Polly.

'You mean it's just for your outfit, not both?' said Boots.

'Just mine, darling,' said Polly. 'Edwin will pay for your mother's, and you'll have the privilege of paying for mine. Does that thrill you?'

'It'll stand me on my head,' said Boots, as a banging and clanging reached his ears, 'but it'll still be a privilege.'

'There's a lovely old scout you are,' said Polly.

'What's going on upstairs?' asked Boots.

'Oh, the twins have formed a band,' said Polly. 'James is banging the drum, and Gemma's thumping around with the tambourine. They want you to join in and blow the trumpet.'

'I'll pass on that one,' said Boots.

Gemma yelled from above.

'Come on up, Daddy! We know you're home, and the trumpet's waiting for you!'

'What a life,' said Boots, 'it's all blow.'

Chapter Nine

Prime Minister Clement Attlee, who always kept a cool head, was doing his best to prevent the back-bench firebrands of the Labour government from promoting bills that related more to Communism than Socialism.

Mr Attlee would have sympathized with Paul Adams in respect of the trouble he had with his own left-wing firebrand, Lulu Saunders. She was holding forth again, this time to two members of the Young Socialists, a young man and a young woman. They had called only to offer help in the matter of distributing leaflets in Bermondsey. They were startled to have her give their ears a bit of a bashing.

'Pushing leaflets through a letter box isn't enough! Make yourselves heard! Protest on behalf of the workers! I'm becoming ashamed of our Labour government. All of us Young Socialists should be. It's letting the workers down by not thumping the bosses. So don't simply leave a leaflet on the mat. Knock and bring people to the door. Talk to them. Ask them to demonstrate. Down with capitalism, that's the thing. Capitalists own ninety-nine per cent of the country's wealth.'

'As much as that?' said the young woman, and glanced at Paul.

'I question ninety-nine per cent,' he said.

'I ain't sure about knocking on doors,' said the young man. 'In Bermondsey you never know what's going to come at you when someone answers your knock.'

'Hungry workers mostly,' said Lulu. 'But if a Tory shows his uncaring face, hit him with the Red Flag. Down with aristocrats, tell him. Bring on the guillotine.'

'Me dad's a docker and a strong trade unionist,' said the young woman, 'but I don't know he'd want a lot to do with that French guillotine.'

'Oh, come on, ducky, we need to chop a few heads off every Bank Holiday,' said Lulu.

'Crikey,' said the young woman, and glanced at Paul again.

'I question the wisdom of chopping any heads off,' he said, 'especially on a Bank Holiday.'

'It does sound a bit grisly, not half it don't,' said the young man. 'I mean, all them heads rolling about. And council road-sweepers ain't going to like clearing them up.'

'Look, fair shares for all,' said Lulu, who always spoke in brisk staccato fashion. 'That's what our Party is after. Which we won't get if we practise finicky Socialism.' Her spectacles glinted with aggression as she added, 'Shut your eyes to any blood. Tell people to march with the workers. Down with the bosses. Tear their hobnailed boots off and chuck 'em in the Serpentine.'

'The bosses or their boots?' asked Paul.

'Them and their boots,' said Lulu. 'Now,' she said

to the visitors, 'you'll take the pamphlets and knock on doors? Paul here will tell you talking to people gets results. Some of 'em don't read the pamphlets. Some can't. And why? Because Tory governments didn't give them a decent education.'

'We'll do our best,' said the young man, 'but I ain't personally going to mention no guillotine.'

'Pity,' said Lulu. 'Still, do some stern talking on doorsteps. Here's the pamphlets.' She handed them a wad each. 'Good luck.'

'Oh, ta,' said the young man, not sure he hadn't been steamrollered.

'Excuse me,' said the young woman to Paul, 'but if you ever need more help in your office, I'd be pleased to do a full-time job for you. I'm learning typing at evening classes, and I could give up me factory job easy.'

'You're a charming girl, and I'll make a note of your offer,' said Paul.

'Oh, thanks, you're nice too. Me name's Betty Clepper and me address is—'

'We're full up,' said Lulu, and hustled her out, along with the young man. She then said to Paul, 'You make me feel ill sometimes. As soon as a skirt comes in here, you're all goggling eyes.'

'I question goggling,' said Paul.

'Turn that record off,' said Lulu.

'You're still wearing those ropey jeans,' said Paul.

'I like 'em,' said Lulu.

'Don't suit your bum,' said Paul.

'You keep saying that ten times a day,' said Lulu.

'I question—'

'Leave off, will you?' said Lulu. 'Listen, there's a reception for Tom Naylor here this evening. You

93

know, our old MP. He's retiring from active politics. I'll attend. You can come and join me, if you want.'

'I'd like that,' said Paul, 'I'd enjoy having a chat with Tom Naylor. He's a fine old-fashioned Labour party man. He belongs to the real people. But unfortunately, I can't, I'm taking Henrietta to a play at the Shaftesbury Theatre.'

'That tarty baggage with a mad old granny?' said Lulu in disgust.

'The mad old granny's one of your heroines,' said Paul, 'or ought to be, seeing she fought for women's equality.'

'Women need to be more equal than men,' said Lulu.

'More equal doesn't make sense,' said Paul.

'It makes sense to me,' said Lulu. 'We're up against dead crafty men. We've got to have the power to free women from slaving at their kitchen sinks.'

'I agree women should be free to make use of their talents,' said Paul, 'but let's start with the up-and-coming ones.'

'And keep all the others still slaving?' said Lulu darkly. 'As a dedicated Labour bloke, aren't you ashamed sometimes?'

'Of what?' said Paul.

'Seeing your haggard, work-weary mother slaving at her kitchen sink?'

'My mother—'

'Yes, how d'you know she wouldn't have blossomed if your father hadn't chained her down?'

'My father—'

'She might have been free to invent the motor car,' said Lulu, spectacles glinting with the light of accusation.

94

'I could point out it was invented before she was born,' said Paul.

Lulu sniffed.

'By men, I suppose,' she said. 'Trust men to invent something that runs people over. Your mother might have—'

'My mother', said Paul, 'is old-fashioned. As a staunch believer in the aims of the Labour Party, I regret I can't get her out of her kitchen to help build ships, but there it is. She likes cooking, baking and jam-making.'

'You mean she seems to,' said Lulu. 'Women are good at hiding their misery.'

'Lulu lovey,' said Paul, 'I'm afraid yours is showing.'

'That's a lie,' said Lulu. 'I pride myself on my courageous front. I fight oppression with dignity. And don't call me lovey. People might think the worst. Listen, you really taking simpering Henrietta out tonight?'

'I really am,' said Paul.

'Poor bloke,' said Lulu pityingly. 'You need your head X-rayed to find out if you're all there.'

'Take a letter,' said Paul.

'Take what?'

'I'm going to dictate a reply to an enquiry.'

'Well, you can dictate it to my grandmother,' said Lulu, 'I don't do shorthand.'

'OK,' said Paul, 'make the coffee, then, while I write the letter out in longhand for you to type.'

'I really am getting to hate you,' said Lulu, 'and I hope the theatre falls on you and lah-di-dah Henrietta tonight.'

'What I like most about you, Lulu,' said Paul, 'is that you're such a happy soul.'

'Glad you think so,' said Lulu. 'Thought you'd never notice. How much cyanide would you like in your coffee?'

Sammy took a phone call from Miss Hilda Campion, manageress of the firm's Oxford Street shop, one that retailed fashions more expensive than the range in his South London branches.

'Hello, Hilda, what can I do for you?' he asked.

'Mr Adams, we're not stocking what many young people are asking for,' said Miss Campion.

'Don't tell me they're asking for what their grandparents wore,' said Sammy.

'Grandparents?'

'My wife tells me there was some female character on *Woman's Hour* talking about the revival of Victorian flannel.'

'Mr Adams, Victorian flannel is dead and buried, and can't be revived.'

'Good, it'll stop me turning grey with worry,' said Sammy. 'So what are a lot of young people asking for?'

'American jeans,' said Miss Campion.

'Eh?' said Sammy hoarsely.

'I think we've got to face the fact that they're going to take on,' said Miss Campion. 'Mr Adams? Mr Adams, are you there?'

'Under the doctor,' said Sammy faintly.

'Mr Adams—'

'Send an ambulance.'

'Can we be serious, please?'

'I am serious, and so's my condition,' said Sammy. 'American jeans? I keep telling people they're not a fashion. They're something invented by hairy cowboys.'

'All the same, I think they're going to be fashion-able,' said Miss Campion. 'Mr Adams, we'll lose out if we don't stock them.'

Sammy turned pale. 'Lose out' represented a term that had sent shivers down his back since the age of nine. Profit was healthy, losing out was a dangerous illness.

'You sure about this, Hilda?'

'I'm sure that if we don't go along with what young customers want, they'll see this shop as behind the times,' said Miss Campion.

'An Oxford Street shop behind the times?' said Sammy, hoarse again. 'Our shop?'

Miss Campion, a very able and attractive woman of thirty-three, as well as an excellent manageress, ventured to declare that this post-war era was devel-oping in favour of the young, who were beginning to think it was old heads and outdated notions that had led to the conflict. They were thinking of a new kind of world, one in which the young had a greater influence than the old. American jeans were associ-ated with the young people of the States, and the young people of Britain would undoubtedly follow that trend.

'I've got to believe this?' said Sammy.

Miss Campion said she was only expressing an opinion, of course. She and her gentleman friend had discussed the matter more than once lately. Sammy asked if her gentleman friend had made a study of what might be called the trendy young. Miss Campion said he was in the trade, that he always kept a close eye on developments, and was convinced the era of young people was about to begin.

'Not in regard to fashions alone, Mr Adams, but

also in regard to social trends,' she said.

'If you're telling me that by the time I'm fifty I'm going to be ordered about by sixteen-year-old kids, I'm going to have a word with your gentleman friend,' said Sammy.

'You're welcome to,' said Miss Campion.

'I've got a fainting feeling,' said Sammy, 'a feeling that our shops are going to end up stocking the kind of reach-me-downs that make girls look like cowboys from the Wild West, and which I consider unfemale. Further, Hilda, to stock 'em in quantity means I might need an import licence. That could take months, seeing I'll be dealing with civil servants.'

'Mr Dickinson is in the trade, Mr Adams, as I mentioned, and has an import licence,' said Miss Campion.

'Mr Dickinson being your gentleman friend?' said Sammy.

'Yes,' said Miss Campion. 'In fact, he has two licences.'

'Two?' said Sammy.

Miss Campion explained that following a successful application by Mr Dickinson two years ago, the first import licence had been followed a week later by a second. Both licences entitled him to import. Her gentleman friend realized his application had been duplicated when processed, the only difference being that the second bore a reference number that was not the same as the first. The duplication was a mistake, of course, but since civil servants were resolutely against being advised of any kind of mistake, Mr Dickinson was tactful enough not to point out this one. Therefore, he was in the position of being able to double his imports. She was sure he would accept orders from Adams Fashions, as long as the amounts were worthy of his consideration.

'Listen, Hilda, are you speaking from behind the door of your shop cubbyhole?' asked Sammy.

'Of course,' said Miss Campion.

'I like that,' said Sammy, 'and if anyone deserves your kind of gentleman friend, you do. Other ladies can have any old friends. Not that it won't grieve me to stock our shops with jeans, particularly when Lilian, our designer, has just come up with something feminine and frilly.'

'Really?' said Miss Campion. 'Tell me more.'

'I'll come up and see you,' said Sammy. 'Listen, if I bring a list detailing the fabrics and materials we need for our new design, and the quantities required, would you be able to have a useful word or two in the ear of Mr Dickinson?'

'I'm sure he'd lend his ear,' said Miss Campion.

That, thought Sammy, could mean her gentleman friend was gone on her, which wasn't surprising, seeing she was a high-class female woman who'd never want to look like a cowboy herself.

'We've got prospects, Hilda?' he said.

'I'm fairly confident, Mr Adams,' said Miss Campion. 'I'm to ask him to supply the jeans as well?'

'It looks like I'll have to go along with the trend,' said Sammy, 'even if it's against me natural-born instincts.'

'We'll have to grin and bear it,' said Miss Campion.

'I'll do what I can to bear it,' said Sammy, 'but I won't be grinning. Anyway, see you on Monday at twelve thirty, say, at Simpson's in the Strand, where I'll book for lunch.'

'You're inviting me to lunch, Mr Adams?'

'Take time off from the shop and leave your assistant in charge,' said Sammy. 'By the way, I might bring brother Boots with me.'

'I'll be happy to see him,' said Miss Campion, 'he's such a personable man.'

'That's not all,' said Sammy. 'Well, it's been an experience talking to you, Hilda, and some of it could've turned me grey and wrinkled, but I can see a bit of light. See you Monday, then, at Simpson's.'

'I shall look forward to it,' said Miss Campion.

Sammy sat alternately brooding and sparking for ten minutes. Then he took himself to Boots's office. Boots was just replacing his phone. He listened as Sammy acquainted him with much of what Hilda Campion had said.

'So it's going to be jeans, after all?' he said.

'Hilda's convinced they're a coming best-seller,' said Sammy, 'which I consider painful on account of my partiality for female women looking feminine. So I tell you, old mate, I need an answer to a serious question. Am I getting old-fashioned or am I already there?'

'Sammy old lad,' said Boots, 'we're being overtaken by change.'

'Change?' said Sammy. 'What from, a pound note?'

'Social change, Sammy, and changes of style. I've news for you.'

'Good or bad?'

'Startling,' said Boots. 'Rosie phoned me. She

wants to know if we can supply all of them with long-lasting chicken-farm wear.'

His adopted daughter Rosie, together with her husband Matthew, and Emma and Jonathan Hardy, ran a chicken farm near Woldingham village in Surrey.

'Exactly what kind of wear is that?' asked Sammy.

'Jeans,' said Boots.

Sammy fell about in the manner of a bloke who'd lost the bones in his legs.

'Blind Amy,' he said, tottering, 'I'm having a nightmare in broad daylight. Rosie and Emma in jeans? If Jonathan and Matt want to dress like cowboys to bring up chickens, well, I can just about go along with that, but Rosie and Emma?'

'Yes, Rosie and Emma,' said Boots solemnly.

'In jeans?'

'Very practical, of course,' said Boots.

'But you feel faint at the idea?'

'Not quite,' said Boots.

'Trust you to be airy-fairy,' said Sammy, 'I've got human failings meself. Ruddy firecrackers, if Chinese Lady finds out, she'll go up in smoke and arrive at the Buckingham Palace do as a pile of ashes under a new hat.'

'And still smouldering if Patsy and Paula follow suit,' said Boots.

'Don't make me feel worse,' said Sammy. 'Besides, Patsy and Paula ain't running a chicken farm, and I'd disallow Paula, in any case.'

Boots said watch out for what the trend might do to the family. Sammy said he'd take up arms against it doing anything horrible, and that he'd start with a shotgun. That'll blow holes in a cartload of jeans, he said. Boots said apart from the family factor, if Hilda Campion was positive the shops would lose out unless they stocked jeans, the answer was to give in. Sammy said he was more than halfway there, that Hilda Campion's friendly gent might be able to supply from imports, and that he and Boots were to meet Hilda for lunch at Simpson's on Monday, and give her a list of requirements. That was if Boots would like to join them.

'I think I'd better,' said Boots.

Chapter Ten

'Don't go on,' said Paul. Lulu was spouting politics of her usual fiery kind again. 'You'll go off pop one day, and I'll have the messy job of sweeping you up and putting you in the dustbin.'

'That's not funny,' said Lulu. 'Listen, I just can't understand you sometimes. That's when you make me wonder if you really want what the Party wants. Fair shares for all. Do you?'

'Not if there's going to be a lot of blood about,' said Paul. 'Don't I keep telling you that?'

'And don't I keep telling you that half-hearted Socialism won't work?' said Lulu. 'By the way, what play are you and tarty Henrietta seeing tonight?'

'*Blithe Spirit* by Noel Coward.'

'Noel Coward's plummy.'

'He writes good plays.'

'Yes, all about life in middle-class drawing rooms,' said Lulu. 'What's good about that? Real life only takes place in the back yards of the working class.'

'You mean that's where they procreate?' said Paul. 'My dad's family had a back yard when they lived in Walworth, but I don't think he and his brothers were procreated there. Or my Aunt Lizzy, their sister.'

Lulu's spectacles sort of glowered.

'Has anyone ever told you you talk like a fruit bun?'

'Only you, Lulu. And can a fruit bun talk?'

'Well, you do, don't you?' said Lulu. 'You're proof of the pudding. Listen, I suppose you're going to take tarty Henrietta home, are you?'

'Of course,' said Paul. 'Being a confirmed Labour bloke doesn't mean you can't act like a gent. I like to think there are times when you behave like a lady.'

'Don't kid yourself,' said Lulu, peering at notes she'd made on how to do away with Eton and Harrow, turn them into bicycle factories and get a consensus of opinions on the matter from Young Socialists. Then petition a backbench MP to promote a private member's Bill. 'I've got better things to do.'

'Is that a fact?' said Paul, stuffing letters from Young Socialists into a large brown envelope. They were to be delivered to the House of Commons, for the attention of the constituency MP, Lulu's dad. 'Who d'you do them with?'

'I wish you'd grow up by improving your mind,' said Lulu. 'Tell me, are you stuck on Henrietta?'

'We're enjoying a growing friendship.'

'Well, I suppose someone as daft as you deserves someone as vacant as her.'

'I've got a feeling I'm going to sack you for your sauce one day,' said Paul. 'By the way, drop this envelope into the House of Commons on your way home.'

'Do what?'

'Tell the bloke on the door it's for your dad. It contains letters from some of his Young Socialist constituents, and they need his attention.'

104

'You'll be lucky,' said Lulu. 'In any case, it's not on my way home. My flat's in the opposite direction.'

'Well, I'll let you leave early,' said Paul graciously. Even more graciously, while hiding a grin because he knew he was getting her goat, he added, 'Take a bus and charge the fare to petty cash.'

Lulu emitted one of her semi-falsetto growls.

'What am I, a pimply errand boy?' she said.

'You look like one in those jeans,' said Paul, 'although I exclude pimples. Do it, anyway, it's an order.'

'Don't make me spit,' said Lulu. His tendency to pull rank on her in this day and age was a betrayal of the principles of equal rights, of which women, the real workers of the world, were entitled to the larger share. Clearing her throat, she said, 'Stop playing the superior being. It's anti-Socialist – wait a tick, didn't I hear about you from upstairs? When I was up there yesterday lunchtime? Didn't I hear you've got an aunt who's the daughter of Sir Somebody-or-other? I meant to mention it.'

'I don't discuss gossip,' said Paul, knowing she meant his Aunt Polly's father, Sir Henry Simms. There were certain things a faithful Socialist liked to keep to himself, but somehow they got around.

'Trying to keep it dark, are you?' said Lulu. 'No wonder you think yourself superior. Actually, it's a positive disgrace. I mean, someone related to an upper-class title being secretary of a Young Socialists' group. You'd get executed for that in Albania.'

'I'm not proposing to go there,' said Paul.

'Just as well,' said Lulu. 'You'd come back without your head.' She mused on that prospect. 'Still, don't get downhearted. It might be an improvement.'

What a character, thought Paul, she'll be my death if she gets to find out my grandma's going to be Lady Finch.

'Anyway,' he said, 'about these letters for your dad—'

'I'm not taking them to the House of Commons,' said Lulu. 'I'll do the obvious thing. Take them round to my dad's home this evening. Why didn't you think of that?'

'I'm failing myself,' said Paul.

That evening, he had an enjoyable time at the theatre with Miss Henrietta Trevalyan. The Noel Coward play was a riot, delighting the audience, and the cast, which included the author himself, took several rapturous curtain calls. If anything could light up these post-war years of austerity, it was the collective offerings of London's theatres.

Henrietta declared herself entranced as she left with Paul, her arm curling around his. Her hip, that had exercised warm contact with his during the play, now caressed his as he hailed a taxi. Paul, though dedicated to the rights of the workers, didn't believe in joining a scrambling workers' queue for a bus or tram on this kind of occasion. Like his dad and his Uncle Boots, he liked to do things in style, never mind if it made a hole in his pocket.

In the taxi he accompanied Henrietta to her home, her grandmother's handsome Victorian house in Kennington Park Road. Her grandmother was Mrs Trevalyan, a sprightly ex-suffragette in her seventies.

In the darkness of the doorway, Henrietta

assumed command of the situation, clasping Paul firmly to her bosom and delivering a succession of smackers on his lips, as well as gushes into his ear.

'Wasn't it a lovely evening?' Smack. 'I did enjoy the play.' Smack. 'Isn't Noel Coward witty?' Smack. 'My, you do kiss sexy, Paul.' Smack, smack. 'Oh, I don't mind, though.' Smack, smack. 'Oh, aren't you a sweetie?' Smack, smack, smack.

Guessing he wasn't the only feller in her saucy life, Paul, excusing himself on the grounds that he had to call on a dying aunt on his way home, detached his person from her bosom with an adroit movement of his chest, and escaped with a flourish of his supple limbs. In any case, a doorway with lighted trams passing by wasn't his idea of where to enjoy a canoodle, despite the smackers sending up his temperature.

When he arrived home, his mum and dad looked a picture of old-fashioned content in their fireside armchairs.

'Hello, me lad, enjoy yourself, did you?' asked Tommy.

'Had to make a run for it,' said Paul.

'You had to run from the theatre?' said his astonished mum.

'It was hot,' said Paul. 'I nearly caught fire.'

'I never heard of any theatre getting as hot as that,' said Vi.

'Oh, well, once in a while,' said Paul.

'What about the girl you took?' asked Tommy.

'She was hot too,' said Paul.

'Well, I hope she doesn't look as scorched as you do,' said Tommy.

'Tommy, Paul doesn't look scorched,' said Vi.

'Pink?' suggested Tommy.

'Your dad's having one of his little jokes, Paul,' said Vi. 'Would you like a nice cup of tea and a sandwich?'

'I'd prefer a cold drink and just a biscuit,' said Paul.

'A cold drink and a biscuit?' said Vi, gaping.

'That'll do,' said Paul. 'No need for you to slave at the sink at this time of night.'

'Beg pardon?' said Vi. 'What's he saying?' she asked Tommy.

'That he needs water to cool himself down,' said Tommy.

'But the bit about me slaving at the sink?' said Vi, not noticing that her Labourite son was sidling out.

'Well, it's either that or slaving as a worker at the gasworks,' said Tommy.

'Me at the gasworks?' said Vi. 'Tommy, that's silly. If I had to work, I'd choose a job in a flower shop.'

'Might I point out you do work, in this house, and most hours of the day?' said Tommy.

'Well, it's nice you've noticed,' said Vi. 'Paul, if you'd like a— here, where's he gone?'

'To the kitchen tap with a glass, that's my guess,' said Tommy.

'He's going to drink cold water and find a biscuit?' said Vi. 'No, that's silly. I'll put the kettle on and make him a nice sandwich.'

It was lucky for Vi that Lulu wasn't around, or she'd have had to listen to what slaving at a kitchen sink was doing to women who might otherwise have invented the power-driven lawnmower.

Boots's wife, Polly, always a woman ahead of her

time, might have told Lulu, if asked, that she was on the right tack, but pursuing an approach that women like those of the Adams family would probably have found too aggressive and too startling. Such women, she might have said, were happy with their lot. She might also have said she was more than happy with her own lot, and that anyone who tried to change it wouldn't get past her front door.

Such women sent Lulu potty. Lulu considered herself a modern kind of suffragette in that she was in the vanguard of a new drive on behalf of women, especially those who had no affinity with a kitchen sink. She was pretty sure Henrietta Trevalyan kept as far away from her granny's sink as she could. Tarty Henrietta could actually be promising material.

Chapter Eleven

Saturday morning.

At Bristol University, Sammy's eldest daughter Bess and Tommy's daughter Alice were chatting over morning coffee in the Students Union. Bess, twenty-one, was in her second year as a student. Alice, twenty-four, and holding a degree in English Literature, was secretary to the bursar, with ambitions to become a lecturer.

'Bess, you say you've had an exciting letter from Jeremy?' she said. She was referring to Jeremy Passmore of Chicago. Bess had met him while on vacation in the Lake District last summer, and they had taken a warm liking to each other. Subsequently, Jeremy, who had been living with English relatives in Kent, returned to Chicago to see his father, terminally ill. When death occurred, Jeremy found he had to stay on to take over management of his father's packaging business. Although he did not intend to make this commitment permanent, he was still in Chicago, trapped by circumstances and his widowed mother's dependence on his help. He had written regularly to Bess, and it was his last letter that excited her.

'Alice, what do you think,' she said, 'Jeremy wants to know if he can come over and spend some time with me during my summer vacation.'

'Heavens, he's thinking of coming all that way to see you?' said Alice, as students entered boisterously, greeted friends noisily, and engaged volubly with each other.

Bess said, smiling, 'Yes, all the way from his home in Chicago, would you believe.'

'That must mean something very positive,' said Alice.

'What's very positive?' asked Bess.

'It could mean he's twitching,' said Alice.

'I think that's a joke,' said Bess and laughed. Studious Alice did not make many jokes. 'Jeremy doesn't twitch.'

'Can you be sure when you've only spent a few hours in his company?' asked Alice.

'Quite sure,' said Bess.

'Are you going to reply in the affirmative?' asked Alice.

'Of course,' said Bess, as fair as her mother and decidedly attractive since losing lingering plumpness. Puppy fat had clung to her for years, right up to the age of seventeen, much to her despair. Sammy, her dad, had called her his Plum Pudding until she was twelve, when he tactfully refrained. Eventually, at seventeen, Bess found the answer, when she gave up certain foods she liked, such as roast potatoes and other fattening items. The dieting did the trick, and when she met Jeremy last summer, she had no cause to be sensitive about her figure. It was as it should be, noticeable but not excessively so. 'I'd love to see him again, and I've

111

'already written to encourage him to come over.'

'Will it be a romantic reunion?' asked Alice.

'Well, there'll be a reunion, of course,' said Bess, 'but I don't know if it'll be romantic or not. You've just reminded me we only spent a few hours together that day in the Lake District.'

'But he's been very persistent in writing so often to you,' said Alice. 'It could have been love at first sight. My, how old-fashioned that sounds.'

'Old-fashioned doesn't mean unacceptable,' said Bess. 'Some modern expressions are hardly the cat's whiskers. But as for love at first sight on Jeremy's part, I couldn't say, could I?'

'Still, would it please you if it were true?' asked Alice.

'Would it please you if it were true of Fergus's feelings for you?' countered Bess.

Alice wrinkled her nose. Fergus MacAllister, a Scot, had made his mark on her life in 1944, before she entered Bristol University. She had thought him a nuisance at first, but he grew on her with his prevailing air of cheerful resolution. He'd been invalided out of the Army after receiving a severe wound during the retreat to Dunkirk in 1940. It left him with shrapnel splinters in his body. However, an emergency operation in King's College Hospital had removed them, and he was taken back into the Army, rejoining his Scottish regiment.

A regular, and now a sergeant, he had been overseas since the end of the war, in trouble spots like Palestine, Cyprus and Malaya, except for one spell of home leave.

He wrote to her every fortnight, making it clear that not until he had served his time would he ask her to marry him. Thanks very much, thought Alice on occasions of frustration, but I'm not waiting indefinitely, I don't intend to go to the altar as an old lady, not for any man, if at all. She still had her mind on a lecturing position, a pleasurable alternative. (A young lady called Lulu would have encouraged her to chuck Fergus, full stop, and go definitely for the career.) All the same, there were moments when Alice wished Fergus was readily accessible, so that she could enjoy their kind of enlivening conversation daily. He had a way of bringing out the best in her, socially.

'Fergus?' she said, responding to Bess. 'I'm not sure about his real feelings. What I am sure is that he's in love with the Army, and more so since he was promoted to sergeant. In any case, he isn't a marrying man at the moment. He's afflicted with reservations.'

'So where does that leave you?' asked Bess.

'Irritated,' said Alice.

'Oh, well,' said Bess, 'he'll turn up sometime, so let's think about happy days.'

'Such as the day of your reunion with Jeremy, and the day when Grandpa and Grandma become Sir Edwin and Lady Finch?' said Alice. 'The family grapevine tells me the prospect is still so unbelievable to Grandma that she'll be taking her smelling salts with her to Buckingham Palace.'

'Oh, she'll come through,' said Bess. 'Grandma would come through even if a horde of Stalin's Bolsheviks landed on her doorstep. You know that's how she sees Russian Communists, and what she thinks of them, that they ought never to have been invented.'

'I do know,' smiled Alice, 'and although it's time she realized the war couldn't have been won without them, every family ought to have a grandma like ours.'

'I wonder what she'll think of Jeremy coming all the way from America to see me?' mused Bess. 'I wonder, in fact, what my parents will say when I phone them this evening?'

'Problems, problems,' said Alice. 'Who'd have one like yours? You would.'

Bess smiled. Alice had made another funny.

Despite the introduction of the five-day week, Paul and Lulu still went to their office on Saturday mornings. That was when Young Socialists liked to show themselves, and to sit around discussing politics and the Party with Paul and Lulu. It kept them keen and made them feel they counted.

Before any of them had turned up, however, Lulu asked Paul if he'd enjoyed the play. Paul said yes, not half, absolutely first-class.

'What about your love life?' asked Lulu, black hair dressed high for a change and held in place with an old-fashioned tortoiseshell comb. It gave her a Spanish look, which Paul thought a definite improvement. 'Yes, what about tarty Henrietta?'

'Why are you so interested in her?' countered Paul.

'I've got compassionate feelings for you,' said Lulu. 'You're bossy, but you're nearly a human being. You're entitled to a bit of protection.'

'From Henrietta?'

'From her gluttony.'

'Gluttony?'

'Yes,' said Lulu. 'It didn't take me long when we first met her to sum her up. She's a man-eater. Bet she swallows men whole. And has young blokes like you for afters.'

'I'll know when that's going to happen,' said Paul.

'When?' asked Lulu.

'When she's made the custard,' said Paul.

Lulu's guardianship of her serious self played truant, and she actually laughed.

'Oh, excuse me,' she said.

'Anything more on your mind?' enquired Paul.

'Yes,' said Lulu. 'Just don't get too near her cooker.'

A knock preceded the entry of the first caller.

'You'll be all right while I'm out?' said Lizzy to husband Ned.

'Is there a reason I might not?' said Ned, fifty-five and thinning of hair, but still pretty mobile despite his tin leg, which was now thirty-three years old.

'Well, I'll be out nearly all morning,' said Lizzy.

'I'll be turning over the vegetable patch,' said Ned, 'getting it ready for spring planting.'

'All right,' said Lizzy, 'only put some thick sweaters on, it's cold today.'

'But crisp and sunny,' said Ned. 'Healthy kind of weather.'

'Yes, but you still ought to wrap up,' said Lizzy. 'Now, like I told you at breakfast, I'm doing a bit of shopping, then taking some nice flowers or grapes to Helene, who's had the flu, then calling on Mum. But I'll be back in time to get lunch.'

'Well, give Helene my best wishes, and my love to

your dear old mum,' said Ned. 'And bring back some grapes for me.'

'But you haven't had flu, not for ages,' said Lizzy.

'And I haven't had any grapes, either,' said Ned. 'At least, not for a fortnight.'

'Oh, dear, what a shame,' said Lizzy, and off she went.

A girl, walking along a beaten path from a farmhouse to a barn, viewed the undulating landscape of the Weald of Kent, the greens sharp in the crisp sunlight of March. Crikey, she thought, I'm right out in the countryside, I can see for miles. It must be lovely here in the summer. Reaching the muddy approach to the barn, the soles of her borrowed wellington boots began to squelch. Yuk, she thought, I don't know I'd fancy living here in the winter.

Squelch, squelch. A young man, hearing the sound, moved from the interior of the barn, showing himself at the moment when her boots found the firm if mud-dotted surface around the timbered building. He was Latin-dark, his black hair thick and curly, his face a deep brown. His old-fashioned blue flannel shirt was open at the neck, his hard-wearing trousers tucked into his boots, which were covered with black smelly stuff. He was holding a stout three-pronged fork.

The moment he saw the girl a smile leapt to reveal white teeth.

'Good-a morning, signorina.'

'Good morning,' said Miss Paula Adams, who had arrived at Kate and David's farm an hour ago, having been driven there by Sammy.

'Ah, a pretty girl,' said Enrico Cellino.

'Beg pardon?' said Paula, clad in a woollen-lined white mackintosh brightly defiant of winter's dark hues.

'Not 'alf, eh?' said Enrico. 'Pretty is good.'

'Excuse me,' said Paula, 'but kindly don't be familiar.'

'Ah, you don't-a like being pretty?'

'I don't like saucy strangers being familiar.'

'You mean we don't-a know who we are?'

'I know who I am,' said Paula, 'and I think you're the young man called Enrico who looks after the cows. My cousin, Mr Adams, told me about you.'

'And you have come to see me, yes?' said Enrico.

'Certainly not,' said Paula.

'Not to see if I am pretty like you?' said Enrico who, although his English was now good, still breathed out an 'a' to soften a hard consonant.

'Pretty?' said Paula.

'I am not, I think.'

'If you were, I'd feel sorry for you,' said Paula. Her nose twitched. A wain, hitched to a tractor, was half-full of a congealed black mass mixed with dirty straw. The smell was pungent. 'What's that?' she asked.

'Muck,' said Enrico, noting English fairness and twitching nose. Her nose was pretty too.

'Pardon?' said Paula, not given to examining farms or farming, but keen to spend an open-air weekend with David and Kate. Open air agreed with her energetic approach to life and she'd accepted an invitation with pleasure, even if it wasn't the best time of the year for the countryside.

'I am mucking out the cow barn,' said Enrico.

'Whatever that is, I'm sorry to say it's making you

smelly,' said Paula, and took a peek at the interior of the barn. Much of the stone floor was thickly covered in the black stuff mingled with dirty straw. 'Ugh,' she said.

'Not pretty?' said Enrico, grinning. 'The cows—'

'Don't tell me,' said Paula, 'I think I know.'

'The muck is for – you have heard of – ah, let me see – yes, small farms?' said Enrico.

'I think you might mean smallholdings,' said Paula, pleased with herself that she at least knew that.

'You are right, I think,' said Enrico. 'That is good, to be right and also pretty.'

'Never mind that, saucy,' said Paula. 'Smallholdings grow things like lettuces and tomatoes for local greengrocers, don't they?' Pleased though she was, that was the extent of her farming knowledge. Paula was a town girl, if with a suburban lifestyle. She liked the hustle and bustle of people and traffic, and the excitements of shops and markets. So did her mum and her Aunt Vi and her grandma. They were all townies, born so.

'They buy muck,' said Enrico, and nodded at what he'd loaded so far on the wain. 'They will buy this.'

'Well, I'm blessed,' said Paula, 'I'd have thought you lucky just to be able to give it away, or even to pay someone to take it away.'

'No, no,' said Enrico, 'it is very valuable. Not like diamonds, no, but still valuable, not 'alf. For giving food to the land.'

'Food?' said Paula.

'Sure,' said Enrico. 'The land gives food, so it must be fed itself.'

'Well, all I can say is that it's a funny kind of food,' said Paula.

'From the cows,' said Enrico. 'It is—'

'Yes, I know,' said Paula, 'it's manure.'

'Pretty good stuff, eh?' said Enrico.

'Smelly,' said Paula.

'Smelly is good,' said Enrico. 'More smelly, more rich. You are a relative of Signor and Signora Adams?'

'Mr Adams is my cousin,' said Paula. 'I told you so.'

'Nice people, very kind,' said Enrico. 'You would like to see the cows and where I milk them, in that shed?'

'I'll do that later,' said Paula, wanting to see all she could, including David and Kate's herd of cows out in the fields. 'I've had my little walk, and I'm going back now to see the dairy.'

'How long you stay here?' asked Enrico.

'Until tomorrow afternoon,' said Paula.

'Good,' said Enrico. 'You would like to see a movie with me tonight, perhaps?'

'Crikey, you're not backward in coming forward, are you?' said Paula.

'Excuse me?'

'I don't go to cinemas except with my friends,' said Paula. She meant girlfriends, for she wasn't yet into any close relationship with a boy.

'You would like me as a friend?' said Enrico, smiling encouragingly.

'Crikey, you think a lot of yourself, don't you?' said Paula.

'Excuse me?' said Enrico.

'Are all Italians like you?' said Paula.

'Italians very good blokes,' said Enrico. 'English girls pretty nice.'

'Well, thanks,' said Paula. 'And personally, I'm particular.'

'Particular is good?' said Enrico.

'It means I don't let saucy young men like you pick me up,' said Paula.

'What is pick you up?'

'Trying it on?'

'Excuse me?'

'Don't keep saying that,' said Paula. 'I bet you know what I mean.'

'I know I like reading books,' said Enrico. 'I am reading one tonight, an English book, but will take you to a movie instead if you would like.'

'Blessed creeps,' said Paula, 'don't I keep telling you no? My dad would land you a thump if he was listening to you trying it on with me, especially as I'm only—' She was going to say she was only fifteen. Instead, she said, 'Especially as I'm only here to be with my cousins. I'm going back to them now.'

'Signor Adams, he is with the cows,' said Enrico. 'I will take you to him, yes?'

'I'll find my own way later, thanks,' said Paula. But she laughed as she left.

She heard Enrico say, 'So pretty.'

Enrico, in fact, had no idea this long-legged girl was only fifteen. He thought her seventeen, which was pretty nice for a girl, not half.

Paula found Kate in the dairy. The dairy, unlike the barn, was spotless, Kate herself in a clean white hat and apron. She was working away at a churn.

'What's that you're doing, Kate?'

'I'm doing my best to turn cream into butter,' said

Kate, whose role as a farmer's wife meant her life was all go. 'Don't stop me now I've started.'

'Is this just one of the things you and David do for a living?' asked Paula.

'Just one,' said Kate, 'and then there's what we do for the Milk Marketing Board as well. Form-filling. Talk about rules and regulations. Your dad says he feels for us because he had to fill in thousands of forms himself during the war. He said it gave him the sort of complaint that makes a bloke wake up in the night yelling for a doctor.'

Paula laughed.

'That's my dad,' she said.

'Mind, David says everything's going to be done by machines as soon as the Government gives us part of the cost and the use of experts to put the machinery in.'

'Kate, d'you like farming?' asked Paula.

'I'm used to it now,' said Kate, winding away, 'I've got over thinking I was born to be the wife of a London bus driver. My old dad was a bus driver, and a trade unionist as well, and a good old dad. Look at me now, a farmer's wife, losing me delicate complexion, and never seeing a London tram in a month of Sundays. Did you meet Rico down at the cow barn?'

'Oh, Enrico?'

'Everyone calls him Rico,' said Kate.

'Oh, I met him all right,' said Paula. 'What a cheeky monkey.'

'How cheeky?' smiled Kate.

'He tried to get me to go to a cinema with him tonight.'

Kate said, 'Actually, for an Italian, he lives a quiet

life with us. He seems to prefer books to the girls in Westerham, though he does go there now and again. I should think some of the girls look forward to it. Well, he's not a bad-looking bloke.' She stopped turning to open up the churn and inspect its contents, thick and creamy. 'Fifteen minutes more at this, then I'll get some lunch.' She resumed her engagement with the churn. 'About the cinema, d'you want to go with our young Italian?'

'Me? Not much I don't,' said Paula. 'Besides, Mum wouldn't let me go with anyone she didn't know.'

'I could phone her,' said Kate.

'Oh, I don't think so,' said Paula. 'Um – how old is he?'

'Rico? He'll be twenty this year.'

'Well, he's grown a lot of sauce in his time,' said Paula. 'Kate, can I do that for you?'

'Can you?' said Kate. 'All right, have a go.'

Paula, always ready to be active, took a turn, finding it needed a bit of stamina to keep the churn moving. Still, she had a fund of energy, and she made the thickening contents reach a buttery firmness.

Chapter Twelve

Midday.

Ned, using a spade to turn over the earth of his vegetable plot, was enjoying the exercise and the sight of the soil crumbling and breaking up. He'd been at it for two hours with a short break for coffee.

Good going, he thought. The exercise was even making him perspire on this cold day. At which precise moment, his energy suddenly ran away, weakness assailed his body, and a giddiness coincided with a tight feeling in his chest. He did the sensible thing and sat down on the grass verge at the side of the plot. He drew deep breaths. Indigestion, that's what I've got, he told himself. I'll have to stop eating fried eggs and bacon for breakfast, especially if Eliza throws in a sausage as well.

He sat for several minutes. The giddiness subsided, and the tight feeling slowly eased. A voice reached his ears.

'Ned? I'm back and I'm going to get lunch.'

He came to his feet.

'Right, Eliza, I'll be with you in a couple of minutes.'

'I've treated you,' called Lizzy.

'What to?'

'Grapes.'

'Lucky old me,' said Ned, and wondered if grapes could cause indigestion. Perhaps the skins could.

He left the plot and went into the house, into the kitchen.

'Had a happy time digging?' said Lizzy, coat off, hat still on, which made Ned think she was like her mother, who often wore hers all day in the fashion of Victorian and Edwardian women.

'Did quite a bit,' he said.

He kept quiet about his indigestion.

Jimmy had received another letter from Jenny.

'Dear Jimmy,

'It was jolly to hear from you, except you sounded a lot too cheerful about me being over here and you being over there. Have you found another girl, then? I hope it's not that sneaky friend of mine, Fiona. I know she fancies you.

'Dad's doing well in his new job on Wall Street, although he says he has to be much more on his toes than in the City of London. Also, most firms start their day at eight o'clock, would you believe, so Dad has to rise at the crack of dawn, or near enough. That's a shock to a man used to City stockbrokers not starting until nine or nine thirty. By nine thirty, Wall Street brokers are thinking about morning coffee. Incidentally, not many New York people drink tea, it's nearly always coffee from breakfast onwards, although some men stop off at a bar on their way home from work for a highball. That's a whisky with ice and soda.

'I'm doing fine at my college of art and science,

getting into the swing of exciting fashion design and trying to cope with lively guys who want to date me. They think English girls have got something a bit special. I wonder what they mean by that?

'Mother-dear has made friends with neighbours, and some neighbours where we live are filthy rich, so she's rubbing shoulders with dollars and diamonds. I think she'll soon be asking Dad for a diamond necklace to go with the pearls he bought her last year. I'm not mad about diamonds and pearls myself, especially not if they're worn together, as per some ladies here. I think it gives them a flashy look. But apparently it's the thing to show you're worth a dollar or two.

'Everyone's very friendly, and neighbours are tickled that we're English. My sister, Caroline, already has a boyfriend, and brother Christopher a following of young American ladies all dying to find out if he's real.

'We had some fierce weather last week, it blanketed New York with snow, which made the streets icy at night. Christopher slipped and bruised his derrière. It gave him a funny walk for a day or two. However, it's sunny and crisp now. I mean the weather, not his derrière.

'Jimmy, write to me again and tell me all your news. And keep away from Fiona. I'm thinking of you. Yours, Jenny.'

Jimmy thought the letter brightly typical of Jenny, although it also had him wondering how long it would be before she let him know one of the lively guys at her college was dating her.

However, he decided to write to her in cheerful vein again, to wish her continuing excitements in

New York, and to assure her he was keeping away from Fiona and looking forward to another summer holiday in Cornwall.

Kate served a light lunch of scrambled eggs, salad and bread rolls. Enrico was present. Kate always cooked for him as well as for herself and David.

The young Italian entered by the back door, his muddy boots off, his feet in his shoes.

'Half a mo,' said Kate. 'Are you smelly, Rico? We've got a guest and smells have to stay outside.'

'Signora, I have washed down,' said Enrico. His brown face had a red tint from soap and cold water, and so did his hands.

'Under the pump?'

'*Si*, signora,' said Enrico, now wearing a warm jersey over his shirt.

'You don't have to punish yourself like that,' said Kate, 'you know you can always have a bowl of warm water.'

'Punishment is good for making a man a better man, you bet,' said Enrico.

'Well, there he is, Paula, he's not too smelly now,' said Kate, 'so we'll let him sit down with us.'

'Ah, that is her name?' said Enrico. 'Paula?'

'Miss Adams,' said Paula.

'Paula I like,' said Enrico.

'Don't embarrass her,' said Kate, 'she's a young girl. And here's David.'

David, entering the kitchen, looked a picture of health and manly fulfilment. Running a farm was his idea of the good life, especially as his cockney wife had adapted so well to what she had originally regarded as frightening in comparison with a back

126

yard, and his Italian help had proved a godsend.

'Well, how d'you like our farm, Paula?' he asked.

'Love what I've seen so far,' said Paula. 'There seems an awful lot more to come. No, not awful, just acres and acres. It must be lovely in the summer.'

'Ah, pretty nice in the summer, you bet,' smiled Enrico, eyeing her with extra pleasure now that she was out of her borrowed wellington boots, and looking a most attractive girl. Also, her orange-gold sweater was very nice, yes, not half.

They all sat down and began lunch. David poured a glass of Kate's home-made lemonade for each of them.

'How far have you been, Paula?' he asked.

'Oh, just to the cow barn,' said Paula.

'Where I was mucking out,' said Enrico.

'Is the trailer fully loaded?' asked David.

'You bet, signor,' said Enrico, devouring a mouthful of Kate's dressed salad. 'All good hot stuff.'

'Good and smelly,' said Paula.

David laughed.

'You can't get away from aromas on a farm, Paula,' he said. 'Rico, get the tractor going this afternoon and haul the load of manure to Mr Jackson's small-holding. He's waiting for it.'

'Ah, will do,' said Enrico. 'The young lady would like to come?'

'Crikey, what an offer,' said Paula. 'Me on a smelly load of muck? I don't think that would do a lot for me.'

'You can ride with Rico on the tractor, Paula,' said Kate.

'Is there room?' asked Paula.

'Pretty nice squeeze,' said Enrico.

Kate laughed, David smiled.

'Take the ride, Paula, if you want,' said Kate. 'Rico will make room.'

'Well, I might think about it,' said Paula, 'but not if it's going to be a small amount of room.'

'You're here to please yourself about what you'd like to do, Paula,' said David, fond of his fair-haired, lively young cousin. 'Just make yourself at home.'

Lunch was soon over. Farm work was too demanding for anyone to linger over the meal.

Paula actually went with Enrico to the small-holding, perched with him on the high metal seat that provided just enough room for the two of them. They were open to the weather, to the crisp air. Fortunately for Paula's girlish nose, the smell of the laden wain trailed out behind them. The young man from Italy, close to her, made cheerful conversation as tractor and trailer crawled along the country lanes. He spoke of how he liked being in England and working on a farm. Life in Italy, very poor for many people, he said, and many Italians hoped to come to England to sell Italian ice cream, or to go to America and be cowboys, like in the movies. His way of speaking made him sound to Paula just like an Italian ice-cream vendor, although in fact he was a brown-faced, strong-looking farmhand.

After a while he began to sing, choosing a song from an Italian opera, his accompaniment being the music of the tractor's engine, except it wasn't music, not to Paula's ears. She protested she could hardly hear herself think in that kind of noise.

'Noise?' said Enrico. 'You no like my singing?'

'Not when the tractor's going,' said Paula.

'Ah, tractor not very pretty, Paula?'

'Not to listen to,' said Paula, enjoying the view from her high seat.

'But my singing you like? Pretty nice, eh?'

Paula glanced at him. He turned his head, smiled at her and winked.

'Might I ask what that's for?' she asked.

'Excuse me?'

'You winked at me, you cheeky thing.'

'To show I like you,' said Enrico.

'I bet you like every girl for miles around,' said Paula, 'and I bet some of them start running as soon as they see you.'

'No, no,' said Enrico, 'I treat English girls very nice. I'm a good Catholic and don't want trouble. How old are you, Paula?'

'Sixteen,' she said. 'Well, I will be next birthday.'

'You are only fifteen now?' Enrico looked surprised. 'Ah, then I will treat you like my sister, see?'

'Thanks very much,' said Paula, not sure how much of a compliment it was for any young man to see her as his sister.

The tractor turned, chugging through an open gate on which a notice board simply stated 'JACKSON'S'. Paula saw greenhouses and two fields, one patterned with long brown furrows, and the other green with young seedlings, a green that was light and sharp under the March sun.

A slightly bow-legged middle-aged man in jersey and corduroys appeared.

'That you, Rico?' he hollered.

The tractor pulled up.

'I'm here, Signor Jackson,' called Enrico.

'Tip the load here, me lad, I'm in a hurry for it,' bawled Mr Jackson. 'Won't do for me late veg if I don't spread it this weekend. Wanted it last week, didn't I, to follow me winter spread.'

'Better this week, very ripe, very good stuff,' said Enrico, and drove to the edge of the ploughed field, close to a shed. Mr Jackson, who had followed on, opened up the back of the wain and shouted, 'Tip her, Rico!' Enrico pulled a lever. The wain rose at an angle and the black mass of manure slid, slopped and formed a huge heap on the ground. Large congealed lumps refused to move from corners and stuck there.

'Ripe all right,' said Mr Jackson, who had a nose for pretty good stuff.

Enrico clambered down and went round the tractor. He looked up at Paula.

'You like to come down?' he said.

Paula wrinkled her nose as a pungent odour rushed at her nostrils.

'If I stay up here, I'll need a gas mask,' she said.

'Who's the young miss?' asked Mr Jackson.

'A cousin to Signor Adams,' said Enrico.

'She can take a look at the greenhouses, if she'd like,' said Mr Jackson. 'You clear the trailer, Rico, while I find me son Harry and his spreading machine.' Off he went, around the shed and hollering for Harry.

Enrico lifted his arms. Paula regarded him suspiciously.

'Long way for a pretty girl to jump, not 'alf,' he said. Paula accepted the option, letting him place his hands on her ribs as she rose from her seat and leaned. Down she came. He swung her clear and her feet landed lightly on the ground.

From the shed emerged a young lady in a full-up sweater and tight breeches, a black beret on her red hair.

'Hey, Rico!' she called.

'Hello, Signorina Jackson,' said Enrico, sounding cautious.

'Who's that with you?'

'A relative, isn't she?'

'Yours?'

'Signor Adams.'

'Well, leave her for a moment and come here. There's something I want to show you in the shed. Jump to it, Musso.'

Crikey, what a female bossyboots, thought Paula, and she's got no manners, either.

'A moment, signorina, eh?' called Enrico. 'I have to clear the trailer, don't I?'

'Leave it, Rico, and come here,' said the redhead. Enrico sighed and walked over to her. They entered the shed together and disappeared.

Blow that for a lark, thought Paula, I'm left here like a dummy with this yukky smell.

She walked away from it.

She stopped and turned as from the shed came a shriek of laughter, followed by the hurried emergence of Enrico, his brown face flushed.

'Rico, come back!' yelled the unseen redhead.

'Not bloody likely, I don't think,' said Enrico to the pile of muck.

'What happened?' asked Paula.

'That young lady isn't a lady,' said Enrico. 'Pretty damn saucy bag of tricks.'

'I don't think much of her, then,' said Paula, who

suspected the young Italian was actually embarrassed.

'Don't you worry, Paula. Stay pretty and nice, eh? Go and look at the greenhouses, you'll see tomato bushes growing very good, not 'alf.' Enrico smiled at her, and Paula found herself beginning to warm to him. 'I must clear out the smelly stuff you don't like.'

'I'll just stand around,' said Paula, thinking that if she went to inspect tomato plants, she'd leave him unprotected. Bossyboots might show herself again and jump on him. Crikey, she thought, I'm daft, he shouldn't need protection, not with his manly muscles and his cheek.

Enrico took a spade from the tractor and set about clearing the wain of its residue of muck. Mr Jackson reappeared, a sturdy young bloke with him.

'Right, Rico,' he shouted, 'all done, are you?'

'All done, signor,' said Rico.

'Off you go, then, and thank Mr Adams for me. Wait a bit, did I hear someone yell?'

'Did you?' said Enrico.

'Not that bloody girl of mine, was it?' Mr Jackson scowled. 'And not you that made her yell, was it?'

'She'd yell if a pin dropped on her head,' said the son, Harry.

'No, she didn't yell,' said Paula, 'she laughed.'

'She'd laugh like crazy even if only a leaf tickled her,' said Harry.

'Can we go?' asked Paula of Enrico.

'Sure,' said Enrico. 'I bring another load tomorrow, Signor Jackson.'

'Early,' said Mr Jackson.

'Here, girlie,' called Harry to Paula, 'doing anything tonight?'

'Yes, knitting,' said Paula.

She and Enrico departed a few minutes later, the emptied wain level again, the afternoon still bright.

'You do knitting, Paula?' said Enrico.

'Me?' said Paula. 'I'm a bit young for that yet. Listen, what did Mr Jackson's daughter do to you that you didn't like?'

'Ah, these girls, they make fun of an Italian,' said Enrico.

'I bet it wasn't fun that made you run,' said Paula.

'Her kind of fun,' said Enrico, 'which can mean trouble, and I don't like trouble. I want my papers, don't I?'

'Papers?'

'*Si*, Paula, papers that will say I am one of you and can make my life here as a good citizen, yes?'

'Oh, you mean you want to be naturalized,' said Paula.

'No, I am already born very natural of my parents,' said Enrico.

'I meant British citizenship,' said Paula.

'Ah, of course. Yes, you are right. Do you like books?'

'Yes, I borrow one from our local library almost every Saturday,' said Paula.

'I read English novels, don't I?'

'So do I,' said Paula, 'I'm not up to reading French ones yet.'

'French ones pretty saucy, eh?' said Enrico.

'I wouldn't know, would I?' said Paula.

Enrico laughed. Paula joined in. They were friends.

Later, talking to Kate in the dairy again, Paula told her of Mr Jackson's daughter, and how she had made Enrico act as if he was running for his life. Kate said Doreen Jackson was a loud piece of vulgarity, and that if she could get Rico in the bushes, he'd lose his virginity.

Paula went pink.

'Lose his virginity?' she said. 'Crikey, you're talking right over my head, Kate.'

'Oh, in the country, with oversexed bulls and rams pawing the ground, you're soon down to earth,' said Kate. 'Rico's got his Italian way of chatting up girls, which David and me gradually found out, but we both think it doesn't go any farther than that. He's so keen on getting a British passport that he keeps clear of anything that might mean trouble. Like angry dads coming after him.'

'Wow,' said Paula, 'I never heard talk like this.'

'We're all hearing things that never used to be mentioned,' smiled Kate. 'In all the years I lived with me mum and dad in Camberwell, I never heard them use the word sex, and me mum would've probably fainted if me dad had mentioned it. Everything's changing now. By the way, when David went to the fields after lunch, he found one of our young bullocks had broken its leg. He had to come back here for his gun, then go and shoot it.'

'Oh, did he have to?' asked Paula.

'You can't treat the broken leg of a farm animal,' said Kate, 'you've got to put it down. Anyway, a local butcher sent a team to collect the carcase and pay for it. It'll be skinned and hung for a week, then he'll saw it up into joints. He'll sell half of them in his shop, and let me and David have the rest.'

'Oh, help,' said Paula. She was well up with all the social trends of the young, like listening to records of American crooners such as Bing Crosby and the rising Frank Sinatra. And going to local youth-club dances with Phoebe and their schoolfriends to indulge in jiving. But she didn't know the ways of farmers and cows and bullocks. 'Crikey, could you actually eat one of your own animals, Kate?'

'Easily, with roast potatoes and horseradish sauce,' said Kate, an accomplished cook who, in her established domestic role, was the kind of wife Lulu sorrowed for.

'Can I come and stay again for a weekend?' asked Paula.

'Anytime,' said Kate, 'it's lovely having you. Just let us know when.'

The male person wandering about in the Denmark Hill library was suffering disappointment. The girl who'd caught his eye more than once was absent. She was always there on Saturdays, but not today.

He waited, but she didn't turn up.

Chapter Thirteen

'Edwin,' said Chinese Lady that evening, 'I don't know how Helene came to catch the flu.'

'Such things happen to all of us, Maisie,' said Mr Finch, settling comfortably down in an armchair beside the fire. Chinese Lady didn't favour central heating, although it was now much recommended by clean-air bodies as preferable to open coal fires. All new commercial buildings and high-rise housing blocks were centrally heated, but a nice homely fire was still Chinese Lady's idea of bliss. And she was impervious to draughts. Well, during her lifetime she'd experienced thousands of them, and they'd rendered her immune. 'Influenza is common in the winter, my dear,' said Mr Finch.

'It didn't ought to be common to Helene,' said Chinese Lady. 'I never saw a healthier young woman, considering she's French.'

'She's also a farmer's daughter,' said Mr Finch, 'and robust.'

'Oh, I'm very admiring of her,' said Chinese Lady, 'she's a good wife and mother.'

'I share that admiration,' said Mr Finch, who knew that Helene, along with Bobby, had served with the French Resistance movement. The thought made him reflect on his own wartime efforts, and how full his life had been since he defected from Germany in 1918. His work with British Intelligence, his marriage to Chinese Lady, her loyalty and affection, and the affection given to him by her children and grandchildren, all had meant a great deal to him. The strenuous efforts of Britain and her Empire in the war against Hitler had confirmed his attachment to his adopted country. He felt pity for Germany's defeated people, pity for their plight and for their misguided worship of their crazy fuehrer, who had committed suicide after declaring they had proved unworthy of him, and that defeat was everyone's fault except his own.

'And I'm admiring of Bobby too,' said Chinese Lady, 'especially for getting medals in the war. Mind, I've never thought medals much good to soldiers that are hard up. Well, I've never heard that medals paid their rent. Perhaps you could write to the Government about it when you get your title.'

'Yes, perhaps I could, Maisie,' agreed Mr Finch.

'They might take more notice of someone titled,' said Chinese Lady. 'Lor', the more I think about that, the more I wonder if my knees are going to hold me up. Edwin, is anyone coming to tea tomorrow?'

Mr Finch smiled. Some family members were nearly always present at Sunday tea.

'Not tomorrow, Maisie,' he said. 'Tomorrow you and I will be enjoying a quiet day.'

'No-one's coming for tea?' said Chinese Lady.

Mr Finch smiled again. He knew her little likings.

'It's a while since we had Lizzy and Ned,' he said.

'Is it?' Chinese Lady looked slightly worried.

'Well, they're the last two I'd want to neglect. We'd best invite them, Edwin.'

'I'll phone them now,' said Mr Finch, and did so. Lizzy said she and Ned would love to come, especially as they had a free Sunday for a change. Usually some of their own family visited on Sundays. Mr Finch was then able to inform Chinese Lady of the outcome.

'Oh, that's nice,' she said, 'it'll make tomorrow more of a proper family Sunday.'

'And that'll please you?' said Mr Finch.

'Yes, it'll please me, Edwin.'

Mr Finch smiled yet again. His Walworth-born wife asked for very little that was in any way extravagant. Simple pleasures, particularly those relating to the family, kept her happy.

'Shall we turn on the radio, Maisie?'

'The wireless? What's on?'

'The Saturday evening play.'

'Well, that's always better than some of the news, Edwin, so turn it on.'

That dialogue was typical of the homely interchanges Chinese Lady enjoyed with her husband, a man of subtle sophistication who might have wished for more challenging conversations, but was content with what obtained.

Sammy answered the ringing phone.

'Hello?'

'It's me,' said Paula. 'How's your whiskers, Dad?'

'Under control,' said Sammy, 'but if they sprout a bit during the night, I'll mow 'em in the morning with me cut-throat. How you doing with Kate and David?'

'I'm ringing to tell you it's all go here,' said Paula.

'I know it,' said Sammy, 'I've been there, several times, to see if the firm's investment ain't loaded with too many overheads. Got to watch overheads, y'know, me pet.'

'You'll get ever such a fitting epitaph, Dad,' said Paula, 'and it'll be something like, "Here lies Sammy Adams, who watched each overhead, in case his bank informed him, his balance was in the red".'

'Hold on, saucebox,' said Sammy, 'where'd you get that from?'

'Uncle Boots,' said Paula with a bit of a giggle.

'One day,' said Sammy, 'I'll have a serious talk with your Uncle Boots. One day. Anyway, d'you like the farm?'

'Well, I haven't seen the cows yet,' said Paula, 'but I've seen a mountain of pongy muck. Crikey, I wouldn't want to live next door to that every day, and not in my best frock, either. David calls it a country aroma, Kate says it's a menace when he brings it into the kitchen and it gets mixed up with the aroma of her cooking. Still, I've been having a lovely time since you dropped me off here.'

'Glad to hear it,' said Sammy, 'but don't bring any home when I fetch you tomorrow.'

'Any what?' asked Paula.

'Any farm pong,' said Sammy. 'Your mum's got a highly delicate nose.'

'Oh, funny ha-ha,' said Paula. 'Anyway, it's been fun here today. I went for a ride on the tractor this afternoon.'

'Where to? Margate?' said Sammy.

'Margate? Be your age, Dad. It was to a small-holding. Enrico took me.'

'The young Italian bloke?' said Sammy.

Paula said yes, that she'd met him this morning, that he was a great help to Kate and David, and had invited her to see a film this evening. Hello, hello, said Sammy, what's he up to with you? Just trying his luck, said Paula, but, of course, I told him no. Crikey, she said, that was only five minutes after I'd met him. I've heard about Italians, said Sammy, but I didn't know they were as quick off the mark as that. I'll have to talk to Antonio when I pick you up tomorrow, he said.

'No, don't do that, Daddy, I'll feel silly if you do,' said Paula. 'And it's Enrico, not Antonio.'

'Same thing,' said Sammy. 'They're all fast workers. If this one fancies you, tell him to point his Italian peepers at a war widow who's a bit lonely.'

'Now tell me another funny story,' said Paula. 'Anyway, give Mum my love and don't forget to collect me tomorrow afternoon about four.'

'I'll be there at four, me pet,' said Sammy, and put the phone down.

He spoke to Susie. Jimmy was out with friends, and Phoebe wasn't yet back from Lily Johnson's birthday party.

'Sammy, are you telling me David's Italian farm-hand has been making eyes at our Paula?' said Susie. 'When she's only fifteen?'

'That piece of news came straight from Paula herself,' said Sammy.

'Well, I hope David and Kate keep an eye on her, and on Enrico,' said Susie.

Sammy showed a good-natured grin.

'What a family,' he said, 'it's got Chinese Lady trying to work out what's happening to it.'

'What d'you mean?' asked Susie.

Sammy delivered his thoughts with a straight face. Might I point out, he said, that our Daniel's married to Patsy from America, Lizzy's son Bobby to Helene from France, and her other son Edward to Leah, a daughter of Abraham. Susie said what of it, they're all love matches. Yes, highly romantic, said Sammy, but it's confusing my dear old ma. Well, said Susie, I admit she often says she doesn't know how these things happened. Further, Susie me love, said Sammy, before they did happen, Emma got churched with Jonathan from the wilds of Sussex, and our Rosie married Matthew, a Dorset bloke. Then there's Eloise, semi-French, he said. Yes, we know how Eloise came about, said Susie, but are you saying your mother thinks Jonathan and Matthew are foreigners?

'Well, you know and I know she thinks anyone born outside Southwark or Lambeth ain't exactly her kind,' said Sammy, 'and she's not too sure about people from Shoreditch and Whitechapel, either. Or Norwood. Now, if Paula brings an Italian geezer home to Sunday tea, and my dear old ma hears about it, which she will, she's going to reach for her smelling salts. She'll think her family's turning into the United Nations.'

'Sammy, you're having a fit,' said Susie. 'Mum's proud of everyone in the family, including French or American or whatever.'

'She's still a bit confused about it,' said Sammy, 'and still trying to work out how Boots got himself an upper-class wife in Polly.'

'That was the best thing Boots could've done when he lost Emily,' said Susie. 'Sammy, go and turn the cold water tap on.'

'Then what?' said Sammy.

'Put your head under it,' said Susie.

It was at this moment that Chinese Lady, listening to the radio play, which featured the intrusion into a stately home of a suspiciously ingratiating visitor from Spain, spoke to her husband.

'Lor', I hope no-one Spanish knocks at any of our doors, Edwin, especially Sammy and Susie's, not when Paula's growing up very attractive, like.'

'Well, Maisie, my dear,' said Mr Finch, 'when you next speak to Susie, tell her not to answer the door unless she knows who's knocking. Now, let's see how this play develops, shall we?'

It was Susie who answered the next phone call. Daughter Bess was on the line from Bristol.

'Hello, Mum love, how's everyone?'

'Everyone's fine,' said Susie. 'And how are you, Bess love, still enjoying university?'

'Very much,' said Bess, and then let her mum know she'd just had an exciting letter from her American friend, Jeremy Passmore of Chicago.

'Oh, you're still keeping in touch with him?' said Susie.

'Yes, he does write regularly,' said Bess, 'and this time, what d'you think?'

'He's proposed in writing?' said Susie. 'Well, I'm sure your dad and me will be happy for you, only so far we've never met him.'

'Mum, it hasn't got anywhere near as far as that,' said Bess, 'we're just good friends.'

'Well, Daniel and Patsy were just good friends once, and so were Edward and Leah,' said Susie.

'Mum, listen,' said Bess. 'Jeremy simply asked if I'd like him to come over and spend some time with me during my summer vacation.'

'He wants to come all the way from America to see you?' said Susie.

'Yes, and I've written to say I'd like it very much,' said Bess. 'I could hardly say no, could I?'

'If he's coming all that way on a boat—'

'A ship, Mum. Boats are what you row on the Serpentine.'

'Oh, pardon me, I'm sure,' said Susie. 'But it sounds to me as if Mr Passmore wants to be more than a good friend.'

'Yes, it does seem like that,' said Bess, 'and I don't think I'm going to fight it. Well, I do like him, very much.'

Susie detected a happy note. She and Sammy, along with others, knew all about the fact that Bess and Jeremy had only been in each other's company once, and then for only a few hours. Still, life was full of little moments that could turn out not to be little at all.

'Let's see, where exactly does he live, Bess?'

'Chicago,' said Bess. 'Mum, you know that.'

'Oh, yes,' said Susie. 'Well, when I tell your dad he's coming over, he'll want to know if he'll be bringing American gangsters with him.'

'Poor old lad,' said Bess. 'Let him know we're living in the Fifties, and that all the gangsters are now senior citizens.'

'Senior citizens?'

'Yes, Jeremy told me it's what old-age pensioners are called in America,' said Bess.

'America,' said Susie, musing. 'America. Well, I wonder what's going to come of it. When's Mr Passmore due to arrive, did he say?'

'No, he only asked if I'd like him to come some-time during my vacation. So I've asked about dates in my reply. Must go now, Mum. Love to Dad and everyone else.'

'Bye, Bess lovey,' said Susie.

Her next step was to acquaint Sammy with the news. Sammy fell about all over America, in a manner of speaking. And when Susie said she'd just remembered that Tommy and Vi's daughter Alice was still in touch with Fergus MacAllister, a Scot, he split his sides. Susie, seeing the funny side of what it all meant, followed suit.

When Phoebe arrived home from the birthday party a few minutes later, she found her mum in fits, and her dad as well. She stared at them.

'Crikey, what's so funny?' she asked.

'It's your grandma's family,' said Susie.

'All of us?' said Phoebe. 'What's all of us done?'

'We've left doors open,' said Sammy.

'And let in all kinds of people from across the seas,' said Susie.

'I haven't noticed,' said Phoebe. 'Who are they, and where have they ended up?'

'Your mum says in the bosom of the family,' said Sammy. 'Like Jonathan, Helene and Patsy. And Eloise, come to that.'

'And there's others who might,' said Susie, looking at Sammy. Their faces seemed to crumple, and they both burst into new laughter.

Phoebe asked for an explanation. What she got

was a lot of garbled stuff about what Grandma Finch was going to make of another American, a possible Scot, and a hint of Italian ice cream landing on family doorsteps.

Susie and Sammy, in fact, were hugely entertained by the prospect of listening to Chinese Lady on the subject. That, of course, was if one of them mentioned it to her.

Young Phoebe thought her mum and dad had gone potty. Much to her relief, it didn't last, and they gave her a coherent explanation of what they found intriguing as well as funny.

Phoebe giggled.

Ned phoned his elder son Bobby to find out if Helene had fully recovered from her attack of flu.

'Well, she's been up on her feet today,' said Bobby, 'but swearing in French about how lousy English flu is. It's not, she insists, as benevolent as French flu. Benevolent, I ask you.'

'You mean she's still feeling a bit under the weather,' said Ned.

'You could say that, Dad old man,' said Bobby, 'you could say it, except that her French is as strong and healthy as your ears could wish for. Good old Dr Mason called this afternoon to give her a final check-up, and told her, apparently, that flu was a swine wherever anyone caught it. It appears Helene disagreed, telling him English flu had a lot more evil microbes than French.'

'Well, I suppose a woman who's as vigorous as she is doesn't take easily to feeling debilitated,' said Ned. 'How are the children?'

'In bed right now, but learning French words of a dubious kind when they're awake,' said Bobby. 'How's yourself, Dad?'

'Fine,' said Ned, 'except for a touch of indigestion now and again.'

'We can all do without that bugbear,' said Bobby. 'What's causing yours, d'you know? Fried onions?'

'I'll find out,' said Ned.

'Yes, take care of your stomach, Dad, and hand it my regards,' said Bobby. 'Thanks for calling, and give my love to your missus.'

'My missus is your respected mother,' said Ned.

'Very respected,' said Bobby. 'Never been known to use language, either French or English – oh, hold on, Helene's on her way, wanting to say hello to you.'

Helene's voice, attractively touched with her French accent, came through.

'Hello, English Papa, how are you?'

'More to the point,' said Ned, 'how are you? Bobby tells me you're now up and about.'

'Yes, I'm much better,' said Helene, 'but feeling a little weak. Dr Mason has told me I must expect that, he said otherwise I'm as good as new. Well, I will be, yes, when Bobby and I, with our young ones, go to France to stay with my parents for Easter.'

'You'll enjoy that,' said Ned, 'but take care you don't catch French flu, even if it is much less weakening than the English kind. Or so I understand from a source I consider the most reliable.'

'Excuse me?' said Helene.

'Yes, I understand French flu is benevolent,' said Ned.

'Benevolent? Who said that?'

'Bobby,' said Ned. 'He mentioned your belief that your native flu is—'

'Ah, the clown. I said it was milder, that's all. Papa, I'm sorry to say your son is an idiot.'

'Don't apologize,' said Ned, 'I've noticed during my lifetime that there's one in almost every family.'

'Ah, well, never mind, Papa,' said Helene, 'I'm not unhappy to have married the one in your family, and you and my English mama both mean much to me.'

'As you do to us,' said Ned.

'Bobby!' Helene called her husband as soon as she came off the phone.

'Here,' called Bobby from the living room. In went Helene, and if flu had left her a little pale, she was still a tall and robust woman, with a strong personality.

Her dark hair showing tints of fiery auburn, she said, 'Bobby, I think I'm going to hit you. What do you mean by telling your father I said French flu was benevolent?'

'Well, my French lily—'

'I only said I was sure it was milder.'

'Ah, well,' said Bobby, getting ready to duck.

'Do you think any kind of flu is a blessing?'

'Well, no—'

'That is what benevolence means, a blessing. And stop saying well, well. I had to tell your father how sorry I was that you're an idiot.'

'And what did he say to that?' asked Bobby.

'That there's one in almost every family.'

'Very consoling,' said Bobby. 'I wouldn't like to think I stood alone.'

Helene looked darkly at him, knowing that not everything he said could be taken literally. Like his

147

cousins Tim and Daniel, and his Uncle Boots, his tongue could be in his cheek twenty times a day.

Bobby eyed her warily, knowing how quick off the mark she could be, especially with a vase in her hand. However, a little sound bubbled in her throat, and the next moment she was laughing.

'Bobby, who cares? We are two of a kind, yes? We are both idiots and could not be happy except with each other. You agree?'

'I will when you put that vase back on its stand,' said Bobby.

Chapter Fourteen

Sunday morning.

The weather was still crisp and bright when Enrico brought the tractor to a stop by Mr Jackson's ploughed field. The field was half covered by lumps of the black manure. The sun was making it steam a bit.

'That you, Rico?' bawled Mr Jackson from the door of a greenhouse.

'New load, signor, more pretty good stuff,' called Enrico.

'I don't know why I've come with it,' said Paula, close beside him on the bucket seat. 'I mean, it'll never be one of my best friends.'

'Tip it, Rico!' hollered Mr Jackson.

'I'll open up the back,' said Paula, keeping the March cold at bay by wearing a cardigan of Kate's over her sweater and skirt.

'No, no, I will do it,' said Enrico, but Paula was climbing down. She went to the rear of the wain and pulled out the bolts. The back of the wain dropped open.

'It's done, Rico,' she called, at which point Mr Jackson's redheaded daughter materialized.

'Who the hell are you exactly?' She thrust the question aggressively at Paula as Enrico pulled the lever.

'Mind your manners,' said Paula, 'and stand back.'

'Push off,' said Doreen Jackson.

Up went the wain at its tipping angle. Down slid a huge mass. Paula was well clear. Doreen, her back to the trailer, wasn't. She yelled as an odorous heap of the manure suddenly surged around her booted feet.

Mr Jackson appeared again at the door of the greenhouse.

'What's going on?' he bawled.

Enrico, startled, jumped down. He gaped as he saw Doreen's booted legs standing in a large amount of black manure. She was still yelling as she pulled one foot free, and then the other.

'Mama mia!' he gasped.

'Is that my bloody girl again?' roared Mr Jackson.

'I'm going to murder someone!' screamed Doreen, boots covered in the messy sludge.

Harry Jackson, showing up, stared at his furious sister, saw what was obvious, that the muck had swamped her boots, and roared with laughter. Mr Jackson came up and took a pop-eyed look.

'Who did that?' he shouted.

'She did!' yelled Doreen, pointing at Paula, who was keeping her distance from the heap and its smell.

'No, no,' protested Enrico. 'She no tipped the load, I did. I'm in trouble, I think.'

Paula, knowing he was set on avoiding trouble, said it was probably her fault in not making sure Miss

Jackson stood well back when the wain began to tip. She'd told her to, she said, but perhaps not loudly enough. Anyway, she said, it certainly wasn't Enrico's fault.

Red-faced father, loud-voiced son and furious daughter bawled and hollered at each other. It spoilt the quiet of the Sunday morning.

Enrico, fastening the back of the wain, which was clear of sludge, whispered to Paula.

'I think we go, eh?'

'Before they chuck us in the pile?' said Paula. 'Not half.'

While the ding-dong was still going on, they climbed up into the tractor's seat, and off they chugged.

'Come back!' yelled Doreen.

The tractor and trailer rolled on.

Heading back to the farm, Enrico said, 'That young lady pretty loud.'

'I'm going to laugh now,' said Paula, and did.

Enrico joined in, and the shared hilarity sounded a lot more acceptable on a Sunday morning than hollering and bawling.

Crikey, thought Paula, I didn't know a Crazy Gang show could take place on a smallholding in the wilds of Kent, and on a Sunday morning. What a yell.

At a few minutes past four in the afternoon, Sammy turned up to collect Paula. Susie and Phoebe were with him. They found Paula looking as if the March sun had touched her. Kate and David said stay for a cup of tea.

'Love to,' said Susie.

They all sat around the kitchen table, drinking hot

tea, with Paula letting her mum and dad know she'd had a lot of fun, and had come to know a thing or two about farm life. She'd seen the cows, she said, which were great walloping beasts, but ever so big-eyed and gentle. Enrico, she said, was out there in the fields, and would be driving the herd to the milking shed in a little while.

'Ah,' said Sammy.

'Yes, Dad?' said Paula.

'This Italian bloke,' said Sammy.

Kate smiled. David winked at Susie. Phoebe glanced at her sister.

'Yes, Dad?' said Paula again.

'Good worker, is he, David?' asked Sammy.

'First-class,' said David. 'Couldn't do without him. Ask the cows.'

'Yes, there's a hundred of them,' said Paula. 'Well, an awful lot, and they follow him about.'

'Well, I'm blessed, that's a happy thing,' said Susie, 'isn't it, Phoebe?'

'Oh, I like to think of cows being happy,' said Phoebe.

'I can't say I've ever been close acquainted with them,' said Sammy. 'Me inclinations always pointed me elsewhere.'

'At profit and loss accounts,' said Susie.

'Granted,' said Sammy. 'Mind, I daresay David and Kate regard their cows as their best friends. Has Enrico got a best friend?'

'A girl, you mean?' said Kate. 'No, no-one special. He's more interested in books.'

'Eh?' said Sammy.

'Fact,' smiled David.

'Well, I'm a monkey,' said Sammy. 'An Italian bloke cuddling books?'

'And singing to the cows,' said Kate. 'He and David are both potty about them.'

'Bust my braces,' said Sammy, 'I'm always learning something new. Well, ta for the tea, Kate. Now we'd better get going. Ready, Paula?'

'Ready, Dad,' said Paula. 'I'm going to come here again later on.'

'Oh, could I come as well next time?' asked Phoebe.

'Lots of room for both of you, Phoebe,' said David, 'and we'd love to have you both.'

Sammy and Susie, and their two younger daughters, were soon out at the car, the girls getting into the back, Kate and David standing by. Kate suddenly darted at Sammy.

'Uncle Sammy,' she said, 'could you do me and David a favour? We've tried to buy ourselves some of those American jeans in Westerham, but no luck. We thought you might be able to get hold of two pairs each for us, you being in the trade.'

Sammy went a bit faint.

'Jeans?' he said hoarsely. 'Jeans? Is it true, then?'

'Is what true?' asked Kate, and Sammy looked into big green eyes that were so like Emily's.

'That jeans might be a coming trend?' he said.

'They're going to be top of the fashions by this time next year,' said Kate.

Sammy sighed.

'They don't have anything to do with fashions,' he said. 'They grieve me rag-trade upbringing. But all right, it seems I've got to go along with the trend, or me shops might go down the drain. I'll see what I can do for you and David.'

'Oh, good on you, Uncle Sammy,' said Kate, and planted a warm kiss on his cheek.

Sammy sighed again, then thought about his lunch date with Hilda Campion at Simpson's tomorrow.

David and Kate called goodbye to everyone, and as soon as the car drove away, they hurried back to resume their farm work. Sundays weren't days off for them.

On the way home, Susie said she'd have liked to have seen Enrico. Paula said he'd be milking the cows now. Sammy said he supposed she liked the bloke. Paula said he was nice, but she'd only ever see him when she had weekends with Kate and David. So you needn't think things, Dad, she said. Phoebe said young Italian men were supposed to be heart-throbs.

'Older ones too,' smiled Susie.

'Well,' said Sammy, on the way to recovering from Kate and David's fancy for jeans, 'if anyone's over the moon about David and Kate's Italian heart-throb, it looks like it's their cows.'

Girlish yelps of laughter ran around the interior of the car.

'Mum, the fruit cake's delicious,' said Lizzy. She and Ned were enjoying Sunday tea with Chinese Lady and Mr Finch. 'You've used a good helping of butter in the mixing, I can tell you have. I simply can't get enough from my grocer. Wouldn't you think there'd be plenty by now? The war's been over nearly five years.'

'Unfortunately, dear Lizzy,' said Mr Finch, 'we're still paying the price of victory.'

'What's the difference, I wonder, between the price of victory and the price of defeat?' mused Ned.

'A small matter of pride, perhaps?' said Mr Finch.

'It's disgraceful,' said Chinese Lady, seated as upright as ever in her command of the large teapot and its embroidered home-made cosy. A pristine white cloth covered the table. Some families were favouring a post-war trend of using place mats instead of tablecloths, which Chinese Lady considered common in view of how much bare table was exposed. 'It was the same after 1918,' she said. 'I just don't know why we bother to win wars, except of course we didn't want the German Kaiser or that monster Hitler trampling in and out of Buckingham Palace.'

'Well said, Maisie,' smiled Mr Finch.

'Oh, Lor', we'll be going there soon, Edwin, you and me,' said Chinese Lady.

'Not in jackboots,' said Ned, 'and not to trample in and out.'

'I should think not,' said Lizzy. 'More like all dressed up and entering very gracious.'

'I don't know my legs will be able to carry me gracious,' sighed Chinese Lady, which Ned thought must have been spoken absently, for Eliza's Victorian mother rarely allowed herself to mention her legs. 'Nor don't I know if I'll be able to walk in a straight line. Lord above, I'll look as if I've had a drop too much to drink.'

Lizzy laughed.

'Not you, Mum,' she said, 'you'll beat all your collywobbles.'

Later, after tea had finished and the washing-up had been done, they all repaired to the large front room that Chinese Lady still called the parlour. As they entered the room, Ned stopped and put his hand to his chest.

'Ned? What's wrong?' asked Lizzy.

'Attack of indigestion,' said Ned, his expression registering pain.

'I hope it wasn't my fruit cake,' said Chinese Lady. 'Ned, sit down for a bit.'

Ned gladly seated himself in an armchair. Mr Finch thought his face drawn.

'An aspirin, Maisie?' he suggested.

'For indigestion?' said Chinese Lady.

'Would you like that, Ned, an aspirin tablet?' asked Lizzy.

'Try me,' said Ned, voice a little strained.

Chinese Lady went back to the kitchen, took a bottle of aspirin tablets from a cabinet, looked at the label and its printed details, and decided two might be better than one. She carried a glass of water and two little tablets back to her parlour. Ned swallowed the tablets and washed them down with gulps of water, Lizzy watching him in concern. He'd never had indigestion before, and certainly not of a painful kind. Well, he'd never said so.

'Is it worrying, Ned love?' she asked.

'Better now,' said Ned.

'Take it easy, old chap,' said Mr Finch.

'I'd be sorry if my fruit cake caused it, if it was a bit too rich,' said Chinese Lady. She was as fond of Ned as if he'd been one of her own. He'd been a good husband to Lizzy, and a caring father to his sons and daughters for many years, and no-one could have said he'd ever acted sorry for himself over his artificial leg, which he'd had to put up with since the Great War. 'Do like Edwin says, Ned, sit back and relax, I think that's best.'

Ned didn't seem inclined to do other than that. He sat back and let the aspirins do their work. After ten minutes, he did relax and gave Lizzy a smile.

'All gone now, Eliza,' he said.

'Oh, that's good,' said Lizzy. Knowing her husband through and through, she was sure the indigestion must have been really painful to have made him sort of collapse into an armchair. And he had a drawn look. 'We'll have to watch his diet, Mum.'

'Perhaps a visit to his doctor?' suggested Mr Finch gently.

'I'll see,' said Ned, 'I'll see.'

Chapter Fifteen

On Monday morning, Lulu arrived for work in a jumper and skirt. Paul noted definitive bosom and visible legs.

'What's happened to your jeans?' he asked.

'They ran up against a leaky dog,' scowled Lulu.

'Pardon?'

'Cocked its leg without asking permission to use me as a lamppost,' said Lulu. 'That's it, laugh.'

'Who's laughing?' asked Paul.

'You look as if you're going to,' said Lulu.

'No, I sincerely feel for you, as I would for anybody who'd been mistaken for a lamppost by a short-sighted bow-wow,' said Paul. 'And that includes an out-and-out Conservative voter. Still, there's a consolation.'

'Which is?'

'Dog's wee rots jeans, so you put on a skirt that suits you a treat,' said Paul. 'It's always a pleasure to see you looking like yourself instead of anonymous.'

'Oh, very witty,' said Lulu.

'Apart from the doggie incident, did you enjoy your weekend?' asked Paul, beginning to open the morning's mail.

'Wonderful,' said Lulu. 'I read my way through a

new biography of Keir Hardie. What a pioneer. Great stuff.'

'Didn't you go out dancing?'

'Dancing? Dancing?' Lulu gave him one of her pitying looks. 'Who's going to tear themselves away from Keir Hardie to jig around with bourgeois people in a sweaty dance hall?'

'It could give you an opportunity to talk some of the fellers into voting for the Labour Party while you're waltzing bosom to bosom with them,' said Paul.

'Waltzing, he says, waltzing,' remarked Lulu, inserting a sheet of paper into her typewriter in a testy way, as if the machine had as much to answer for as Paul.

Paul, unfolding a letter, saw a postal order drop out. Examining it, he found it was for five bob. The writer, a female, had made a donation to funds.

'Lulu, look at that, a five-bob postal order from a young lady member,' he said. 'It's probably more than she can afford, probably a far greater sacrifice than Mrs Trevalyan made when she handed us a cheque for ten quid.'

'Mrs Trevalyan, oh, yes,' said Lulu. 'Tarty Henrietta's dear old granny.'

'Not that I didn't appreciate it,' said Paul, 'but this postal order from a young working lady shows devotion worthy of an angel. I'm touched.'

'Let's send her a touching acknowledgement, then,' said Lulu. 'We don't run across angels every day.'

'I'll scribble something out,' said Paul.

'How jolly good,' said Lulu, and began to type suggestions for a new campaign by the Young Socialists.

*　　*　　*

Paul went upstairs to the main offices of the headquarters at eleven o'clock to talk to the constituency's agent. Lulu took the opportunity to phone Henrietta Trevalyan.

Henrietta's old and eccentric grandmother answered the call.

'Yes, yes, who is it?'

'Lulu Saunders—'

'Who?'

'Lulu Saunders, Mrs Trevalyan, of the Young Socialists. I met you when I called on you some time ago. With our secretary, Paul Adams. You kindly gave us a cheque for ten pounds for our funds.'

'Upon my soul, you're that belly dancer. I hope you've given up that kind of thing and got yourself a respectable job.'

'Mrs Trevalyan, I was never—'

'Belly dancing disgraces our sex, and if our leader, Emmeline Pankhurst, was still alive, you'd feel the weight of her umbrella.'

'I assure you, Mrs Trevalyan—'

'You have given it up?'

'I work at the Labour Party headquarters with Mr Adams. We share the responsibility of looking after the affairs of our Young Socialists group. Excuse me, but is Henrietta there?'

'That granddaughter of mine is a hussy, but she's here. Wait a minute.'

'I'll hold on,' said Lulu. She heard Mrs Trevalyan raise her voice.

'Henrietta, come down here.' A pause. 'What, what? Who wants you? It's that belly dancer.'

Lulu sorrowed for the silly old biddy.

Henrietta arrived at the phone.

'Hello?'

'Oh, hello,' said Lulu, and introduced herself.

'Oh, yes, you work with Paul, such a sweet young man,' said Henrietta.

'Look,' said Lulu, 'I'm keen to start a new women's movement for more equality with men. It's something the Labour Party encourages. We've only got partial equality so far. And only in some spheres. What we need is more in all spheres.'

'More?' said Henrietta.

'Yes, we need to be more equal than men. That's the only way to put 'em in their rightful place. We need to have the whip hand. Get them working for us. Instead of us for them. Make them bow the knee to our ambitions. You'd like to have men do as you desire, wouldn't you?'

'Well, frankly,' trilled Henrietta, 'I do have desires, but I like men to be manly, I'd have no interest in men who bowed their knees. They'd make me feel they were limp. Limp men, how frightful, there's nothing they could do for a girl.'

'But you don't agree with men exercising domination, do you?' said Lulu.

'Rather,' said Henrietta. 'With a bit of encouragement, of course, in case their domination had reservations.'

'You disappoint me,' said Lulu. 'I was sure you'd like to join me in my new movement. I'm calling it "Women in Command".'

'Oh, I beg you won't, Miss Saunders,' entreated Henrietta. 'It sounds like a trade union for women who carry whips about, looking for a peculiar kind of limp men.'

'Nothing of the sort,' said Lulu. 'Not what modern women have in mind at all. Let's give them their due. They can be quite useful in many ways. But they've got to make room for us. You know Paul fairly well, don't you?'

'Yes, isn't he manly? And very useful, I should think.'

'Well, he's in favour of my movement. And he shares the Labour Party's sympathy for the lot of women. He feels for our oppressed sex. He'd like us to spring free. Which is the aim of Women in Command.'

'Well, what a sweet man. I'd love to assist him in helping you yourself to spring free. I don't mind being oppressed myself, I'm quite happy as a yielding woman.'

'Happy? You mean you think you are,' said Lulu. 'It's simply the result of centuries of indoctrination. We've got to fight our way out of any suggestion that we're happy.'

'Oh, such a lovely idea,' trilled Henrietta, 'and although I'm content myself with things as they are, I'm sure Paul and I really could help you towards your kind of happiness in your own kind of—' She broke off, then said, 'What's that, Granny dear?'

Lulu heard Mrs Trevalyan in a loud voice again.

'Henrietta, you wretched girl, what's this bill for two dresses and six pairs of satin knickers?'

'Must go, Miss Saunders,' said Henrietta. 'Lovely to have had this little talk. Do remember me to Paul. Isn't he adorable?' She hung up.

That tarty ha'porth, thought Lulu, can be counted among women's worst enemies. And if any man's adorable, I'm Joan of Arc. Still, I'll admit that although Paul's a bit cocky, he's not a bad bloke. He ought to be saved from Henrietta.

Paul, reappearing, caught her silently musing.

'Picture of a thinker,' he said.

'What's the next line?' asked Lulu.

'You look soft and relaxed when you're deep in thought,' said Paul.

'Soft and relaxed?'

'As if you're yielding to dreamy content,' said Paul.

'Yielding?' Lulu had visions of tarty Henrietta happy with her lot. 'Yielding?'

'Suits you,' said Paul. 'It goes with your skirt and jumper. By the way, God upstairs wants us to double our membership over the next six months. He says voters who are caught young are supporters for life.'

'So what do we do?' asked Lulu, struggling with her mixed-up thoughts. 'Start campaigning in nurseries?'

'We'll put our heads together after lunch,' said Paul.

'Oh, right.' Lulu shook herself. 'I'll have a large bunch of ideas and suggestions ready by then.'

Yielding? she thought. Wishful thinking on his part. It's my skirt. I'll have a look at my jeans this evening, and find out if washing them five times has taken the smell out. For the sake of my career, I've got to avoid being one of the yielding.

A little after one o'clock, Boots and Sammy were lunching at Simpson's in the Strand with Miss Campion from the Adams shop in Oxford Street. Miss Campion, in her thirties, was a tall slender brunette, very stylish in appearance.

They were dining on one of the restaurant's specialities, roast saddle of mutton. Sammy was holding forth on the matter pertaining to the import licences owned by Mr Roland Dickinson, Miss Campion's gentleman friend.

'I've got a feeling there's prospects, Hilda, if his shipments are large enough to oblige our requirements. In which case, I can say brother Boots and yours truly will consider ourselves much obliged if you could get Charlie Dickens to help us out.'

'Mr Dickinson,' said Miss Campion, slightly reproachful.

'Manners, Sammy, manners,' said Boots.

'Slip of the tongue, Hilda,' said Sammy. 'Accept my apologies.'

'As for how large Roland's shipments are, I only know he doesn't deal with insignificant customers,' said Miss Campion. She addressed Boots. 'Mr Adams, I did tell Mr Sammy that the firm would have to come up with large orders.'

'What could suit us more?' said Boots.

'When I mentioned to Roland – Mr Dickinson – that young people were coming into the shop asking for American jeans,' said Miss Campion, 'he informed me he was having to increase his imports of them to cope with increasing demand, and that we'd be wise to stock them in all our shops.'

'That coincides with requests for them from some of our young relatives, including my elder daughter,' smiled Boots.

'Oh, I've come to believe we must stock them,' said Miss Campion, 'and I'm sure Roland will be able to help us.'

Roland, thought Boots, is an operator who's

164

holding two import licences and keeping the Ministry's mistake to himself. He probably started, like Sammy, with a market stall. Now he's a close friend to Hilda Campion, a stylish woman. Well, women are delightful creatures, but not many men can tell which way they'll jump a gate when they're in their thirties.

'Any help from your obliging friend, Hilda, will be considerably appreciated,' said Sammy.

'I'm sure he'll think positively about it, Mr Sammy,' said Miss Campion, smiling at him, although most of her attention was being given to Boots. She had seen him only once before today, not long after the end of the war, when he had visited the shop with Sammy. His easy-going air, his good-humoured face and his firm features gave him a singular masculine charm. 'I'm also sure there's going to be a steady demand by the end of the year.'

'For jeans?' said Sammy, glooming a bit. 'Well, Hilda, I've got to say again that it near breaks my heart to go along with girls looking like cowboys. It didn't surprise me that last night I had one shocking dream about our shops giving away a horse and saddle with every pair of jeans. I woke up suffering all over. Still, if it's a question of sacrifice, I'll have to suffer in silence, like the duchess said to her saucy butler.'

'Mr Sammy, that's quite a mouthful,' said Miss Campion.

'Sammy has many gifts,' said Boots.

'Granted,' said Sammy, never held back by modesty. Modesty was for violets, and not at any time in his life had he qualified as a shy flower.

'Do you do after-dinner speeches, Mr Sammy?' asked Miss Campion with another smile.

'Only to my better half,' said Sammy, 'and she mostly forgets to listen.'

The restaurant, alive with clatter and conversation, was full. Keen-eyed businessmen, dapper gents with lady friends, and some uniformed American officers were lunching in this famous establishment with its English menu and its unfading Edwardian decor. An American military presence was still seen in Britain, mainly in the form of air force bases whose squadrons were held in readiness against the threat of what might develop out of the Cold War. American headquarters in London were fully staffed.

'Mr Adams,' said Miss Campion to Boots, 'what kind of order for jeans and fabrics does the firm have in mind?'

'Sammy has a list of requirements he's going to give you,' said Boots.

'Jeans for example? Six gross as a starter,' said Sammy. He had in mind one gross each for the shops in Kennington, Brixton, Peckham and Clapham, and two gross for the Oxford Street branch.

'How does that sound, Hilda?' asked Boots.

'Promising, Mr Adams,' said Miss Campion.

Blow me, thought Sammy, it's always the same. In this kind of company, Boots gets to be Mr Adams, and I get to be Sammy, the errand boy. What's he got that I haven't? Not that I don't know. It's his education and his aristocracy. Education, well, lots of people have got that, but where did he get aristocracy from? Fell on him out of the sky, I suppose.

166

'Sammy, I suggest you hand Hilda the list of everything we want, including the fabrics and materials for turning out the new design,' said Boots, at which point a plump, well-fed waiter arrived to refill wine glasses. Sammy used the little break to give Miss Campion the list. Finishing her main course, she studied requirements and quantities.

'My word, this really does amount to a large order,' she said, 'but Roland does import all these fabrics, I'm sure. He's a well-established rag-trade man, and –' She laughed. 'And, in his own words, a somebody.'

'A somebody?' said Boots drily.

'Oh, he's informed me that he was never cut out to be a nobody, that nearly everybody's a nobody,' said Miss Campion. 'I suppose that's true, that there's only room at the top for a few somebodies.'

'Sammy could tell us if it's crowded up there,' said Boots. 'He's been a somebody for years.'

'Granted,' said Sammy, 'and I'll admit I get elbowed at times. Anyway, what d'you seriously think about these requirements, Hilda?'

'I seriously think I must talk to Roland,' said Miss Campion.

'We'll be happy to leave that to you,' said Boots.

'I'll do my very best for the firm, Mr Adams,' said Miss Campion.

'It'll earn you a bonus, Hilda,' said Sammy.

'What a nice thought,' said the lady. 'I'll let you know what Roland can do for us.'

'And when we might expect delivery if he can oblige us?' said Sammy.

'I'll let you know,' said Miss Campion.

On that promising note, they all chose Simpson's famous syrup pudding as a dessert, with a fresh bottle of white wine, although Miss Campion said she really shouldn't.

Chapter Sixteen

On the way back to Camberwell, Sammy said, 'How d'you feel, Boots?'

'Full up,' said Boots.

'I wasn't asking after your Aunt Nelly,' said Sammy, 'I was asking how you felt about Charlie Dickens.'

'Dickinson?' said Boots. 'He sounds sharp, yes, but we've had our own moments.'

'He's lovey-dovey with Hilda,' said Sammy, 'and Hilda's a bit classy.'

'Which would make her a woman of special appeal to him, if he started as a barrow boy,' said Boots.

'Point is, is he a married cove?' said Sammy.

'And is Hilda his mistress?' said Boots. 'Is she that kind of woman? Whatever, it looks as if there's some kind of close relationship.'

'But will we get the goods for sure?' asked Sammy.

'If there's a definite promise,' said Boots, 'I think we should meet the gentleman who classes himself as a somebody.'

'I can't wait,' said Sammy, 'I like a face-to-face with a supplier. Mind you, I had a face-to-face with crafty

Claude and still got taken in. Me, Sammy Adams. Talk about mortified.'

'Perhaps we've got a guarantor,' said Boots.

'First I've heard of a guarantor,' said Sammy. 'Half a tick, though, could you mean Hilda?'

'Well, if he's hooked,' said Boots, 'let's assume he won't want to let her down.'

'If he's seriously lovey-dovey with her, it won't surprise me,' said Sammy. 'Hilda's got style. It also won't surprise me if he asked for a backhander. There's a lot of untaxable backhanders about these days.'

'It's all synonymous with post-war business gymnastics,' said Boots.

'Don't start talking educated,' said Sammy. 'And listen, don't put Roland's hooter out of joint by getting Hilda to give you the eye too frequent. It might hold up our order.'

'I pass on that one, Sammy,' said Boots.

'You ain't that innocent,' said Sammy. 'Strike me happy, Gertie and Lilian, and Rachel as well, are going to show a leg or two in a knees-up when they know the factory might be in line for turning out the new design. Well, a female leg or two never hurt my peepers. We've had a satisfactory lunch, Boots, would you say?'

'We can't complain,' said Boots, 'except for punishing our constitutions with the syrup pudding.'

'By the way,' said Sammy, eyes paining him a bit as he glimpsed bomb sites still looking stark and ugly in Waterloo Road, 'do we get lunch at Buckingham Palace next month when our dear old ma gets to be a lady and our stepdad a lord?'

'We get the privilege of watching the ceremony,' said Boots.

'No lunch?' said Sammy.

'No lunch, Sammy.'

'Not even a helping of Royal syrup pudding?' said Sammy, grinning.

'I think I can do without that,' said Boots.

Sammy, threading into the traffic of London Road, made his approach to the Elephant and Castle with a marked degree of interest. The junction that had teemed with hustle and bustle, surrounded by buildings, now looked vast with space. Buildings by the score had been destroyed during the prolonged air blitz. As elsewhere, development of cleared sites was proceeding apace. Immense structures of scaffolding scarred the scene, and the pre-war hustle and bustle of people was now the hustle and bustle of swarms of building workers.

'Look at it,' said Sammy. 'It's me firm conviction we could have asked double the price for the sites we sold while the war was still going on like the ruddy clappers.'

'That's a thought for today, Sammy,' said Boots, 'not for yesterday. It's called hindsight.'

'Have I heard of hindsight?' said Sammy.

'Sammy,' said Boots, 'what you did get at the time was probably as much as you could get, and it put the property company in clover.'

'I ain't complaining,' said Sammy, entering the old and familiar thoroughfare of the Walworth Road. 'Listen, I keep hearing that Chinese Lady's still carrying her smelling salts around.'

'If, like you, she's thinking she and Edwin might have to eat lunch off gold plates, let her know she won't,' said Boots. 'That should cure some of her nerves.'

'I'll bet she'll still have her smelling salts in her handbag,' said Sammy.

'What a woman,' smiled Boots.

'Not many like her, Boots old soldier,' said Sammy.

'Hardly any, Sammy old cock,' said Boots.

Honest John Saunders, Labour MP, called on his daughter Lulu at her Kennington flat that evening. The first thing he noticed when he followed her into her living room was that, as always, it resembled the quarters of a bachelor, a notoriously untidy species. Books, newspapers, pamphlets and various odds and ends were everywhere. Only one of the armchairs was empty, that which Lulu usually occupied.

'Don't you ever tidy up?' he asked.

'Of course I do, once a month,' said Lulu.

'I think you missed last month,' said her dad.

'Now look here,' said Lulu, 'I've got more important things to do than turning myself into a skivvy. The day's going to come when skivvying's in the dustbin. The day when it won't be a priority with certain women. Women who've got more to offer the world than a brush and pan.'

'Young lady,' said her dad, 'tidying up the place you live in isn't skivvying, it's putting order into your life. Tidy habits mean a tidy mind, y'know.'

'My mind's tidy enough,' said Lulu. 'It's got my own priorities in order.'

'I'm getting worried about your priorities,' said Mr Saunders. 'I'm not sure they won't take you up the garden path.'

'What garden path?' demanded Lulu.

'It's another name for wishful thinking,' said her dad. 'I did a lot of wishful thinking myself when I was your age, but it wasn't until my brain grew up that I realized I wasn't getting anywhere, and that the world was full of people up against the plain facts of life.'

'It's still full of struggling workers, Dad,' said Lulu. 'And I'm one of them.'

'Well, that's something, girlie, being a worker.'

'Don't call me girlie.'

'You're still young, y'know.'

'That's not going to stop me qualifying as a Labour Party candidate for local elections in a year or so,' said Lulu. 'And you can help me do some pushing when the time comes.'

'I'll give you what help I think you deserve,' said Mr Saunders. 'I won't do any pushing simply because I'm your dad.'

'Good old Honest John,' said Lulu.

'How are you getting on with Paul Adams?' he asked. 'I hear the pair of you are turning into a pretty good combination.'

'Well, he contributes middle-class morality, and I contribute brains and initiative,' said Lulu.

Her dad coughed.

'Middle-class morality?' he said. 'Well, there's a lot of that about in Purley and Hampstead. Now it's in your office, is it?'

'It's holding him back,' said Lulu.

'Paul Adams?'

'For instance,' said Lulu, 'if I had the power, I'd use my brains and initiative to turn Buckingham Palace into a home. For retired dockers and miners.

Paul Adams, well, his idea is not to interfere with the royal family. That's in case moving to Clapham upsets them. I keep wondering if he really is a genuine Socialist.'

'He's done a lot of good work with the Young Socialists,' said Mr Saunders. 'And I'm told he's a practical-minded bloke. I'll be frank and tell you we've got MPs on our side of the House who wouldn't know how to saw up a plank of wood. They're the ones who think we can do wonders for the workers overnight.'

'Paul Adams isn't imaginative enough,' said Lulu. 'He'll get a mental block when I tell him about my new idea.'

'What new idea?' asked Mr Saunders, looking slightly apprehensive.

'A movement to promote more equality for women,' said Lulu. 'I'm calling it Women in Command. It'll strike chords, you bet. I don't want to criticize our Government, but it's got no real agenda for asserting women's rights. Tell you what, Dad. Mention Women in Command to the PM. Yes, and put my name to it. Remind him what my kind of women did in the war.'

'Ran off with American GIs, if I remember right,' said Honest John.

'What?' said Lulu, spectacles glinting with outrage. It made her dad hasten into correction.

'No, not all of them, of course,' he said. 'Most did their bit, along with other women, as well as any of the men. I've got total admiration for the courage and valour of all of 'em. Er, Women in Command, you said? I'm not sure the new PM won't think you're suggesting Mrs Attlee should take his place.'

'Oh, come on, Dad,' said Lulu. 'There's got to be a woman Prime Minister one day. It's what more equality is all about. It's why I'm founding the movement.'

'Now I get you,' said Honest John, 'now I know what your number one priority is.' He chuckled. 'Well, good luck to you, me girl, and if I'm in a wheelchair by the time you're sworn in as Prime Minister, I'll still get up and cheer. But pick up a few happy days on the way.'

'Happy days?' said Lulu.

'Yes, treat yourself to a decent bloke who'll give you something to remember every weekend,' said her dad.

'There you go again,' said Lulu, spectacles slipping indignantly to the end of her nose. 'My own dad. Encouraging me to let some male moron accost me in my bed.'

'Nothing like that, Lulu,' said Honest John. 'I'd be the first to knock his head off. But existing isn't the same as living. Existing's a matter of all work and no play. Living's good for a woman, especially if there's a marriage certificate on the mantelpiece.'

'Marriage certificate?' said Lulu. 'That's not even at the bottom of the pile. It's non-existent as a possibility. I'm not taking up slavery. I've got my political career in front of me. Not a kitchen sink and an apron.'

'Still, what about Paul Adams?' suggested Mr Saunders. 'He seems a very decent bloke.'

'Listen, Dad. Paul Adams is more non-existent in my life design than even a marriage certificate or an Ancient Roman centurion.'

'You wouldn't find an ancient centurion very

exciting,' said Honest John, 'not with all his rusty armour to cope with.'

'There's a hammer somewhere under those newspapers,' said Lulu. 'I'm going to hit you with it in a minute. I don't like having to bash my own dad. But you're asking for it.'

'Lulu, I'm only suggesting that if you don't get your priorities rearranged,' said Honest John, 'you'll end up like a hermit.'

'I'll end up as a Labour MP,' said Lulu. 'Fighting for the cause of women.'

'Well, it'll be your own choice,' said her dad. 'Um, speaking of marriage—'

'Don't bother,' said Lulu. 'Not on my account.'

Her dad, coughing a bit, went on, 'I was going to say that now your mother's been gone for quite some time, I'm thinking of it for myself.'

Lulu blinked.

'You're thinking of getting married again?' she said. 'Well, I'm not against it for you. You're still in your prime, Dad.'

'I pride myself I've still got health and strength,' said Honest John, who did indeed look in his prime.

'Who's the lady?' asked Lulu.

'Ah, yes,' said her dad, shifting his feet about. 'Um, Sylvia Jennings.'

'What?'

'Sylvia—'

'I heard. She's your Parliamentary Secretary.'

'A good woman,' said Honest John.

'She's only a few years older than I am,' said Lulu, spectacles steaming a bit. 'You're twice her age. Dad, it's indecent.'

'It'll be legal once we're married,' said Honest

John. 'She's willing, and so am I. Nice to know you're pleased for me, Lulu.'

Lulu laughed. Her dad perked up.

'Oh, all right,' she said, 'go ahead. Some people like getting married. Sorry I don't have any bubbly. But if I can find the kettle, we could have a cup of tea as a celebration.'

'Kind of you, Lulu,' said Honest John, 'but I've got to get back to the House. There's a division tonight.'

'All right, pop off,' said Lulu. 'Give my best wishes to Sylvia. What a life. I'm going to have a stepmother nearly young enough to be my sister.'

'She'll get to be your best friend,' said Honest John.

'I'm my best friend,' said Lulu.

Chapter Seventeen

The following day.

'Ned, you've been overdoing it,' said Dr Mason, letting his stethoscope dangle.

'No, I haven't,' said Ned, who had left his office early to catch his GP's afternoon surgery before it closed. 'I live a quiet life, I don't go with naughty ladies, or jump up and down, or climb lampposts.'

'What about the demands of your business?' said Dr Mason.

'My job's no more of a strain than it's always been,' said Ned, buttoning his shirt.

'You mean it's stressful?'

'Not to me after all these years,' said Ned.

'But after all these years, stress is something to bear in mind,' said Dr Mason. 'You're still gardening?' The GP and Ned were on friendly terms, and both enjoyed garden work.

'I'll admit the first attack came when I was digging my vegetable plot over on Saturday,' said Ned. 'I thought the tightness was indigestion. I think you're going to tell me it wasn't.'

'You've managed to develop a slight hardening of the arteries,' said Dr Mason, 'and the pain was

178

caused by your blood struggling to reach your heart. Both attacks were a warning. I'm going to prescribe an aspirin a day to help keep your blood thin. Are you allergic?'

'To the smell of cats?'

'To aspirin?'

'I can't remember any unpleasant effects,' said Ned.

'Well, we'll go for a daily aspirin first thing every morning,' said Dr Mason, giving Ned an encouraging smile that suggested there was no great worry. He knew Ned was fifty-five, but with his grey, thinning hair and lines around his eyes, he looked older. Dr Mason suspected that business stress could have been largely responsible for his attack, especially after the strain of keeping things going all through the war. 'Your blood pressure's good, very good, but I'd advise no strenuous gardening for the time being.'

'Curse that,' said Ned, 'gardening's my main recreation, and I don't think Eliza's forte is spadework.'

'You can potter, prune and do other light jobs,' said Dr Mason, 'but no heavy work, and try to avoid business stress. I suggest you let your wife know your condition. It's always advisable, Ned.'

'If I know Eliza at all, she'll wrap me in cotton wool,' said Ned.

'A sign of a caring wife,' said Dr Mason, writing out the prescription.

'Cotton wool's not my favourite overcoat,' said Ned, putting his jacket on. 'By the way, how d'you like being part of the National Health Service?'

'Well, my patients like free treatment,' said Dr

Mason, 'it brings them far more often to the surgery.'

'Free treatment brings on more illness?' said Ned.

'If you could call a common cold an illness,' smiled Dr Mason. 'By the way, I'll arrange an appointment for you at King's College Hospital. I think you should be tested there.'

'If you say so,' said Ned. 'Anyway, increased demands on your time mean you've got stress yourself, have you?'

'I'll survive. Here's your prescription, Ned. Make sure you take one tablet daily, and I'm glad you called to see me. I'll let you know the date for your hospital appointment.'

'What would we do without our GPs?' said Ned.

'Consult a witch doctor, I imagine,' said Dr Mason. 'Good luck now. And do let your wife know.'

'Oh, Lor',' said Lizzy in distress, 'how rotten for you, Ned love. I've heard about hardening of the arteries, but I never thought you'd get that complaint.'

'There's no real problem as long as I take the daily aspirin,' said Ned.

'Oh, we'll manage,' said Lizzy over-brightly, 'I'll make sure about the aspirins, and perhaps it would help a bit if you went to bed earlier. And on really cold mornings, you've got to wear your warmest overcoat. I'm sure going out in the cold could affect you. And never mind about the gardening, we'll pay someone to do it for us. Ned, sit down now and I'll make you a nice hot cup of tea before I start supper.'

'I suppose a nice hot cup of tea is the equal of cotton wool,' murmured Ned.

'What's that, what did you say?' asked Lizzy.

'That I fancy the offer of a nice hot cup of tea,' said Ned.

Lizzy phoned Bobby that evening. Helene answered the call. The mother now of two children, Estelle and Robert, she was still as resilient as she'd been during the war, and her recovery from the flu was indicative of that. She and Bobby lived in Thurlow Park Road, Herne Hill, from where Bobby commuted daily to his job at the Foreign Office.

Helene, having a very soft spot for her mother-in-law, was happy to take the call.

'Hello, Mama, are you well?'

'I can't complain, dear, and I'm pleased you're so much better yourself,' said Lizzy. 'It's Bobby's dad that's not too good.'

'Oh, I am sorry,' said Helene. 'He hasn't caught my flu, has he?'

'No, it's not the flu, love, it's his heart, his doctor says he's got slight hardening of the arteries.'

'Oh, I am really sorry,' said Helene, 'Papa Somers is such a nice man. Is it serious?'

'Not if he acts sensible, and takes an aspirin a day, and goes to the doctor regular for a check-up,' said Lizzy.

'Mama, you would like to talk to Bobby?'

'Yes, is he there?'

'I'll call him,' said Helene.

Bobby came to the phone.

'Hello, Mum, what's this about Dad?'

Lizzy repeated what she had said to Helene, adding that Ned had to avoid stress, and would be going to the hospital for a proper test of his condition.

'I didn't tell him I was worried,' she said, 'but I am, of course.'

'So am I,' said Bobby. 'You know, Mum, going up and down to his wine merchant's premises in town all through the war must have taken its toll, and he had to cope with limited stocks. He had the sense to see the war coming, and to build up his reserves, but he still had the extra worry of not knowing if a bomb would ruin the whole place and every bit of stock. He was a valiant old lad to keep things going the way he did.'

'Now he's been told by Dr Mason not to do any heavy gardening, like digging,' said Lizzy, 'and you know how much he likes the garden and growing our own vegetables.'

'Tell him not to worry,' said Bobby, 'I'll come and do a stint every Saturday morning.'

'I was thinking of finding some gardening man,' said Lizzy.

'Don't worry about finding anybody,' said Bobby. 'Leave the work to me, Mum, it'll be my pleasure, and a small return for all you and Dad have done for me and Helene.'

'Well, I'm sure your dad will like that,' said Lizzy, 'and it'll be nice for both of us to see you on Saturdays, if you're sure Helene won't mind.'

'She'll tell me it's the least I can do,' said Bobby. 'What's Dad doing at the moment?'

'Listening to the radio and reading his news-paper,' said Lizzy. 'Oh, and sipping a little whisky.'

'A sign of helpful therapy, I call that, and it's not something I can do myself too easily, three things at once,' said Bobby.

'Well, he's listening one moment, and reading the next,' said Lizzy.

'Sounds fairly relaxing,' said Bobby. 'Give him my love, tell him to take care and to enjoy watching me bend my back on Saturdays while he takes a rest cure. Phone at any time, Mum, if you're ever worried, and I'll be right over. D'you want me to pop in this evening?'

'No, it's all right, Bobby, I just wanted to let you know about his arteries,' said Lizzy.

'Leave it to me to tell Annabelle, Emma and Edward,' said Bobby.

'Oh, thanks, love, but don't make them feel their dad's actually bedridden,' said Lizzy. 'He won't want them to come rushing round.'

'Understood,' said Bobby. 'I know you'll be looking after Dad, so look after yourself as well, and don't forget to phone whenever you want to. So long now.'

'Bye, Bobby, it's been a nice relief talking to you,' said Lizzy.

Bobby spoke to Helene, and, with their children in bed, they discussed the practical help they could give.

'We'll both do the gardening,' said Helene.

'Where will that leave your Saturday morning shopping?' asked Bobby.

'I will do that on Fridays,' said Helene. 'We must help your father on Saturday mornings.'

'It'll mean taking the children with us,' said Bobby. Little Estelle was three, small Robert sixteen months.

'Of course,' said Helene, 'and Mama will keep an eye on them. I can use a spade and fork.'

'So you can,' said Bobby, 'you're a farmer's daughter, with a nice set of fine female muscles.'

'Muscles? Muscles?' said Helene. 'You are saying I have big biceps and lumpy calves like a Russian weight-lifter?'

'Not exactly—'

'My figure is perfect,' said Helene. 'I have given you two children, but my figure is still perfect.'

'Believe me,' said Bobby, 'I never cease to wonder at how well nature put you together. You're not lumpy, no, nor skinny, you're just the job.'

'Just the job?'

'And sexy as well.'

'Bobby, I am still sexy to you?'

'Not half,' said Bobby. 'Show us your stocking-tops.'

'My— oh, you idiot, your jokes are still terrible,' said Helene, but she laughed. 'Bobby, we should not be laughing when your father isn't very well.'

'We'll keep an eye on him, my little French chicken,' said Bobby, not wanting to be alarmist, 'and he wouldn't want us to gloom about him.'

'Bobby, your parents have been like my own to me,' said Helene.

'Well, we'll be popping over to France to see yours at Easter,' said Bobby.

'Ah, even if you are an idiot, I am glad to be married to you, *chéri*,' said Helene.

'Well, I'm glad you're glad,' said Bobby. 'Look, although Ma said it wasn't necessary, I think I will go round and see Dad. I won't be long.'

'Yes, I think you should go and see him,' said Helene.

So off Bobby went, and it was his dad himself who opened the door to him.

'Hello, what's this?' said Ned. 'Run out of milk? I

daresay your mother can find some spare for you.'

'Good guess, Dad, but incorrect,' said Bobby, stepping in. 'I've just called to see how you are.'

'Still on my feet and I don't need a nurse,' said Ned.

Lizzy came out into the hall of the house in which she and Ned had lived for almost thirty-four years, and where they had acquired the art of making their marriage entirely worthwhile. Ups and downs had no effect on their abiding affection for each other, and they were heading now towards their Darby and Joan years of uncomplaining companionship.

'Bobby?' she said.

'Oh, just a quick call to make sure Dad's not swinging from the ceiling like Tarzan,' said Bobby, delivering a kiss on his mum's cheek.

'Listen, my lad,' said Ned, 'don't get ideas about me and Tarzan. He can monkey about all he likes. I was never a trapeze artist myself, and I'm not starting now.'

'Very sensible,' said Bobby. 'Still, let's have a look at you.' He surveyed his dad, and noted that although there were no outward signs of a man about to go downhill, he was looking his age. But so he had been for several years. It hadn't limited his activities. All the same, age and stress could be a pointer. Bobby, extremely attached to his father, as good-natured as Uncle Boots, felt a definite surge of worry. 'Has he had his aspirin for today, Mum?'

'Yes, I made sure he took one,' said Lizzy.

'Eliza,' said Ned, 'your son's come round to fuss me.'

'Well, it's only natural,' said Lizzy, 'he's your son as well.'

'I've called just to tell you to take it easy, Dad,' said Bobby, 'and to confirm I'll be here on Saturday mornings to do a spot of gardening – which reminds me, Helene insists she'll give a hand too. That means we'll bring the tots with us.'

'Oh, that'll be really nice,' said Lizzy. 'I'll look after them, Bobby, and all of you might as well stay for a light lunch.'

'I'm going to put a notice on the front door,' said Ned, 'a notice that fusspots won't be admitted. Anyway, now you're here, old son, have a quick drink with me.'

Bobby accepted a beer, and Ned had a nip of whisky. Lizzy kind of hovered. Ned growled a bit.

On his return home, Bobby informed Helene that he realized his dad really was looking his age.

'We must persuade him to retire,' said Helene. 'That will help, retirement and rest.'

'He's only fifty-five,' said Bobby.

'Never mind, no,' said Helene, 'you must talk to him from time to time until he's willing to accept early retirement. Your father is a good man, Bobby, and it's our duty, yes, to care for him.'

'You're right,' said Bobby.

A little later, feeling he should, he phoned Annabelle, Emma and brother Edward in turn. They all expressed concern and an intention of looking in on their dad, but Bobby said what Lizzy had said to him, not to go rushing round, but to drop in casually. In passing, as it were.

Annabelle, eldest of her parents' offspring, said to drop in casually wasn't her idea of a caring daughter. Emma said she and Jonathan would do it so casually that her dad would hardly know they'd arrived.

Edward said he had a new crime novel, just the kind his dad liked, and he'd take it round to him, say on his way home from work one evening.

Bobby told each of them that if there was a notice on the front door forbidding fusspots, to take the hint.

Earlier, at their chicken farm in Surrey, Boots's adopted daughter Rosie and her husband Matthew Chapman were relaxing with their partners, Emma and Jonathan Hardy.

Rosie, at thirty-four, could see forty waiting for her. Polly had dreaded the advent of that milestone, but Rosie was a more serene woman than Boots's second wife. If she sometimes wondered where all the years had gone, those ahead of her had their own promise of enjoyment. She was still striking enough to make many a man wish for the moon and to find her its sole inhabitant if it landed on his doorstep. Husband Matthew thought her one of nature's first-class creations. Her children, Giles and Emily, when asking their dad where their mum had come from, were told she'd been a gift from a very generous Father Christmas. Subsequently, they were heard arguing about that.

'But I don't see he could have dropped her down a chimney,' said Giles, nearly eight.

'Well, of course not, soppy,' said six-year-old Emily, named after Rosie's late adoptive mother. 'He would've knocked on the front door.'

'What, like a postman with a parcel?' said Giles.

'Well, he'd have had to knock,' said Emily, 'he couldn't have pushed her through the letter box.'

'No, I suppose not,' said Giles. 'Still, I just don't

think I ever heard of Father Christmas carrying presents like our mum in his sack.'

'Oh, he can put anything in his sack,' said Emily. She thought. 'Like even a bicycle.' She thought some more. 'Or even a pony.'

'Crikey, he'd need a sack as big as a balloon,' said Giles.

'Yes, he sort of floats on it,' said Emily imaginatively.

Giles, however, wasn't convinced that his mum arrived as a Christmas present for his dad from inside some kind of balloon. He just couldn't picture it.

This evening, he and his sister were asleep in their beds, and Emma and Jonathan's four-year-old daughter Jessie was also tucked up. The parents were resting their weary limbs after a full day's work. A full day's work meant, among other chores, feeding the chickens, collecting and packing eggs, making deliveries, and attending to the welfare of lambs newly born to the small flock of sheep.

'Frankly,' said Rosie, 'I'm whacked.'

'I need a new pair of legs,' said Emma.

'Don't like the sound of that,' said Sussex-born Jonathan.

'I don't like the feel of it,' said Emma.

'One thing's for sure, the foxes will be wide awake and sniffing around,' said Matthew, a Dorset man. He and Jonathan had spent months trying to get rid of foxes that pestered the chickens and lay in wait for ailing lambs. They had managed to shoot one here, and another there, but there were always others. A month ago they had erected a defensive wire fence on all sides of the hedge, something they hadn't wanted to do, but it had kept the foxes at bay. Cursedly, however, there were now signs that the predators were burrowing.

Rosie said it wasn't the foxes alone that were a problem. There was the fact that the work was pretty full-time for all of them. It prevented either couple from ever enjoying a decent holiday.

'But we're prospering,' she said, 'and prosperity, according to Uncle Sammy, is highly desirable.'

'Uncle Sammy', said Emma, a picturesque and effervescent brunette, 'speaks for all of us.'

'And don't we all know it?' said Jonathan. 'I'm a believer in Uncle Sammy's regard for profits.'

'What Rosie and I have been thinking of is that we can now afford to take on a couple of extra hands,' said Matthew. 'That'll mean we can find time for holidays. There's the kids, and kids ought to be able to enjoy a beach and buckets and spades once a year.'

'I second that,' said Emma.

'And I don't be far behind a seconder,' said Jonathan.

'We'll advertise for helpers,' said Rosie.

'For the kind that cherish the land,' said Jonathan. 'I be a cherisher myself of what the land can provide.'

'Ah, you be fond of farms and cows and chickens and suchlike, Jonathan?' said Emma, taking him off.

'Weren't I born in a cow barn?' said Jonathan.

'Heavens, were you?' asked Rosie.

'So I were told,' said Jonathan. 'It seems that Ma had an emergency, and Pa had to take her to the hospital on the vicar's horse. Well, the emergency being what it was, he had to stop at a barn after a tidy while, and just in time. My, I didn't enjoy the ride, Ma were joggling side-saddle all the way.'

Emma yelled with laughter. Rosie joined in. Matthew roared.

'Jonathan, you're incurable,' gasped Emma.

'Born that way on account of being joggled,' said Jonathan.

'An up-and-down beginning,' said Matthew, 'but you've made the grade, Jonathan, and with honours. For that and the prospect of being able to consider holidays, let's break open a bottle of Somerset scrumpy.'

'Scrumpy cider makes me tiddly,' said Emma.

'Well, Emma, I never did see any woman look more lively than you when you're a tidy bit tiddly,' said Jonathan. 'Regular French dancing you do and all.'

'What's on offer?' said Matthew. 'Something like the cancan?'

'You'll be lucky,' said Emma.

'I'm reminded there's a Dorset rhyme about scrumpy,' said Matthew. 'It goes like this.

"Down by Dorset land they say
Scrumpy's drunk each summer day,
And Dorset mums do sit and pray
Their girls aren't rolling in the hay."

'As usual,' said Rosie, 'that's the Dorset equivalent of cockney codswallop.'

'I like it,' said Emma, 'I grew up close to Uncle Sammy's cockney codswallop, all of which has earned him his place as a self-made marvel.'

'Like your grandpa, Emma, your Uncle Sammy

might also earn his place on an honours list one day,' said Matthew.

'My oh my,' said Emma, 'can someone earn that for cockney codswallop? I'd be the first to congratulate Uncle Sammy.'

The doorbell of the farmhouse rang.

'Who can that be?' asked Rosie.

'Some old dog fox with enough good manners to ask for permission to make feathers fly,' said Matthew, getting up. He went to answer the ring. When he returned, he had a neighbour with him, a retired old soldier, Major Gorringe.

'Hello there,' said the major, upright of figure, florid of countenance and brisk of delivery. 'Apologies for disturbing your evening, but thought I'd just drop in. Got something useful for you.'

'Sit down, Major,' said Rosie.

'Kind of you, but no, won't stop,' said the major. 'Mildred's got a bellyache.' Mildred was his wife. 'Had tea with the vicar's wife this afternoon. The cucumber sandwiches did it. Can't take cucumber. But look here now, I've got a dog you can have. It'll sort out the foxes for you. An old regimental brother officer landed me with it. Gone off to farm in South Africa. Can't keep the dog myself. Mildred's allergic to hounds.'

'What breed?' asked Matthew.

'Mildred? Oh, she's a Wokingham Pringle. Good family on the whole.' Major Gorringe went on unstoppably. 'Her sister married Knightley of the Foreign Office. Bit of a squirt, I always thought. All wind and squeaks. Where was I? Ah, yes, Matt, about the dog, hope you'll accept it.'

'What kind is it?' asked Matthew. 'The last one we

had was fearsome enough, but barked all night every night.'

'And spent most of the daytime chasing Mrs Purcell's Pekinese filly,' said Emma.

'Filly, eh?' Major Gorringe issued a bark of laughter. 'Bit of a yappy young bitch, I'd say. Well, this one's a sheepdog, and a good worker, I'm told. Got a friendly feeling for sheep and hates foxes. So there you are, just the ticket for you people, I thought. Brought it with me, tied its lead to your front beech tree. Name of Cecil. Damn silly name for a dog, but it won't answer to Fido or Buster. It's all yours, with my compliments.'

'That's very neighbourly of you,' said Rosie.

'Pleasure,' said the major. 'Glad to get it off my hands. Friendly hound, tried to sit on Mildred's lap, which didn't do her bellyache much good. Well, must get back to feed her another dose of bismuth. Better if she'd had one of your eggs, lightly boiled, instead of cucumber sandwiches. Good night now, see myself out.'

Off he went, at a brisk march.

'Blowed if I don't have a ringing in my ears,' said Jonathan.

'Still, what a lovely old soldier,' said Emma.

'Who's going to fetch Cecil?' asked Rosie.

'I will,' said Matthew, looking highly amused. Out he went and brought the dog in.

Cecil proved friendly indeed, considering he'd never been introduced to any of them before. His tail beat the air of the living room, and his nose investigated everything interesting, including Rosie's feet.

'I'm flattered,' she said, 'but what can we expect

of a dog trying to make a meal of my big toe?'

'Down, Cecil,' commanded Matthew, and Cecil sat on his haunches. 'Up, Cecil.' Up the dog came.

'Promising,' said Jonathan. 'Let's put him in the field for the night, Matt, and see how he performs.'

'You mean someone's going to watch him all night?' said Emma.

'I suggest a happy alternative,' said Rosie, 'I suggest we all try for a night of uninterrupted sleep.'

'Can we rely on you, Cecil?' asked Matthew.

Cecil's tail wagged and thumped.

'Let's take him out,' said Jonathan.

He and Matthew took Cecil into the field. In the grey dusk, the dog at once went to say hello to the sheep and the baby lambs. It frisked around the bunched flock, stopped, crouched and waited for instructions.

'Down, Cecil,' called Matthew. Cecil lay relaxed but watchful.

'Looks as if we've got an intelligent dog,' said Jonathan.

'We'll give him a go,' said Matthew.

It was on their return to the house that the phone rang, and Emma received the news about her father from her brother Bobby. When she came back into the living room, she was sober of expression. Jonathan, Rosie and Matthew listened sympathetically as she told them that her dad had a heart problem.

'That's worrying, Emma,' said Jonathan.

'Oh, Bobby said he doesn't think it's serious at the moment,' sighed Emma, 'but that Dad's got to take care. Also, he said, the family shouldn't start rushing round, as that might make Dad feel he's worse than he is. Bobby suggested calling on a casual basis. Jonathan, could you and I drop in sometime this week?'

'We must,' said Jonathan. 'I'm sure we could manage that, if Rosie and Matt could spare us the time.'

'Of course,' said Matthew.

'Thanks,' said Emma.

'Uncle Ned is Boots's oldest friend,' said Rosie quietly, 'and they both served in the Great War.'

'Which makes them old comrades,' said Matthew. 'And of a special kind.'

'I'll keep in touch with Aunt Lizzy,' said Rosie. 'Emma, did Bobby say if Boots knew?' She had taken to calling her adoptive father by his nickname years ago, simply because she felt so close to him.

'No, he didn't mention Uncle Boots,' said Emma.

In fact, Bobby telephoned Boots last thing that evening, and it sobered Boots as much as it had sobered Ned's sons and daughters. He said, however, that everyone should wait for the diagnosis of the hospital's heart specialist before giving way to real concern.

The following morning, Matthew was woken up by a subconscious stirring of instinct. He slipped from the bed, went to the window, drew the curtains back and picked up his binoculars from the window sill. He focussed them, and in the misty light of dawn he spotted Cecil. The sheepdog was far up the field, at the wire-covered gate. On the other side were two foxes. All three animals were on their haunches, Cecil beginning to emit friendly barks, the foxes not in the least unreceptive.

'By God,' muttered Matthew, 'what have we got here?'

'Matt?' Rosie was awake. 'Is that Cecil barking?'

'It is,' said Matthew. 'Cecil is a fraud, Rosie. He's starting a friendship with the foxes, up at the gate.'

Rosie laughed.

There were dogs and dogs.

Life was very entertaining.

Chapter Eighteen

'Now look here, wondergirl,' said Paul the next morning, 'the bosses upstairs don't think we're putting together the right kind of ideas for a strong enough campaign on behalf of the Party.'

'The bosses upstairs need to get off their bums,' said Lulu. Her laundered jeans were back in place, which Paul thought regrettable. Modern though he was in his outlook and his fixed belief in the ideals of the Labour Party, he was like his dad and his Uncle Sammy in favouring fashions that gave the opposite sex a look of inviting femininity. Jeans did nothing for Lulu, except to make her look a bit short of sex appeal, and a bit bumpy of bottom. However, jeans generally did not make him feel as his Uncle Sammy did, that life for people in the rag trade was hardly worth living. He simply preferred Lulu in a skirt.

'It's the bosses' heads that count, Lulu, not their bums,' he said.

'Sitting on them turns their heads into rice puddings,' said Lulu, using a blue pencil to cross out some of her personal ideas, those sniffed at by the people upstairs. She did so with an air of ferocious martyrdom. 'They only come to at election times.'

'The Party's in trouble,' said Paul. Clement Attlee's government was struggling in debates, due to its narrow majority. 'We've got to get out more, to stir up the people. We've got to rubbish the Conservatives, and emphasize Labour's value to the working classes. Labour's given them the National Health Service and welfare benefits for the old and the poor. We don't want them to forget that. It's the responsibility of all Young Socialists to make sure there's a hundred per cent turnout in the event that the Prime Minister might have to consider a snap General Election by this time next year. He'll be asking the electorate for a larger majority.'

'You really think so?' said Lulu.

'So do some of the activists upstairs,' said Paul.

'Then we've got to go for a rousing campaign,' said Lulu. 'How about a new idea of mine?' Her spectacles gleamed with the light of inspiration. 'A Sunday march by the Young Socialists through London. Tons of banners and Red Flags.'

'Lulu, the Red Flag makes nervous people feel we're aiming to import Stalin and his commissars,' said Paul. 'It sends some of them into hiding under their beds.'

'Best place for them if they're as nervous as that,' said Lulu. 'Someone should tell 'em that Stalin at least knew what to do with his capitalists.'

'That won't impress those who know what he also did to millions of dissidents and German prisoners of war,' said Paul.

'He'd had a lot to put up with from Hitler's butchers,' said Lulu. 'Listen. This march. It stops at regular intervals and uses loudspeakers to address the crowds. To let them know what could happen if

Winston Churchill and the Tories were ever returned to power.'

'Oh?' said Paul, trying to work out what to do about an unemployed member who wanted someone important to visit him and let him know why the Labour Party had done nothing for him. The bloke had sent the letter in an unstamped envelope, and it had cost the funds double postage out of the petty cash. Still, it could have meant the bloke was on his beam ends. 'And what would happen if the Tories did get back?'

'Persecution, discrimination, starvation wages and sending children down mines,' said Lulu curtly.

'Lulu, stop living in the 1850s,' said Paul.

'Under the Tories we'd still be in the 1850s,' said Lulu. 'Look, I'm making a firm suggestion that we organize this march. Yes, and with our Red Flags raised high. That alone will command attention.'

'And a few bricks,' said Paul. 'And we'll need permission from the police. To get down to serious stuff, there's a letter here from an unemployed member who wants to know if my assistant will call and explain why our Labour government hasn't done anything for him. He lives in Manor Place. You can make your call after lunch on Thursday afternoon. We'll send him a letter by today's post to let him know you're coming.'

'Don't bother on my account,' said Lulu. 'I'm not going.'

'Dear oh dear,' said Paul, 'what a problem you are, Lulu. I'm sure you're a nice girl under your suit of armour. I wonder, would you like me to recommend you for a job upstairs among the grass-roots activists?'

'What?' said Lulu, lifting her chin and throwing her hair back.

'Upstairs is where the professionals do their supportive work for their MP, your dad,' said Paul, leaving his desk to advance on hers. 'I could find out if Henrietta Trevalyan would like to take your place down here.'

Lulu smouldered and growled.

'That sugarplum fairy?' she said. 'Not bloody likely. She'd turn you into a cream bun. D'you want that?'

'I think I'd fight it,' said Paul.

'You'd lose,' said Lulu. 'You're already halfway there, you poor bloke.' She fidgeted, took her glasses off, and rubbed each lens clean. She glanced up at Paul, her unguarded eyes seeming soft and misty with myopia. Years and years ago, Boots had looked into the myopic eyes of Elsie Chivers and thought them fascinating. Now his nephew Paul looked into Lulu's eyes and thought them too appealing to live permanently behind her spectacles. She put them back on. 'You need protection,' she said. 'I feel it's up to me to give it. I can't do that if I work upstairs. All right, I'll go and see this unemployed bloke.'

'Good girl,' said Paul.

'Forget girl,' said Lulu irritably. 'I'm a woman.'

'I'm looking forward to when you will be,' said Paul.

Lulu emitted another of her semi-falsetto growls.

But she smiled when the constituency's agency sent word down later in the day that he liked the idea of a march and a demonstration by a horde of Young Socialists. Splendid. Well done, well done. Just the job. Capital.

She did, however, dissociate her suggestion from the word 'capital'. It conjured up what profiteers had in their bank accounts at the expense of the workers, and it might have disgusted her to know just how much the firm run by Paul's Uncle Sammy had in its own account.

'Hello, Lizzy,' said Boots. He was on the phone to his sister from his office.

'Oh, it's you, Boots,' said Lizzy.

'I heard about Ned from Bobby last night,' said Boots.

'Oh, Lor',' said Lizzy, 'I suppose everyone in the family's going to know he's got a heart problem, and he doesn't want anyone to fuss about it. He says he's fit enough for it to go away in time.'

'Well, it can't be too serious,' said Boots, 'or Dr Mason would have had him admitted to hospital for tests immediately.'

'I'm glad you said that, Boots. Yes, of course, that's got to be the case, I'm sure. I suppose it's why Dr Mason just prescribed an aspirin a day for the time being. What actually does an aspirin do, d'you know? Dr Mason said it thins the blood.'

'So it does, Lizzy old girl,' said Boots, 'and that allows the blood to reach the heart more easily. It's a common condition.'

'Well, I hope it stays common with Ned, and doesn't turn nasty,' said Lizzy.

'It shouldn't, providing he takes care,' said Boots. 'Did he go to work this morning?'

'Yes,' said Lizzy. 'He sort of insisted that doing what he does every day was better for him than sitting around. But he promised not to rush about and to catch an earlier train home so as to avoid the crush. I didn't argue.'

'Good psychology, Lizzie. Keep arguments at a distance.'

'Lord,' said Lizzy, 'none of us ever heard the word psychology when we were young, and I'm sure Chinese Lady's never said it all her life. Now you can hear it every day. Well, I think it's just a fancy word for common sense.'

'Something you've always had your share of, old girl,' said Boots.

'You and your old girl,' said Lizzy. 'Watch out you don't give me cause to call you old codger.'

'I think I'm already that to the twins,' said Boots. 'Lizzy, give my regards to Ned. I'll look in on him sometime.'

'Yes, sometime,' said Lizzy. 'I'm telling everyone not to rush round. Ned's not keen on being fussed.'

'Ned's special, Lizzy,' said Boots. 'The first to enter the family on the day he married you.'

'When you were his best man,' said Lizzy.

'On that day, Lizzy,' said Boots, 'Ned was the best man.'

In a splendid residence situated in a suburb of Chicago's city limits, Jeremy Passmore was at breakfast with his widowed mother. Mrs Passmore, elegant of style and bearing, was in her graceful fifties, and inclined, in unAmerican fashion, to carry herself as if superior to even the foremost of Chicago's more distinguished citizens.

Jeremy, twenty-nine, belied his dark looks that were emphasized by his jet-black hair and tanned, strong-boned features. He was a man of a singularly quiet and temperate nature. In England last year he had met a young lady who, in her fair English looks and delightful modesty, had taken immediate hold of his sensibilities. In the space of a few hours in her company, he came to feel a deep empathy with her, not too difficult for a man who, having lived in England since the end of the war, had acquired an understanding of the reservations inherent in the natives. Only the illness of his father, a giant in the booming packaging industry, had made him return to Chicago. His mother had entreated his support.

Over breakfast he was reading one of the letters that had come with the morning mail. He was not only reading it, he was so absorbed in its contents that Mrs Passmore felt he was totally unaware of her presence. She fidgeted. She spoke.

'Jeremy, that letter, who's it from?'

Jeremy looked up.

'Bess Adams,' he said. He had told her about meeting Bess last summer. His account interested her, but not in a pleasurable way. Nor had his long stay in England pleased her. She had borne it sufferingly, and was only able to put up with it because she and her husband were constantly involved with social events, the kind the best people simply had to attend. Once she was widowed, all that stopped. Widows were never at the top of invitation lists, however exalted their status. 'The young English lady,' said Jeremy, returning to the letter.

'Do you mean to go through breakfast in silence?'

'Do I ever?'

'No. I simply hope this is not a beginning. What is in the letter?'

'Some amusing university anecdotes and an answer to my request.'

'What request?'

'Come along, Mother, you know that in my last letter to Bess, I asked her if she'd like me to join her during her summer vacation. I made a point of telling you so.'

'It slipped my mind, probably because I felt you weren't serious. If you are, is there a special reason?'

'What's your idea of a special reason?'

'I'm wondering, naturally, exactly how you regard a young woman you have seen and spoken to only once.'

Jeremy smiled. He was quite prepared to be tolerant of his mother's possessive attitude now that she had lost his father. However, if she intended to have the last word on the kind of woman he should marry, then that intention was misguided.

'Mother, I've talked to you about Bess Adams several times, and I've let you know I think her a young lady of great charm.'

'First impressions, Jeremy, aren't always the right impressions. Where did you say she comes from?'

'South London.'

Mrs Passmore applied butter and jam to an English muffin and bit delicately into its sweetness.

'South London, yes, I see. What is her voice like?'

'Her voice?'

'You must know Americans find a London accent unattractive. It turns every sentence into an incoherent gabble.'

'That, Mother, strikes me as an extraordinary statement. Have you made up your mind that if you ever meet her, you aren't going to like her?'

'I hope I'm not as prejudiced as that. I hope, indeed, that I'm not prejudiced at all. In the event of meeting her, I shall take her as I find her, which is the civilized thing to do. Is such an event likely?'

'Right now,' said Jeremy, 'that's a question I can't answer, but I can assure you you'd have no cause to fret about her voice or her accent. You'll find them delightful. I think you're mixing her up with London cockneys.'

Jeremy, never having met Bess's parents, had no idea they had been born and bred in the cockney heart of South London. However, he would not have found they gabbled. Susie and Sammy both spoke clearly, their cockney undertones now slight.

'Jeremy,' said Mrs Passmore, 'you know how delighted I am to have you home again, and my one wish for you is a fulfilling future in taking your father's place in the business and in your personal and private life. Which prompts me to suggest that if you go to England to see Miss Adams, you'll give Charlotte Gilligan reason to feel a little hurt.'

'If she does feel so, I guess Charlotte will survive it,' said Jeremy. 'Are you pointing her at me, or me at her?'

'Jeremy, you've known Charlotte since her days at high school, and your father and I always understood the two of you would come to a happy arrangement. The war interfered with that, but not, I'm sure, with Charlotte's expectations.'

Jeremy shook his head at his mother for being way off track.

'There were no expectations, only those fashioned by you and Father. Take note that Charlotte has a very promising career in City Hall, and that we've only seen each other a few times since I returned. And, I might say, just as good friends.'

'But I've given you pause for thought. You're not eating any breakfast.'

'I've had all I want.'

'All you've had wouldn't feed a cat.'

'Not a fat cat, perhaps. I'll admit, however, that my thoughts are entirely with this letter from Bess. I'll be frank, Mother. I'm an obsessed man.'

'Obsessed? How can you be?' Mrs Passmore looked as if something unwelcome had popped up. 'Jeremy, that's frankly ridiculous.'

'I guess it's even absurd after such a brief encounter.' Jeremy smiled. 'On the other hand, four or five hours can create lasting impressions, and there it is. I can't wait to see Bess again.'

Mrs Passmore sighed.

'Well, I shall have to go along with absurdity, it seems,' she said, 'but I hope you won't forget your responsibilities as your father's heir.'

Jeremy knew what that meant. A lifetime in the packaging industry. But he wasn't interested in industry, or a permanent occupation of his father's palatial office and chair. He had been a farm manager during his years in England, and developed a love of the life. Here in America that life was easy to come by. Its farmlands were almost limitless. But did he want to spend his days amid the great flat wheatfields of the Midwest? And if it happened that he married Bess, would she want that? His feelings had actually taken him as far as thinking of marriage. Or, at least, proposing it. It was damned frustrating to have her three thousand miles away. However, she had said she would love to see him again, and could he let her know when to expect him and for how long? He had in mind the month of August.

He wrote accordingly, and by air mail, as usual.

Bess, on receipt of his letter, felt like doing a bit of a knees-up. Half a mo, she thought, is this feeling meaningful? Well, all I can say in answer to myself is that I think August could turn out to be my nicest month of the year.

That's meaningful.

She rang her parents in the evening. Her dad answered.

'Hello, Dad old love, it's me.'

'Happy is the day,' said Sammy. 'How's Bristol looking?'

'Still wounded,' said Bess. Bristol had been heavily bombed during the war. 'Listen, I've heard from Jeremy again, and he's coming over for the whole of August.'

'That's definite?' said Sammy.

'Definite.'

'And you're happy about it?' said Sammy.

'Very.'

Sammy grinned down the phone, in a manner of speaking.

'Well, let Jeremiah know there'll be a welcome mat on our doorstep,' he said.

'Jeremy, Dad.'

'Slip of me tongue, love, and let him further know your mum and me are going to look forward to meeting him.'

'You'll like him, I know you will,' said Bess, and they talked some more before they rang off.

Sammy then acquainted Susie with the news that Bess's American bloke would arrive on their doorstep at the beginning of August.

'That's happy news,' said Susie. 'I can't wait to meet him, except we'll be in Cornwall the last week in July, and the first week in August.'

'Did I remember that when I was talking to Bess?' said Sammy. 'No, blowed if I did, and blowed if Bess did, either. Tricky. I mean, can we let the two of them be alone in the house until we get back?'

'We can trust Bess,' said Susie, 'but we'll have to talk to her when she next phones.' She smiled. 'Sammy, an American on our doorstep.'

Sammy laughed.

Chapter Nineteen

Chinese Lady, inevitably, had found out about Ned during a phone conversation with Susie. On informing her husband, she received a typically understanding response to the effect that Ned's condition could definitely be taken care of by the daily aspirin.

'One is concerned, of course,' he said, 'but not unduly worried.'

Chinese Lady, who regarded her husband as a fount of mature knowledge, said, 'Well, it's a relief you think so, Edwin.' Then she issued a little grumble. 'Boots must of known about Ned, and should of told me.'

'Perhaps he didn't want to worry you, Maisie.'

'Still, I ought to of been told,' said Chinese Lady. 'Well, I'd best put my hat and coat on.'

'Your hat is on, Maisie,' said Mr Finch, 'and has been since you returned from shopping this morning. Might I know why you now have to put your coat on?'

'Well, Lizzy will want a bit of comforting,' said Chinese Lady, 'so I'd best go and see her.'

'Phone her first,' said Mr Finch.

'Well, perhaps I will,' said Chinese Lady. 'Oh, and

there's something else. I couldn't hardly believe my ears when Susie told me that young Bess's American friend is coming over to see her, and for a month, would you believe.'

'Young Bess is twenty-one, Maisie.'

'All the same, I hope the American gentleman is respectable, which some of their soldiers weren't when they were here during the war,' said Chinese Lady. 'I heard some stories I couldn't hardly believe, and I remember Susie's mother telling me some such stories were in the *News of the World*.'

'I think we both know Bess well enough to be sure that all her friends are entirely respectable, Maisie,' said Mr Finch.

'Well, if you think so, Edwin,' said Chinese Lady, deferring to her belief in his wisdom. 'Edwin, you don't suppose Bess might be thinking of marrying this American, do you?'

'Did Susie say there was a hint from Bess?'

'I asked, of course, but Susie said Bess didn't know if anything like that would happen,' said Chinese Lady. 'Lor', suppose it did, with Daniel already married to an American girl? I don't know I could believe it.'

'Well, let's wait, shall we, Maisie, to see if the un-believable happens,' said Mr Finch.

'Oh, if you say so, Edwin,' said Chinese Lady. 'Would you like a nice cup of tea?'

Mr Finch had long lost count of the number of times that that homely question had been asked of him.

'Well, yes, I would, Maisie, thank you,' he said, which was the answer he had always given.

* * *

Bernard Gibbs, the Young Socialist who had written asking for someone in authority, specifically Paul's assistant, to come and talk to him, lodged in a back room on the first floor of a house in Manor Place.

Lulu, arriving at the house on Thursday afternoon, knocked on the front door. It was opened by a woman in a pink jumper and black trousers. If her jumper looked very nice, her trousers looked aggressive in their confrontation with Lulu's blue jeans. However, the jeans did not flinch. They remained firm-fitting.

'Yes?' said the woman, somewhere in her thirties and wearing make-up that Lulu thought tarty.

'Good afternoon,' she said, 'does Mr Gibbs live here?'

'What, young Bernie?' said the woman. 'Well, 'e don't live anywhere else, I can tell yer that. Can't afford to, seeing he only collects dole money. He's lucky I'm a landlady with a soft heart.'

'Is he in?' asked Lulu. 'I've got an appointment to see him.'

'An appointment?' The woman chortled and her pink jumper quivered a bit. 'I dunno we ever get appointments knockin' on the door, they're a bit posh, ain't they?'

'I'm not,' said Lulu, 'I'm one of the people.'

'Are yer?' said the woman. 'My, we've all got some problems, ain't we? But go on up, then. Turn right at the top of the stairs, and 'elp yerself – er, what d'you want to see 'im for?'

'Just to have a chat,' said Lulu.

'I wish yer luck,' said the woman.

Up went Lulu, noting the stairs were covered with brown pre-war linoleum, cracked in places. She turned right on the landing, and tapped on the door facing her. When it opened, she saw a young man in a shirt and tie. He was quite nice-looking, even if he needed a haircut.

'Hello, Bernard,' said Lulu, opting for informality, 'I'm assistant to Paul Adams. You're expecting me?'

'You bet I am,' said Bernard, 'you're Lulu Saunders, and your old man's our MP. Come in.' He reached, shook her hand vigorously and ushered her in. 'It touched me, yer know, getting the letter to say you were coming.' He gave her shoulder a welcoming slap.

'Watch your manners,' said Lulu, noting an unmade bed, a little table, a couple of chairs, a cupboard, a gas ring, some shelves, an electric fire and other paraphernalia associated with a bedsit. A suitcase peeped from under the bed.

'Don't mind me enthusiasm,' said Bernard, 'I'm a bit pent-up, like. It ain't every day I get to meet an MP's daughter. I've seen you at meetings, of course, and been highly impressed. I've been telling meself that if anyone can inform me why I'm unemployed, you can. I want to ask you, don't I, why there's unemployed when we've got a Labour government?'

'Good question,' said Lulu, 'but even—'

'I know what you mean, and I wouldn't belong to the Young Socialists, would I, if I didn't have faith in the Party, but here I am, going on twenty and out of work since last November – no, I tell a lie, last October – which is reducing me circumstances to humble poverty, like.'

'Tell me,' said Lulu, 'what was your—'

'Job?' said Bernard. 'Plumber's mate – here, would you like a cup of tea?'

'Thanks, but—'

'Just as well, seeing I ain't got a penny for me gas ring right now,' said Bernard. 'Ain't that heart-breaking under a Labour government, a willing worker like me with no job and nothing coming in except me dole?'

'How did you come to lose—'

'Lose me job? Crying shame, that was, me acci-dentally dropping a new lav pan on a doorstep and seeing it end up in bits. What got me was getting the sack just for an accident, which I thought was unlawful under a Labour government. Ain't it unlawful, a worker being given his cards for an accident, didn't the Government make regulations to protect the workers from that sort of thing?'

'There is an Act that protects—'

'Well, it didn't protect me,' said Bernard. 'Here, sit down if you want to, Lulu. Don't mind me calling you Lulu, do you? Or telling you them specs of yourn don't 'alf suit you? I never seen any specs that made a girl look more high-class than yourn. Might say highly intelligent too. I got respect for intelligent girls.'

'I'm out of girlhood, Bernard, I'm a—'

'You're a treat, you are,' said Bernard, 'and you know what you're talking about too, it's a pleasure listening to you.'

'Chance would be a fine thing if—'

'And what I'm wondering is if you know any plumbers that need an apprentice, like. That's it, I said to meself when I wrote to your boss, Paul Adams, I bet our MP's daughter could help me.'

'I don't consider Paul Adams my boss,' said Lulu, 'I'm equal in—'

'I know what you mean,' said Bernard, 'it's being intelligent that does it. I bet you could equal Finkelstein.'

'If you mean Einstein—'

'What, him that runs the Walworth Road hock shop? No, not him, Lulu, he ain't in your class. Anyway, would you or your dad know any plumber looking for a mate that's as keen as I am? I ain't partial to being unemployed, and it's hurtful, y'know, being out of work under a Labour government. It ain't what they promised. What they did promise was work for all, and milk and honey for everyone, like, and as you can see I ain't wallowing in any milk or honey meself.'

'I'm sorry, of course,' said Lulu, 'it's not—'

'You're right, Lulu, it ain't, it's humiliating, and by the time I've managed to keep body and soul together each week, there ain't much left to pay me rent. If it wasn't for Gloria, me landlady, letting me pay the rent in kind, like, I'd have to go back to me parents in Hackney, and I ain't keen on that. Me dad says every time I put a foot in the house, something falls over and breaks. Now, would you know a plumber that's in need?'

'I'm sorry—'

'Well, would your dad know? As me MP, he ought to be able to help. I've given the party me genuine support as a Young Socialist – by the way, would you tell Paul Adams I might have to defer paying me next subscription?'

'I'll tell him,' said Lulu, 'but I'm not sure about my dad and what he knows of—'

'Plumbers?' said Bernard. 'Well, he could ask around, and I'd show me gratitude, I'd be happy to treat you to the pictures at Camberwell Green, and fish and chips afterwards. We could go on the day I get me dole.'

'Bernard,' said Lulu, 'I didn't come here to—'

'To get an invitation to the flicks? Well, I'm sure you didn't, anyone can see you've got more class than Gloria, who's a war widow. Mind, she's got a heart of gold, especially about the way I pay off me rent. Funny, though, that she wouldn't accept me offer to do a bit of plumbing for her when she had a blocked drain. I wouldn't have charged her, would I? Anyway, it's a promise, y'know, treating you to the pictures if your dad can help me. Well, if an MP like your dad can't find a plumber that requires a mate, who can, eh, Lulu? D'you know, you're the first Lulu I ever met. I always thought Lulus wore grass skirts.'

Lulu, halfway to going bonkers, said, 'You're thinking of Honolulu and the—'

'It would suit you, y'know.'

'What would?'

'A grass skirt,' said Bernard. 'I ain't quarrelling with your jeans, but I know I could like you a lot in a grass skirt and selling pineapples.'

'Not my style,' said Lulu, 'and look here, Bernard, about the Labour government. I can tell you what it's done for the workers so far, and what it's going to do. Especially for the unemployed. You can rely on—'

'I'm sure I can,' said Bernard, an earnest look on his face, 'and I could listen to you all day, but all I'm asking is for the Party to find me a job in plumbing, which is me natural direction. If it can't, I'm going to have to complain. In which case, could you tell me how I can get to see your dad so's I can have a little talk with him?'

'I don't think—'

'Here, why don't you sit down?' Bernard reached and took hold of a chair to bring it forward. It fell over. 'Look at that, even me furniture don't seem to owe me a living. You can understand, I'm sure, that no job and unreliable furniture reduces me dignity as a human being.'

'Shut up,' said Lulu.

'Beg yer pardon?'

'You talk too much,' said Lulu.

'Eh?'

'And somehow,' said Lulu, 'I don't think you're cut out to be a plumber, or even a furniture remover. Now, there's a—'

'I only want—'

'Shut up and listen,' said Lulu. 'There's a firm turning cleared bomb sites into car parks in the City. It's called National Car Parks Limited. They're looking for full-time attendants. Go to the Walworth Road Labour Exchange. They'll give you the address of the firm's City offices. There you can apply for a job as an attendant.'

'But what about me feel for plumbing work and—'

'Bernard, shut up,' said Lulu. 'Concentrate on being a car-park attendant. But for God's sake don't touch any of the cars in case they fall to pieces and earn you the sack. Be polite to the drivers. But don't talk to them about the Labour government or your dignity. Just tell 'em good morning and thank you. You got that, Bernard?'

'Well, I got to say you're coming up trumps, Lulu,'

said Bernard, 'and as soon as I land the job I'll keep me promise to take you out to the flicks and treat you to fish and chips as well. I was right in thinking you could—'

'That's all,' said Lulu. 'I don't go to cinemas, I'm too busy studying politics every evening.'

'Still, when I get the job,' said Bernard, 'I'll come and see you at your office to make me gesture of gratitude, like with a bunch of flowers. Daffodils, they're nice at this time of the year.'

'I don't have any flower vases,' said Lulu. 'Good afternoon, Bernard. It's been a bit of a fight meeting you, but we're both still alive. So long.'

'Lulu, you don't have to go—'

But Lulu opened the door and escaped. Downstairs, the landlady reappeared, a sly smile on her face.

''Ad a nice chat with Bernie, did yer, love?'

'That's one way of putting it,' said Lulu.

'What a caution, eh? Talk about a tongue that never stops wagging. Did it hurt your ears a bit?'

'I'm immune to male prattle,' said Lulu.

'You sure?' said Gloria. 'Only you look sort of wore out. Mind, Bernie's got his other ways.'

'What other ways?'

'Oh, the kind where he don't have to do any talkin',' said Gloria, and gave Lulu a wink as she saw her out. It made Lulu wonder at the infinite variations of human nature, and ask herself if as an adult woman of nineteen she still had something to learn about life, after all.

'How'd you get on?' asked Paul on her return to the office.

'That's the first and last time I'm going to let you send me to listen to any member who's got a complaint,' said Lulu. 'What a gasbag. Treated me like a donkey.'

'A donkey? You, Lulu?'

'Yes, he talked my bloody hind leg off,' said Lulu, and gave details of the encounter. Paul laughed. 'You've got a lousy sense of humour if you think it was funny,' she said.

'I wouldn't say it was something to cry about,' said Paul. 'You did well, putting him in the way of a job and accordingly strengthening his faith in the Party. With the Prime Minister struggling to cope with his narrow majority, we need blokes like Bernard Gibbs to spread his faith.'

'Among his friends?' said Lulu. 'You've got a hope. I bet even his closest friends do a quick bunk as soon as they see him coming.'

'Still, cultivate him—'

'Do what?'

'Pop in on him occasionally and keep his enthusiasm going,' said Paul. 'Give him a bundle of leaflets to hand out in Manor Place and Walworth Road.'

'I'm getting bitter feelings about you,' scowled Lulu.

'What are Bernie's feelings about you?' asked Paul.

'Only that the barmy plumbing misfit would like to see me in a grass skirt,' said Lulu.

'Well, well,' said Paul, 'he's a misfit with imagination.'

'Don't say any more.'

'Still, he's obviously—'

'Shut up.'

'Well, talk to him about the proposed march of the Young Socialists through London,' said Paul. 'He sounds to me as if he'd willingly carry a banner or a Red Flag. Has he got the muscles for it?'

'Listen, brainless,' said Lulu, 'if I had a banner right now, I'd flatten you with it. I'm not putting myself anywhere near that talking machine again. Ever. Any tea going?'

'I've been waiting for you,' said Paul.

'Well, put the kettle on,' said Lulu. 'It's your turn, and I'm worn out. Oh, there was just one thing about Bernard I liked.'

'What was that?' asked Paul.

'He recognized me as a woman of intelligence.'

'In or out of a grass skirt?' said Paul.

'Grow up,' said Lulu.

'I believe it's a fact that not every woman likes her intelligence to be noticed ahead of her charm, especially when she's still a girl,' said Paul, and ducked out to put the kettle on before Lulu heaved her typewriter at him.

Later, over their cups of tea, he spoke of the work they were now both doing in respect of the proposed march and demonstration.

'It's taking up most of my time,' said Lulu.

'I was thinking, let's see how far we've got by Saturday,' said Paul. 'Then I suggest you bring all your notes to my home on Sunday afternoon. We'll spend a quiet time going through yours and mine before tea and after tea.'

'Eh?' said Lulu.

'Yes, have Sunday tea with me and my family,' said Paul.

'Sunday tea?' said Lulu. 'Sunday tea?'

'Probably with shrimps and winkles,' said Paul, 'and my mother's home-made cake.'

'Shrimps and winkles?' said Lulu, gaping. 'Shrimps and winkles?'

'You ought to know about them as a Kennington girl, and that they're a good old cockney treat,' said Paul. 'My parents grew up on such treats, and I've spent hundreds of Sundays growing up on them myself.'

'I can't believe this,' said Lulu. 'Are you and your family still living in Queen Victoria's time?'

'My grandma will tell you Queen Victoria was the last monarch who could put the wind up a Prime Minister,' said Paul.

'She ought to have stayed the last,' said Lulu. 'All the others since her time should have been put in a home for the unwanted.'

'Now, Lulu, don't start all that Marxist stuff again,' said Paul. 'The Labour government and the workers can live comfortably with a constitutional monarchy.'

'Not the real workers,' said Lulu. 'Not the miners and dockers. You sure you're a Socialist and not a closet Conservative?'

'I'm sure,' said Paul. 'Anyway, see you at my home Sunday afternoon, say about three.'

'If I turn up,' said Lulu, 'where, I'd like to know, will we be able to do some quiet studying? Without your family looking over our shoulders?'

'Oh, we'll do it in my bedroom,' said Paul.

'I'm not doing anything with you in your bedroom,' said Lulu.

'We'll find somewhere,' said Paul. 'By the way, wear a nice Sunday frock.'

'A what?'

'Don't wear your jeans,' said Paul, 'or my mother will think the end of her world is nigh. She's a sweet lady, so I'd be obliged if you'd settle for a nice Sunday frock.'

'I don't have a nice Sunday frock,' said Lulu. 'As far as I'm concerned, they went out with Alice in Wonderland. All right, I'll wear a blouse and skirt. Listen, didn't you tell me your father's a capitalist?'

'I did, yes, but he's not a bad old dad, so try not to talk about doing away with him and my uncles over tea.'

'Your dad and your uncles are all capitalists?' said Lulu.

'Afraid so,' said Paul. 'I think about it with regret sometimes, but I console myself by remembering they're very fair-minded employers.'

'But all capitalists,' murmured Lulu, as if she was having sad thoughts. 'Well, I feel for you, having to live that down. No wonder you're a bit of a funny bloke.'

Chapter Twenty

Over supper that evening, Paul surprised his parents.

'You've heard me talk about my assistant, Lulu Saunders,' he said.

'Several times,' said Tommy.

'Yes, imagine you having an assistant, Paul, when you're not twenty yet,' said Vi.

'Bit of a feather in his cap,' said Tommy.

Paul came up with his surprise.

'I've invited her to tea on Sunday,' he said.

'Eh?' said Tommy.

'My oh my,' smiled Vi, 'that's got to mean something.'

'Yes,' said Paul, 'it means that instead of trying to work things out in our noisy office, we're going to have a quiet time here looking over our plans for organizing a Young Socialists march through London.'

'Do what?' said Tommy.

'A march?' said Vi. 'D'you mean with a band?'

'That's a point, Mum,' said Paul. 'A band, yes. I'll make a note of that.'

'Half a mo,' said Tommy, 'what's the march all about?'

'Promoting the cause of the Labour Party,' said Paul.

Tommy groaned.

'I don't think your dad likes that,' said Vi, still a very equable woman.

'Listen, me lad,' said Tommy, 'might I point out this family, from your grandma downwards, has come up on hard work and private enterprise, and without any help from the Labour Party?'

'Well, good for you, Dad,' said Paul, 'but to my sorrow it's turned us all into capitalists and made me feel I owe something to the workers. I'll probably spend the rest of my life doing what I can for them.'

'Well, you can include me and your mum,' said Tommy, 'we're workers. So's your brother David and your sister-in-law Kate, and everyone else in the family, with your Uncle Sammy on top of the pile.'

'Dad, I've got to point out you're all working for capitalism,' said Paul. 'It's not the same as digging coal out of the bowels of a mine or unloading ships at the docks, and all for low wages.'

'Paul, lovey,' said Vi, 'do mind what you're saying.' She was sure it was vulgar for anyone to mention bowels. Vi wasn't in the least prudish, even though she'd been brought up by a prudish mother. But she was sensitive.

'I suppose your assistant, Lulu Whatsername, thinks the same as you, does she, me lad?' said Tommy.

'More so,' said Paul. 'She's red-hot on the sins of capitalism.'

'Oh, dear,' said Vi.

'Well, if she's coming to tea on Sunday, tell her to cool down before she knocks on the door,' said

Tommy. He was trying to enjoy his homely supper of liver, bacon, fried onions and mashed potato. But he relegated his enjoyment to second place in favour of defending capitalism, first informing Paul that it was business and industry that did a lot more for the country's health, wealth and strength than anything politics could do. Politics were hot air and politicians were gasbags. Politicians and civil servants couldn't even mend a tin kettle or run a market stall. If the Labour government ordered some of its civil servants to do that, to run a market stall, they'd turn up for their daily stint in their swaddling clothes.

'Swaddling clothes?' said Paul.

'What they were born in, suit, bowler hat and umbrella,' said Tommy, and went on to say they'd get things chucked at them. It beats me, he said, that people keep believing governments will make them well off in a week, and give them new curtains as well. 'It hurts me, Paul me lad, that you go round telling people that's what the Labour government will do for 'em. What we all get out of life depends on what we put into it. Good ideas, a bit of initiative and hard work. That's what made your Uncle Sammy a capitalist, which I suppose red-hot Lulu Whatsername wants to knock off on account of him making a profit.'

'Now, Tommy, don't get worked up,' said Vi, 'and don't let your supper get cold.'

Tommy forked a lump of tenderly cooked liver into his mouth, and chomped on it.

'I ain't worked up,' he said.

'I've got sympathy for Dad's feelings, Mum,' said Paul, 'and even though we're on opposite sides, I'll admit he can do a good talking job for the Conservative Party.'

'Oh, I'm sure he'll be nice to your lady assistant on Sunday,' said Vi in her pacific way. 'Is she nice-looking, love?'

'I couldn't say,' said Paul, 'I've never seen much of her face. She keeps most of it hidden behind her specs and hair. But I've a feeling she's good at heart. Of course, being a modern female, she likes to think she's a tough cookie.'

'A what?' said Vi.

'A tough cookie,' said Tommy, grinning.

'Paul, I don't think you ought to call a young lady a name like that,' said Vi.

'Oh, there's a lot of them about,' said Paul.

'I'm beginning to run into some meself,' said Tommy.

'Some what?' asked Vi.

'Tough young cookies,' said Tommy, 'at the factory.'

'Oh, I expect they're mostly young women that served in the Army,' said Vi.

'That's it,' said Tommy, 'it's the war that did it, me lad. Your grandma always said it would.'

'Lulu's not ex-Army,' said Paul, 'she wasn't old enough to be conscripted. If she had been, she'd now be an ex-sergeant major. She's that kind of character.'

'I hope your mother can cope with having an ex-sergeant major to Sunday tea,' said Tommy.

'Oh, I'm sure she won't be a worry,' said Vi.

'By the way,' said Paul, 'while she's here, don't mention that Grandpa Finch is going to get a title.'

'Why not?' asked Tommy.

Paul said that in the first place it was against the principles of his Socialist ideology to be related to a title. Vi asked what Socialist ideology was. Daft, said Tommy. In the second place, said Paul, if Lulu got to know she'd shout it about and the Young Socialists would ask for his resignation. Vi said well, she just didn't know what to call that kind of thing. Daft, said Tommy. In the third place, said Paul, he'd probably be ostracized by the Party. What's that? asked Vi. Bloody daft, said Tommy.

'Oh, dear,' said Vi.

'But what can you expect from people that don't understand profit?' said Tommy.

'Paul lovey,' said Vi, 'your Uncle Sammy's spent all his life making friends with profit.'

'Don't tell Lulu,' said Paul, 'or Uncle Sammy will be the first to be ostracized.'

'A fat lot he'll care,' said Tommy.

'Oh, well, don't let's argue about it,' said Vi, 'let's give a nice welcome to Lulu, Tommy, and I'll serve a really proper Sunday tea.'

'How really proper?' asked Paul.

'I'll buy some shrimps and winkles,' said Vi.

Paul yelled with laughter.

Boots dropped into Sammy's office the next morning.

'Heard from Hilda Campion yet, Sammy?'

'Not yet,' said Sammy.

'It's been four days,' said Boots, 'but don't rush her, of course.'

'Ta for the advice,' said Sammy. 'Which, I might say, I don't need.'

'I'm under pressure myself,' said Boots, 'from Kate and David.'

'Hard luck,' said Sammy.

'And from Emma and Rosie.'

'More hard luck,' said Sammy.

'I'll try to cope,' said Boots. 'Sammy, you've got a worried look.'

'It's not worry,' said Sammy, 'it's me twitching state.'

'Brought on by what?'

'The thought of some of me favourite female relatives in jeans,' said Sammy. 'I don't like keeping on, nor repeating myself. People start walking away from that kind of bloke, but don't you get twitches too?'

'I'm taking the easy way out,' said Boots, 'I'm resigning myself.'

'Wait till the time comes when Chinese Lady gets a sight of some of her granddaughters looking like cowboys,' said Sammy. 'She'll read them the riding act.'

'Riot Act?' said Boots.

'Riding,' said Sammy. 'On how they weren't brought up on horseback.'

'I'll try not to be there when it happens,' said Boots. His easy smile surfaced. 'Meanwhile, keep in touch with Hilda, Sammy.' Out he went.

'He's still Lord-I-Am,' muttered Sammy.

Boots looked in on Tim and Daniel, who shared a large office as joint managers of the property company. Tim, an ex-commando, was twenty-eight. Daniel, an ex-infantryman, was twenty-three, having volunteered when he was eighteen. Both made Chinese Lady think of her first husband, a fine-looking man who'd soldiered with the West Kents on the North-West Frontier when Britain's Empire was at its peak. She thought Tim and Daniel, like their soldier grandfather, both looked more suited to the great outdoors than to office desks. But each had his own agile mind, and each was proving an asset to the expanding family business.

'Any problems with negotiations?' asked Boots.

'None,' said Tim. 'In fact, we're on the verge of completing the sale of two of our three sites.' Sammy had acquired more than a few sites for the property company during the war. All had been sold except these three.

'The developers have settled for our asking price,' said Daniel. 'Further, we've two firms enquiring after the third site.'

'I'll recommend both of you for a bottle of champagne,' said Boots. 'How's the new factory at Bethnal Green coming along?'

'We'll be going there again with the architects on Monday to inspect progress,' said Tim. 'I think you'd be pleased with the brickwork so far, and so would Uncle Sammy.'

'Well, he needs some good news,' said Boots.

'Not half he doesn't,' said Daniel. 'He's going off his chump about the prospects of our shops stocking jeans.'

Boots said there was a large amount of repetitive chat about jeans going on, but it wasn't wise to mention those prospects too often to Sammy. Daniel said his mum was tickled by his dad trying to forbid any kind of talk about jeans in case it gave Paula and Phoebe ideas. But Patsy, he said, was sure his dad was fighting a lost cause, since London was bound to come into line with New York eventually. Also, she was after jeans for herself. Boots asked Daniel if he'd mentioned that to his dad. Daniel said he didn't want to give him more cause for gloom. Tim said he could understand Uncle Sammy's feelings, since he'd been in the rag trade for years and accordingly was married to the kind of fashions he considered complimentary to females. Unfortunately, grinned Tim, he's being overtaken by something that's driving him barmy.

'He'll get over it,' said Boots. 'In business, he's instinctively adaptable.'

'If jeans in our shops turn out to be profitable,' said Daniel, 'he'll adapt to that like a duckling to water.'

'So will we all,' said Boots, 'we've all got dependants.'

When he was back in his office, Rachel Goodman came in. Boots, like Sammy, was never unappreciative of how well-preserved she was in looks and figure, nor of the fact that she'd always been a heart-and-soul member of the firm's executive team. In view of the unspeakable horrors he had witnessed at Belsen concentration camp, he often wondered how many Jewish women as warm-hearted and full-figured as Rachel had been reduced to skeletons before being exterminated. His regard for nephew Edward's mother-in-law was one of long-standing affection.

She asked him if progress was being made with Hilda Campion's gentleman friend. Boots said that if Hilda was making the right kind of progress with the gentleman, then the outcome could be nicely in favour of Adams Fashions. Rachel said Sammy was chewing his lip. And twitching, said Boots. Poor dear, said Rachel, I've stopped worrying him about all those materials and fabrics the factory needs. But as you're not chewing your own lip or twitching, she said, I can confer with you. It's going to be a case of yes or no, said Boots, and we're going to have to settle for that. By the way, said Rachel, Leah thinks jeans would make lovely casual wear. The walls of Jericho are all falling, said Boots, but tell Leah that her Uncle Sammy can't see anything casual about them, only the ruination of genuine fashion. It's hard on Sammy's sensitivities, said Rachel. It's hard on everyone's ears, the constant mention of these American casuals, smiled Boots, but Daniel has just pointed out to me that Sammy's sensitivities will stand up to the trend if it proves profitable. Rachel laughed.

'Profit can bring a silver lining to Sammy's darkest clouds,' she said.

'We're all in favour of that kind of lining, Rachel,' said Boots.

'Business is business,' said Rachel.

'Sammy himself couldn't have put it better,' said Boots.

Sammy was now on the phone to the Oxford Street shop, and talking to Miss Campion.

'Morning to you, Hilda. Any news from Flanagan?'

'Flanagan?' said Hilda.

'Mr Dickinson,' said Sammy.

'Oh. Oh, yes,' said Hilda. 'I've seen him and he's promised to let me know as soon as he can.'

'Was he optimistic?' asked Sammy.

'Optimistic, Mr Adams?'

'Cheerful.'

'Oh, very,' said Hilda.

'Does as soon as he can mean in a couple of days, say?' asked Sammy, treating her to gentle verbiage in case she felt he was rushing her.

'I'll be seeing him again tomorrow evening, Saturday,' said Hilda. 'He's taking me to the theatre.'

'I like that,' said Sammy. 'A theatre seat and a couple of gin and tonics during the interval ought to help you mix pleasure with business.'

'Pardon?' said Hilda.

'What I meant, Hilda, was that while you're working on behalf of Adams Fashions, enjoy yourself as well. And remember the bonus I promised.'

'Thank you, Mr Adams, I'll do my very best for the firm.'

'I know I can rely on you,' said Sammy. 'By the way, any customers in the shop this morning? I mean customers asking for jeans?'

'Oh, yes,' said Hilda, 'a mother and daughter.'

'Eh?' said Sammy.

'A mother and daughter.'

'Blind O'Reilly,' said Sammy, 'what's my life coming to? A girl fancying jeans, that's painful enough, but her mum as well? If my own dear old ma knew, she'd order me to blow up the Board of Trade. I'd be obliged, Hilda, if you'd tell me you're joking.'

'No, I'm quite serious,' said Hilda.

'That's done it,' said Sammy, 'I'm ringing off now. I need to put my head in some place where it won't hurt so much. Like a bucket of floating kippers. Keep in touch, Hilda.'

He put the phone down.

Gorblimey Amy, he thought, this cowboy clobber is haunting me, and my twitches need an operation.

Chapter Twenty-One

Paul and Lulu were busy, very. The morning's mail had been quite heavy, and if some of the letters contained impractical suggestions, the whole represented the enthusiasm of Young Socialists for a rally. Paul said this was typical of young people, that they were still staunch supporters of the Party, while older voters were losing a bit of faith.

'It's because Labour ministers aren't making the right decisions,' said Lulu. 'They're actually afraid of genuine Socialism. They're backing away from nationalizing all means of production. Even my own dad spoke against nationalizing the Stock Exchange.'

'The Stock Exchange doesn't produce anything except share prices,' said Paul.

'It's the City's cosy kingdom of parasites,' said Lulu. 'It exists for the benefit of brokers and shareholders. It doesn't benefit the workers. Ought to be nationalized and turned into a factory for making fridges. At a price cheap enough for working-class families.'

'Would it pay for itself?' asked Paul, scribbling answers to letters.

'That's a question a genuine Socialist wouldn't

ask,' said Lulu, head bent, hair flopping, spectacles directed at her pages of notes. 'Nationalized industries shouldn't have to pay for themselves. There should be a yearly government subsidy for all of 'em. Still, you come from a capitalist family. You're thinking of profit. I hope I'm not working with a dissident.'

'Me too,' said Paul, 'or I'd be on your list for the chop. By the way, there's a photograph of your dad in my morning newspaper, with a lady he's going to marry. The blurb said very complimentary things about him as Honest John Saunders, an MP of integrity, and I must say the lady looked dishy.'

'She's his secretary,' muttered Lulu.

'So it said. I'd like one like her.'

'You've got me, so count your blessings,' said Lulu.

'You're pleased for your dad, are you?' said Paul.

'About him getting married again?' said Lulu. 'Why not? I'm not against marriage for old-fashioned people like my dad. I simply believe it's something intelligent women don't need.'

'Cheer up,' said Paul, 'with luck it'll pass you by. As it is, I'll be giving you a daffy of work for typing in a few minutes.'

'I'm busy,' said Lulu. 'Working on all these ideas for the march.'

'I'll still want letters typed,' said Paul.

Lulu swept her hair back and fixed him with an aggressive look.

'One day,' she said, 'I'm going to sock you.'

'Lulu, I'm sure that by the time one day arrives, you and I will have learned to love each other,' said Paul.

'What a happy thought,' said Lulu.

'Incidentally,' said Paul, 'among my own ideas for the march, I've included a band.'

'A band?'

'Actually, my mother suggested it.'

'A band?'

'It could be a rousing factor,' said Paul, 'it could draw the crowds and make us all step lively on our march.'

'Where do we get the right kind of band?' asked Lulu.

'Grenadier Guards, with kind permission of the King?' suggested Paul.

'Does that mean I'm going to have to type a letter to His Noble Majesty?' asked Lulu.

'You could phone, I suppose,' said Paul.

'Oh, yes, I'm that kind of idiot, I don't think,' said Lulu. 'No, nothing doing. As for the band of the Grenadier Guards, you're off your fat head. It's got to be a workers' brass band, full stop.'

Her dad came in then. He breezed into the office, smiling all over.

'Morning, Lulu, morning, Paul, lovely day,' he said.

Paul came to his feet.

'Well, it's a day for congratulating you, Mr Saunders,' he said, and shook hands with the pleasant-looking backbencher, an MP he considered a really genuine bloke, whose years as a young man in the printing shop of a national newspaper had turned him into an active trade unionist, but not a firebrand. He was a staunch Labour man, well thought of by his constituents for his good humour, his common sense and his approachable nature.

Paul could understand why he'd been a back-bencher for years. In Parliament's corridors of power, it was the scheming kind of MPs who fostered their ambitions. Honest John never seemed to let ambition affect his opinions or make him a creature of Labour's whips. Paul liked him, very much, and his congratulations were sincere.

'Well, thanks, Paul,' said Lulu's dad, 'I'm a lucky old lad, and I've popped in to invite you to meet Miss Jennings at lunchtime. Lulu's already met her, several times. She'll be here in a while, mingling with the staff, and I'll be drawing the champagne corks. How'd the two of you feel about that?'

'I feel good,' said Paul.

'I feel I'm going to watch what happens to my glass,' said Lulu. 'Still, you're on the ball, Dad.'

At lunchtime, Paul had the pleasure of meeting Sylvia Jennings. He found her a pretty and slightly plump young woman, vivacious of personality and frankly happy about attaching herself in wedlock to Lulu's likeable dad. She carried off the ordeal of being the centrepiece of a humming crowd of Party workers without looking either shy or harassed.

The champagne corks popped, the bubbly flowed and prepared sandwiches were gobbled.

At one point, Honest John managed to draw Paul aside.

'In a couple of years, Paul,' he said, 'you'll want something more serious than looking after your Young Socialists' group, won't you?'

'I'll always want something that'll keep me in active support of the Party,' said Paul.

'Good man,' said Honest John. 'Have you thought

about doing that as a local councillor?'

'Great stuff,' said Paul, 'but I'll need to get elected first, Mr Saunders.'

'I'll back you in a way that'll help you get adopted as a candidate,' said Lulu's dad.

'Won't you be doing that for Lulu?' asked Paul.

'Not till she calms down, which'll take more than a few years,' said Honest John. 'Local government's no place for a firecracker. It turns council debates into a circus, and members start chucking things at each other. Of course, don't tell Lulu I said so, me lad.'

'No, right,' said Paul.

'In a couple of years, then, we'll have a chat,' said Honest John.

'Well, thanks a lot, Mr Saunders,' said Paul.

'You're welcome.'

Paul went in search of Lulu, not to talk about what might be in store for him in a couple of years, but to find out if she needed protecting from too much champagne. Her glass had just been refilled for the fourth time.

'You all right, Lulu?' he said.

'This stuff's – oops – this stuff's a bit fizzy,' said Lulu.

'Try not to drink too much of it,' said Paul. 'By the way, your dad's found himself a very nice fiancée. She's a charmer.'

'Er?' said Lulu, whose eyes behind her spectacles were beginning to look crossed. Despite her resolution not to get tiddly, she was already there. She was no drinker. 'Who?'

'Miss Jennings, I like her,' said Paul.

'Oh, you mean my stepmother,' said Lulu, slurring a bit.

'Well, she will be once she and your dad leave the church,' said Paul.

'What?'

'Once they're married.'

'Hope she knows Dad will put her into an apron the moment he gets her home.'

'Is she likely to kick about that?'

'Hope so – oops – hope every bride kicks,' said Lulu.

The lunchtime revelry in honour of the constituency's MP and his fiancée was enjoyed by all, but it put Lulu into the kind of state where she didn't know if her legs were with her or if she'd left them at home. Seeing she was the daughter of Honest John, her glass was under constant pressure from people carrying bottles around.

After the party broke up, she was pretty useless in the office all afternoon, peering at the keys of her typewriter, tapping them with tiddly optimism and giggling at what emerged on paper. Her glasses kept falling off, and her curtain of hair kept shutting out her face.

Paul took her home early, helping her onto a bus to begin with. In return for his gallant assistance, she told him to watch what he was doing, or else. He stopped her trying to climb the stairs to the upper deck, and ushered her inside. She fell into a seat, and gave him a cross-eyed look when he sat down beside her.

When they reached her stop and he helped her off, she wanted to know who he was and why he was touching her person.

'You're lucky I'm here,' said Paul, 'so come on, wonky legs.'

He managed to get her to the door of her flat, by which time her glasses were at a lopsided angle and her eyes misty. He helped her find her keys and he opened her flat door for her. At which point she fell against him.

'Get away,' she said.

Paul grinned.

'Hello, bosom chum,' he said. Lulu lifted her face, her spectacles somewhere around her neck, her shining black hair at least tucked safely up inside her beret.

'I know you,' she said.

'See you in the morning, if your head's better,' said Paul.

'All right, give us – oops – give us a kiss, then,' said Lulu, bosom breathing warmly against his chest.

Paul gave her a kiss. She returned it with a wine-induced headiness.

'Lulu, you've got promise,' he said.

'Here, let go of me, clear off, you swine,' said Lulu, coming to for a brief moment.

He saw her into her flat first, however, in case her legs gave way at her door, and someone uncaring swept her up. He was smiling when he made his way home, thinking she'd shown, as once before, that there was a female girl struggling to get out.

Chapter Twenty-Two

Jimmy received another letter from Jenny. It contained further news of the life she and her family were living in New York, including how they were wallowing in seas of plenty. There were no shortages of anything. People dined on T-bone steaks of huge proportions, and young people gluttonized on hamburgers and treated them just as a snack. Clothes were in sumptuous supply, materials and fabrics ranging from the highest and most expensive quality to the cheapest. New York women looked marvellous, and businesswomen looked smart and elegant, except the outsized ones, who bulged a bit and had to kind of heave themselves out of the city's low-slung taxis. Central Park was a playground for young people and a relaxing place for the retired.

She was doing well at the college, and a fellow student was dating her, but she had reservations about what he was after, a friendly relationship or something much too personal. Was Jimmy dating someone else, some new girlfriend? If so, well, it was understandable, but she hoped it wouldn't mean he would stop writing to her.

Jimmy replied saying that if that fellow student of hers had something personal in mind, it was probably because T-bone steaks were pepping up his hormones. He also said that neither he nor any of his family had seen a T-bone steak since about 1939, and that not even his clever old pa had seen any fall off the back of a meat truck. Result, no-one in the family had pepped-up hormones. Well, not as far as he knew.

He gave Jenny an account of his activities, and said he wasn't dating anyone else, that all his dates were outings with a group of old friends, girls and fellers. And no, he wasn't thinking about chucking his pen-pal relationship with her, since he had very nice memories of their times together and would always be interested in how her life developed. By the way, he added, my old dad, who's been in the rag trade for years, has got his knickers in a twist regarding imported American jeans. He thinks they'll kill real fashions stone dead. Have they killed American fashions yet? He signed off with affection and added a couple of kisses.

Lulu had suffered no hangover. Paul said that was one of the welcome things about champagne, that it didn't cause a hangover. Lulu said thanks for small mercies, but all the same she was going to sue him for pouring so much of the stuff into her.

'Not guilty,' said Paul.

'Listen,' said Lulu, 'what did you do to me on my way home?'

'Put you on a bus, sat beside you to keep you from flopping, helped you off the bus, carried you to your flat—'

'You carried me?'

'Good as,' said Paul, 'your legs were wonky. I got

you to your flat, then left you sitting on your floor. It was where you wanted to be.'

'What a swine,' said Lulu. 'Did you kiss me?'

'Not while you were sitting on the floor,' said Paul.

'When, then?'

'While you were hanging onto me at your door,' said Paul.

'You took rotten advantage of me?'

'Not rotten, no, we enjoyed a few kisses together, and you breathed a bit heavy,' said Paul.

'I did what?' said Lulu.

'You were probably feeling emotional about your dad getting engaged,' said Paul.

'Big deal,' said Lulu. 'I don't believe any of it.'

'Fair enough,' said Paul. 'Now, with that settled, will you type the letters you weren't able to yesterday afternoon?'

'Hand 'em over,' said Lulu, and spent the morning doing an efficient job of work, while Paul dealt with a few callers.

When they left at midday, Paul reminded her not to forget to turn up for Sunday tea at his home. Three o'clock. Lulu said it would be the first time she'd had Sunday tea with a capitalist family.

'Well, be nice about it,' said Paul, 'leave your guillotine at home.'

'You're a laugh a minute,' said Lulu.

At one of the Army's training camps in Aldershot, the parade ground echoed to the clump of Army boots moving in unison. A regiment of National Service conscripts had finished its four months of training to become part of Britain's modern Army, a force imbued with technical skills and the art of mobility. That, however, had not meant the elimination of old-fashioned square drill or taking the traditional end-of-training salute from the camp commandant, Colonel Bill Lucas, known as Luke to his friends.

A wartime commando, he was thirty-nine and still a man of strong physique and rugged looks. He had lost his left arm during the British drive for Germany late in the war, but as a regular Army officer, with outstanding combat honours, he was offered a continuation of his military career. That landed him in this Aldershot training camp with the responsibility of turning intakes of National Servicemen into efficient soldiers. He was assisted by a cadre of officers and NCOs, who soon discovered him to be a tough taskmaster. Results were accordingly excellent, even if most recruits, at some stage or other, wished they'd never had to join.

The day was cold, but the men, rifles shouldered, marched in strict defiance of the temperature. It was what Colonel Lucas expected and demanded of them.

The cadre's regimental sergeant major bawled.

'Eyes r-r-r-right!'

Every head turned, and Colonel Lucas saluted the parading column for the time it took to pass by. A suspicion of a scowl flickered as a man in the last rank lost step. But a fleeting grin followed. The martinet, more than satisfied generally with the accomplishments of this intake, had his sense of humour and let it show for a moment.

Beside him, his second in command, Major John Whyburn, murmured, 'What will their mothers think of them now that they've developed their iron chests?'

'Write me letters complaining that Wally or Willy could do with better boots,' said Colonel Lucas, watching as the regiment was brought to a halt and ceremoniously dismissed. This meant the men were to disperse in orderly fashion, and not as a rabble. They were due now for leave before reassembling and posting. Posting would probably take them to a troublesome hot spot, such as Malaya or Cyprus.

'Fairly promising bunch, this lot,' said Major Whyburn.

'These intakes come and go,' said Colonel Lucas. 'Damned if I'm not beginning to think the routine is turning me into a dummy. I'll end up in a shop window, modelling the King's uniform.'

'What's bugging you, a touch of restless corpuscles?'

'I need a spell of active service,' said Colonel Lucas.

'You'll be lucky,' said Major Whyburn, himself missing his right eye by reason of a war wound. He wore a patch over it. 'So would I be. We're both crocks.'

'Better than being dead, so I'm not actually complaining,' said Colonel Lucas, and went off duty to depart for his home and his French-born wife in the countryside just west of Aldershot. He did not live in the officers' quarters, which were mostly occupied by single commissioned men.

Eloise, with her three-year-old son Charles beside her, welcomed her husband's arrival. She did so with a rush of words while he was treating the boy to a bear hug.

'Luke, I'm having such a happy day. Yes, isn't it amazing that life is so good to us. I had the results of my test from Dr Harvey. Positive, would you believe. We're going to have another.'

'Another bottle of pills?' said Luke.

'Pills? Pills? No, you silly man, another child. There, what do you say to that?'

'I can say I've been keeping my fingers crossed for you, and that I'm now delighted,' said Luke, and planted a warm kiss on her mouth. 'I'm proud of you, you sweet woman.'

'Oh, you can take a bow too,' said Eloise, glowing because his delight was so visible. Nearly thirty-three now, she had a French flair for being exhibitionist, something she had inherited from her mother. It amused her down-to-earth husband, who found her permanently entertaining. 'I'm pleased to have made you happy,' she said.

Young Charles, a sturdy little chap, piped up. He'd been told he was going to have a baby brother or sister before Christmas.

'Daddy, who's going to bring us the baby?'

'Good question, young 'un,' said Luke. 'Probably the postman.'

'What, in a parcel?' asked Charles.

'Bound to be wrapped up,' said Luke. 'And stamped.'

'Golly,' said Charles, highly impressed by the usefulness of their postman.

'Luke, I phoned my father,' said Eloise. 'He expressed immense pleasure.'

'At your condition or my performance?'

'Performance?' said Eloise. 'You're not a circus act.'

'By God, I hope not,' said Luke.

'According to my father, it's only God Himself who knows what Grandma Finch is going to say about the prospect of one more great-grandchild.' Eloise laughed.

'I've heard', said Luke, 'that she has trouble in counting those she already has.'

'Oh, I'm sure she won't worry about that kind of thing on the day she goes to Buckingham Palace with Grandpa Finch,' said Eloise.

'There's one thing she will worry about,' said Luke. 'That's if her hat's on straight and if it's the right kind of hat.'

'Oh, hats on such occasions are very important,' said Eloise. 'Luke, my father sent you his regards and congratulations.'

'Your father, dear woman, is a man for all of us,' said Luke. 'Now, I think there's a bottle of bubbly somewhere in the house, unless Rosy Roberts has snaffled it and shared it with one of his NAAFI girls.' Corporal Roberts was his bat-man, called Rosy because his face always wore a rosy hue.

'No, of course not,' said Eloise, 'he wouldn't dream of doing such a thing.'

'Good,' said Luke, 'we'll pop the cork and have the bubbly with our lunch.'

'Could I have some?' asked Charles.

'Little man, it'll get up your nose,' said Luke, 'but sure you can have some on an occasion like this. In an egg cup.'

'What about the postman, Daddy?'

'If it's all the same to you, young 'un, he can wait until he arrives with the parcel.'

'Lord above,' said Chinese Lady, when she received the news that Eloise was expectant again, 'I just don't know how I'm going to count all my family up.'

'Start from the beginning, with Boots, your first-born,' said Mr Finch.

'Edwin, it's not like you to be unsensible,' said Chinese Lady. 'If I started with Boots and poor Emily, I'd never stop counting.'

'Your accomplishment, Maisie, as the fount of all, is something to be proud of,' said Mr Finch.

'Never mind that, whatever it means,' said Chinese Lady. 'I wasn't talking about everybody, I was talking more about our grandchildren and great-grandchildren.'

'Ah,' said Mr Finch, 'that should be a little easier.'

'Easier?' said Chinese Lady. 'I don't know how many times I've mentioned I can't hardly remember them all.'

'True, many times,' said Mr Finch, and hid himself behind his newspaper.

'Mind, I'm pleased for Eloise and Colonel Lucas. Lor', and there's Patsy and Daniel as well.'

She went on in this vein, and Mr Finch, knowing she was on her favourite hobby horse, accepted it all with a smile while reading about how the Labour government was struggling to preserve its authority in the face of its narrow majority.

Meanwhile, expectant Patsy was letting husband Daniel know on a daily basis that she sure was intrigued about Bess's American guy coming over from Chicago. As the guy was from Chicago, Daniel responded repeatedly, did Patsy think he'd bring a tommy gun with him? Patsy said Daniel was a scatty echo of his dad, who thought Chicago was still full of gangsters and hoodlums.

Chapter Twenty-Three

The girl, carrying a book, left the Denmark Hill public library that afternoon. The sun had broken through, taking the chill off the day. The male person, who had been hovering and casting his eyes at her, made up his mind. He followed her. He had no book, but he did have a purpose, particularly as there were no other people around.

He made a silent and speedy advance as the girl approached the point where an old car was parked at the kerbside.

From the direction of Herne Hill on the other side of the road a white farm van came motoring slowly, the driver looking for a particular house. He was suddenly alerted by an astonishing sight, that of a man coming up behind a girl and throwing a hand around her head. He clapped his paw over her mouth and began to drag her to the parked car, she dropping the library book and kicking wildly, her screams muffled by his hand.

The white farm van roared across the quiet road and stopped with a screech of tyres. Out leapt the driver and ran at the assailant. He wrenched him away from the struggling girl and struck his temple a ferocious blow. The man staggered, reeled, recovered, issued a spit-flecked curse, and ran for the old car. The girl collapsed against the chest of the hero of the moment.

He stared at her. She, white-faced, stared back. At the kerbside, the engine of the shabby car fired and away the vehicle went with a bang of its exhaust and a rattle of its body.

'I don't-a believe it,' said Enrico Cellino, Italian farmhand, gazing into dizzy blue eyes.

'Oh, crikey,' gasped Miss Paula Adams, 'where did you come from?'

'From the farm van, didn't I?' said Enrico.

'That man – the rotten beast – oh, I'd faint if you weren't holding me – I can't believe how you got here just in time.'

'God, He knows,' said Enrico, 'I don't. Paula, you are shaking.'

'I should think I am,' said Paula, quite sure the sound of her knocking knees could be heard. Her heart was pumping in scared tumult. 'Oh, help, what a beast. Thanks ever so for turning up like a miracle.'

'Come, sit in the van,' said Enrico. 'Sit and get your breath, eh? Come.'

He picked up the library book, and with his arm around her he walked her to the van, the sides of which bore the inscription, 'ADAMS DAIRY FARM, WESTERHAM VALE'. He helped her into the passenger seat. A bus rumbled by as he circled the van and folded himself into the driver's seat.

'I still can't believe the way you were suddenly there,' said Paula.

'Paula, do you know that man?'

'I don't know him, but I've seen him in the library,' said Paula, still a little pale of face. She looked very girlish in a warm sweater and skirt, a pull-on knitted hat over her head. Enrico thought how terribly frightened and vulnerable she must have felt. 'Did you get the number of his rotten old car?' she asked.

'Ah, no, I was too concerned for you,' said Enrico. 'I must take you to your home, and tell your father. That swine of a pig, he must be caught.'

'But what brought you to Denmark Hill?' asked Paula, breathing a little easier.

Enrico explained. Signora Adams had asked him to deliver many joints of beef to her parents, enough for them and their close relatives. Signora Adams did not think he could make the delivery to everyone, but this could be done by Paula's parents. It was because the bullock had been shot a week ago, and there was much beef to be shared out. Signora Adams had given him instructions on how to reach Paula's home in Denmark Hill, so see, this was how he had arrived here, wasn't it, eh?

'I am happy I did,' he said.

'So am I, I should say so,' breathed Paula. 'Gosh, what a coincidence out of the blue. Look, my home is only a little way from here, on the other side of the road. I'll show you.'

'You are better?' said Enrico.

'Much,' said Paula.

'Good, then so am I,' said Enrico, 'but I don't think your parents will like what we must tell them.'

Sammy and Susie's house, built after the war on the site of their bombed one, impressed Enrico. He opened his eyes wide as he surveyed its handsome frontage, its front door adorned with an ancient but gleaming brass knocker and a matching letter box.

These had been obtained from Eli Greenberg, who could always find such items for Sammy, even if he swore that what Sammy offered for them took the shirt off his back.

Sammy and Susie were at home, Phoebe out in the park with a girlfriend. Sammy and Susie were appalled by what Paula and Enrico told them. Sammy, on hearing that the number of the pervert's car had not been noted, at once drove to the library in his own car, taking Susie, Paula and Enrico with him. A counter assistant, given a description of the man, was immediately responsive.

'Yes, we know him,' she said, 'he's here every Saturday afternoon. He was here up to about half an hour ago. You say he actually attacked you, Miss Adams?'

'He did,' said Paula.

'And I saw him, didn't I?' said Enrico, looking a little out of place in a darned sweater and worn corduroy trousers, his thick black hair in need of a trim and a brush.

'I'm terribly shocked,' said the assistant.

'I'm livid,' said Sammy. 'What's his name and address?'

'His name is William Jarvis, I know that,' said the assistant. 'He regularly takes out a book. His address? Just a moment.' She referred to the library's file of borrowers. 'He lives in Kimpton Road, Camberwell.' She gave the house number. 'Will you inform the police?'

'I'll do some of my own informing at first, person to person,' said Sammy, expression a fixed one of grim intent. 'Thanks for your help. Much obliged.'

*   *   *

Outside the house in question was a parked car, ancient and dirty. The house had been divided into two flats, ground and upper floor. A large and lumpy woman, answering Sammy's knock, fixed him with a look of aggression, much as if people who knocked on her front door without being asked to could be considered suspect. Sammy had Enrico with him, having dropped Susie and Paula at home.

'Yes?' said the woman.

'Afternoon to you, missus,' said Sammy with a deceptive smile. 'I'm looking for Willy.'

'Eh?'

'Mr Jarvis.'

'Oh, him.'

'Is he in?'

'Not in my place he ain't, seeing he gives me the creeps, and I don't mind who hears me say so,' said the woman. Her aggressive look gave way to an expression of hope. 'Here, if he owes yer money, you can turn him inside out as far as I'm concerned. Is that what you're after?'

'I'm after his shirt tail,' said Sammy.

'You got my blessing, then,' said the woman. 'He's upstairs, in his own flat. Go on, up you go, if you want.'

'Much obliged,' said Sammy, and up he and Enrico went. A closed door confronted them. Sammy rang the bell. The door opened after a while, and Sammy found himself looking at a face that was as pink and soft as a child's, an ageless face with no suggestion that it had ever needed shaving. The eyes, however, were an ugly protruding blue, the lids a waxy pale yellow, the mouth a thin-lipped slit. Ruddy hell, he thought, imagine having that evil baby-face wandering round a public library. I never saw a plainer bad egg. 'Good afternoon, Mr Jarvis,' he said, lifting his hat and leaving it in his hand.

The protruding eyes fell on Enrico, in a manner of speaking. The waxy lids twitched.

'Don't know either of you,' said Jarvis, his voice oddly silky. 'Can't spare time for you. Goodbye.'

He made an attempt to slam the door. Sammy and Enrico each put a foot against it. Sammy barged, and the door hit Jarvis. More accurately, it thumped him, eliminating him as an impediment to entry. Well, Sammy and Enrico weren't there with any intention of respecting the bloke's person. In they went, closing the door behind them. Jarvis backed off into his living room, a place of junk and erotic literature.

'This is him, Rico?' said Sammy, placing his hat on a chair.

'I say so for sure, don't I?' said Enrico.

Sammy looked at his prey and, noting his strangely repulsive appearance, felt sick at what kind of perversion he might have committed on Paula.

'You horrible lump of garbage,' he said, 'I've got a feeling we'd be doing Camberwell a favour by chopping you into little bits. But we're not staying long enough for that, and we forgot the chopper, anyway. We've just got the right amount of time to make sure you never get yourself within a mile of my daughter again. A mile. You got that? See a doctor about your complaint, you sick sack of wormy horse-meat. Well, you'll have to see him for a new complaint, in any case. Broken legs.'

'I'll see the police first,' said Jarvis in the voice that didn't go with his unpleasant looks. 'So let me warn you that you'll be making a serious mistake if—'

Sammy shut him up by hitting him on the mouth, his fist crunching lips and teeth. Then he took his jacket off. Enrico stood by, watching in admiration as Paula's father set about giving the pervert the hiding of his life. There was some initial resistance, a wild and vicious kind. Sammy, tall, well-muscled and unspoiled by any kind of debilitating living, made mincemeat of all resistance. He considered the law unlikely to deal suitably with this kind of blot on the Adams landscape. What was called for was a bit of personal brutality.

It was the Adams way to make a personal thing of dealing with crooks and misfits who seriously upset the family, especially as seriously as this, although Boots would have advised Sammy on the merits of hiring an outsider to put a character as obnoxious as Jarvis into a condition of near paralysis.

Sammy's gorge was too heated for him to consider anything but instant justice. Downstairs the large woman heard a chair crash.

'Now that's what I call a real man,' she said to her meek and mild husband.

'Him?' said meek-and-mild. 'Jarvis?'

'No, yer silly bugger, the bloke that spoke to me.'

'Upright and true, was he, me love?' said meek-and-mild.

'A man.' The ceiling rumbled. 'You can hear he is, can't you?'

'It don't sound too peaceful, I'll admit,' said meek-and-mild.

It wasn't for Jarvis. He finished up bruised and agonized all over, his head singing, his mouth bleeding, some front teeth very loose, and his left eye closed and swollen. He lay on the floor and stayed there, hissing bubbles.

'How's that, Rico?' asked Sammy.

'Bloody good, Signor Adams,' said Enrico. 'Very hurt, I think, but not dead. Dead would not be good.'

'If there's a next time,' said Sammy, putting his jacket back on, 'dead might be the word.' He looked down at Jarvis. 'I hope you heard that.'

Jarvis whimpered.

Susie pounced as soon as Sammy and Enrico were back. She was still furious.

'Did you get him?'

'He won't be seen near Paula again,' said Sammy.

'He's at the police station under arrest?' said Susie.

'No, on his floor,' said Sammy. 'I don't fancy he'll be up too quick, either.'

'Sammy? Sammy, what have you done?'

'Flattened him,' said Sammy.

'Not half, you bet,' said Enrico.

'You had a fight with him?' said Susie.

'I hit him a few times,' said Sammy.

'You didn't call the police?'

'Didn't need them, I had a referee,' said Sammy. 'Rico saw fair play.'

'Sammy, that man should be charged,' said Susie.

'It would mean Paula appearing in court,' said Sammy, 'and I ain't having that, Susie. Where is she?'

'In the lounge.'

'Crying?'

'No, reading her library book.'

'What a trouper,' said Sammy with a breath of

relief. 'If any girl has got what it takes to get over that ponce laying hands on her, it's our Paula.'

'A fine girl, not half, isn't she?' said Enrico.

'Enrico,' said Susie, 'we can't thank you enough for being there at the right time, and for what you did. But the man's a danger, Sammy, and ought to be locked up.'

Sammy thought. He was still resistant to any idea of Paula having to appear in court at the tender age of fifteen.

'I'll have a word with Boots,' he said.

'Yes, do that, Sammy,' said Susie, long a believer in Boots's aptitude for dealing with family crises. 'See what he says.'

'Ah, he's a lawyer, yes?' said Enrico.

'He could have been,' said Sammy. 'As it is, he's my eldest brother and the family's Lord High-Up.'

'Excuse me, signore?' said Enrico.

'Just my husband's funny idea about his eldest brother,' said Susie.

Enrico smiled, and Susie thought what an attractive young man he was, and typically Italian with his dark Latin looks.

'It's a joke?' he said.

'It's no joke,' said Sammy.

'Ah,' said Enrico, uncomprehending. But then, only people who knew the Adams family intimately would have known what Sammy meant.

Susie said how good Enrico had been about Paula. And having been told why Kate and David's farmhand happened to be in Denmark Hill, she thanked him for bringing the joints of beef. Enrico said they were still in the van, and that he would now bring them in.

'Well, good on you, Rico,' said Sammy.

'And I'll make a pot of tea,' said Susie. She smiled at Enrico. 'Or would you prefer coffee?'

'*Si*, signora, thank you,' said Enrico. 'Then I must go, see? I still have much to do at the farm before dark.'

Sammy went to see Paula, finding her curled up on a settee by the window. She did have the library book with her, but wasn't reading it. She was looking out of the window.

'Paula me pet?' Sammy felt she was suffering reaction.

She turned her head.

'Oh, hello, Daddy,' she said, 'did you get to see that man?'

'I did,' said Sammy.

'What happened?' asked Paula.

'I've got to be frank,' said Sammy, 'I gave him a hiding and took a few of his teeth out.'

'Oh, good, that'll teach the beast,' said Paula, and Sammy experienced a flood of relief at how normal she sounded. 'Thanks, Daddy. Did Enrico help?'

Sammy swallowed a lump, cleared his throat and said briskly, 'He refereed the contest. Very fair about it, and did a good job counting the bloke out. He's a first-class Eyetie, Paula.'

'Italian,' said Paula.

'He's still first-class,' said Sammy.

'Did you get bruised?' asked Paula.

'You can take it as gospel, all the bruises were exclusive to weird Willy,' said Sammy. 'It wouldn't surprise me if he was still on his floor.' With a residue of concern, he asked, 'You all right, Paula love?'

'I'm fine, apart from my knees still feeling a bit

shaky,' said Paula. 'I'm glad you sorted the beast out, Daddy, and we don't have to tell the rest of the family about him, do we?'

'Understood,' said Sammy.

'Oh, good,' said Paula, accepting that Enrico knew and that her mum had phoned David and Kate to explain why their farmhand would be late back. 'I really am fine now and I've been enjoying my library book.'

'Bless you,' said Sammy, a little huskiness indicating he was emotionally touched. 'Well,' he said, brisk again, 'your mum's making a pot of tea for us, and coffee for Rico. Come and join us, eh?'

'Love to,' said Paula, uncurling herself. 'Dad, I think I like Rico.'

'So do I,' said Sammy. 'Bit of all right, and that's a fact.'

'Of course, I wouldn't be able to see much of him,' said Paula, getting to her feet. 'I mean, him living at the farm and me living here.'

'Eh?' said Sammy. 'Is something going to happen to surprise me?'

'I don't know why it should surprise you,' said Paula. 'After all, I'm fifteen, not twelve, and just fancy, I've never had a boyfriend. Supposing Rico would like me as a girlfriend? He did ask if he could take me to the pictures, even when he'd only known me for five minutes, so I'm sure he likes me.'

'He's a bit older than you,' said Sammy. 'You're only fifteen and he's nearly twenty.'

'Well, fancy that, it's hardly anything,' said Paula with all the blitheness of the carefree young.

Well, blind O'Reilly, thought Sammy, it's come to pass. We're going to have to tell Chinese Lady there's an Italian bloke who'll probably be knocking at our door.

He laughed.

'All right, Paula girl, let's see how it turns out, shall we?' he said indulgently.

By the time Enrico left, Paula had said she would visit the farm again, if Kate and David would have her. Which made Enrico depart greatly relieved at her healthy recovery from something very bad, and whistling the overture to an Italian opera.

Chapter Twenty-Four

Sunday afternoon.

The month of March, without being asked, was taking on the mantle of April to bestow alternating sunshine and showers on London.

Wearing a raincoat, Lulu arrived at the home of Paul's parents on Denmark Hill. On the bus she hadn't failed to notice the middle-class aspect of this residential thoroughfare. And when she reached Tommy and Vi's abode, it was as she expected, imposing enough for a family of middle-class capitalists, and worth at least fifteen hundred quid. However, when introduced by Paul to his parents, she quickly identified them as cockneys, even if time and their environment had taken the basic nuances out of their accents.

'So you're Paul's assistant,' smiled Vi.

'Heard a lot about you,' said Tommy.

'Oh, really?' said Lulu, raincoat off and a folder under her arm. 'Good or bad stuff?'

'Oh, he's said lots of nice things about you,' said Vi, noting brown eyes behind the spectacles, a clear if rather pale complexion and straight shining black hair worn in a style that reminded Vi of depictions of Cleopatra.

'What about the other things?' asked Lulu, clad in a mannish brown pullover, a white shirt-blouse, and a dark maroon skirt, thus showing she didn't bother with matching colours. Her one concession to glamour was a pair of silk stockings, pulled on at the last moment. 'I bet there's been other things.'

'Nothing you'd black his eye for,' said Tommy. Lulu thought him quite handsome, and his wife kind of gentle. But they were moneyed all right. One could tell that from their clothes and their front-room furniture, which included a handsome polished walnut radiogram and some very attractive table lamps.

'Well, parents,' said Paul, 'now that you've met the office wondergirl, excuse us while we get together to do our homework.'

'On this London march?' said Tommy.

'Oh, he's told you about that, has he?' said Lulu.

'Several times,' said Tommy.

'Did he tell you it was my idea?'

'Did he?' asked Tommy of Vi.

'Did you, lovey?' asked Vi of Paul.

'Several times,' grinned Paul. 'And I told her a band was your idea, Mum.'

'Well, I did think that would be nice,' said Vi. 'You could get a Salvation Army band.'

Lulu blinked.

'You can get gusto out of a Salvation Army band,' observed Tommy, keeping his face straight.

'I don't think Lulu had a religious march in mind,' said Paul. 'Still, she might consider a bit of rousing religious music, like "Onward, Christian Soldiers".'

'I hope we're going to improve on that this afternoon,' said Lulu.

'Come on,' said Paul, 'we'll get out of the way and find somewhere quiet.'

'You can have this room,' said Vi, 'while your dad and me use the living room. We'll have tea at five, shall we?'

'Fine, Mum,' said Paul.

'Enjoy yourselves,' said Tommy, 'but don't bring the house down if you're going to sing "The Red Flag".'

'Don't you vote Labour, Mr Adams?' asked Lulu.

'Can't afford to,' said Tommy. 'I'd be voting for a lot of increased taxes. I ain't fond of increased taxes.'

'It's all for the benefit of the poor,' said Lulu.

'I'll be one of them myself if we don't get rid of the Labour government,' said Tommy, and Vi steered him gently out of the room before a political argument started in earnest.

'Your dad needs converting,' said Lulu.

'I've tried it many times,' said Paul. 'No go. Come on, take a seat, and we'll go through our notes, first about the route of the march.'

They sat down on a settee, Lulu determinedly keeping space between them. Paul spread a map of London over his knees. The march was timed for the second Sunday in May, and Lulu's dad had said he'd help through the Home Office to get police permission. The police would want to know exact details of the route well in advance. So this afternoon, Paul and Lulu had to settle the matter. Lulu, consulting her notes, said the march should start in the graveyard of the poor, Shoreditch High Street.

'Graveyard?' said Paul.

'What else?' said Lulu. 'That's where the poor starved to death before the war, got bombed to death during the war, and are starving to death again now.'

'Under our Labour government?' said Paul.

'I mean they still can't afford the kind of food that loads the tables of the middle classes,' said Lulu.

'No-one's starving,' said Paul, 'the Party's made sure of that with Social Welfare. In any case, ought we to start in a graveyard?'

'That's a figure of speech,' said Lulu. 'From Shoreditch High Street. After I've made the opening speech.'

'I do that,' said Paul.

'We'll talk about it,' said Lulu.

'I'll make the speech as chief organizer and the bloke in charge,' said Paul.

'No, the local MP and my dad will be in charge,' said Lulu. 'Then we'll march down Bishopsgate into Threadneedle Street. We'll have our first stop outside the Bank. That's the citadel of capitalist power. The Shoreditch MP and my dad will both address the people there.'

'There won't be many of 'em, not on a Sunday,' said Paul. 'My notes tell me we should start at St Paul's Cathedral just after the main morning service ends.'

'No, that's our second stop,' said Lulu.

'Listen, woolly ears, this is supposed to be a consultation, not a formal adoption of your ideas,' said Paul.

'My ideas are better,' said Lulu. 'They come from my working-class roots. Look, you're not a bad bloke. But you don't have any real Socialist fire.'

'Yours will go up in smoke if you keep giving me sauce,' said Paul.

'Oh, yes? You and who else?' said Lulu.

The consultation turned into an argument. Suggestions for the route, the stops, and who addressed the anticipated multitudes, were all chucked at each other, with Lulu beginning to burn.

Finally, Paul said, 'Take an order, my girl. Only speak when you're asked to.' Lulu hit him with her folder, jumped up to belabour him, but fell over his feet and landed on the carpet. Her skirt looked any-old-how, but her silk stockings looked fabulous all the way up to her thighs. 'Legs, Lulu, legs,' said Paul. Lulu actually blushed. He stood up, reached and helped her to her feet. Her glasses were on the end of her nose, her eyes confused. Paul, realizing she was far from being a tarty girl, felt quite tender towards her then, simply because she seemed genuinely embarrassed. 'Sorry about that,' he said.

'Where are my specs?' asked Lulu vaguely.

'There,' said Paul, and pushed them into place. 'Come on, let's be friends, let's consult as if we like each other.'

Lulu, still a little flushed, sat down again, and they began a friendlier discussion. Paul agreed that the march should start in Shoreditch, and Lulu agreed he should make his share of speeches. The amicable discussion flowed on, Lulu almost chummy and Paul refraining from throwing his weight around. He demurred, however, about ending the march at Buckingham Palace. He said he didn't, in any case, think they'd be allowed to.

'Well, we ought to be,' said Lulu. She blinked, frowned, and recovered the senses that had floated away from her. 'Yes, we ought to be allowed. Especially if him and her come out to see what's going on.'

'Him and her?' said Paul.

'Our capitalist Majesties,' said Lulu. 'What a great chance we'd have.'

'Chance for what?'

'Turning the megaphone on them.'

'And?'

'Addressing them directly.'

'Oh, I see,' said Paul. 'We suggest they might like to vacate the Palace, do we?'

'Yes, and turn it over to retired workers,' said Lulu. 'I'll admit it all sounds drastic, but—'

'Fatuous, more like,' said Paul. 'What a crackpot. Lulu, you'll give fiery Socialism a bad name if you keep on like this.'

'Don't get personal,' said Lulu.

Tommy put his head in.

'Tea's ready,' he said.

'What's on the table?' asked Paul.

'Shrimps and winkles,' said Tommy.

Lulu rolled her eyes.

When they were all seated at the dining-room table, Vi said, 'I always think shrimps and winkles make a nice Sunday tea. My old dad, bless him, just loved them.' She didn't mention her mother served them under protest. Her mother regarded them as common.

'I never thought middle classes ate shrimps and winkles,' said Lulu.

'Oh, I don't know hardly anything about the middle classes,' said Vi, 'except for the vicar and some of the ladies I meet at the Women's Institute.

Are you middle class, dear? Only you speak very nicely.'

Paul counted that innocent remark as one in the eye for Lulu. It made Tommy grin.

'I'm working class by birth and struggle,' said Lulu.

'Oh, you're one of us, then,' said Vi. 'Mind, we're a lot better off than we used to be, thank goodness. Have some bread and butter with your shrimps and winkles.' Vi had removed all the winkles from their shells, which Paul thought spoiled the fun of watching Lulu use a pin.

Lulu began her tea. She did know all about shrimps and winkles, of course, and she enjoyed the tasty mixture of shellfish, consuming it with a thin slice of bread and butter. I don't suppose they're eating anything very much of a meal in Shoreditch, she thought, and I ought to feel guilty about enjoying mine. Still, I won't. It would be uncomplimentary to Paul's mother, especially as she's quite a nice woman. What's Paul grinning about, I wonder? My legs, probably. If he says something sexy about my silk stockings later, I'll hit him again.

'How did your consulting lark go?' asked Tommy, openly studying the young people.

'We got through quite a lot,' said Paul, 'but we're stuck on whether or not to end the march at Buckingham Palace.'

'With the Red Flags flying?' said Tommy.

'Oh, goodness, I hope not, the King and Queen might be at home,' said Vi.

'Well, we hope they'll come out and listen to us,' said Lulu.

'You mean you're hoping,' said Paul.

'Barmy,' said Tommy.

'Now, Tommy,' said Vi.

'We'd like to have the chance of addressing him and her,' said Lulu, who didn't believe in making a secret of her Socialist ideals.

'Him and her?' said Tommy.

'Lulu means King George and Queen Liz,' said Paul.

'Oh,' said Vi, who'd never heard anyone else refer to the monarchs as him and her.

'Well,' said Lulu, 'it does seem to me a bit wasteful. Just the two of them and their daughters living in the Palace. There's probably about five hundred rooms. And probably a conservatory as big as Alexandra Palace.'

'Lor', five hundred rooms?' said Vi. 'And one of those glass conservatories? Oh, well, they've got to keep up appearances, I suppose. Have some more shrimps, dear.'

Lulu helped herself, saying, 'Thanks. Don't you think the Palace could be used as a retirement home for the poor?'

'Barmy,' said Tommy.

'There was ever such a thrilling mystery play on the wireless last night,' said Vi.

'Yes, I wonder if him and her were listening to it?' mused Paul.

'Don't you start,' said Tommy.

'Yes, it's a bit disrespectful, Paul lovey,' said Vi.

'But we all ought to be equal,' said Lulu.

'We can't be,' said Tommy, 'we're all born to be different, except for loonies. They're all equally barmy.'

'We had ever such a handsome joint of beef for our dinner today,' said Vi. 'Our other son, David, is a farmer and sent it to us. Paul's Uncle Sammy brought it round last night. Have you met Paul's Uncle Sammy, Lulu?'

'Is he the family's leading capitalist?' asked Lulu.

'Oh, nothing like that,' said Vi, 'just a hard-working businessman, like his brothers. He doesn't have anything to do with people like – like –'

'Rockefeller?' said Tommy.

'Ought to be tried for criminal exploitation of the masses,' said Lulu.

'My Uncle Sammy?' said Paul.

'Rockefeller,' said Lulu. Addressing Tommy, she said, 'I hope you don't mind my being frank, Mr Adams.'

'I like it,' said Tommy, 'but I'm glad I'm not Rockefeller.'

Lulu enjoyed her tea, taking a great liking to Vi's home-made fruit cake. She ate simple shop food herself, she said, like pork pies or corned beef. Vi said oh, don't you do any savoury cooking? Lulu said she only cooked when she had to, as it wasn't one of her targets in life. Paul explained to his parents that her targets were all to do with making the world a better place for the poor and deprived. Well, said Tommy, savoury cooking for a start wouldn't half improve their lot.

'If young Lulu here took some cookery courses,' he said, 'she could make a target of poor old grannies just waiting for a plate of home-cooked fish and chips, and I couldn't say fairer.'

'Rattling good idea, Dad,' said Paul. 'I'm behind Lulu all the way on some of her targets, and I'd be right behind her if she did cookery at evening classes. What d'you say, Lulu, d'you fancy learning to be a first-class cook for the benefit of hungry old grannies and the like?'

'It does sound Christian,' said Vi.

'It's not my style,' said Lulu. 'But if Paul fancies it, he's got my best wishes.'

Vi had a bit of a coughing fit.

That over, she said, 'Would you like another cup of tea, Lulu?'

'Thanks, but no,' said Lulu. 'I don't think I could manage another. Oh, and thanks too for a lovely tea. Now Paul and I ought to finish our homework.'

It didn't take long to finalize their notes in readiness for Lulu to type out tomorrow.

'Well, that's it,' said Paul. 'Now, if you ever did think of getting married, would you mind if the bloke belonged to a middle-class family?'

'Listen,' said Lulu, 'I'm married to my career. And the last thing I'd ever do would be to let myself get chained to a middle-class sink.'

'Still, you never know,' said Paul. 'Supposing in a couple of years I popped the question –'

'What?'

'If I did, I'd leave out the kitchen sink.'

'Oh, you poor bloke, you're out of your tiny mind,' said Lulu, and regarded him sadly.

'All I'd ask is that you get your hair curled for the wedding day,' said Paul.

'Oh, that's all, is it?' said Lulu. 'What's up with you? Are you trying to tell me you fancy me as much as that? And what about Henrietta?'

'Never mind Henrietta, I fancy you've got more

'promise than you think,' said Paul.

'It's for the Party,' said Lulu. 'And I'm off before you start molesting me. Come on.'

She said goodbye to Tommy and Vi, thanked them again for the tea and their kindness, and allowed Paul to walk her to the bus stop. On the way she said she wouldn't have thought his parents really were capitalists, since they were a homely couple and genuinely nice people. But they obviously lived in style. Paul said they'd both worked very hard for what they had now, which was why he could put up with them voting Conservative.

'Going back to your possible change of mind in a year or so,' he said, as they waited for a bus, 'take your time to—'

'Nothing doing,' said Lulu. 'Forget it.'

'I'm in favour of marriage myself,' said Paul.

'So are most men,' said Lulu. 'They get an unpaid slave.' Unexpectedly then, she gave him a smile. 'Still, some blokes are nicer than others. So don't think I'm unappreciative.'

'Oh, well,' said Paul, 'let's settle for a partnership dedicated to the cause of the workers.'

'And the march of the Young Socialists,' said Lulu.

A bus arrived. Two people alighted, and Lulu boarded.

'See you tomorrow morning,' said Paul.

'You bet,' said Lulu. 'And thanks for the Sunday tea. Lovely.'

The bus moved off, and Paul walked back home. When he arrived, his mum said it was nice to meet Lulu, but what a funny girl.

'Yes,' said Paul, 'I'm going to have to marry her and quieten her down, or she'll end up as a

Commie and get expelled from the Party. It'll be her ruination.'

'Marry her, you said?' breathed Vi, and sank weakly into an armchair.

'Barmy,' said Tommy, 'both of 'em.'

Chapter Twenty-Five

Monday morning.

Paul arrived wearing a brisk, businesslike air. Lulu, already at her desk, was her usual practical self in her jeans. She was also wearing the shirt and mannish pullover of yesterday. This thing she has about looking more like a bloke than a female, thought Paul, has got to be cured. It's hurting my eyes.

'Morning, Lulu,' he said.

'Same to you,' said Lulu.

'I suggest you start by typing out all those finalized notes on the march,' said Paul. 'Any letters can be done later. That all right with you?'

'It's just what I had in mind,' said Lulu, spectacles gleaming with enthusiasm.

'Right, get cracking, then,' said Paul.

'Yes, sir, will do, sir,' said Lulu, and took the cover off her typewriter. 'Oh, yes, and might I say again it was a pleasure meeting your parents? Your mum reminded me of my own mum. She's a dear. And your dad's nice too. I bet he voted Labour before he got rich.'

'He's not rich, he's comfortably off,' said Paul.

'Oh, well, he's still nice,' said Lulu generously, and got down to her work.

The morning began to advance pleasantly. Much to Lulu's disgust, however, Henrietta Trevalyan came in just after ten, and without knocking.

'Good morning, Lulu, good morning, Paul,' she trilled, looking like a garden nymph in a primrose-coloured spring coat and a green hat. To Lulu's eyes, the hat looked soppy.

'Well, hello, Henrietta,' said Paul.

'I can't stay,' said Henrietta. Hoo-blimey-hooray, thought Lulu. 'I've just popped in, Paul, to let you know I've got two stalls tickets for the musical *Oklahoma!* on Saturday evening.'

Oklahoma! being a great hit in the West End, Paul asked, 'Who's going to be your lucky escort?'

Henrietta leaned over his desk, gave him a sweet smile, and said, 'I do hope it'll be you. Can you make Saturday evening?'

'I won't need dragging,' said Paul.

'Lovely,' trilled Henrietta. 'Will you call for me at seven, then?'

'I'll be there,' said Paul.

'Oh, jolly good, but must dash,' said Henrietta, and Paul saw her out, not just from the office, but from the building.

It left Lulu fuming. And there was something else. A worried feeling. Not for herself, of course. For Paul. As a marrying kind of bloke, he might end up with gushing Henrietta on his arm. She'd turn him into some kind of pet.

Lulu ground her teeth.

When Paul came back, she said, 'You're not getting serious about tarty Henrietta, are you?'

'Not while I'm serious about you,' said Paul, 'but I like her curly hair.'

'Ugh,' said Lulu, and worried a bit more. Not for herself, of course.

Sammy was talking to Boots in the latter's office, giving him confidential details about what had happened to Paula on Saturday after she left the public library, and how David and Kate's Italian farmhand, on the way to deliver beef to Susie, had played his part in saving Paula from what the sick assailant had in mind for her.

Boots's grey eyes showed a glint of steel, but he only said, 'Then what, Sammy?'

'What do you think?' said Sammy, and recounted the rest of the unpleasant story, finishing with what William Jarvis looked like on the floor of his flat. Battered, bruised, bleeding and half-dead.

'But Susie thinks the coppers should be told,' he said. 'Myself, I'm against Paula having to appear in court.'

'Susie, I suppose, feels it'll happen to some other girl if the bugger isn't put away,' said Boots. 'Well, we'll send Mitch round to him once a week.' Mitch was the firm's van driver. 'With a note.'

'Oh, yes? Wishing him a happy birthday?' said Sammy.

'Just say, "Fungus, you're being watched".'

'Eh?'

'That's all,' said Boots, 'but once a week regularly. If he's out, Mitch can slip it under his door. If he's in, Mitch can hand it over personally. That would be preferable. Mitch is no lightweight, any more than you are, Sammy.'

'Got you, Boots,' said Sammy. 'Fungus is what we might call appropriate.'

'Yes, fungi grow out of rotting wood,' said Boots.

'Eh?' said Sammy. 'What's fungi?'

'Plural of fungus,' said Boots.

'Stop showing off,' said Sammy. 'Still, I like the message, all of it. It's – let's see, educated?'

'Once a week will add up to an exercise in psychology,' said Boots.

'That's educated,' said Sammy. 'Yes, got you, Boots. Ta.'

'You're welcome,' said Boots. 'How is Paula?'

'Good as a first-class trouper,' said Sammy, 'and with a fancy for having Italian Rico as her first boyfriend.'

'Girls like heroes,' said Boots, 'and I suppose you could say Paula deserves one. Any news from Hilda Campion?'

'Not yet,' said Sammy.

'You'll have to think about chasing her,' said Boots.

'I ain't in the market for chasing females,' said Sammy. 'Susie's against it. Still, I know what you mean. I'll give Hilda until tomorrow, and then I'll have a word with her. By the way, Paula would like it if no-one else in the family got to know about Saturday.'

'Understood, Sammy,' said Boots, 'although I'd like to discuss it with Polly.'

'No further than Polly,' said Sammy.

'No further,' promised Boots.

'Well, I've got a busload of work on me desk and I'd better get on with it, or the overheads might pile up behind my back,' said Sammy.

'Off you go, then,' said Boots.

He's done it again, thought Sammy as he went back to his office, he's turned me into the office boy again with his pat on my head. One day it'll do my brainbox an injury, and who'll look after the overheads then, someone tell me that.

'Sammy?' Rachel appeared at his door as he sat down at his large and handsome desk, the desk that always made him feel in command of the business.

'Come in,' said Sammy. 'That's if you're not thinking of patting my head.'

'Patting your head?' said Rachel.

'It's just been done by Boots,' said Sammy. 'He's a knowing old soldier, and I respect him for it, but he's still got his lordly habits, and more so since coming out of the war as a general.'

'A colonel, Sammy,' said Rachel.

'Same thing, good as,' said Sammy.

'Boots, of course, does wear his lordly crown with style,' said Rachel.

'Don't I know it?' said Sammy. 'I ought to, seeing I've lived with it all me life. Anyway, what's on your mind, Rachel me old friend?'

'Sammy, I've just had a phone call from Mr Blenkinsop,' said Rachel.

'What, good old Oswald from the Air Ministry, the bloke that kept contracts coming our way all through the war?' said Sammy, perking up.

'That's the gentleman,' said Rachel. 'Sammy, he wants to know if we'd like to tender for the new RAF uniforms, men's and women's. I said we'd be delighted, and he invited me to go up and see him on Friday morning.'

'Well, bless me soul,' said Sammy, 'ain't you a

fetching female woman, Rachel? No wonder Osbald the Good took a fancy to you. Yes, you go up solo and see him, Rachel. I'll stay put. Even in business there's times when three's a crowd. Get the specifications and a guarantee all materials will be delivered, and I'll give you a signed certificate stating you're Queen Piccalilli of Camberwell.'

'Never mind the certificate, Sammy,' said Rachel. She laughed. 'My life, isn't it enough to know that at my age I'm still fetching?'

'Well, you go and let Osbert see you are,' said Sammy. 'Give his mince pies a treat. That'll help him to mix honest pleasure with generous business.'

'I should show him my legs?' said Rachel.

'I'm not recommending that,' said Sammy. 'He might jump his desk and make you leave premature without a contract.'

'Very good, Sammy,' smiled Rachel.

'I've got faith in you, Rachel,' said Sammy, which sentiment was a pleasure to her.

During the afternoon, the constituency's agent came down to impart sad news to Paul and Lulu. The march was off.

'Off?' said Paul.

'Off,' said the agent.

Lulu's spectacles dulled over.

'Off?' she said.

'Off,' repeated the agent.

'For what reason?' asked Paul.

The agent said the Home Office Minister wouldn't allow it, and that the Party had decided the time wasn't right. The Government was under constant attack during debates in the House, and too many people among the electorate were becoming critical about issues that weren't being resolved. Like a higher wages policy. If the march took place, all kinds of wavering Labour voters would take umbrage at a mass of Young Socialists waving Joe Stalin's Red Flag and bawling for an economic revolution. Any kind of revolution wasn't popular with the broad masses of British people. They'd probably see the march as an effort by the Party to encourage riots. And riots, said the agent, led to revolution.

Lulu ground her teeth.

'We don't intend to go in for anything like that,' she said.

'And certainly not on a Sunday,' said Paul.

'We're aiming for stirring stuff that would get the waverers cheering,' said Lulu. 'And revive their belief in the Party.'

'What we'd like in place of the march', said the agent, 'is to see you and Paul doing your stuff from a good old-fashioned soapbox at Speakers' Corner for several Sundays.'

'Come again?' said Paul.

'With a backing of Young Socialists to help you cope with hecklers.'

'But there'd only be a comparatively small crowd of people listening,' said Lulu. 'Whereas a rousing march with stops for speeches would reach thousands of ears.'

'That's what the Party's afraid of,' said the agent, 'that the ears wouldn't be receptive to what they'd be hearing. Too much like political agitation. That's out just now. The PM himself is backing moderation for the time being. He's emphasizing the fact that the

British people on the whole are conservative. Conservative with a small "c". Try your luck at Speakers' Corner. Sorry and all that, but no march, full stop.'

At which point the agent beat a retreat from the glare of Lulu's heated glasses.

'Suddenly,' said Paul, 'all our work's going up in smoke.'

'So am I,' said Lulu. 'I'm so hot and fuming, it's a wonder I don't explode out of my jeans like a rocket.'

'Go ahead,' said Paul.

'Oh, you'd like that, would you?' said Lulu. 'Me shooting upwards in my knickers?'

'Sight for the gods,' said Paul. 'That's if they're pretty. Are they?'

'Don't get kinky,' said Lulu. 'Especially not at a time like this. The march cancelled? That's a blow to the core of my being.'

'Yes, I know, and it's rotten bad luck, Lulu ducky,' said Paul, conscious of how much work she'd put in, and how many circulars she'd composed and sent out to members. 'Well, we'll have to go for the alternative, addressing the proletariat at Speakers' Corner. Give 'em some of this stirring stuff, and lay into the Tories.'

'It won't have anything like the impact of a march from Shoreditch to Buckingham Palace,' gloomed Lulu.

'True,' said Paul, 'and I don't suppose it'll bring King George and Queen Liz out, either. But it'll be a useful experience for us, outdoor speaking, so let's settle for it, without advocating revolution. At Speakers' Corner, they chuck rotten eggs at revolutionaries.'

'Anything else?' said Lulu.

'Yes, as it'll be on Sundays when we're performing,' said Paul, 'wear something pretty.'

'Big joke,' said Lulu. 'Something pretty is for dolls.'

'It pulls in the blokes,' said Paul. 'We don't want to find ourselves addressing just a few old geezers and half a dozen hecklers. Get your hair curled and wear a Sunday frock, eh?'

'That's for someone like tarty Henrietta, not serious-minded women like me,' said Lulu.

'Well, I suppose I could ask her to stand in for you,' said Paul.

'Over my dead body,' said Lulu.

'There's always room for a bit of sex appeal on a soapbox,' said Paul, musing on the possibility of co-opting Henrietta.

Lulu ground her teeth again.

'Oh, all right,' she said.

'What does that mean?' asked Paul.

'I'll wear a dress,' said Lulu.

'Good on you, Lulu.'

'Under protest,' said Lulu. Paul smiled. 'That silly grin of yours isn't your best feature,' she said.

'Sorry about that,' said Paul, 'but it's the only one I've got.'

'Pity,' said Lulu.

That evening, when the twins were in bed, Boots told Polly about what had happened to Paula on Saturday afternoon. Polly, appalled, then listened to what had happened to the assailant when Sammy laid heavy hands on him. That put a happier light in her eyes.

'Good for Sammy,' she said. 'And where's the

four-legged creep now? In a dark, damp dungeon, ridden with rats, while he waits for his trial?'

'I fancy he's at home,' said Boots, 'but I don't know if any rats have arrived.'

'Are you telling me he's not in custody?' said Polly.

'Sammy's not keen on Paula having to appear in court,' said Boots.

'Boots, old love, a man like that is a danger to any girl who takes his depraved fancy,' said Polly.

'Well, Sammy and I both favour a routine that'll keep him twitching,' said Boots, and told her about the idea of Mitch delivering a weekly note of discouragement.

'Ye gods, what a family,' said Polly. 'It makes its own rules, its own laws, delivers its own verdicts and its own penalties. It's like a primitive Saxon court.'

'So you don't approve?' said Boots.

'My dear old Saxon, for better or worse, I'm with you all the way,' said Polly. 'I'm that kind of Saxon myself. I'd even suggest that to add to the discouraging motif of the weekly note, Sammy gives the creep a further going-over every month. Yes, anything to spare Paula a court appearance at the awesome Old Bailey, which is where a trial would certainly take place.'

'Glad to hear you say so, Polly old girl,' said Boots.

'Don't mention it, Boots old boy,' said Polly. 'Your world may be that of the family, and it may be parochial thereby, but it's my world too, and I'm hanging onto it for all the years left to me. Bring on the dragons, and we'll slay them together.'

'Dragons or not, I'll come along for the ride,' said Boots.

Chapter Twenty-Six

The following day, Ned kept an appointment with the cardiac unit at King's College Hospital, and underwent tests to establish the exact reason for his heart condition. He was asked to visit Dr Mason in three days' time, when his GP would let him know the result.

Lizzy fretted.

Sammy phoned the Oxford Street shop and was informed by the assistant manageress, Connie Phillips, that Miss Campion was out.

'Out where?' asked Sammy.

'She said she had to see a special friend.'

That has to be Dickinson, thought Sammy.

'Fair enough,' he said. 'When she gets back, ask her to ring me, would you, Connie?'

'I'll do that, Mr Adams.'

By three thirty, Sammy had received no phone call, but five minutes later Miss Campion arrived at his office in person, and in a state of upset.

'I need to talk to you, Mr Adams,' she said.

'Well, I'll be frank, Hilda,' said Sammy, 'you look as if you need to. Sit down.' Hilda gratefully seated herself. 'Hold on,' said Sammy, 'what's that rusty mark on your coat?'

'A bloodstain,' said Hilda huskily.

'You've had a nosebleed?' said Sammy.

'It's not a mark of my blood,' said Hilda, 'it's Mr Dickinson's.'

'Come again?' said Sammy, startled.

'I'm here to explain,' said Hilda.

'I smell something I'm not going to like,' said Sammy.

Hilda explained. She had met Mr Dickinson in December, at a reception for people in the retail fashion trade. He said he was an importer, and she thought him a lively, outgoing man. She told him what her job was and he called at the shop one day after Christmas and invited her to lunch. To cut a long story short, said Hilda, they became close friends, very close, and as he was about to divorce his wife, she slept with him at his Bloomsbury flat one night, in the expectation that his intentions meant he would marry her when the divorce came through.

She spoke to him about his business as an importer, and he told her how he'd secured two licences by reason of a Civil Service mistake. Some weeks later, she mentioned that Adams Fashions needed a large and regular supply of certain materials and that American jeans were also going to be on the required list. He said he'd be able to oblige, that he'd be pleased to. Since when, following her meeting at Simpson's with Sammy and Boots, he'd been so evasive that she became suspicious. She hadn't wanted to admit to Sammy that Dickinson might be making a fool of her. She slept with him again, and that gave her the chance to discover that he actually lived in Clapham. She went there one evening and watched the house. Eventually, a taxi arrived, and Dickinson came out with a woman. They entered the taxi, and it drove off. She had a certainty that the woman was Mrs Dickinson, although he'd said they no longer lived together.

Hilda stopped for a moment.

'Take your time, Hilda,' said Sammy gently.

She said she'd been to the Clapham house again today, driven by anger and disillusion. She caught Dickinson at home, but by himself. He attempted bluff, but eventually admitted there was no divorce pending, so would she care to be his dolly bird. She turned that proposition down flat, and asked where she stood in respect of his promise to supply Adams Fashions with the needed imports. He said he'd been dealt a body blow only that morning, that the Ministry had discovered the mistake and revoked the duplicated import licence.

Hilda saw through that and lost her temper. She picked up a whisky bottle and hit him with it. Yes, she lost her temper very badly.

'If you think that surprises me, it doesn't,' said Sammy. 'How hard did you hit him, and how many times?'

'Oh, hard enough,' said Hilda, 'but only once. The bottle broke. So did his head. A little of his blood marked my coat. He panicked about the state of his head, and when I left he was on the phone to the ambulance service, groaning that his skull was fractured and bleeding.'

Sammy couldn't help himself, even though the promise of certain imports had gone down the drain. He leaned back in his chair and laughed.

'What a performance,' he said.

Hilda, unable herself to see anything to laugh about, said stiffly, 'Mr Adams?'

'Sorry, Hilda, but I can't help picturing what the geezer's face was like when he saw that whisky bottle coming his way,' said Sammy. Actually, he was thinking that only a few days after he'd left a pervert, name of Jarvis, bruised, flattened and whimpering, the highly classy Miss Campion had left Loverboy battered, bleeding and groaning. Talk about happy coincidences. 'He wasn't dying when you left, was he, Hilda?'

'Unfortunately, no,' said Hilda bitterly.

'Now, now, Hilda,' said Sammy, trying a soothing touch.

'Just as I was leaving by the front door,' said Hilda, 'I heard him yelling impatiently down the phone.'

'Well, no-one's ever heard of a dying bloke being able to yell,' said Sammy. 'In any case, it wouldn't have been too clever, Hilda, to have turned him into a stiff. The law's a bit hot on manslaughter.'

'Damn the law,' said Hilda fervently.

'Not to worry,' said Sammy. 'He won't mention you, that's for sure. He's got too much egg on his face. He'll tell the ambulance crew – yes, and his wife – that he had an accident. Something about falling over his whisky bottle, I shouldn't wonder.'

'Sod him,' said Hilda. That, coming from the classy manageress, made Sammy's ears twitch a bit.

'Well, I know how you feel,' he said, 'the same as I do. We've been done down, Hilda, and much to me sorrow, it ain't the first time for me lately. I'll wager Dickinson's no legit importer. Ten to one he's a black-market operator, and the reason why he kept stringing us along was probably because he's been tapping his sources in hope, and his sources can't or won't oblige him. But he didn't want to tell you that. Why not, you might ask.'

'I'm not asking,' said Hilda.

'Black-market operators don't like losing face, that's why not,' said Sammy. 'I'm betting the regular large quantities we were after were making him lick his lips, so he kept hoping he'd strike lucky with his sources.'

'Bugger his sources,' said Hilda, and Sammy's ears twitched again.

'Steady, Hilda, we'll both get over it,' said Sammy. 'And he'll get over his cracked head. He's onto a nice little earner with what business he does do. That's obvious, seeing he's got a castle in Clapham for living in, and a flat in Bloomsbury for a bit of recreation. It looks to me like he was also hoping to have you on the side as his favourite custard tart.'

'His what?' said Hilda with umbrage.

'Slip of the tongue,' said Sammy. 'I meant his extra piece of love life. Still, you're well out of—'

'Talk, talk, talk, don't your kind ever shut up?' said Hilda.

'Eh?' said Sammy.

'That's what I got from him, talk, talk, talk,' said Hilda, 'and I fell for it. Men, they're all the same. It happened to me before, during the war, when a Yankee officer in London talked me into letting him share my bed. All his talk included a promise to marry me, but what happened when the war was over?'

'Don't tell me he did a quick bunk,' said Sammy.

'The lousy swine told me he had to go back home to his wife and kids,' said Hilda, seething.

'Hilda, I can see you're upset, but—'

'Don't start more talking,' said Hilda, 'not after my falling into another man-made trap, and you and your big ideas about new designs made it worse. You used me to get at Dickinson. You're just another scheming swine.'

'Here, steady on,' said Sammy.

Hilda jumped up, took hold of his tray that was full of paperwork and chucked it at him. It bounced on his head and showered him with its contents.

'Sod you, Sammy Adams, and your job,' she said, and rushed out, leaving him wondering if it was today, tomorrow or next week.

'Flaming coconuts,' he breathed, 'what a carry-on. I'm lucky there wasn't a bottle handy, or me own head would've been as seriously injured as Dickinson's.'

He sat there, musing more in sorrow than anger on Hilda's behaviour. She couldn't be blamed, not after she'd twice suffered the kind of misfortune damaging to any woman's pride. Humiliation, that was it. He came to his feet after a while, picked up the tray and retrieved the scattered paperwork. Then he went to see Boots.

'I've got news for you, matey,' he said.

'New news?' said Boots.

'Well, it's not old yet,' said Sammy.

'Is it good or bad?' asked Boots.

'Believe me, I didn't like it,' said Sammy, 'and I don't suppose you will.' He went on to say Hilda had called in to let him know that the Dickinson gent was no gent, but a first-class washout with nothing to

286

offer except a load of talking codswallop. Hilda was upset very considerable, and had lost faith in blokes and more or less had given notice.

'What do we have, then,' said Boots, 'a disillusioned lady and no fabrics or materials?'

'We've got all of that,' said Sammy, 'and Dickinson's got a damaged head.'

'Hilda dropped a brick on it?' said Boots.

'No, she broke a bottle of whisky over it,' said Sammy.

'Shame about the whisky,' said Boots. 'Well, that's one more chapter of upside-down events in the life of the firm.'

'Trust you to be airy-fairy,' said Sammy. 'If anyone invented it, you did. There's poor old Hilda losing her virginity again, and—'

'Again?' said Boots.

'It seems she first lost it to a sweet-talking Yank during the war,' said Sammy. 'Losing it again to Charlie Dickinson, and all for nothing, has made her think all male geezers are swines. That includes you and me.'

'Natural reaction, I suppose,' said Boots. 'Well, write her a kind letter, Sammy. Tell her we sincerely feel for her, and that we can't accept her notice because the shop can't do without her. Be appreciative of her work, but not flowery.'

'Flowery?' said Sammy.

'Yes, too much sugary stuff might remind her of Dickinson and his codswallop,' said Boots. 'You know what I mean, so get it down on paper in your best handwriting. To her home address.'

'Pardon me, I'm sure,' said Sammy, 'but is that an order, guv?'

'Just a suggestion,' said Boots.

'So why's it hurting my lugholes?' asked Sammy.

'You're feeling sensitive at the moment,' said Boots, 'but there's better news on the way. That is, there will be if Rachel comes back with an Air Ministry contract on Friday.'

'I've got confidence in Rachel,' said Sammy. 'Mind you, I've had the kind of setbacks lately that make me wonder if this is me year of doom and gloom. I wouldn't like to think that on the day our respected parents get to be a lord and lady, I'll be officially bankrupted.'

'I think we can avoid that, old chap,' said Boots. 'About Hilda, would you like me to write the letter?'

'Now you're talking, and good on yer, old soldier,' said Sammy, 'but might I make a suggestion?'

'Fire away,' said Boots.

'Enclose a signed photograph,' said Sammy.

Boots laughed.

Over supper, Sammy did not go into full details of this latest setback. Not in front of Paula and Phoebe. Certain aspects concerning Hilda's private life weren't for their young ears. He merely said she'd been taken in by a talking geezer, the result of which was painful to her, to Boots and to himself.

'And the firm,' he said. 'Can you believe that, Jimmy me lad, some bloke I've never met dropping a clanger on Adams Fashions from the top of the Eiffel Tower?'

'The Eiffel Tower's in Paris, Dad,' said Jimmy.

'Well, I know when it landed that it was from a long way off,' said Sammy. 'I've still got a headache.'

'Oh, I'm sorry, Daddy,' said Phoebe.

'Yes, hard luck,' said Paula.

'Granted,' said Sammy, 'so can anyone tell me why your mum's giggling?'

'Answer up, Mum,' said Jimmy.

'Well, it does have its funny side,' said Susie, 'your dad and his brainbox taken in by – um—'

'Pie in the sky?' suggested Jimmy.

'Was that what dropped on him from the top of the Eiffel Tower?' asked Paula.

'Was it a meat pie, Daddy?' asked Phoebe.

'Listen, family,' said Sammy, 'I'm definitely not in favour of comical stuff, not while I'm still feeling injured.'

Titters ran round the supper table, in a manner of speaking.

Sammy smiled indulgently, so Susie gave him a little pat for his good humour. Well, he thought, what's one more pat?

Jimmy's thoughts turned on New York and Jenny, two thousand miles away. The blight of it was that he couldn't interest himself in any other girl.

Chapter Twenty-Seven

It looked as if Lulu was going to be late for work on Friday morning, for at twenty to ten there was no sign of her. However, her father walked in at that moment.

'Morning, Paul,' he said, 'can you manage by yourself today? Lulu's in bed. Had a troublesome wisdom tooth extracted under gas on her way home yesterday evening, and it's left her with a sick headache.'

'I'm sorry, poor old Lulu,' said Paul. 'She did mention she had a dental appointment at five, and I let her leave early.'

'I saw her last night, when the headache was already giving her cause to complain about heavy-handed male dentists,' said Honest John, 'and I called in again this morning on my way here. I've a suspicion she's allergic to gas. Some people are, but what the hell, you can't have a wisdom tooth pulled without some kind of anaesthetic.'

'I'll take her a bunch of flowers on my way home this evening,' said Paul.

Honest John's countenance creased in a broad grin.

'Flowers for Lulu?' he said. 'She'll chuck them at

you, Paul. Don't you know about the bees in her bonnet? One of them is that a gift of flowers from a feller is a sure sign he's after turning her into a weak and sentimental female. Very dangerous, y'know, to her independence.'

'Oh, well, we've all got our funny ways,' said Paul.

'So we have, m'lad, and I'd be the last to deny Lulu her fair share,' said Honest John, 'especially about her independence. When I asked her, some time after her mother died, why she was moving out to live in a flat, she informed me it was to get away from my kitchen sink. She had a feeling, she said, that she'd wake up one morning and find herself chained to it. Bang would go her independence. It didn't mean she wasn't fond of me, she said, but as I was pretty self-sufficient, she didn't have to worry about my welfare. So I've got a daily help, a good old-fashioned char who also does the shopping for me.'

'You've got to admire the way Lulu argues her case,' said Paul.

'Listen, young feller, no-one admires my daughter more than I do,' said Honest John solemnly. 'I just wish –' His solemnity gave way to another broad grin. 'I just wish she wasn't such a crackpot at times. Anyway, would you do me a favour?'

'Of course,' said Paul.

'Would you look in on your way home this evening?' asked Honest John. 'There's this critical Defence debate in the House today, and God knows when I'll be able to leave. It could be well after midnight.'

'I'll drop in on her with pleasure,' said Paul.

'Just see how she is and make her a pot of tea. Something like that. If she's up and about, all well and good. Here's the key to her flat.' Honest John removed the key from a ring and handed it to Paul. 'You can leave it with her.'

'If she's all well and good, but hasn't fed herself, shall I do something for her?' asked Paul. 'Something bland, like a poached fillet of fish?'

'You'll be lucky to find much in her larder,' said Honest John. 'Her idea of how to live in a practical way is to buy herself fried fish and chips or a Kennedy's pork pie.'

'If she's had the mother and father of sick headaches, I shouldn't think she'd fancy either of those,' said Paul.

'Well, I'll leave it to you, Paul, thanks,' said Honest John, and made for the door. He turned, smiling. 'I know one thing, she's determined to be herself by Sunday afternoon, when the two of you are up for a stint at Speakers' Corner.'

'A case of her challenging spirit overcoming any will to stay in bed,' said Paul.

'You've got talent, m'lad, and like I've mentioned, you could do well as a local councillor in a couple of years,' said Honest John, and disappeared.

Rachel's appointment with Mr Blenkinsop was at ten o'clock. She departed for Whitehall with Sammy's good wishes ringing agreeably in her ears. Mr Blenkinsop, slightly portly and slightly bald, but nonetheless pleasant-looking, received her in his office with the kind of cordiality civil servants usually avoided, in case it made their renowned impartiality look a bit crinkly round the edges.

'Mrs Goodman – good morning – how very nice to see you again – I trust these post-war years have been kind to you – do sit down. Would you like coffee? Yes, I'm sure you would. I'll ring for some.'

Mr Blenkinsop was undoubtedly an admirer, which wasn't surprising, since Mrs Blenkinsop was pudding-faced, sexless and a bit of a disaster. Rachel, by contrast, was warm-hearted, picturesque and charming. And, in her expansive Jewish way, she knew how to turn it on.

The time she spent in very pleasant discussion with Mr Blenkinsop was not only rewarding, it culminated in such an unexpected and happy finale that she could have kissed him. Mr Blenkinsop would probably have been embarrassed, and might even have blushed. Mrs Blenkinsop, had she known, would have thrown a fit and done him a grievous injury below the belt.

Sammy's phone rang mid-morning.

'Hello?'

'Miss Campion's on the line, Mr Sammy,' said the switchboard girl. 'I'm putting her through.'

A click.

'Hello?' said Sammy again, not sure if he was going to receive another uncomplimentary earful, or a straightforward demand for damages, for which Hilda might consider him indirectly responsible. 'Hello?'

'Mr Sammy, I feel dreadful about my behaviour yesterday.' Over the line Hilda's voice sounded as if her anger had turned to womanly woe. 'I really didn't expect to receive such a lovely letter from Mr Adams senior this morning.'

Mr Adams senior? Well, thought Sammy, if that last straw don't break the camel's back, it's only because this camel has got an outsize hump.

'You mean my general manager, Hilda?'

'Yes, such a lovely man and so understanding,' said Hilda. I'll need my dear old ma's smelling salts in a minute, thought Sammy. 'I woke up feeling rotten about everything,' said Hilda, 'but the letter was a welcome tonic, except that it filled me with remorse. I really must apologize for all the horrid things I said to you and about you.'

'Think nothing of it,' said Sammy, 'I'd have let off steam myself in your place.'

'How kind,' said Hilda. 'In his letter, Mr Adams spoke so well of you that I'm sure you're as understanding as he is.'

Sammy's sense of humour crept up on him and took over. He laughed.

'Don't mention it, Hilda,' he said.

'Mr Sammy, did I hear you laugh?'

'If it doesn't upset you,' he said, 'it's got its funny side, including you giving Dickinson a funny head. Might I ask if you're not going to leave us, after all?'

'I'm going back to the shop this afternoon to resume work,' said Hilda, 'and thanks for wanting me to do that. Tell Mr Adams how much I appreciated his letter, won't you?'

'I'll tell him,' said Sammy, and Hilda rang off.

Sammy, of course, took himself into Boots's office. Boots was just finishing a spell of dictation to his shorthand typist, Marjorie Trapper, a young lady who had dreams about being shipwrecked on a desert island in tropical shorts and a damp shirt, with Boots undoing her buttons in a bamboo hut to make sure her bosom was still beating. Not half.

'Is that all, Mr Adams?' she asked.

'That's all for the time being, Marjorie,' said Boots.

'Oh, righty-oh,' said Marjorie, and spoke to Sammy on her way out. 'D'you think one could live on dates and coconut milk, Mr Sammy?'

'One what?' asked Sammy.

'Anyone,' said Marjorie.

'Count me out,' said Sammy.

'Oh, righty-oh,' said Marjorie, and exited.

'What's she talking about?' asked Sammy of Boots.

'Getting away from it all, I fancy,' said Boots.

'What's her problem, then?' asked Sammy.

'Trams, buses and crowded pavements, probably,' said Boots.

'Tell her trams are being done away with,' said Sammy. 'Listen, I've just had Hilda on the phone. She got your letter and liked it. It's sent her back to her job. Just thought I'd let you know I'm pleased with you. Accept me compliments.' He patted Boots on his shoulder and left at a smart pace while the advantage was his. Boots could always turn the tables.

Rachel was back from her appointment with Mr Blenkinsop at midday, entering Sammy's office with a spring in her step.

'Well, well, who's been a clever girl, then?' he asked. 'I hope you're going to say you have.'

'I don't think you'll be disappointed,' smiled Rachel.

'In that case, Rachel me sport, take a pew, make yourself at home and fill me in,' said Sammy.

Rachel sat down. There was a delicate swish of covered limbs as she crossed her legs. Blow me, thought Sammy, she's still got sex appeal. She'd been a widow for several years now, and he wondered if some appreciative son of Abraham wasn't knocking regularly on her door. There ought to be. Even at forty-seven, Rachel was still some wise bloke's dream.

'Sammy?' she said, conscious he was looking at her with a kind of thoughtful smile.

'I'm all ears, Rachel.'

'There,' she said. She had two large brown envelopes with her, and she placed one on his desk. 'There's the contract form for the new RAF uniforms, with two copies. All copies are to be signed by you as chairman and by one director – well, you know the routine, don't you, from all the wartime contracts that landed in this office.'

'Rachel, what can I say that befits your remarkable self?' said Sammy.

'Should I turn down your compliments?' smiled Rachel. 'Pile them on, Sammy.'

'Consider yourself a one and only wonder,' said Sammy. 'Also and what's more, Tommy, Lilian and Gertie at the factory are going to talk very loving about you for this contract. That's if Blenky has guaranteed delivery of the materials.'

'More than that, Sammy,' said Rachel.

'More?' said Sammy. 'What kind of more?'

Rachel said that by the time she and Mr Blenkinsop were discussing the supply of necessary materials, they'd reached a state of mutual happiness. Sammy said reaching mutual happiness with any Ministry official ought to be recorded in the

Book of Geniuses.

'Genesis, Sammy?'

'Yes, that as well, Rachel.'

Rachel, smiling, said that because Mr Blenkinsop was so receptive, she mentioned how difficult it was for Adams Fashions to obtain certain fabrics and materials for new designs. What they needed was an import licence, which she knew would be difficult to get. Mr Blenkinsop said that was a matter for the Board of Trade, but he followed that up by making a phone call to a colleague there concerning Adams Fashions, a firm that had handled government contracts during the war, and was now to deal with new contracts. A most efficient firm that wished to extend its business by securing an import licence. What could be done for them?

When he came off the phone, he said, 'Mrs Goodman, if you could stay a little longer, a messenger will bring something for you.'

'Something?' said Rachel.

'An application for an import licence,' said the estimable Mr Blenkinsop.

Subsequently, said Rachel, a messenger from the Board of Trade arrived.

'And then?' said Sammy, fired up.

'Here is what he brought,' said Rachel, and placed the second brown envelope on the desk.

'In which is what?' asked Sammy.

'The forms relating to the application,' said Rachel.

'Oh, the forms,' said Sammy, a little deflated. 'Not the licence? Well, much to my regret, Rachel, I've got to point out we've applied before, more than once, and been turned down each time.'

'My life, don't I know that?' said Rachel. 'But this time will be different, this time I'm sure we'll get it. Just before I left, Mr Blenkinsop said to me, "Be of good cheer, Mrs Goodman, your time here will bear fruit, I'm sure".'

'He said what?' asked Sammy.

'Something on those lines, the dear man,' said Rachel. 'So go to it, Sammy, fill in the application, and the copies, and send them.'

Sammy beamed. What a woman.

'Rachel, I'm up to my eyebrows with admiration,' he said, and gave her an affectionate look. 'People come and go, Rachel, but old friends stay for ever.' He coughed to clear his throat. 'Let's see, exactly how long have you and me known each other?'

'Thirty-three years, Sammy.'

'Half a lifetime,' said Sammy, 'and every year a prime one. Thirty-three years? I'm a privileged bloke, Rachel, especially now Leah's a niece and you're a sister-in-law. Well, good as.'

'I'm happy if you're happy,' said Rachel.

'Everybody's going to be happy,' said Sammy, 'especially Lilian. All right, let's include jeans on our list of required imports and risk any damage they might do to our sales of Sunday frocks and such-like.'

'Sunday frocks, Sammy, don't have quite the same place in a girl's social life as they used to,' said Rachel. 'There's a change in attitudes to face up to.'

'Don't tell me I'm going to have to face up to Sunday jeans,' said Sammy.

'I should like that myself?' said Rachel. 'Not much. But we'll have to go with the tide, Sammy, especially if it lands us with more of what will keep the firm healthy.'

'More of what?'

'Profit, Sammy.'

'Now you're talking,' said Sammy.

Chapter Twenty-Eight

Paul slipped the key into the lock, turned it, and opened the door. At once a voice was heard.

'Who's that? Whoever it is, buzz off.'

Well, thought Paul, the lady can't be too bad, she's talking.

'It's only me, Lulu,' he called.

'Only you sounds like the enemy. Buzz off.'

Paul traced the direction of the voice, reached a half-open door and knocked.

'I've just called to see how you are,' he said.

'Bloody rough, but all right, come in now you're here.'

Paul entered. Lulu was out of her bed, but sitting on the edge, an old brown woollen dressing gown draped over a plain white nightdress. Her black hair was hanging, her glasses off, her eyes peering, her face peaky.

'Good-oh,' said Paul.

'What d'you mean, good-oh?'

'You're better.'

'Oh, really?' said Lulu. 'How did I look before, then?'

'I wasn't here before,' said Paul, 'but your dad was. He mentioned he'd seen you this morning and that you were under the weather. I'm just guessing you're feeling better now.'

'I felt lousy then,' said Lulu, 'I just feel rough now. Who'd have thought it? I only had a tooth pulled. Listen, how'd you get in?'

'Your dad lent me your key. Have you had any nourishment, anything to eat or drink?'

'All I've had is a lousy head,' said Lulu, uncovered eyes a bit cloudy.

'Well, you'd better have a little nourishment now,' said Paul. 'Will your missing tooth be able to cope?'

'You mean is my gap still sore?' said Lulu. 'No, not much.'

'Tell you what, then, I'll make you a pot of tea first, and then some porridge.'

'Porridge? Porridge? I hate porridge.'

'Something else that's bland, then?' said Paul. 'Say cereal in hot milk? D'you have any cereal?'

'In the larder,' said Lulu.

'Right,' said Paul. 'You get back into bed and I'll see to things.'

'Well, all right,' said Lulu, and she wormed her way in between the sheets. Paul tucked her in. 'Listen, I don't need nursing,' she said, squinting up at him. 'Also, if there's one thing I don't allow in my bedroom, it's a bloke handling my bedclothes.'

'Yes, I'm sure you're much better than you were,' said Paul, 'you sound as if you're nearly yourself. Still, lie back and relax, and your Uncle Paul will find out where your kitchen sink is.'

He explored the flat. It consisted of a bedroom, living room, kitchen and bathroom. The living room looked a bit like a junk shop, but the kitchen was tidy enough, except for the sink being laden with dishes and crockery that needed washing. He filled the kettle, and lit a gas ring on the cooker. On went the kettle. He found a teapot on a shelf and a packet of Lyons tea in the larder, with a half-full bottle of milk. While he waited for the kettle to boil, he started the washing-up. He'd phoned his mum from the office to let her know he'd be late. Vi asked why. He told her.

'Well, I never, you must be getting fond of that funny girl,' said Vi, who had, however, convinced herself Paul had only been joking when he said he was going to marry her.

'She's good at heart,' said Paul, 'but she's trying to fight it in case people might think she's not tough enough to be an MP.'

'An MP?' said Vi.

'Member of Parliament,' said Paul. 'Sometime in the future.'

'Well, bless me,' said Vi, 'I just don't know what to say to that. Still, I'll keep your supper hot, love.'

'Ta, Mum.'

In Lulu's kitchen, the kettle boiled and Paul made the tea. On a tray, he carried the pot, cup and saucer, small jug of milk and a little bowl of sugar into the bedroom. Lulu sat up, the loose dressing gown falling away to reveal the V of her nightie. My word, thought Paul, I can see for certain that there's a real girl struggling to get out.

'What's this?' she asked, her spectacles in place.

'Girl in a nightie, what else?' said Paul.

Lulu looked down at herself and a slight flush turned her peaky look a faint pink. She brought her dressing gown back into place.

'Trust you to be pathetic,' she said. 'I meant what's on that tray?'

'Pot of tea, cup and saucer, sugar and milk,' said Paul, and placed the tray on the blanket covering her lap. 'Enjoy it, and drink it while it's hot. Hot tea's reckoned to be a stimulant. If it stings your gum, drink it on the other side.'

'If it stings my gum and makes it bleed, I'll sue you,' said Lulu.

'You won't get much in the way of damages,' said Paul. 'I'm only a working bloke on low wages.'

'Well, thanks, anyway,' said Lulu. 'No, I mean thanks.'

'Pleasure,' said Paul, 'and I'll see to the cereal in five minutes.'

He found an open packet of cereal in the larder. Not much else was there, just a tin of baked beans, a tin of sardines, half a loaf of bread, and some butter in a small covered dish. Vegetables were conspicuous by their complete absence. Well, there it was, visible proof that Lulu wasn't greatly attached to her kitchen. Studying the life of Keir Hardie no doubt rated a lot higher than cooking herself a roast Sunday dinner.

He finished the washing-up, prepared a dish of cereal in hot milk, and took it to her. The tray was on her bedside table. She was still sitting up, an open book in her hands.

'The cereal?' she said.

'Well, your sick headache –'

'It's gone.'

'Good. Would you like sardines with baked beans after you've eaten the cereal?'

'Ugh, no sardines, thanks,' said Lulu, 'just the cereal.'

Paul gave it to her. She put the book aside, and took the dish, plus a spoon.

'What's the book?' asked Paul.

'*The Rise of Socialism in the Great War*,' said Lulu.

'Wouldn't something by Agatha Christie be more relaxing?' asked Paul.

'Agatha Christie is for Brighton holidaymakers on a rainy day,' said Lulu.

'How about Rebecca West?'

'Now she's brilliant,' said Lulu, spooning milky cereal into her mouth.

'I think my Aunt Polly's got some of her novels,' said Paul. 'I'll see if she'll lend you one.'

'Well, thanks – here, wait a tick, isn't she the relative with a titled upper-class father?'

'I'd like you to know my Aunt Polly's one of the people,' said Paul, 'she served as an ambulance driver all through the Great War.'

'I like the sound of that,' said Lulu, 'but she's still—'

'Listen, there's something I'd like to do for you before I leave,' said Paul. What she was on about reminded him that Grandpa and Grandma Finch were due at Buckingham Palace on the third Tuesday in April, and that they'd come out titled. It was something that as a confirmed Labour voter he'd have to live down, and most of all keep from Lulu. 'Yes, if you'll point me to your hairbrush, I'll give your locks a brushing before I buzz off.'

'You'll do what?' said Lulu.

'Lulu, your hair, it's all over the place.'

'So are you,' said Lulu. 'Buzz off.'

'Tomorrow's Saturday,' said Paul, 'so don't worry about doing your morning stint. Take time off to get yourself fit for Sunday and Speakers' Corner.'

'I'll be fit for that,' said Lulu, 'you can bet I will. It'll be my first time for open-air speaking. We're getting back-up, aren't we?'

'Yes, quite a few Young Socialists,' said Paul, 'including your most ardent admirer.'

'My most what?' said Lulu.

'You know, that unemployed bloke Bernard Gibbs, the one you went to see,' said Paul. 'He's now got his job as a car-park attendant. He's looking forward to giving you personal back-up. He phoned to say so.'

'Send him a telegram,' said Lulu. 'Care of the car park. Tell him to get himself run over.'

'You sure you wouldn't like me to give your hair a brush?' said Paul.

Since that only made Lulu look as if she was about to throw the dish and what was left of the cereal at him, Paul departed in a wise hurry.

Oh well, thought Lulu, he's not a bad bloke. Bossy, of course, but aren't they all. Still, he's better than most. Not that that's saying a lot.

She slipped from the bed and sat down at her dressing table to examine her reflection in the mirror. Her peaky look made her grimace, and her hair wasn't exactly a shining glory. She gave it a brush. Perhaps she should see what the local hair-dresser could make of it sometime tomorrow. Then she remembered it was tomorrow that Paul was going to the theatre with tarty Henrietta.

Well, if he didn't mind being turned into Henrietta's poodle, he'd got a sick future in front of him.

*   *   *

'Oh, there you are, love,' said Vi, when Paul arrived home.

'Yup, here I am,' said Paul.

'Your supper's keeping warm in the oven,' said Vi.

'Good, I'll have it in a minute,' said Paul. 'How's work at the factory going, Dad?'

'Steady,' said Tommy, 'just steady, like it has been since the end of the war on account of your Labour lot restricting imports of materials. But it's going to buck up like a dog's tail now that there's a contract for new RAF clobber in the pipeline. So your Uncle Sammy told me by phone this afternoon. Your Aunt Rachel came back from the Air Ministry with the good news.'

'She's such a credit to the business,' said Vi, 'and the family.'

On the occasion of Lizzy and Ned's son Edward marrying Rachel's daughter Leah, the family had welcomed Rachel into its bosom as one of their own.

'Now, what's this about you dropping in on the girl Lulu to feed her some medicine?' asked Tommy of Paul.

'Her dad asked me to look in on her sick headache,' said Paul. 'My diagnosis is that she's over it, and that I'm not expecting a relapse.'

'My, we've got a doctor in the house,' said Vi, smiling.

'That reminds me,' said Tommy, 'Ned was seeing Dr Mason today to get the result of his test. I'd better phone Lizzy sometime this evening.'

Ned, in fact, was home from his call on Dr Mason. Lizzy had gone with him, just to keep him company, she said. It's my belief you feel I might have to be carried home, said Ned. No, of course not, said

Lizzy. Subsequently, when they left the surgery, she tucked her arm around his in loving fashion.

'There, I knew you wouldn't have to be carried,' she said, 'I was sure you'd just have to keep taking care.'

Dr Mason had said his original diagnosis stood, that Ned's problem was indeed a slight hardening of the arteries. So an aspirin a day was to continue, stress was to be avoided, and a saltless diet to be initiated.

'I don't mind taking care,' said Ned, who was to visit Dr Mason for a check-up once a fortnight, 'I do mind potatoes and green veg being cooked without salt.'

'Oh, I'll find a recipe for spicing them up so you won't notice,' said Lizzy. 'It's got to be a relief, Ned love, that you don't have a weak heart. If you did have, well, you'd probably have to miss going to Buckingham Palace in case the excitement was too much for you.'

'Don't worry about me,' said Ned. 'Just keep an eye on your mum in case she forgets her smelling salts.'

'She won't forget, not on that special day,' said Lizzy. 'Oh, I'll phone Bobby later and let him know the result of your test, and he'll let Annabelle, Emma and Edward know.'

'And all the Adamses,' said Ned, 'and tomorrow's *Daily Express* as well.'

'*Daily Express*?' said Lizzy. 'Of course not, you silly.'

'I hope that's a promise,' said Ned.

Through their ever-active grapevine, the whole family soon came to know Ned's problem had been confirmed as a hardening of the arteries, but no more than that. Some still felt concerned, others were relieved. Chinese Lady, among the latter, was thankfully so. She'd had her mind on the dread possibility of the worst, which would mean another family funeral. There had already been two in recent times. Emily's and old Uncle Tom's. The fact that Emily's dated back nearly ten years didn't prevent Chinese Lady from counting it as recent.

She felt all funerals ought to be exclusive to other families. The fact that Edwin was seventy-six and might not have much longer to go was something she always pushed to the back of her mind. And perhaps, in her inimitable way, she saw herself as lasting for ever. Well, since being cured of TB many years ago, she had never known a day's illness.

Chapter Twenty-Nine

Feeling much better, Lulu arrived at the office the following morning.

'Welcome,' said Paul.

'Thanks,' said Lulu, 'and thanks for being a good bloke yesterday evening.'

'It's what friends are for,' said Paul. 'Are you OK? No headache and no sore gum?'

'I'm fine,' said Lulu, removing her coat. Paul blinked at what she was wearing, a dark grey costume with a pleated skirt, and a white blouse with red bow tie.

'Very smart,' he said, although he thought the costume a bit severe, the skirt too long. However, the red bow tie hit the eye. 'Lulu, that looks like a touch of the Red Flag.'

'My bow tie?' said Lulu. 'It's a symbol of my devotion to red-blooded Socialism. And to the rights of the workers.'

'What's on your mind for tomorrow?' asked Paul, opening up the morning's mail.

'I've got some notes here,' said Lulu, and consulted them. 'Yes, I'm going to talk about keeping the Labour government in, and the Tories out.'

'Fair enough,' said Paul.

'And what are you going to say to the audience?' asked Lulu.

'I'm hoping first of all that we'll get a decent crowd,' said Paul, 'and then I'll remind them of what the Labour Party has done for the workers so far, and what they intend to do next. Listen, as you weren't here yesterday, no typing was done. So before our back-up team arrives to confer with us, d'you think you could do some letters?'

'Hand 'em over,' said Lulu briskly. 'Oh, how many in the team?'

'Six,' said Paul, 'including Bernard Gibbs.'

'Don't let him get anywhere near me,' said Lulu. 'Take him outside and push him under a bus.'

Unfortunately, Paul refused to take that seriously, and when the back-up team arrived an hour later, Bernard the goon made straight for Lulu's desk, plonked his bottom on the corner and addressed her with enthusiasm.

'Well, what a pleasure, seeing you again, Lulu. Don't mind me calling you Lulu, do you, Lulu?'

'Drop dead,' said Lulu, as the other members crowded around Paul's desk. He was a popular figure in the Young Socialists group.

'Here, I got that job with National Car Parks,' said Bernard. 'Mind, it grieves me that I ain't making use of me plumbing talents, but I'm still grateful for your help. I never met anyone kinder, except for me landlady—'

'Get off my desk,' said Lulu. 'Push off to your car park.'

'I'm off till Monday,' said Bernard, 'I could be all yours till then. Fancy the pictures tonight? You just say what film you'd like to see, and it'll be me particular pleasure to take you.'

'Oh, it will, will it?'

'I'm better off now I've got this job,' said Bernard. 'I've got useful dibs in me pocket and human desire in me heart.'

'You've got what?' said Lulu, quite sure that some blokes, if not most, belonged to another planet.

'I'll be frank, Lulu,' said Bernard, 'I fancy you something chronic, and I'm hoping you'll return me affection. I don't suppose it'll happen right now, but after we've got together a bit, I daresay you might feel I'm what you've been waiting for, eh?'

'How would you like your legs chopped off?'

'Beg yer pardon?'

'Get 'em out of here,' said Lulu.

'If you two would give up your private conversation,' called Paul, 'we'll all discuss tomorrow's plans.'

That rescued Lulu. Also, when Paul exercised his talents for leadership by reducing Bernard's babble to an indistinct mutter, her ears took a happy holiday.

The conference on how to make the most of tomorrow's assignment at Speakers' Corner went well, although when Bernard was on his way out with the rest of the team, he managed to get himself back into Lulu's ears.

'Where we going to meet tonight, Lulu?'

'Be at the Tower of London at seven,' said Lulu. 'By the execution block.'

'Er?'

'You bring your neck, I'll bring the chopper,'

said Lulu, and closed the door behind him.

Another door opened at that moment, the door of a flat in Camberwell, and the unpleasant face of William Jarvis twitched as he beheld the caller, a sturdy middle-aged man who had an envelope in his hand.

'Message for yer,' said Mitch, driver of the Adams delivery van, and he plonked the envelope into Jarvis's mitt.

'Another one?' hissed Jarvis in silky sibilance.

'Just a reminder, according to me guv'nor,' said Mitch, and departed, leaving the unholy character twitching all over.

During the afternoon, Bobby and Helene, with their children, three-year-old Estelle and eighteen-month-old Robert, called on Boots and Polly, together with Edward and Leah. Edward and Leah were the parents of two-year-old Eliza, named after her paternal grandmother.

Twenty-three, Leah took after Rachel, her mother, in her lush brunette looks and her warm personality. Typical of her friendly nature was the way she had achieved a compatible relationship with domesticity from the day she and Edward took up residence in their home in Addiscombe, close to Croydon. Edward's job was with Croydon's main public library.

Still following her Jewish religion, Leah served meals that allowed her to introduce kosher food to Edward quite frequently. She regarded Edward as the kindest of men. His tolerance of people and their vexing quirks or awkward failings echoed that of his Uncle Boots. If he was more serious-minded than most of his cousins, he did have teasing moments that were good for many a giggle. Their marriage was what society called mixed. Leah simply thought it a mixture of their feelings for each other, all of which merged without any complaints or reluctance, especially when they made love.

Now, with Flossie taking charge of the children, including her employers' twins – no mean feat – Leah, Edward, Helene and Bobby began a discussion with Boots and Polly concerning the reason for this prearranged get-together.

'Frankly,' said Bobby, 'I'm worried. Some might think a slight hardening of Dad's arteries isn't too serious, but the fact that Dr Mason wants to see him once a fortnight tells me there's cause for concern.'

'Yes, your papa doesn't look well, Edward,' said Helene.

'Don't think I haven't noticed,' said Edward.

'We've both noticed,' said Leah.

'Everyone's noticed,' said Polly, which fact didn't surprise her. The problems of any one member of the family never escaped the attention of the rest.

'What's exactly on your mind, Bobby?' asked Boots.

'I'm going to propose that we persuade Dad to retire,' said Bobby. 'It's a fact, surely, that his journey to his business every day has to be a strain.'

'But who is going to persuade a man like your father to retire when he's only fifty-five?' asked Leah.

'And wouldn't Dr Mason have suggested it if he'd thought it right for his patient?' said Polly.

'Early retirement for Ned?' mused Boots. 'That needs thinking about.'

'I'm personally in favour,' said Edward, 'although

I think Dad would find retirement a bit of a bore.'

Helene said it was better to be a little bored than to be at risk. Leah said she wondered how Edward's mother would feel about that. Helene said oh yes, Leah, that was something to consider. She had not been sure of how Leah regarded her during the days when they were both newly wedded into the Somers family in 1946, for by then stories of the French rounding up Jews for Himmler's concentration camps were becoming widely known. She suspected Leah would think the worst of her as a Frenchwoman. Leah, however, simply took her as she found her, a woman of strong character who had bravely served with the French Resistance.

'Perhaps what's best for Dad is more to do with Mum than us,' said Bobby. 'I came here certain he ought to retire. Now I'm not so sure. He loves his job and his wine cellars.'

'It seems to me it's not for us or Mum to decide, it's for Dad to make his own decision,' said Edward.

Boots, standing within the arc of the picturesque bow window, regarded the green of the garden with his mind on Ned, his oldest and closest friend. They had known each other since 1912. The long years had cemented the friendship.

'Are you with us, old scout?' asked Polly.

Boots turned.

'I think it should be Ned's own decision, yes,' he said, 'and the best person to mention retirement to him is his doctor.'

'Bobby,' said Leah, 'why don't you go to see Dr Mason, and ask him if your father's condition will remain as it is or get worse?'

'Good point, Leah dear girl,' said Polly. 'That will

help Bobby decide if he should ask Dr Mason to suggest retirement. If so, let's all sit back and leave it to Ned.'

Bobby said he thought his mother had the impression that Dr Mason wasn't worried about the condition worsening. Impressions could be wishful thinking, said Edward. My life, said Leah, we should be worried about wishful thinking? Yes, we should, she said.

'Yes,' said Helene, 'because your papa is such a nice man, Bobby.'

'I'll call on Dr Mason,' said Bobby, mind made up, particularly as Boots and Polly were in favour. Boots rarely offered the wrong kind of advice.

In came Gemma at that moment, bouncing up to Boots.

'Daddy, could Robert and Estelle and Eliza have some cake?' she asked. 'And me and James as well?'

'It looks to me, poppet,' said Boots, 'as if it's Polly put the kettle on and we'll all have tea. Except Flossie will see to it.'

'Tea?' said Edward. 'Count me in.'

'We're all in,' said Bobby.

Polly smiled. Tea. The source of life to every branch of this family, as it was to all the people Boots had known in his younger days, the Walworth cockneys.

In the grand house south of Chicago, Jeremy Passmore was reading another letter from Bess Adams, a reply to the last one he'd sent her. Bess informed him that because her parents would be away in Cornwall, he and she would stay with her Aunt Vi and Uncle Tommy for two weeks, and then with her parents, who simply wouldn't hear of him putting up at a hotel.

Jeremy's mother, the stylish but touch-me-not Mrs Passmore, had been trying to come to terms with what she considered was her son's absurd infatuation with the young Englishwoman he'd only ever met once. Such an infatuation could not last. But there he was, again ruining a breakfast for her by devoting himself to the letter from England.

'You're still set on going to England, Jeremy?'

Jeremy looked up, smiling.

'To see Bess?' he said. 'Yes, and she's written to let me know I'm to be the guest of an aunt and uncle, and then of her parents.'

'Well, although I think the situation ridiculous, I must accept it, even to the point of being left alone for a month,' said Mrs Passmore.

'You needn't be alone, Mother,' said Jeremy, 'you could stay with your sister.'

'You know very well I don't get on with Mayflower.'

I don't get on with having to address her as Aunt Mayflower, thought Jeremy. My grandparents went way over the top in giving her a name like that.

'We'll work something out, Mother old girl,' he said.

'That's a stupid English expression,' said Mrs Passmore. 'Something you picked up during your time in England. You'll be saying tophole next, or what jolly good fun.'

'Bess would laugh her head off if I did,' said Jeremy.

'Heaven help me, does that mean she giggles?' said Mrs Passmore. 'Our neighbours, the

Wetherfields, have a ten-year-old daughter who giggles.'

'No, Bess doesn't giggle,' said Jeremy, 'she's a young lady of character and charm, not a girlish adolescent.' He returned to the letter.

Mrs Passmore remained unimpressed, as she would have about any woman she had not herself chosen for her son.

Oklahoma! lived up to its reputation as an American musical of outstanding songs and infectious vitality. Paul and Henrietta thoroughly enjoyed it, and since the seats had been Henrietta's treat, Paul engaged a taxi for the drive to her home. She snuggled close, hip to hip and thigh to thigh.

'Wasn't that an absolutely lovely show, Mark?' she murmured.

'You're with me, not Mark,' said Paul. Her slip of the tongue hadn't surprised him. He always felt she dispensed her favours liberally.

'Oh, silly me,' she said, 'did I say Mark?'

'No worries,' said Paul, 'I don't mind about Mark, or Tom, Dick and Harry.'

'Oh, really, that's an unkind dig,' protested Henrietta as the taxi crossed Waterloo Bridge, with a full moon streaking the river with light. 'I'm not that kind of girl, you know.'

'I'm sure you aren't,' said Paul. 'But in any case, what does one more friendship, or several more, matter when we're young?'

'Paul, you're quite special to me,' said Henrietta.

So's Mark, I daresay, thought Paul. And Tom, Dick and Harry too. Oh well, let her enjoy herself, she was an entertaining girl, but not the kind he'd want to marry and live with. He was pretty certain her eyes would always be travelling elsewhere.

'That's something, being quite special,' he said.

'Well, you are, sweetie,' purred Henrietta, who did indeed favour him. He had decidedly masculine qualities, along with an infectious personality. 'By the way, is that odd girl, the one my grandma thinks is a belly dancer, still being odd?'

'I think she'll turn out to be as much of a character as your grandma,' said Paul.

'Poor thing,' said Henrietta.

When the taxi reached her home in Kennington, she invited Paul to come in and see if Granny Dear was in bed. If so, they could have a little time together. Paul, who saw himself being floored, in a manner of speaking, said, 'Nice of you, Henrietta, but I think I'll let the taxi take me on to my own home. I've had a long day, and I'm a bit fagged.'

'Oh, righty-oh,' she said, and her pouting lips delivered a kiss that seemed like an attempt to buck him up, especially as her hand was on his thigh. It didn't work, but she was a good-natured girl, not given to taking offence. There was always a next time. 'Well, sweet dreams, Paul, and I hope they're of me.'

'If they are, they'll wake me up,' said Paul. 'Thanks a buzz for the seats.'

'Keep in touch, ducky,' said Henrietta, and slipped out.

The taxi took Paul home, where his mum asked if he'd like a nice cup of tea, which he declined in favour of sharing a hot toddy with his dad before they all went to bed.

Before they did, Vi asked, 'Paul, are your dad and me going to meet this other girl?'

'It's not likely,' said Paul.

'It's not serious, then?' said Tommy.

'It all amounts to a passing flight of fancy,' said Paul.

'My oh my, listen to you,' said Vi.

'That's all this girl is, a flight of your fancy?' grinned Tommy.

'No, I'm the passing fancy,' said Paul, 'and I won't last long.'

'I get you,' said Tommy, 'flight means flighty, eh?'

'She's still a nice girl,' said Paul. 'She simply likes spreading her wings.'

'Well, we're all only young once,' said Tommy tolerantly.

In her flat, Lulu was about to retire with a good book, an account of events that led up to the General Strike of 1926, when the workers valiantly took on the might of the Conservative government.

Seated in her plain nightie at her dressing table, she was regarding her reflection in the mirror for one more time since early afternoon.

She'd had her hair styled, and it was a mass of springy curls.

'Lulu Saunders,' she said to her reflection, 'you're pathetic.'

Chapter Thirty

Hyde Park, Sunday afternoon.

The weather was bright, if cool, and there were the usual crowds at Speakers' Corner, mostly for the purpose of being entertained in one way or another by the usual array of soapbox orators. Among such were amateur politicians, fanatical anarchists, confirmed vegetarians and eccentrics who'd got religion so badly they were always capable of delivering a scorching amount of fire and brimstone. All orators attracted ribald hecklers.

From her collapsible stand, a well-dressed lady exhorted her audience to consider not only the health-giving nature of vegetarian food, but also how unkind and unnatural it was to eat animals that wanted only to exist quietly in God's green meadows.

'Lady, I ain't ever eaten no sheep standing up in a meadow,' said a heckler.

'You're not alone, my friend,' said the lady speaker.

'It ain't unkind to eat 'em when they're dead, missus,' bawled another heckler, a noisy one, 'and I never heard no lamb chop making a fuss.'

'My good man,' said the lady speaker, 'try asking

a lamb chop while it's still part of a living animal.'

The audience chortled.

'Got you there, Smiffy,' said someone to the heckler, 'eat your greens.'

'I hate greens, don't I?' said the heckler. 'Here, lady, is fried fish 'n' chips all right to eat?'

'Try to realize that a fried plaice was once a fish happily swimming about in the sea,' said the lady vegetarian.

Elsewhere, an anarchist was trying to convince his listeners that individual freedom could only come about if governments, monarchies, police forces, local councils and all other forms of authority were blown up.

'What about my old lady?' called a heckler.

'Whose old lady?' chanted other hecklers in chorus. This kind of performance was routine.

'My old lady,' said heckler number one, 'she's me personal authority.'

'Oh, what a great big awful sight, blow her up with dynamite!'

'If you can't be serious,' said the anarchist, who had to put up with this kind of heckling every week, 'go and play with your toy trains.'

'Here, don't be cross, Hector.'

'He ain't cross, he's careful, like.'

'So he should be, he's sitting on his dynamite.'

Paul and Lulu were among the orators. They were standing on sturdy wooden crates fronted by a waist-high collapsible frame on which a banner proclaimed their credentials.

'The YOUNG SOCIALISTS Support The LABOUR PARTY – So Should YOU.'

Their back-up team of six provided strength and

encouragement in the face of a small crowd obviously ready to bawl disagreement.

Lulu, wearing her dark grey costume, her bright red bow tie, and a woollen hat pulled right down to her eyebrows, was declaiming.

'Only a Labour government can look after the interests of the workers, only a Labour government will fight the capitalists—'

'Hear, hear!' yelled Bernard, making himself the leader of the back-up team.

'Only a Labour government will protect the rights of our trade unions,' declared Lulu, her spectacles dancing with reflected light, 'only a Labour government—'

'Half a mo, girlie,' called a heckler, 'do yer mum and dad know you're out?'

'Shut up!' yelled Bernard and the rest of the team. Beside Lulu, Paul grinned.

'Who's that piece of ancient furniture?' demanded Lulu scathingly.

'Percy Juggins,' said an informative bloke.

'Huggins,' said the heckler, 'and what I want to know is can the little girl tell me what the Labour government's done for me, me wife, me kids and me widdered grandma?'

'Shut up!' yelled Bernard.

'I can answer the question,' said Paul, as the audience swelled with newcomers. 'The Labour government's given you free medical treatment, decent unemployment pay-outs, welfare benefits, better schooling, and a better pension for your grandma. How's that for starters?'

'Hear, hear!' yelled the back-up team.

'Does yer grandma know all that, Percy?' said a thin party to the heckler.

'She ain't short of sense,' said Percy, 'she just don't say much, not since she left her false teeth on a bus.'

'Shut up!' bawled Bernard.

'Might I point out your grandma can get new dentures from a National Health dentist at low cost?' said Lulu.

'Could yer write her a letter?' asked Percy. 'Here, can yer see what you're looking at under that woolly titfer? You ain't bald, are yer, at your age?'

'Shut up!' yelled Bernard, working his tonsils off in defence of the speakers, Lulu in particular.

'Who's he?' asked the thin party.

'Never seen him here before,' said a tall woman in company with her short husband, 'what's he shouting about?'

'Ladies and gents,' said Lulu, 'pay attention. If Winston Churchill and the Tories ever get back—'

'Three cheers for Winston!' cried the tall woman.

'Good old bloke, our Winnie,' said Percy.

'Oh, yes?' said Lulu. 'What's he ever done for your grandma?'

'Ten to one he ain't kept 'er in fur coats nor egg custards,' said Percy, thereby causing Lulu to tell Paul to get down and chuck the bloke under a bus.

Someone arriving at the edge of the audience shouted, 'Here, me friends, there's an old soldier over there talking about a German prisoner-of-war camp that was mostly run by German Army women guards that liked a bit of the old malarky every Saturday night!'

The audience melted away in a rush.

'What a farce,' said Lulu. 'Waste of time. I'd have done better staying at home and washing my hair. No, never mind, forget it,' she added hastily, in case Paul wanted to know what she looked like under her hat.

'If you ask me,' said Bernard, gazing up at her, 'all we got was a crowd of ignoramuses that didn't appreciate you, Lulu. Me, I'm all of appreciative—'

'Leave off,' said Lulu.

'I propose we pack up and go home,' said Paul.

'Seconded,' said Lulu.

So they packed up, the team taking care of the soapboxes, the collapsible frame and the banner. Bernard did his best to persuade Lulu he could give her a blissful time if she let him take her home.

'Want to try that, Lulu?' said Paul.

Lulu's glasses steamed up.

'Call yourself a friend?' she hissed.

'What's that?' asked Bernard, trying to come between them.

'Paul's taking me home,' said Lulu. He better had, she thought. 'Unfortunately, Bernie, you talk too much.'

'Lulu, if you fancy doing more than talking,' said Bernard, 'I could—'

'Not with me you couldn't,' said Lulu. 'Goodbye.'

'Oh, well,' said Bernard, 'I'll have to see what me landlady's got for Sunday tea. Hope it ain't rock cakes,' he burbled, as Paul and Lulu went their way. 'She's a kind woman, but her rock cakes ain't like me mum's.'

On the upper deck of a bus travelling through the Sunday quiet of London's streets, Lulu and Paul were very much by themselves. Lulu, accordingly, was in clear voice, declaring the afternoon a disaster, the first and last time for her on a Hyde Park soapbox. It was for the old stagers, the characters who'd been doing it for years.

'And they're all a bit potty, of course. And they all turn themselves into Aunt Sallys for the benefit of the hecklers. I ought to have remembered that. So ought you.'

'Tomorrow,' said Paul, 'we'll put together a report on the unsuitability of Speakers' Corner until we're a lot older and tougher. When you've typed it, you can deliver it upstairs.'

'Listen, bossy-pants,' said Lulu, 'stop trying to turn me into your office skivvy.'

'Comment noted,' said Paul. 'By the way, are your ears cold?'

'What d'you mean?'

'Your woolly's covering them up,' said Paul.

'Oh, really?' said Lulu.

'Yes, haven't you noticed?'

'What's it to you?'

'Lulu, you're fighting it too much.'

'Fighting what?'

'Your gender,' said Paul.

'I'm just fighting for the right of women to be heard.'

'Well, you won't hear much yourself if you use your woolly hat as an ear muff,' said Paul.

'It saves you giving me earache,' said Lulu.

'Would you like to come home with me and have Sunday tea again?' asked Paul.

Lulu made a face.

'You should have asked me before today,' she said.

'As it is, I'm having tea with my dad and Sylvia.'

'His bride-to-be?' smiled Paul.

'Yes, and I've got a duty to warn her about domestic servitude,' said Lulu.

'If she's like my mum,' said Paul, 'she might take to it.'

'Listen, you're not a bad bloke,' said Lulu. 'Just a pity you sometimes talk like a dinosaur.'

When the bus reached her stop in Kennington, she thanked Paul for standing up with her on the soapboxes, said she'd see him in the office tomorrow, and alighted.

What a character, thought Paul.

'Well, how d'you get on, me lad?' asked Tommy when Paul arrived home.

'Talk about a riot of hecklers,' said Paul, 'they had more to say than we did.'

'Told you,' said Tommy.

'Did you?' said Paul.

'Well, I meant to,' said Tommy, 'but it slipped me mind. Anyway, who won?'

'We didn't,' said Paul. 'We lost our audience. They all faded away to listen to some ex-soldier talking about a German prisoner-of-war camp run by female guards.'

'Goodness me, I've never heard anything like that before,' said Vi.

'I wonder if Boots has?' mused Tommy. 'I mean, larky talk about naughty goings-on behind the barbed wire could have got around the Army.'

'Now, Tommy,' said Vi.

'And the Marines,' said Tommy. 'So your audience scarpered, Paul?'

'Yup, we lost 'em,' said Paul.

'Oh, never mind, lovey,' said Vi, 'I've baked a nice cake for tea, and I'll bake a special one when Alice comes home for a week during Easter.'

'It'll be great to see Alice again,' said Paul.

'You bet it will, and we'll find out if anything's still going on between her and Fergus MacAllister,' said Tommy. 'Listen, me lad, how did Lulu take losing the audience?'

'Like a good Socialist,' said Paul, 'and with her ears covered up.'

'What a funny girl,' said Vi.

Paul discovered what had happened to Lulu's hair when she arrived in the office. First off, she was wearing her jeans and a jumper defiantly. Second, when she removed that same woollen hat, she disclosed a head of shining springy curls.

'What am I looking at?' he asked.

'What my local hairdresser made a mess of on Saturday afternoon,' muttered Lulu.

'Pardon?'

'All right, I know, it's a sight,' said Lulu. 'I must've been unconscious to let it happen.'

'Lulu, it's lovely,' said Paul.

'What?'

'Great,' said Paul.

Lulu, cleaning her glasses, said, 'You're serious?'

'Of course I am,' said Paul, 'that's a seriously smashing hairdo.'

It was to his eyes, it took away the plain look of her straight curtains and turned her into what his Uncle Sammy would have called a genuine female girl. That's if a bloke discounted her mannish jeans.

'Oh, pleasured, I'm sure,' said Lulu offhandedly, putting her spectacles on. But she was a little pink.

'I can't think why you covered it up yesterday,' said Paul.

'Didn't want hecklers chucking bags of flour at it,' said Lulu. 'Now what about this report on Speakers' Corner? Its unsuitability for any speaker except cranks?'

'You start making some notes while I go through the post,' said Paul. 'Then we'll get together. Lulu?'

'Well?' said Lulu cautiously.

'I seriously like your curls,' said Paul.

Lulu went a little pink again. I need help, she thought, I've got a shocking feeling I'm going soft in the head.

Later, over coffee, she asked Paul if he'd enjoyed his theatre visit with tarty Henrietta.

'Great show,' said Paul, 'enjoyed it from beginning to end.'

'And then?' said Lulu.

'We took a taxi to her home,' said Paul.

'And then?' said Lulu.

'End of the evening,' said Paul. 'Why are you interested?'

'I'm a sister human being,' said Lulu. 'Don't want to see you turned into a poodle. And put on a lead. By the way, how's that nice mother of yours?'

'Getting nicer all the time,' said Paul. 'How did Sunday tea go with your dad and his fiancée?'

'Oh, I took her aside and pointed out what she was up against,' said Lulu. 'I told her I liked the idea of her marrying my dad. But keep out of the kitchen, I said, or you'll be enslaved.'

'What did she say to that?' asked Paul.

'Something I couldn't believe,' said Lulu. 'That she was going to have the kitchen done up, with everything new. What she wanted, she said, was a new-looking and pretty kitchen. Talk about grief and sorrow. She's done for already.'

'Cheer up,' said Paul, 'she's proved herself as one of your women in command.'

'Command of what?' asked disgusted Lulu.

'Of your dad's kitchen,' said Paul.

Lulu eyed him over her coffee cup, and put a hand over her mouth. A muffled little sound emerged.

Then she burst into laughter.

Blimey, thought Paul, her sense of humour has struggled out. Very promising, especially as she's had her hair styled.

At six thirty, Alice Adams left the office of Bristol University's bursar. She'd had a long working day, and was looking forward to a restful evening at her lodgings in the heart of the city. Arriving at the terraced house of three storeys and a basement, she stopped at the sight of a uniformed Army sergeant sitting on the stone steps, a valise beside him.

'I don't believe it,' she breathed.

'It's no' a wee goblin, Alice, it's me,' said Sergeant Fergus MacAllister of a Scots Highland regiment. His dark looks, darker because of a deep tan, were topped by his beret, his eyes bright and teasing. 'I'd almost forgotten what a sweet-looking lassie you are.'

Alice, fair and slender, studious and somewhat reserved, took a deep breath. She was never quite sure of her feelings for Fergus, although his presence and his challenging nature always aroused her.

But that hadn't happened for ages. He'd been away far too long.

'Fergus, for heaven's sake, where have you sprung from?' she asked.

'Singapore and Southampton,' said Fergus. 'The regiment's home, y'ken.'

'Why didn't you let me know?'

'I didna have time. We only disembarked this morning.' Fergus came to his feet, a lean and sinewy man, looking like a pirate in khaki. 'Are ye no' pleased to see me?'

'Yes, of course I am,' said Alice. 'Where are you staying?'

'Wi' you, I'm hoping,' said Fergus. 'You've two rooms here, so you've said in your letters.'

'Don't be absurd,' said Alice, 'you can't share with me, not even if I had a suite of rooms.'

'I'll sleep on the sofa,' said Fergus. 'I'll no' enter your bed.'

'You certainly won't,' said Alice.

'Well now,' said Fergus, 'I thought a few days here wi' you would give us a chance to fix a date for the wedding.'

'What?'

'Aye, I'm on a full month's leave, and out of the Army a month later, and I mean to marry you, Alice. Haven't I always said so?'

'Several times,' said Alice, fair hair stirring in the breeze, and the skirt of her white-cuffed blue dress coyly fluttering. 'But I don't recall either of us being positive.'

'Whisht, lassie, I'm more positive than a stalking tiger,' said Fergus. 'Will you keep me standing here and no' open your door for the two of us?'

Alice regarded him intently. He smiled and her pulses twitched. The students who were all around her each day, and about to take off for the Easter vacation, were young, chattering and making hard work of growing up. Fergus was well beyond that stage. He had known the front lines of the war, and the Communist terrorists of Malaya. He looked supremely fit and self-assured, but there was still a touch of the devil about him. If Alice had thought marriage to a university professor would suit her, she was less sure of it these days.

'Fergus,' she said, 'let's go in and up to my rooms. I'll make some supper and we can talk. Oh, and you can bed down on the sofa for the sake of what my grandmother would call my good name.'

'I've a like grandmother, Alice my bonny,' said Fergus, 'with her eyes always at my back.'

'In that case, let's put the door between her and your back,' said Alice. She opened the solid-looking door and stepped into the house.

Fergus picked up his valise and followed her in. He closed the door and shut out the hustle and bustle of Bristol.

Chapter Thirty-One

Paula, by arrangement, was going to spend time with Kate and David at Easter, from Good Friday to Monday. Phoebe was going with her. She'd said she didn't ought to spend the Easter weekend feeling deprived.

'Deprived of what, me pet?' asked Sammy.

'Of seeing Cousin David's cows,' said Phoebe. 'Crikey, no-one ever sees cows in Denmark Hill or Camberwell Green. Or even Ruskin Park.'

'Oh, dear, what a shame,' said Susie.

'Well, I daresay we can arrange for you to go with Paula,' said Sammy.

'Mind where you walk,' said Jimmy.

'What d'you mean?' asked Phoebe.

'You'll find out when you're chatting up the cows,' said Jimmy.

Bess arrived home from university, and enjoyed long talks with her family about Jeremy and his arrival in August. Susie noted her visible pleasure, and also that she was much more outgoing. Like her cousin, Alice, she'd been a little reserved. Not now. She was quite a vibrant young woman. In the animated way she talked of seeing Jeremy again, she made Susie wonder if she was starry-eyed about the man.

'Sammy,' she said later, 'is our Bess in love, d'you think?'

'If you're asking me, Susie,' said Sammy, 'you're asking a bloke who's scratching his head.'

'You're not sure, you mean?' said Susie.

'Well, it could be she's in a bit of dream about the bloke,' said Sammy.

'I wonder,' said Susie.

'I know what you mean,' said Sammy. 'It's what we've talked about before, that one day we might find we've got another American relative.'

'What a mixed lot we'll be,' said Susie.

'League of Nations,' said Sammy. 'Mind, that bunch of half-hearted officials didn't come to much.'

'Not like the Adamses,' smiled Susie.

'Granted,' said Sammy.

Two days later, a letter from the Board of Trade arrived on his desk. It said, in effect, that the application from Adams Fashions Ltd for a textiles import licence was under consideration, and that the result would be communicated to him in due course. Sammy wasn't keen on 'due course'. He'd had some of it from the Ministry of Supply during the war, and it usually meant a long wait.

'We'll have to be patient,' said Rachel.

'Unfortunately,' said Sammy, 'waiting gives my kind of patience a gorblimey headache.'

Bobby had seen Dr Mason, and the GP had advised him that his father's condition, common to many men, was not to be considered serious. He had assured Ned of that following the result of his examination by a specialist. A saltless diet and a daily aspirin, together with an avoidance of stress, could keep his condition stable. If it did worsen, however, then retirement could be a sensible move. In which case, I'll suggest it myself, said the caring doctor.

Bobby informed his mother accordingly.

'Well, as your dad will be having a check-up every fortnight,' said Lizzy, 'I suppose we can leave everything to our doctor, can't we?'

'Best thing, Mum,' said Bobby.

'I'll try to stop worrying, then,' said Lizzy.

'I'll do that myself while Helene and I, with the kids, are visiting her parents in France for a week over Easter,' said Bobby. 'Let Dad know we'll put in some extra work in your garden when we come back.'

'Yes, all right, Bobby,' said Lizzy, relieved that Dr Mason had again insisted there was no cause for real concern.

Tommy received a phone call from daughter Alice one evening. She reminded him she was coming home for a week just before Good Friday.

'Your mum and me are looking forward to that,' said Tommy.

'So am I,' said Alice, 'it's been ages since I was last at home.'

'We miss you, y'know,' said Tommy, 'all that way down in Bristol. Your grandma never stops worrying about you living somewhere as foreign as that.'

'Grandma never changes,' said Alice, 'any more than Queen Victoria ever did.'

'She'll change when she gets to be Lady Finch,' said Tommy, 'she'll be in a permanent tizzy.'

'Dad, you don't know your own mother if you think that,' said Alice. 'She'll have one day of trying to work out what happened, then she'll be back on her family roundabout as if nothing out of the ordinary had happened at all.'

'Except she'll be wearing a tiara,' said Tommy.

'That'll be the day,' said Alice. 'Listen, Dad, I'd like to bring a friend home with me.'

'One of your university friends?' said Tommy.

'No, a special friend,' said Alice. 'Fergus.'

'What, Fergus MacAllister that used to service our gas boiler?' said Tommy. 'Your mum and me wondered if he was still around in your life. We thought he was overseas.'

Alice told him of Fergus's arrival on the steps of her lodgings, and of the fact that he was staying in Bristol. She didn't say she was putting him up herself. She knew her parents were of the old-fashioned school, and might think she and Fergus were living in sin. Not that that was likely. She had her own principles about right and wrong, as Fergus knew. He had strict instructions to sleep on her living-room sofa, and to stay there.

'He's on a full month's leave, Dad,' she said. 'Then he's going back to his unit to wait for the date of his discharge. So would you and Mum mind if I brought him home with me?'

'You do that, Alice, your mum and me have always liked your Scotch bloke,' said Tommy.

'Scottish, Dad,' said Alice. 'Scotch is whisky.'

'I like that as well,' said Tommy. 'A nip now and again was recommended for me health by your

Uncle Boots years ago. Would you mind telling me if there's something special going on with you and Fergus, something to do with him leaving the Army?'

Alice said Fergus kept talking about marrying her, that she wasn't talking about it herself, she had to do some serious thinking about the prospect of what she'd had in mind for ages, a career as a university lecturer. Tommy said well, it's got to be one thing or the other, and she ought to make a decision about it, and not keep Fergus on a string. She'd got to be fair to the bloke, he added. Alice said she felt she'd know what decision to make after a week at home with him. Tommy said bring him, then.

'Thanks, Dad,' said Alice, 'I'm glad you understand.'

'I'm not sure I do,' said Tommy, thinking she ought to know her mind already, considering she was spending time with Fergus in Bristol. She said goodbye then and rang off. He spoke to Vi.

'Oh dear,' said Vi, 'our Alice is just the same, liking a career more than the idea of marriage.'

'Well, it's her life, her choice,' said Tommy.

'It can't be very nice for Fergus,' said Vi. 'I mean, all this time and Alice still not able to make up her mind. Tommy, she could end up an old maid.' Vi could think of nothing more sad for a woman.

'Like I said, it'll be her own choice,' murmured Tommy, who wasn't oblivious to the fact that the war had brought a social change, that more than a few young women had the kind of independent outlook rarely known in the past. Such an outlook sprang from all that women had accomplished during the war.

*   *   *

Saturday, and Lulu had Paul gaping. She'd arrived in a New Look patterned dress which, with her styled hairdo, made her a young lady to behold.

'I'm dreaming,' he said.

'Oh, yes?' said Lulu.

'What's happened?' asked Paul.

'Meaning have I had a funny experience on my way here?' suggested Lulu.

'Meaning why are you dressed like a Mayfair deb?' said Paul.

'Oh, my dad and Sylvia are taking me to meet her parents,' said Lulu. 'They live in Blackheath.'

'Blackheath?' said Paul. 'Some fine houses there, by the heath, and a lot of middle-class bods.'

'All right, so Sylvia's middle class,' said Lulu. 'Not her fault. Unfortunate accident of birth. We're having lunch and afternoon tea with her parents. Sylvia turned up with this dress last night. With strict instructions from my dad that I was to wear it. I hoped it wouldn't fit, but it did. I feel like a freak in frilly wrappings.'

'You don't look it, not from here,' said Paul.

'It's not me,' said Lulu.

'Listen, sexy, it's the real you,' said Paul, 'the other one's just—'

'What did you call me?' Lulu's spectacles gleamed.

'The real you,' said Paul, 'the other one's just fallen overboard. Hope it sinks. But half a mo, I'm not sure you ought to be seen in Blackheath looking like that. You'll get propositioned.'

'Shut up,' said Lulu. 'Trust a bloke like you to have evil thoughts. And what d'you mean, I'm sexy?'

'Oh, just the kind of girl who'd make a lot of

337

fellers think of you and springtime,' said Paul.

'Oh, really?' said Lulu. 'Very funny, I don't think. Under this soppy dress is a woman trying to make a serious name for herself.'

'My sister's like that,' said Paul, 'but there's a Scotsman chasing her.'

'Hope she can outrun him,' said Lulu. 'Listen, I don't want to be considered sexy. You sure you meant that?'

'Positive,' said Paul.

'Oh, well, I must have taken a wrong turning,' said Lulu. 'Anyway, my dad and Sylvia are picking me up here at eleven thirty, and we're all going straight to Blackheath for lunch and tea with her parents. So I'll be leaving early.'

'Enjoy yourself,' said Paul, 'and try not to worry about Sylvia's parents being middle class.'

'Oh, they've both got a saving grace,' said Lulu.

'Which is?'

'They're both Labour voters,' said Lulu, thus grabbing the last word of a dialogue she needed to win. Well, what young woman devoted to a political career with the Labour Party wanted to be considered sexy in preference to seriously dedicated?

Still, she couldn't say she actually felt insulted.

Shortly before the Easter weekend arrived in early April, Alice came home, bringing Fergus MacAllister with her. Tommy and Vi welcomed them warmly, since they both liked Fergus. He was the kind of man much favoured by the family, from Chinese Lady downwards. That is, he looked as if he could take good care of himself and a wife. He seemed on very easy terms with Alice, and she seemed happy enough

338

with their relationship, even if she did not show the emotions of a young woman in love. But then, she had always been reserved.

Bobby and Helene, with their children, travelled to France to stay with Helene's parents for a week. Jacob and Estelle Aarlberg, now middle-aged, but still running their farm, welcomed them with unreserved delight. Both had a great fondness for their English son-in-law, acquired during the dangerous days when they had sheltered him from scouring Germans for several weeks immediately following the Dunkirk evacuation. His eventual return to England in company with Helene, by crossing the Channel in her small yacht, was regarded by Jacob as an act of sheer bravery. How happy and relieved he and his wife had been when they received news by a roundabout way that they had landed safely.

Madame Aarlberg accepted a hug and a kiss from Bobby and from Helene, then bestowed hugs and kisses on her grandchildren, three-year-old Estelle, named after herself, and little Robert, eighteen months.

The holiday at the Aarlberg farm was enjoyed in an atmosphere of limitless hospitality.

Paula and Phoebe commenced their long weekend at David and Kate's farm, mostly in places where they were in contact with the engaging young Enrico. After some while, Paula suggested that Phoebe might like to go and help Kate in the dairy.

'But I like being in the fields near the cows,' said Phoebe.

'Yes, but you're following me about,' said Paula.

'Crikey, I know what you're after,' said Phoebe, laughing, 'you want to be alone with Rico.'

'Fat chance I've got of that, when you're always in the way,' said Paula.

'Well, I like him too,' said Phoebe.

'You're not old enough to start liking young men,' said Paula, lofty in the knowledge that she herself was in her sixteenth year, the age when a girl could accept a kiss if she wanted to. 'Go and like Kate's dairy.'

'All right,' said Phoebe, in her agreeable way, 'and if she asks me what you're doing, I won't say you're doing it with Rico.'

'Don't you dare,' said Paula, and Phoebe departed giggling.

That left Paula to enjoy time with Enrico, while David was sowing a ploughed field with swedes, food for the cows.

'Paula,' said Enrico, herding the Jerseys from one field to another, 'I would like to say you get prettier, don't-a you?'

'Oh, I can't disagree, can I?' said Paula. 'It wouldn't be fair to myself.'

'When you are older, I would like you for my best girl,' said Enrico.

'Well, thanks,' said Paula, 'how jolly good of you, especially if no-one else is interested in me, and I just get older and older.'

'No-one?' said Enrico. 'That's a joke, I think. You are much too nice for no-one to take notice of you.'

'Oh, my pleasure, I'm sure,' said Paula. 'Rico, stop hitting the cows.' She was holding the gate open, the herd lumbering through, Enrico slapping the flanks of those inclined to blunder about.

'It's a caress, little signorina,' said Enrico, stopping as the last of the animals went through. He glanced at Paula, just inches away from him. In a cream jumper, knitted by her mum, and a neat blue skirt, she looked alive, enchanting, and very kissable, of course, to a young man of Italy. Enrico, however, checked a natural impulse to deliver a kiss. He was held back by the instant memory of that moment when he had seen a pervert pounce on her. It would not do to remind her of that by giving in to a natural impulse. Further, Kate had warned him not to take liberties. But Paula sensed what he had intended.

'Blessed cheek,' she said, 'you were going to kiss me.'

'See, I'm sorry,' said Enrico.

'Don't think about it again,' said Paula. 'Well, not till I'm ready.'

'No, no, I must wait until you're older,' said Enrico.

'Oh, I'll be older by this time tomorrow,' said Paula, and laughed. Enrico, happy about such a healthy reaction, split his sides, and in the April sunshine their combined laughter sailed over the heads of the cows.

Boots, Polly and the twins were spending a day at the chicken farm. The fine weather saw the twins scampering about with the other children. Giles and Emily, born of Rosie and Matthew, and Jessie, born of Emma and Jonathan, were in joyful and yelling companionship with Gemma and James. They ran about amid the sheep, tried to cuddle the lambs, and chased the multitude of chickens and the yellow swarms of chicks. Squawking added its own note to the yelling. So did the barking of Cecil, the dog that had proved useless in keeping foxes away.

'Boots old love,' said Polly, 'listen to all that yelling.' She and Boots were sitting on a long bench with Rosie, Matthew, Emma and Jonathan. 'Were you just as noisy when you were a little fiend?'

'Probably,' said Boots, watching the running youngsters and thinking, not for the first time, of the many thousands of Jewish children deprived by the gas chambers of ever knowing the joys of growing up.

'Polly,' said Matthew, 'I dispute that Boots ever squawked.'

'So do I,' said Emma, enjoying a welcome break from plucking chickens for local butchers. 'Well, I mean, you might have been a fiend, Uncle Boots, but never a chicken.'

'By rights,' said Jonathan, 'chickens should be seen and not heard.'

'Baa,' said a sheep in apparent disagreement.

'Is that a relative of yours, Jonathan?' asked Rosie.

'It's old Fanny,' grinned Jonathan, 'but I won't say she's not got a likeness to my old Aunt Martha that ever was.'

Young James, galloping, tripped, tumbled and lay winded. All the other kids jumped on him. So did Cecil. The racket sent the chickens scurrying for cover. The fluffy chicks took no notice.

'Kids,' smiled Boots.

'Who'd have them?' said Rosie.

'Well, we've all got 'em,' said Matthew.

'Happy are the blessed,' said Polly, 'but who are the blessed, I wonder, we or them?'

'Not James right now,' said Boots, 'he's at the

bottom of the pile. By the way, Matt, any luck with extra help?'

'We've interviewed two young couples,' said Matthew.

'Hopeless,' said Rosie.

'They didn't like the long hours,' said Emma.

'Or the prospect of hard work,' said Jonathan.

James's muffled gasps suddenly died away and stopped. The other children scrambled off him. He lay inert. Boots, instantly suspecting suffocation, came to his feet and ran. Reaching his son he was at once aware that the boy seemed to have stopped breathing. He dropped and straddled him, using his hands to dig strongly into James's chest. The other children looked on in frightened bewilderment. Polly came rushing up, white-faced.

'Boots – oh, my God!' she gasped.

Boots kept going, pressing hard and repeatedly at James's chest. Up came Matthew. He flung himself down on his knees behind the boy's head, framed the closed mouth with his fingers, forced it open, dipped his head and blew strong breaths of air into the throat, a reviving technique lately finding favour with first-aid teams.

Matthew blew into the boy's lungs, and Boots dug harder into the chest, with Polly, looking stricken, down on her knees beside him. During her momentous years as an ambulance driver in the Great War, she had known emergencies when only immediate treatment of a battlefield casualty could save him from dying. But she had never witnessed this kind of resuscitation. She did what she rarely did, she prayed with desperate fervour. She prayed for the life of her son.

The other children were still silent and staring. Rosie, Emma and Jonathan, close by, were just as silent. Emma had a hand over her shaking mouth.

Something happened that gave everyone hope.

James issued a tiny cough. Matthew, taking a deep breath, blew more air into the boy's lungs, and the next moment he was breathing. His eyes opened.

'So there you are,' said Boots gently, his working hands easing a little.

James gulped air and his chest heaved. Matthew straightened up.

'Welcome back, Jamie,' he said.

James coughed again and said something that sounded like 'Erk?' It represented a gasping enquiry about what had happened to him.

Gemma began to cry. Rosie soothed her, while James began to breathe freely.

'Dad, what happened?' he asked faintly, as Boots stood up.

Boots might have said a large bundle of imps fell on him, but he knew that would distress the other children.

'Oh, just a kind of passing-out parade, old chap,' he said. 'You're fine now.' He brought the boy to his feet and gave him a hug. 'How about a cup of hot sweet tea, if Rosie would put the kettle on?'

'Hot tea? Just the thing,' said Matthew briskly. There was nothing mundane about hot tea as a reviving stimulant for a shaken boy, and as a welcome pick-me-up for nerve-racked adults. It was the first thing Chinese Lady would have recommended.

Polly, on her feet now, gave James a hug of her

344

own, a lingering one. She looked at Boots, and then at Matthew, her eyes overbright.

'Thanks for that, old dears,' she said huskily.

Rosie and Emma quickly made their way to the house to put the kettle on and to find some cake for the upset children.

Over the tea, Rosie tried to raise the level of the subdued conversation, while the children became subconsciously aware that parental care was on a very affectionate plane. Emma and Jonathan sat close to Jessie, Rosie and Matthew paid indulgent attention to the little wants of Emily and Giles, and Polly and Boots were a reassuring unit to the still shaken James and a soothing one to his still upset sister.

In time it brought the children back to active life.

In these immediate post-war years, young ones were precious to their parents, especially so because of a conflict that had been terrifying to the children of Europe and had cost the lives of untold numbers of them.

The Swinging Sixties, which would see a gradual diminishing of parental love and care in favour of careers, were yet to come.

Chapter Thirty-Two

Fergus left the home of Tommy and Vi a day earlier than planned.

'But we thought you weren't going until tomorrow,' said Vi.

'Och aye,' said Fergus, 'nor was I, Mrs Adams, but I canna get Alice to make up her mind, y'ken, so I'm away up to Aberdeen and my family until my leave ends. I'll no' press Alice any longer. I'm thanking you and Mr Adams for your kindness in putting me up, and I'd like it fine if you'd give my regards to Paul.' He and Paul had found each other very agreeable, especially when discussing politics, since Fergus supported the Labour Party. 'I'll say goodbye, with hopes of seeing you again sometime.'

After he'd gone, Tommy and Vi spoke to Alice, who confessed she'd been unable to commit herself to a definite understanding with Fergus. He'd wanted her to agree to marriage, but at the moment she still couldn't see that as her first priority, which was to become a lecturer. After all, she'd spent several years with that ambition in mind. Fergus had known this.

'Well, your mum and me hope you're not making a mistake,' said Tommy.

'Fergus is such a fine man, honest and straight-forward,' said Vi.

'Yes, I know,' said Alice, 'and he's good company, but I just don't feel I need marriage.'

Such a comment mystified her parents, born of the old school, but they didn't press her, and she returned to Bristol the following day. Paul said she wasn't the only young woman who had modern ideas concerning their future.

'What's modern ideas, might I ask?' said Vi.

'It means it's a new way of looking at life,' said Paul.

'Daft,' said Tommy.

'Paul lovey,' said Vi, 'have you got modern ideas?'

'In some respects,' said Paul, 'but I'm not set on becoming a stuffy and cranky old bachelor with egg stains on my waistcoat.'

'Thank goodness for that,' said Vi, 'you can't get rid of egg stains very easy, and thank goodness too that your brother David doesn't have modern ideas, and did what was right and sensible.'

'Sensible?' said Paul.

'Yes, when he married Kate,' said Vi.

'I call that better than sensible,' said Paul.

'You can say that again,' remarked Tommy. 'It was what comes natural, or should do. Modern ideas?' He shook his head. 'Daft,' he said.

During the afternoon of Saturday, two burly Walworth stallholders made a citizens' arrest of a man who'd attempted a quick and very sick assault on a girl in the East Street market under cover of a crowd around a fruit stall. The market bobby was summoned and, amid a mass of irate shoppers, the

347

man was officially arrested and taken to the police station. There, in the presence of witnesses and the girl herself, he was charged with an act of indecency and held in custody prior to appearing before the magistrates on Monday.

On Monday at the court, his solicitor pleaded not guilty on his behalf, and on the grounds that it was all a mistake. His client, he pleaded, had accidentally stumbled against the girl from behind, and simply held onto her to prevent himself falling. Nevertheless, the man was committed for trial at the Old Bailey. However, since there was no record of previous misdemeanours, he was allowed bail. He returned to his home.

Late that evening, the large and lumpy woman who lived with her meek and mild husband on the ground-floor flat of a house in Kimpton Road, Camberwell, heard a crash that made their ceiling vibrate.

'What was that?' she asked.

'Sounded like Jarvis dropping a crate of eggs,' said her husband.

'Talk sense,' she said, 'what's he want a whole crate for, you gormless loon?'

'I only said it sounded like that.'

'Well, it didn't to me,' said the woman. They listened. The quiet caused uneasiness. 'Look, I don't like the man, I never have and never will, but you'd better go up and see if he's all right.'

'Can't we mind our own business?' said meek-and-mild.

'If he's just fallen down dead drunk, leave him,' said the woman, 'but if he's broke his neck, we'll

348

have to do something about getting an ambulance.'

'Supposing his door's locked?'

'Well, knock on it till he answers.'

'I ain't particularly keen— oh, all right, me love, no need to get vexatious, like, I'm on me way,' said meek-and-mild, and up he went. He found the door of the upper flat open.

He was shaking like a beanpole in the wind when he reappeared only a minute later with frightening news.

William Jarvis, an incurable deviant, had done himself and his immediate world a favour by hanging himself, kicking a heavy chair over in the process.

The following day, Sammy had a word with Mitch, the van driver.

'Seen the morning paper, Mitch?'

'Not half, guv,' said Mitch. 'Our queer bloke's done himself in.'

'No need for any more notes,' said Sammy.

'Thought you might say so,' murmured Mitch.

'I wonder,' mused Sammy, 'could they have started him on the way to a suicide job?'

'Them and an Old Bailey trial,' said Mitch. 'A bit of an uncomfortable place for bad 'uns, the Old Bailey. You ain't bothered, are you, guv?'

'It won't keep me awake,' said Sammy, thinking of Paula. He and Susie had known immense relief at how well and how quickly she'd got over the shock of being attacked. Boots had said she was a girl of such well-balanced mental resilience that if she accidentally walked into a nudist camp, she'd come out giggling at the lumpy, bumpy or wrinkled look of unclothed bodies. Sammy supposed well-balanced mental resilience simply meant it would take a lot to send Paula round the bend, but Boots, who got more educated every year, used his own kind of wordage, and very often as if it concerned something highly amusing. This did not apply to anything concerning Jarvis, however. 'No, it won't keep me awake, Mitch. Ta muchly for delivering the notes.'

'Pleasure, guv.'

The news was frankly welcome to Susie. She had never been quite sure that Sammy's way of dealing with Jarvis had been the right way. It had left the man free to give in to his sexual fantasies whenever he lost control of himself, as such men did. He'd lost that control in the Walworth market. By hanging himself he'd left Susie a completely relieved woman. She made sure that the newspaper carrying the report, and the details of why Jarvis had been awaiting trial, was quickly destroyed before Paula had a chance to read it. However, when she was alone with the girl, she told her that the man had died.

'Mum, how d'you know?' asked Paula.

'Oh, our van driver, Mr Mitchell, was talking to your dad,' said Susie, 'and he mentioned that a man called Jarvis, who lived near to him, died very sudden and unexpected.'

'But Mitch didn't know he was the man who attacked me, did he?' said Paula.

'Well, your dad and me have only talked to a few people about it,' said Susie truthfully. 'Like David and Kate.'

'Oh, well, poor bloke, what a sad case,' said Paula.

'I suppose you could call him that,' said Susie.

Paula did some thinking, then said in artless fashion, 'I expect he got overexcited about something and had a heart attack.'

'You could be right, Paula love,' said Susie.

That closed the chapter.

Something else happened that was welcome to Sammy. He was granted an import licence on behalf of Adams Fashions Ltd.

He popped into Rachel's office to give her the good news.

'I'm blissed,' said Rachel.

'I ain't far behind you,' said Sammy, 'and I like it that it was all your own work. What a woman, credit to the firm, and what's more, you're a corblimey marvel as well.'

'My life, Sammy,' smiled Rachel, 'hasn't it always been a wish of mine to be known as a corblimey marvel?'

'Glad you've made it,' said Sammy. 'Next thing we need is a list of textile importers.'

'Board of Trade again,' said Rachel.

'Ring 'em up,' said Sammy, 'you've got the kind of voice they like.'

'What kind of a voice is that, Sammy?'

'I'm not much good at poetry, so don't ask me,' said Sammy, 'ask Shakespeare.'

'My life, Sammy, I've got a voice for a poet?' said Rachel, and laughed.

'By the way,' said Sammy, 'much to me sorrow, we've got to get the Board of Trade to include an importer of American jeans on their list.'

'Better an importer of denim, so that we can manufacture our own,' said Rachel. 'Under licence, of course. I know you're fed up talking about them, but jeans are going to sell, Sammy, I'm sure of it.'

'Oh, well,' said Sammy, 'a decent profit margin might just help me to think a bit kinder of American cowboys.'

'Edwin, I've been talking to Lizzy,' said Chinese Lady, having just come off the phone.

'About Ned?' said Mr Finch. 'Or about next Tuesday?' Their day at the Palace was only a week away.

'Lord, I still get chronic flutters every time I think about that,' said Chinese Lady. 'It's my one relief I don't have to meet the King myself and do a curtsey. I know I'd fall over, and then what? I'd be in the *News of the World* for people to read about. All my life I never wanted to be read about in the *News of the World*. It's common.' Chinese Lady had never been on friendly terms with anything she considered common or vulgar. 'No, I've been talking to Lizzy about Ned.'

'About his present condition?' enquired Mr Finch, in good health himself at seventy-six.

'Yes, I was thinking next Tuesday might be too much for him,' said Chinese Lady.

'So the great day did come into it, Maisie?'

'Well, it's been on my mind that it's not like going to listen to the band in Hyde Park,' said Chinese Lady anxiously. 'I mean, all the people and the Palace and lords and ladies, and seeing you doing your bow to the King himself, it could be a bit much for Ned.'

'Um – too much nervous excitement, you mean, my dear?' said Mr Finch. 'What did Lizzy say?'

'Oh, just that Ned's feeling fine and wouldn't miss the day, not for anything,' said Chinese Lady. 'Well, I'm feeling fine myself, except for my troublesome trembles occasional, but only the Lord knows if I'll be able to keep standing up, which I don't know I could if I had a weak heart.'

'Ned doesn't have a weak heart, Maisie,' said Mr Finch, 'and you'll be sitting, not standing, throughout the ceremony.'

'Well, if you think it'll be all right for Ned – ?'

'I'd never dream of persuading him to stay away,' said Mr Finch. 'There are occasions, Maisie, when we must let our nearest and dearest do what they most wish.'

'Yes, all right, Edwin,' said Chinese Lady, 'I just hope for myself that no-one hears my knees knocking – oh, Lor', supposing the King does?'

'Be in no doubt, Maisie, knees rarely knock when one is sitting down,' said her ever-reassuring husband.

Saturday morning.

Polly and Boots, keeping a promise to the twins, had taken them to see Buckingham Palace and the Changing of the Guard. The day was fine enough to emphasize the colour of the spectacle. Sightseers lined the approach to the Palace as the new guard, jackets a bright scarlet and bearskins a glossy black, came marching in step to their band music. Gemma and James, standing between their parents, were thrilled and excited, and they leaned forward to take in more of the brave look of the guardsmen. Polly, holding Gemma's hand, clasped it tighter. Boots, an arm around James's neck, placed a firm hand on the boy's shoulder. The memory of the incident at the chicken farm was still fresh.

Fascinated, the twins watched the ceremonial changing of the sentries and then, through the railings, the replacement of the retiring guard by the new.

Impressed, James said in serious vein, 'I think I'd like to be a soldier.'

'But you'd have to go away,' protested Gemma, not in favour of being parted from him.

The spectacle was coming to an end. The twins, however, were still goggle-eyed. Polly glanced at Boots, and they smiled at each other in mutual acknowledgement of their children's enjoyment.

'Time to go in a moment, old sport,' said Polly. They were due to meet her father and stepmother for lunch at Fortnum and Mason in Piccadilly, as a further treat for the twins.

'Right,' said Boots, thinking about a surprise he had arranged for his family, with Flossie's co-operation. It was to do with the installation of a very modern piece of furniture, and Flossie, he was sure, would see that it was carried out satisfactorily.

The ceremony ended. Some onlookers began to move away, others lingered. So did the twins. At this point, the crowds began to buzz. A sleek black limousine, chauffeur-driven, appeared from the Mall, and slowed in its approach to the Palace gates. People clapped and cheered. James and Gemma, and their parents, spotted the occupants of the car, none other than the popular Princess Elizabeth and her husband, the dashing Prince Philip, she in a light spring coat and a fetching hat, he in the

354

uniform of a naval officer. The Princess acknowl-
edged the applause of people with smiles and hand
gestures. The Palace gates opened, and the limousine drove through.

'Oh, goodness me,' breathed Gemma, 'who was
that, Daddy?'

'You've just seen Princess Elizabeth and Prince
Philip,' said Boots.

'Crikey,' said James, impressed.

'Has that made the morning worthwhile for you
and Gemma?' smiled Polly, who never stopped
thinking their children made every day worthwhile
for herself and Boots.

'Not half,' said James, and they all departed for
Piccadilly and lunch with the twins' maternal grandparents, Sir Henry and Lady Simms.

When they finally arrived home, at four in the afternoon, the surprise was in place in the living room, a
handsome television set of cabinet construction.
Britain's BBC had pioneered a limited television
service before the war, had closed it down on the
outbreak of hostilities, and recently resumed it on a
nationwide basis, although not every household was
able to obtain a set or afford one. Like so much else,
sets were in short supply, and there was a licence fee
to pay for, as well as the cost of the set itself.

'Boots, you lovely old dog,' said Polly, delighted.

'Yes, ain't it a marvel, mum?' enthused Flossie.
'There's instructions, but the men from the shop
showed me how to switch it on. Shall I show you?'

'Do that, Flossie,' said Boots, 'we're all agog.'

Flossie switched on the set. After a few seconds,
the screen began to hum lightly and then suddenly

355

came to miraculous life with a clear black and white picture of *Children's Hour*.

'There, what d'you think of that, kiddies?' said Flossie.

Gemma and James blinked, gazed, and went into a hypnotized trance that was close to rapture.

'The thing works,' said Boots.

'Well, we've seen the sets of some of our neighbours, haven't we?' said Polly.

'True,' said Boots, 'but the fact that ours works means we're now keeping up with the Joneses.'

James came out of his trance to request, 'Mum, could you and Dad stop talking, so's Gemma and me can hear what they're saying in the picture?'

'Yes, would you mind, please?' said Gemma, then thought. 'Daddy, we don't know any Joneses.'

'Oh, your daddy means that what some of the neighbours 'ave got, we've now got as well,' said Flossie, always made to feel she was one of the family herself, a family that was now a television-owning entity, and well up with all the Joneses.

Chapter Thirty-Three

Monday morning found Chinese Lady on very sensitive tenterhooks, for tomorrow was the day of her husband's investiture.

Over breakfast, he said with a smile, 'Maisie, my dear, why are you spooning cornflakes into your tea? You usually take just a little sugar.'

'Oh, Lor', I'm already that nervous, I can't think what I'm doing of,' she said, 'and I know I'll be worse tomorrow.'

'Well, just before we leave for the Palace, you shall have a nip of brandy,' said Mr Finch.

'Brandy? Edwin, I'll be drunk when we get there.'

'You'll be relaxed and happy, Maisie.'

'Well, I just hope I'll be able to stay on my feet,' said Chinese Lady not for the first time, and showing she still didn't quite know what she was doing as she sipped at the tea infested with cornflakes.

Mr Finch's smile was indulgent. His affection for his enduring, cockney-born wife was constant and unchanging.

'What's up with you?' asked Lulu, fingers coming to a halt on the keys of her typewriter. Paul was unusually quiet.

'I'm thinking,' he said.

'If it's about tarty Henrietta, don't bother,' said Lulu, whose styled hairdo was now receiving regular attention from her hairdresser, even if she did keep telling herself she was letting some kind of biological weakness undermine her nonconformist strengths.

'No, I'm not thinking about Henrietta,' said Paul, chewing over notes he was making.

'I hope that's a promising sign,' said Lulu.

'It's like this,' said Paul, deciding to tell her before she eventually found out in one way or another. 'Tomorrow my good old grandpa's attending an investiture at Buckingham Palace to receive a knighthood.'

Lulu's spectacles quivered on her nose.

'He's what?'

'I think you heard,' said Paul.

'What's he done for it, then?' asked Lulu. 'Run charities for retired millionaires?'

'No, working for successive governments since I don't know when,' said Paul.

'Well, of course, I'm against honours and titles on principle,' said Lulu. 'Ought to have been done away with by Oliver Cromwell. By an irreversible Act of Parliament.'

'No such thing,' said Paul. 'No Parliament can bind its successors.'

'Ought to be exceptions,' said Lulu. 'Anyway, if your grandpa's been useful to the country and a loyal Labour voter, what's the problem?'

'I've no idea which Party he votes for,' said Paul.

'Well, let's give him the benefit of the doubt,' said Lulu generously. 'So you don't have to be too ashamed about his title. After all, it's not your fault. Still, you'd better not let our Young Socialist group know.'

'What I'm chiefly thinking about is should I resign?' muttered Paul.

'Eh?' Lulu looked shocked.

'And get your dad or the agent to find someone suitable to take my place,' said Paul.

'Don't talk daft,' said Lulu.

'But you'd prefer someone not related to a title, wouldn't you, Lulu?'

'Have I ever said so?' demanded Lulu.

'Good as,' said Paul.

'Forget it,' said Lulu.

'I've always thought myself that a genuine Labour bloke should be far distant from titles, which—'

'Shut up,' said Lulu.

'The point is—'

'Shut up. You're not to resign. Not to. You get that?' Lulu was quite fiery. 'Just thinking about it is feeble. Feeble. Is your grandpa a capitalist?'

'I can honestly say no.'

'He's a worker?'

'Well, he was for years until he retired,' said Paul.

'There you are, then, he's one of us,' said Lulu. 'And listen, in thinking about resigning, were you thinking about my feelings?'

'What feelings?'

'All right, I'll tell you,' said Lulu. 'First off, I don't want to work with some other bloke who'd probably try to boss me even more than you do.'

'He'd have a job,' muttered Paul.

'What's that?'

'Oh, nothing much,' said Paul.

'Secondly,' said Lulu, 'out of human kindness, I need to keep an eye on you.'

359

'Pardon?'

'Well, someone's got to see you don't talk yourself into marrying Henrietta in a couple of years or so. It'll do you no good and it'll upset me.'

'Upset you?'

'Yes. I'd have to watch you slowly falling to pieces. After all, you're not a bad bloke. If you must stick to your old-fashioned idea that marriage is necessary to your life, you deserve an improvement on Henrietta.'

'D'you have someone in mind?' asked Paul.

'Don't look at me,' said Lulu. 'Oh, all right,' she said, 'now that I've had my hair done there must be some soppy reason for it.'

'Name the soppy reason,' said Paul.

'I'm searching for it,' said Lulu. 'All I can say is that it's about time you took me to a theatre instead of Henrietta.'

'Would you repeat that?' asked Paul.

'Once is enough,' said Lulu, and took her glasses off to polish the lenses. Paul got up and crossed to her desk. He looked down into her myopic eyes.

'Lulu, did you get your hair curled to please me?' he asked.

'Well, it wasn't for Bonnie Prince Charlie, was it?' said Lulu. 'He's dead. And I like your mum and dad, don't I, even if they are capitalists.'

Paul laughed, and brought her boldly to her feet.

'Lulu, the real you is out at last, so come here,' he said.

When the constituency's agent looked in a few minutes later, he stared, then made a tactful retreat. The secretary of the Young Socialists group and the daughter of Honest John were in a close huddle, exchanging kisses. Not the kind of thing that ought to go on in working hours, but one could turn a blind eye to two young people like Lulu Saunders and Paul Adams.

It was finished, the new Adams factory in Bethnal Green. It had been proudly built by the contractors, and had cost a large outlay of capital. However, Sammy, in masterminding the project with the backing of Boots, had always had an instinct for knowing when expenditure would bring its happy return.

He and Boots, together with Tommy, Daniel, Tim, Rachel, and Gertie and Bert Roper, were inspecting the rectangular two-storeyed building of commodious design in company with the contractors' site manager and one of the architects. Its tall windows supplied maximum light, its central heating system was able to offer its workers the comfort of warmth on the severest winter days, and its size able to accommodate more than two hundred machinists and seamstresses. There was also a fire-extinguishing system of ceiling water jets.

'My life,' said Rachel, 'such a first-class place for first-class outputs.'

'Oh, blimey, Mister Sammy,' breathed Gertie, 'we've got a real 'andsome place for the girls.'

'I'll say,' said Bert, still a loyal stalwart. 'I never did see a more 'andsome fact'ry, and I've seen a few in me time around the old docks.'

There were spacious offices, a studio for the designer, fully equipped canteen, toilets, and a rest room with a compartment for a first-aid treasure chest.

'It's made a painful hole in the firm's bank

account,' said Sammy, 'but I ain't complaining. Is anyone?'

'Well, it ain't my money,' grinned Bert.

'Bert,' said Boots, 'are you and Gertie sure you'll be able to stay on long enough to help see the factory reach full working order?' He knew Bert and Gertie were now past sixty and considering retirement. He also knew their way with the staff was an invaluable asset, and would be more so in regard to winning the loyalty of extra workers.

'We ain't going to give up yet, Mister Adams,' said Gertie, 'not when we've 'ad thirty 'appy years with you and yer brothers. We're still ready to go two more. Speak up, Bert.'

'Ain't I already spoke up?' said Bert. 'Good as?'

'Good as is good enough,' said Tommy. 'Two more years then?'

'Be a pleasure,' said Bert, ex-docker and a wartime volunteer in the AFS, which had helped the regulars fight the catastrophic fires during the Blitz on London.

Tim and Daniel, joint managers of the property company, were wandering around together.

'I like it,' said Tim.

'One up to us,' said Daniel.

'You're admiring our contribution?' said Tim. They had been involved with Sammy and Boots in approving the architects' final design, when it then became their responsibility to make regular inspections of progress, and to help settle any disputes between the architects and the builders. Sammy had kept a surreptitious eye on how they were coping. Boots had simply left them to prove themselves, earning from Sammy the rebuke that it didn't do to be airy-fairy about some things. Boots said he had faith in Tim and Daniel, and that in any case he didn't intend to let business give him ulcers. I don't have ulcers, said Sammy, so why should you? Well, Sammy old lad, said Boots, there's a difference between your stomach and mine. Sammy asked what difference? Yours is armed with armour plating, said Boots. Oh, that's a fact, is it? said Sammy. Well, I ain't amused.

'Looking over this building,' said Daniel, 'I'm giving myself a pat on the back.'

'Include me in,' said Tim.

'Patsy wants to see the finished job,' said Daniel.

'Felicity would like to,' said Tim wryly.

'Like to, oh hell,' said Daniel, 'it's a swine of a life she's living, and it's something she's got to put up with for ever. I'd go crazy myself.'

'She has her moments,' said Tim, 'but most of the time no-one could fault her. Come to that, Danny boy, can you fault this canteen?'

Spotless and shining, with tables and chairs installed, and the recessed kitchen gleaming and ready for use, the canteen looked like a gesture of generous hospitality on the part of the employers.

'No complaints from me, Tim, but cut out Danny boy. If Patsy heard you, she'd make funnies about it all day. On the other hand, she's concentrating exclusively right now on when the baby's due.' Patsy was close to her time.

The overall inspection by everyone came to a satisfactory conclusion, and they all departed, but not before Boots, Tommy and Sammy received good wishes for a happy and glorious day at Buckingham Palace tomorrow.

'And long may you reign over us, Dad,' said Tim to Boots.

'Hear, hear,' said Gertie and Bert.

'Dad, you said?' remarked Daniel to Tim. 'Dad? Don't you mean Your Majesty?'

'I think you're muddling me up with your grandpa,' said Boots.

'Not much,' grinned Sammy. 'As the family's Lord-I-Am, you were bound to end up at Buckingham Palace one day.'

'You never spoke a truer word, Sammy old cock,' said Tommy.

'God save me from more of the same,' said Boots.

That evening, Lizzy gave Ned an affectionate but searching look when he arrived home from his work. On her mind, of course, was the fact that he was having to cope with a lot of excitement tomorrow.

'How d'you feel, Ned love?' she asked.

'By touch, usually,' said Ned, and placed a hand on her bottom, applying a light squeeze.

'Ned Somers, I didn't ask for that kind of answer,' said Lizzy.

'Is there another kind, then, Eliza old girl?' said Ned.

'What I meant was d'you feel you'll be all right for tomorrow?'

'Can't wait,' said Ned. 'Especially as my hired topper fits. If it didn't, I'd stay in bed.'

'Try being serious,' said Lizzy. 'And then get ready for us going out to have supper with Polly and Boots.'

'Oh, yes, we did get an invite,' said Ned, and Lizzy gave him another look. He was smiling, and she knew he was feeling fine. Otherwise, he would have grimaced about not spending the evening at home. 'It's always a pleasure to see Polly,' he said. 'Still a bit of a charmer, and she's been a great consolation to Boots ever since he lost Emily.'

'Well, yes,' said Lizzy. But loyalty towards Boots's first wife, who had been her oldest friend, made her add, 'Mind, I don't think anyone could mean as much to him as Emily did.'

At the home of Boots and Polly in Dulwich, supper, prepared as usual by the indefatigable Flossie, was over, the twins in bed, Ned and Lizzy, accompanied by their hosts, were strolling around the extensive garden. The spring twilight was quite balmy.

'I envy you your large vegetable plot, Boots,' said Ned, glancing at the green shoots of planted seeds. 'You and Polly always make the most of it.'

'You're speaking of my plot, mine,' said Polly. 'The lord and master has nothing to do with it.'

'There's a notice,' said Lizzy, and examined a little board mounted on a stick. A square piece of white cardboard pinned to it contained a warning.

'Trespassers will be prosecuted or stoned to death. By order of the keeper, Polly Adams.'

'That sounds serious,' said Ned.

'No, it's just a joke of Polly's,' said Lizzy.

'You sure?' said Ned. 'I'm not. Polly's had a love affair with vegetable cultivation for years.'

'Yes, I know,' said Lizzy, 'but—'

'No, Ned's right, Lizzy,' said Boots, 'it's serious.'

'Deadly serious, believe me, dear old things,' said Polly. 'If it weren't, Boots and the twins would be treating it as part of their cricket pitch. Every seed or seedling is planted and nurtured by my own fair hands. You've seen my runner beans every autumn, haven't you, Lizzy?'

'Yes,' said Lizzy, and gave vent to a girlish giggle. 'But I've never seen Boots being stoned to death.'

'Well, of course you haven't, Lizzy old sport,' said Polly, 'it's not the kind of event for spectators. Far too gruesome, unlike tomorrow's event at the Palace, at which we'll all present ourselves in full dress order. Look, there's my spinach coming through. And there's the first of my garden peas, and there's my spring onions.'

Boots made a grave inspection of the green shoots, Lizzy a polite one. Ned turned ostensibly to regard rhododendrons coming into flower, and to hold his breath as the little sharp pain in his chest made itself known for the first time in weeks. He bore it without making a sound, and to his relief it receded before Boots spoke to him.

'Coffee and a brandy, Ned?'

'I'll do the honours,' said Polly, happy about the fact that she could now brew excellent coffee, as well as prepare eggs and bacon for Sunday breakfasts.

Ned drew in a lungful of the soft evening air and said, 'Sounds welcome to me, Boots old man.'

'Just coffee for me,' said Lizzy.

I hope to hell, thought Ned, that I haven't had a signal warning me off tomorrow's excitements.

'Polly,' he said, 'while we're having coffee, let's see how your television works.'

'What made you buy one?' asked Lizzy.

'Oh, Boots, the proud old sport, thought we ought to keep up with the Joneses,' said Polly.

'If you believe that, Lizzy, you can believe I'm Henry the Eighth,' said Boots.

Chapter Thirty-Four

Nerves were eased by the cheerful courtesies of Palace officials, who shepherded the recipients of honours, with their attendant nearest and dearest, into the Palace. Bomb-damaged during the war, all necessary repairs had been effected, and everyone entering was immediately in awe of stately grandeur.

At seventy-three, Chinese Lady had a bucketful of nerves to cope with, but if her dark brown hair showed gathering tints of grey, her slim body was as upright as ever, her bosom as proud as ever. The three-quarter-length sleeves of her ankle-length dress allowed for long silver-grey gloves to enhance her appearance. Her wide-brimmed hat of dark blue was perched neatly on her head, secured by one of her old-fashioned hatpins. Not on any account, she had said, was she going to risk the hat being blown off.

Mr Finch, silver haired, but as upright as his wife, carried his grey topper in his hand. In his morning suit, he looked to Chinese Lady unruffled as well as distinguished. Lord, she thought, how did all this happen? It's not making me feel unruffled myself.

Blinking at the Palace's interior splendour, she whispered, 'Oh, Lor', Edwin, I'm that nervous I'm sure I'll faint.'

'I'm sure you won't, my dear,' murmured Mr Finch.

As the stream of men and women moved slowly forward, an usher kept repeating certain words of information.

'Ladies' cloakrooms to the right, gentlemen's to the left.'

There, the ladies were able to attend to any last-minute adjustments of this or that, and those wearing coats were smilingly requested to remove and leave them.

'Oh, help,' breathed Chinese Lady, 'do you feel as nervous as I do, Polly?'

'Frightfully,' said Polly, who didn't, 'but I'm looking forward to seeing Georgie.'

'Georgie?'

'Our Britannic Majesty,' said Polly. Chinese Lady wanted to know if her hat was on straight. Polly assured her it was, and that it looked perfect. 'And so do you, you dear woman,' whispered Polly, which touched Chinese Lady to the quick.

In their own place, the gentlemen left their toppers, bemedalled officers their caps.

'Do you feel up to scratch, Edwin?' asked Boots.

'As much as I ever will be, Boots,' said Mr Finch.

'Enjoy it,' said Boots.

'I intend to, Boots, since you must know this is the most memorable day of my life,' said Mr Finch.

Boots, the keeper of his stepfather's secrets, smiled.

'It's not far short of being the most memorable day for your family,' he said.

This made Mr Finch himself feel deeply touched.

While the recipients of honours were being drawn aside, the guests were escorted by liveried ushers to the magnificent ballroom, the venue for State functions and banquets, and a blaze of red and gold. The red carpeting leapt to the eye. Told by the very agreeable usher to relax and enjoy the ceremonies, which would begin with the arrival of His Majesty at eleven o'clock precisely, the guests were shown to their allocated seats among serried ranks of red and gold chairs.

Chinese Lady sank gratefully into her chair, and Boots sat between her and Polly. All three took in the splendour of the ballroom and the colourful livery of the ushers and other officials.

'Boots, I went and forgot,' breathed Chinese Lady.

'Forgot what?' murmured Boots.

'My smelling salts,' whispered Chinese Lady.

'Don't worry, old girl,' said Boots, 'you'll pull through.'

'Well, I do worry,' whispered Chinese Lady, 'and must you call me old girl when we're sitting here, right in the middle of Buckingham Palace?'

'Certainly, we don't find ourselves here every day,' said Boots.

Polly, hearing these exchanges, smothered a laugh and took in the railed-off area where the red carpet led to the dais awaiting the arrival of the King. All court officials present were going about their duties with smiles and a complete lack of stuffiness, thereby creating an atmosphere of ceremonial informality. Polly thought that although the atmosphere and the grandeur related unmistakably to pomp and circumstance, the proceedings so far had been decidedly informal.

She glanced at Boots, still exchanging murmured talk with his nervous mother. He, of course, showed no nerves at all. Typically, in his easy-going way, he was able to take pomp and circumstance as calmly as he took a phone call. What an old charmer he was.

Meanwhile, in an ante-room, the gentleman in charge of the ceremonies, a lieutenant colonel of the royal household, was outlining procedures to the candidates for honours, and doing so with a welcome touch of humour. It was, of course, he said, an occasion perhaps a little overwhelming, but every lady and gentleman must do his or her best to remember it as somewhat more enjoyable than a visit to the dentist.

'You will be escorted to the ballroom by ushers, and please halt when requested to. Each of you will in turn hear his or her name called, and your citation stated for the benefit of His Majesty and your families. Then advance forward, and turn left to face the King. If a lady, please curtsey. If a gentleman, and I presume you all are – yes, I'm sure you are – you bow. Then walk to the dais, but not onto it, for there won't be room for you and His Majesty together. You will then receive your decoration – ah, yes, the gentlemen to be knighted will go down on one knee. His Majesty will lightly touch your left shoulder, then your right, with the ceremonial sword, when you may then rise and perhaps find him exchanging a few friendly words with you. After which he will shake your hand, as he will with all recipients, when you will then please take a few steps backward and be escorted out by an usher. Not backwards, I hasten to assure you. Your decoration will immediately be taken from you, much to your surprise, I daresay, but just as immediately it will be handed back to you in a rather handsome little box. Now, if any of you forget precisely what to do, watch the gentleman preceding you, and do what he does, unless he's forgotten as well. Oh, by the way, should a lady precede you, I recommend you don't do as she will, for a curtsey by a gentleman is foreign to this court. Now, do please endeavour to enjoy the ceremony. My best wishes to all of you.'

In the ballroom, precisely on the dot, a quiet fell, heralding the arrival of King George the Sixth from the throne room. A tall lean man of good looks, but a little careworn, he was uniformed in Guards' blues. He halted on the dais, and bandsmen in the gallery began the National Anthem. The whole assembly came to its feet. Chinese Lady did her very best to stay quite still, but couldn't prevent little vibrations travelling up and down her spine.

As soon as the anthem finished, the investiture commenced to the accompaniment of light music. The name and citation of the first recipient were announced clearly.

'Mr Clive Goodliffe, for services in aid of returned prisoners of war, a knighthood.'

Mr Goodliffe, looking like a ruddy-faced yeoman of the countryside, walked sturdily to the railed-off area, halted, turned left to face the King, and advanced to the dais. There he went down on one knee. The King lightly touched his left shoulder, then his right, with the sword.

The recipient came to his feet, the King placed the ribboned decoration around his neck, smiled, exchanged some brief words with him and shook his hand. The new knight then retreated and was escorted out by an usher.

Oh, Lord, Edwin's got to do all that, thought Chinese Lady. I just hope he does it right and proper.

Mr Finch's turn was not long in coming.

'Mr Edwin Finch, for years of courageous and devoted service to Great Britain and its Empire.'

Looking extremely self-controlled, Chinese Lady's distinguished husband did all the right things and presented himself to the King before going down on one knee. The sword performed its investiture touches, and he came to his feet.

The King smiled. Mr Finch noted shadows around his eyes, the shadows of a careworn man on the way to becoming terminally ill.

'Congratulations, Sir Edwin, and our thanks to you for your very invaluable services.'

'Your Majesty, it's been a great privilege for me, every day of my service, and this day most of all,' said Sir Edwin in total sincerity.

'Today is our pleasure,' said the King. They shook hands, Sir Edwin took a few steps backwards and an usher escorted him from the ballroom to the strains of 'Greensleeves'.

When the ceremonies were over, recipients and their nearest and dearest all met up outside the Palace and posed for official photographers on the forecourt, crowds looking on from outside the railings. Among these intrigued people were various younger members of the Adams family, including Emma and Rosie, taking time off from the chicken farm, and Lizzy and Ned's elder daughter Annabelle and husband Nick. Also there was Cassie Brown from Walworth. Patsy had wanted to be present, but at this particular moment she was in the maternity unit of King's College Hospital, having been rushed there by ambulance two hours ago, Daniel with her.

The photographs having been taken, Chinese

Lady, short of breath, managed to say, 'Oh, my goodness, I never knew anything like this before.'

'But you enjoyed it, Mum, didn't you?' said Susie, who imagined, correctly, that everything had gone off marvellously.

'Well, Susie, all of it took my breath away,' said Chinese Lady.

'But was it lovely?' asked Vi.

'Absolutely delightful,' said Polly.

'I can't help it, I'm still dizzy,' said Chinese Lady, 'but I must say our King looked handsome and dignified. Edwin, I can't hardly believe you're knighted.'

'Maisie, I share that feeling with you,' said Mr Finch, now Sir Edwin Finch. He studied the Palace, the colourful picture of the forecourt and the animated people outside. He thought again of his life, of his first loyalties to and his work for the Imperial Germany of Kaiser Wilhelm. And he thought of his acquired affection for the United Kingdom and all it had meant to him since his defection from Germany in 1918. No, he thought, I would not change any of the circumstances that have brought me here with my inimitable wife and my family. Yes, my family.

She was saying something, his wife.

'Edwin, can we get a pot of tea somewhere?'

'We're all going to Brown's Hotel for a celebratory lunch,' said Sir Edwin.

'Brown's?'

'A hotel, Maisie, of quiet distinction, with a staff and a service of unequalled renown,' said Sir Edwin. 'We have a lunchtime reservation.'

'Oh, my goodness, Edwin.'

Catching sight of Rosie and Emma, Sir Edwin

373

added, 'And everyone in the family who can be there, will celebrate with us at Boots and Polly's house this evening.'

'I just don't know I'll last the day out,' breathed Chinese Lady.

'You will, old lady,' said Boots. 'Sammy, find out if we can pick up our cars now, would you?'

'Certainly, me lord,' said Sammy, 'I'm only the Palace bootboy.'

'Sammy, you're the most invaluable and reliable member of our family,' said Boots.

'Granted,' said Sammy, and did his stuff in cheerful awareness that his worth had been recognized by none other than his respected eldest brother.

'We're all going to this place, Brown's Hotel?' said Vi, thrilled.

'All ten of us,' said Ned, triumphant that he'd suffered not a single suspicion of a struggling circulation.

'Is it posh?' asked Susie, spotting Annabelle and Cassie, and waving to them.

'Civilized,' smiled Polly.

'The table,' said Boots, 'is booked for Sir Edwin and Lady Finch and party.'

'Oh, Lor', someone hold me up,' breathed Lady Finch.

In Chicago, Jeremy Passmore was counting the days to August.

In Aberdeen, Fergus MacAllister was still thinking of Alice, and in King's College Hospital a young American lady, Mrs Patsy Adams, was being delivered of a baby boy.

Chapter Thirty-Five

Late July

The new knight, Sir Edwin Finch, and his wife, Lady Finch, had begun their holiday in Cornwall together with Boots, Polly, and the twins. Also there, in an adjacent holiday home, were Sammy, Susie, Jimmy, Paula and Phoebe. And with them were Daniel, Patsy, little Arabella and baby Andrew of two months. Mother and child were in fine fettle, father Daniel not too sure that, by way of help, he was a born nappy-changer.

'Daniel, you're doing swell,' said Patsy.

'Ugh,' said Daniel.

'Here's the talc.'

'What's that for?'

'Powdering his little butt.'

'Listen, Patsy, I'm his dad, not his mum. Powdering's a mum's job.'

'But you promised this kind of help, so that we could both enjoy the vacation.'

'If I'm right, Patsy,' said Daniel, 'I suffer too many weak moments in my relationship with you.'

'Oh dear Daniel, what a shame, but never mind,'

said Patsy, sounding like Susie, her mother-in-law, 'I like your weak moments.'

'What a cherub,' said Daniel.

'Me?'

'Our infant.'

'Well, sure, Daniel, aren't they all when they've been changed and powdered by their daddies?'

'Once we get back home, this one's going to be exclusively changed and powdered by his mummy,' said Daniel. 'Which reminds me, I wonder how Bess is getting on all by herself at home?'

'Oh, she'll like being by herself when her guy from Chicago turns up,' said Patsy. 'Three would be more than a crowd for lovers, more of a multitude.'

'Lovers?' said Daniel, working at the problem of getting their bawling infant's clothes off. 'That's going too far, Patsy. They've only met once.'

'Everyone says that,' said Patsy, 'but no guy is going to cross the Atlantic all the way from Chicago just to say hello to Bess.'

'So what's going to come of it?' asked Daniel, handing the cherub to Patsy for safe keeping.

'You'll be surprised, I guess,' said Patsy, cuddling her baby, 'but I won't.'

Daniel smiled. Patsy was flying high. But he knew Bess. She might not be as reserved as formerly. She was, however, very unlikely to be swept off her feet by a bloke she'd only known face to face for a few hours.

On the way to Daymer Beach, with her husband, Chinese Lady, who refused to be known by her title as far as family, friends and acquaintances were concerned, said, 'Edwin, if Boots or Polly want to introduce us to any people they know here, I want it to be as Mr and Mrs Finch.'

'I've already made that clear to them,' said Sir Edwin, sporting a light panama, a blue blazer twenty years old, and cream-coloured ducks even older. He was carrying two deckchairs, for the sunny day invited a long restful morning on the beach.

'Still, I don't know I could ever trust Boots not to say something he didn't ought to.'

'I think we can trust him on this particular matter, Maisie.'

'Where is he?' asked Chinese Lady, carrying a fringed pearly-coloured parasol in the true spirit of an incurable Victorian, which meant she didn't believe in letting the sun affect her complexion.

'He and Polly are following on behind, with the twins,' said Sir Edwin. 'And I daresay Sammy and Susie, with their family, aren't far away.'

'I can't help thinking they shouldn't of left Bess at home all by herself, Edwin.'

'Bess is staying at home in anticipation of the arrival of her American friend, Maisie.'

Reaching the bottom of Daymer Lane, the broad sunlit vista of sand, sea and bay opened out. The beach was dotted with active holidaymakers, and in the sea families splashed about. Shapely girls in skintight swimsuits ran into the blue waters.

'Well, I must say bathing costumes aren't like what they were when I was a girl,' said Chinese Lady, descending a worn path to the beach with Sir Edwin beside her.

'Um – a little too little by comparison?' he smiled.

'Oh, there was a bit too much of them old-fashioned costumes,' said Chinese Lady, not at all

377

disapproving of the modern styles. Prim in many ways she might have been, but never prudish. 'Well, I suppose we shouldn't worry about Bess staying at home, except she'd of looked very nice in a costume like those girls are wearing.'

'I'm sure she would,' murmured Sir Edwin, 'she's a very attractive young lady, and I fancy her American gentleman hasn't failed to notice that.'

The subject had been a matter of family interest for many a month.

Well behind everyone else, Jimmy was strolling slowly down the lane, beach towel over his shoulder. He looked a lithe young man in brief blue shorts and an open white shirt, sandals on his feet. He wasn't thinking about his sister Bess, or her American bloke. He was thinking of the good and the not so good. The good was in the fact that his dad was promoting him from his routine job in the family's Walworth store to a position as his Uncle Tommy's assistant in the new Bethnal Green store, now operating.

He was to start when this holiday was over. It would mean his first leg-up on the family business ladder, with a corresponding rise in earnings. He'd have useful dibs in his pocket, something a bloke of his age, twenty, ought to have in order to take a girl-friend out and about. There wasn't one in his life right now. There had been, in the shape of Jenny Osborne, even though she had settled down in New York with her family.

The not-so-good factor had intruded three days ago, when he received another letter from Jenny. It caused him a bit of grief, for she informed him she was dating a very dishy guy, a fellow student at the city's College of Art and Science. She hoped the news wouldn't upset him, and, anyway, as they were far away from each other, their friendship couldn't come to anything serious. Even so, she wrote, she'd always be pleased to hear from him. At one stroke of her pen, Jimmy saw himself reduced to a mere pen pal. But he took the blow manfully, and he couldn't say it was unexpected. As a modest young man, he'd never thought himself a great catch for a stunner like Jenny.

Jimmy underrated himself. He was as personable as most members of the Adams family, the young and the mature. Chinese Lady, whenever she took note of this collective trait, always thought of her first husband, Corporal Daniel Adams, a man as handsome as any woman could have wished. Accordingly, she considered him the main source of her extensive family's good looks. In thinking so, she too underrated herself, for as a young woman and then a wife, no-one in those days would have called her less than engagingly attractive.

Jimmy, catching up with Paula and Phoebe as they reached the beach, drew in the invigorating ozone and tried to console himself with the prospect of meeting another stunner like Jenny on Cornwall's sunny sands.

Some hopes. Still, a bloke with good business prospects could always be more confident about catching up with a desirable social prospect, preferably one wearing a skirt. Or a figure-hugging swimsuit.

But there was still a lingering lament for having lost Jenny.

Saturday arrived and, with it, the beginning of August.

At home in the handsome family house on Denmark Hill, Bess Adams, unusually fluttery, was waiting. Jeremy had confirmed the date of his arrival, and that it would be sometime during the morning if all went well. He would be flying overnight from New York on the now established transatlantic air route to London Airport, and taking a cab from there.

Bess kept telling herself to calm down, that it was ridiculous to have a high pulse rate over a reunion with a man whom people would insist she hardly knew. But she felt she knew him very well, not only from the one time they had been together, but from his many letters. It was all enough to think him totally likeable. So she frequently looked at herself in a mirror, made little adjustments to her hair and wondered if she had slightly overdone the lipstick effect. Yes, perhaps a little. No, not really. Lord, what a goose. Be your age, Bess.

Despite the expectation of a knock on the front door, she jumped when it did happen. Was it him or the milkman? The milkman always called later than usual on Saturdays, when he collected the weekly owings from his customers. No, he'd been at half nine, and it was now nearly ten thirty.

She answered the knock.

A man stood on the doorstep, a suitcase at his feet. He lifted his hat.

'Hello, Bess,' said Jeremy Passmore, his fine light

grey suit tailored to his muscular figure, his smile warm but slightly enquiring, as if he wasn't sure whether his arrival was happily or moderately welcome to her.

He was not a brash American, he was a quiet man in the main, if frank and open in his attitudes. With his hat lifted, his features showed strong-boned and tanned, his hair black and thick, his fine and clear eyes searching hers.

'Jeremy?' Bess sounded a little husky.

'Bess? It's a delight to see you again.'

'Jeremy?' Bess, obviously, was not quite herself. She was giddy, in fact. But she made an effort, she came to and said in a rush, 'Oh, come in, come in.'

He stepped in, placing his suitcase on the floor. He closed the door. They looked at each other in what some people would have called a meaningful silence. A flush coloured Bess's face.

'Bess,' said Jeremy, 'I've never stopped thinking of you.'

She let emotion speak then.

'Jeremy, oh, I'm so happy to see you,' she said.

Jeremy acted on the natural impulse of a man who knew himself in love. He dropped his hat, took her into his arms and kissed her, ardently. Bess, giddy again, responded blissfully. That said more than a multitude of words from either of them. It was definitely meaningful.

A telegram arrived at a holiday home in Cornwall late that afternoon when the tenants were just back from the beach. It was addressed to Mr and Mrs S. Adams.

'DEAR ONES STOP HAVE RECEIVED A MARRIAGE
PROPOSAL STOP HAVE SAID YES STOP AM VERY
HAPPY HOPE YOU ARE TOO STOP LOVE FROM
BESS AND JEREMY'

'Stone me,' said Sammy, 'what's my old ma going
to say to this?'

'Not "stone me",' said Jimmy, 'she's a lady now.'

'Not half,' said Paula. 'So she's more likely to say
"Goodness gracious me, how delightful".'

Susie laughed.

Phoebe giggled.

THE END